PASSIONATE ALLIANCE

LORETTA BEAVER

PublishAmerica
Baltimore

ISBN: 978-1-4489-5804-7
PUBLISHED BY PUBLISHAMERICA, LLLP
www.publishamerica.com
Baltimore

Printed in the United States of America

This book is dedicated to Herman and Ruby Reum:
Without their faith in me I would never have finished writing this
book, may they both rest in peace.

PROLOGUE

Montana

A bright flash of lightning streaked towards earth. As it got closer it split into three separate bolts. The man walking out of the cabin stopped short in astonishment, he stared in awe as the whole sky lit up unexpectedly in front of him. But even the wonder he felt at nature's fury didn't lesson the tears streaming down his face. Suddenly before he could count to two the cabin behind him shook as a deafening clap of thunder made him duck, it was an instinctive reaction even though death right now would be welcomed, it was so loud the very ground beneath him trembled in reaction.

Looking up infuriated at the black and purple clouds hovering above him, he grimaced in rage, as the rain began to fall unexpectedly. Several drops fell on the bundle he carried as he sighed resignedly. He clutched his burden protectively trying to shield it from the rain as he strolled purposely to the grave he had dug earlier that day. He mumbled to himself irritably. "What a lousy day for a burial."

Any day was a bad day of course especially one of this sort.

He knelt and gently set the white bundle down beside the grave to look one last time. His hand trembled slightly in reaction as he eased the cloth away from the faces of the woman and child. He glared up at the heavens, though he couldn't see much in the pouring rain, screaming in rage and frustration. The agony in his voice was plain to hear as he managed to gasp out past his constricted throat. "WHY?"

He looked again at the woman in remorse. He reached out gently and lovingly stroking her cold cheek, shaking his head in bewilderment and anger. How could anyone do something so unspeakable? How anyone could hurt a woman, especially one so obviously with child! Then his gaze turned to the young boy and his breath caught on another sob as his hand dropped from the women cheek to his son's coal black hair. He brushed it back sadly. His son had just turned ten this past summer, but now he would never reach manhood.

He dropped his hand into his lap as he bent his head then wept bitterly as he recalled that his son had still been alive when he had found them. There was nothing he could do to save him, although he had tried desperately.

His son was still lucid when he had first arrived from his trap line. It appeared to the man that his son had kept himself alive by shear will alone; long enough to tell his father what had happened to them so he could die in peace…

"I tried to help Mom, but there were three of them. After the attack, they thought we were all dead so started talking about Dakota and revenge against a woman who had killed their brothers. Then they started laughing about how Mom put up such a good fight, but not as good as the Indian squaws they had came across two years ago."

The boy lived long enough to give a vague description of the three men for his father before he died. Fortunately, he had heard them call each other by their first names. His son's fascination with horses meant he remembered what they looked like as well…

"There was a man with blonde hair who rode a black gelding. They called him Marty. The second man had hair that was very black, and rode a big grey mare. His name was Sam. The third man had greasy brown hair and he was even taller than you Dad. His horse was a red stallion, a mean brute. I heard them call this man Jimmy. The only thing that was the same on all three was that they all had the same dark blue eyes."

With his dying breath the boy described what the men had done to his mother, but the man pushed that thought away. It was just too painful to remember.

The man gazed at his family one last time in anguish and disbelief. He gently wrapped them back in the sheet before jumping into the grave, pulling the bundle towards him. He carefully lifted his wife and son then put them into the deep pit. He jumped out of the grave with a shiver of reaction then picked up the waiting shovel. Slowly, he began filling in the grave, his heart hardening with each scoop of wet soil. Tossing the dirt over the shell of his dead wife and son, would he ever feel anything but hate and anger again.

When he finished, he dropped the shovel in distaste. He began piling the large rocks that he had collected earlier to mark the grave and to keep scavengers from digging up his family. He placed a makeshift cross on top of the fresh mound of dirt, having painstakingly carved 'My beloved family' with his own two hands.

Although he knew no prayers he spoke a few private words of love, asking forgiveness for having left them for so long. He looked up towards the heavens and made a solemn oath to his family. As he made his vow he lifted his fist towards the sky in fury and shook it threateningly, his voice becoming lethal in promise. "I won't rest until I have found and punished those bastards; no matter how long it takes, even if I have to pursue them into hell itself!"

Before he dropped his hand, lightning lit up all around him and a crack of thunder shook the very earth, and seemed to seal his vow as if God himself approved.

* * *

A dark skinned man was watching the burial from the safety of the woods. He finally stepped out and let himself be seen. He hadn't understood the words the white man was saying but he could guess at their meaning, as he remembered his own pain that was still with him after two long years.

The white man tensed slightly at a whisper of sound behind him then he spun away from the grave quickly. As he turned, his hand moved in a blur of motion as he drew his gun, and pointed it steadily at the stranger standing behind him.

The Indian gazed at the revolver pointed at him without flinching. Looking up at the white man with no fear, he spoke calmly in his own language. "You are the white man the Indians speak of as 'Grey Wolf'."

Grey Wolf gave the man a searching look. He had never seen this particular Indian before. By the war paint on his face he was obviously Cheyenne Grey Wolf had him measured in moments. Slowly he lowered his gun feeling no threat from the Indian as he put his gun away.

Grey Wolf spoke in the Cheyenne language guessing that the Indian didn't speak English. Very few could or would. He nodded in confirmation and curiosity. "Yes I'm Grey Wolf. What do you want with me?"

For a moment the Indian was silent, as he took in the white man's size wondering again if this was a good idea. Most whites were untrustworthy but he had heard good things about Grey Wolf. Things like how he had always spoken truthfully to both whites and Indians. He had also heard that this man was quick to anger, but never drew his gun unless given no other choice. There were also great tales of how he helped both whites and Indians when trouble brewed between the two nations. He was almost always successful in quelling any disputes that arose.

He hadn't missed the speed with which Grey Wolf had moved and he knew that everything that had been said about this man was true. He smiled in satisfaction, knowing he'd found the white man he had been searching for all this time.

Finally the Indian broke his long silence as he motioned in sympathy at the mound of dirt and rocks that marked the white man's family grave. "I am sorry about your family."

Grey Wolf looked assessingly into the Indian's eyes for a long moment then relaxed his stance slightly at what he saw in the Cheyenne's eyes. He nodded in acceptance of the condolences before he repeated his question more persistently, unsure where this was leading. "What do you want from me?"

The Indian frowned slightly in disapproval at the abrupt tone the white man used. He wasn't very patient. He pointed at himself in introduction. "I am Chief Giant Bear."

That was a very good description of the man. He was huge for a Cheyenne, about six feet and so husky he almost looked like a bear. Especially with that bear skin wrapped around his shoulders. Most Indians were slight, almost skinny and not quite as tall, but not this one.

Grey Wolf smiled knowingly, guessing at how Giant Bear had gotten some of his name. He knew that the Cheyenne Indians named their sons on merit but wondered how Giant Bear had earned the rest of his name. 'Bear' in particular. Maybe it was just because he looked like a bear. The polite curiosity was plain to hear in Grey Wolf's tone. "How did you get your name?"

Giant Bear kept his face impassive, proud of how he had gotten his name but not wanting to seem boastful, he spoke without a trace of arrogance. "I saved a small boy from a grizzly bear when I was eleven summers. I killed it with only a small eating knife and so earned the name 'Giant Bear'."

Grey Wolf nodded, impressed. A bear as large as the skin hanging from the Indians shoulders would be almost impossible to kill with just a knife. He guessed correctly when he figured that was the skin that Giant Bear was wearing now. Giant Bear must have jumped the bear from behind then went for its throat in order to get a kill; since a bear's thick fur and hide would stop a knife easily anywhere else.

Grey Wolf didn't speak again, knowing that Giant Bear had seen the approval on his face, and that's all that would be needed. He waited impatiently for Giant Bear to tell him why he was here and what he wanted.

Giant Bear finally waved to the grave behind Grey Wolf in explanation, but didn't look away from the white man trying to convey how serious he was as he made his offer. "I would like to help in your search for your family's killers."

Grey Wolf was taken aback by Giant Bear's offer. Not having expected that in the least, he hid his surprise well as he gestured in curiosity. "Why would you do that?"

Giant Bear gazed at the horizon for a moment. His face void of all emotions as he remembered the pain of two summers ago, at the death of his own wife and sister. Finally, looking back at Grey Wolf, he let his emotions blaze to the surface for a moment.

Grey Wolf saw the agony on Giant Bear's face then watched as the pain was replaced by hate and vengeance before his face became impassive once again. Grey Wolf recognized the hidden sorrow instantly and was very surprised that Giant Bear would show it to him at all.

Giant Bear finally balled up his fist in fury as he shook it. That was all the emotion he now showed as he explained. "Two years ago the same men that killed your family also raped and killed my wife. They raped my sister as well and left her and my young daughter to die. But they made a mistake. My sister did not die on that day. Three days later she told me what they did, and then she took her own life because she could not live with her dishonour. It was then that I vowed to hunt them down. But they are always a step ahead of me."

After a silent pause Giant Bear continued, as he motioned sharply in frustration clearly enraged. "It is difficult for a lone Indian to hunt in white man's territory. I tracked them here, but I was too late to help your family. I only arrived a few minutes after you did."

Grey Wolf turned gazing sadly one last time at his family's grave wishing Giant Bear had arrived in time. He didn't blame the Indian, though he blamed himself. He put his family in danger by ignoring his father's warning not to bring them. Why did I not listen?

He brought his attention once more to Giant Bear. His face turned pensive as he tried to decide whether he should bring an Indian Chief into white man's territory. He sighed resignedly and knew that if he were Giant Bear he too would find a way, regardless of the consequences. Grey Wolf finally conceded his mind made up. "I would be honoured to have you by my side. I cannot do anything more here so let's head out."

Giant Bear inclined his head slightly in relief, and relaxed noticeably at that good news, he watched Grey Wolf turn then walk towards the cabin before disappearing inside. The Great Spirit had been right after all, he mused to himself. He had meditated in the sweat lodge for several days before he left his people, until he was shown the way to his wife's killers.

Giant Bear had not understood at the time why he was to go northeast to find this cabin, but now he understood because he had just found the man the Great Spirit had promised would not only become his friend, but would help him find the killers. Without Grey Wolf to help him and teach him about white people, he would fail and be dead within a year. Giant Bear smiled unemotionally in satisfaction and turned to get his horse.

A few minutes later Grey Wolf rode up to Giant Bear with a packhorse in tow and nodded in approval at Giant Bears sturdy looking Indian pony. "Let's go!"

Giant Bear motioned to Grey Wolf that he was ready, and stayed close to his new friend and ally. The closer the better, he had been told by the Great Spirit and he definitely agreed.

CHAPTER ONE

North Dakota

Melissa Ray stopped her high-strung stallion and looked around suspiciously, instantly knowing something was amiss. A quiver of foreboding rippled down her spine as she felt the hair on the back of her neck suddenly standing erect. Glancing around again, she touched the butt of her revolver at her side in reassurance. She unhooked the strap that held the gun in place, looking around nervously. What was making her so jumpy? Nothing seemed out of the ordinary? Once again, a shiver of forewarning rippled down her spin unexpectedly, and that was all the warning she needed as she kicked her horse into a desperate run. "Ayah!"

Lightning squealed in surprise as he instantly surged forward at his mistress's urgent command. Soon he was in a full gallop as a shot rang out behind them.

Melissa glanced over her shoulder searchingly, wondering if she should turn back to find out who had taken that shot at her. It was then she saw three men charging out of the trees and she grinned knowingly as she kept going. The men finally gave up and turned back into the trees. When Melissa decided it was safe she slowed her horse to a slow lope and laughed in exhilaration. She had won again as she patted her horse in apology for the rough handling.

Anyone watching her from a distance wouldn't believe that she was a woman. She wore a man's checkered flannel shirt, a tan coloured oversized vest, and dark blue pants. A black cowboy hat pulled low over her forehead effectively hid her hair, and she carried two colt revolvers at her hips. The people in town where use to seeing her in this strange attire, but most strangers laughed at the guns in disbelief. That is, until they saw how well she could handle them.

Melissa held her horse at a lope as she continued north. The thick forest on her left kept her going straight. She looked to her right smiling in satisfaction at the new growth of trees. Her men had done an excellent job at replanting, and she would make sure that she mentioned it to them tonight.

She skirted the new baby trees and was once again surrounded by thick forest on either side. She headed west following a small game trail that was almost invisible, unless you knew it was there. She continued on the trail as it twisted and turned for a quarter of a mile then finally reached a small open valley. A creek meandered through the valley, which was almost hidden by the trees that surrounded it. Here the grass was lush with new growth and wild flowers of every description were starting to bud.

This was Melissa's favourite spot, and her eyes sparkled in pleasure at finding it just as lovely and peaceful as she remembered. She dropped the reins and slid off her horse prepared to enjoy the peace and quiet of her haven, having been gone far too long.

Melissa was tall for a woman. At five feet eleven inches she topped most men. However, she was every bit a woman. This was evident when she removed her hat, as she did now. As Melissa stood with her blonde hair flowing around her, she was a beauty. Clouds of curly hair framed her delicate features, of which the most striking were her large eyes. Looking into the depths of those turquoise eyes would make a person feel that she could read their very soul. That made a lot of people nervous, particularly if you were a man.

At this moment, Melissa's eyes sparkled in satisfaction at the thrill of the chase. She wondered if her men had finally given up on her. They tried several times a month to surprise her but hadn't yet caught her off her guard.

If anyone asked her why she was still unmarried at the unheard of age of twenty-seven she would laugh heartily, and answer that she had yet to find the man who could outshoot or outride her. That her life became quite lonely at times she would admit to no one, not even to herself.

Melissa walked to the creek and sat down by the edge to gaze into the clear clean water. She didn't worry about her horse straying for the bond between this horse and his rider was unbreakable. She turned slightly to admire him as he nibbled at the tender sprouts of green grass growing along the edge of the forest. Her thoughts went back to the first time she had seen him as a small, frightened silver grey colt.

The mare she was riding at the time was scrambling up a steep ridge when she heard a horse screaming in terror. She urged her horse to pick up more speed as the desperate sound continued. When she crested the knoll in front of her she saw a man cruelly beating a small silver grey stud, so she quickly made her way down.

Melissa jumped off her horse infuriated and rushed forward to prevent the man from hitting the frightened colt again. She grabbed the whip from the man's hand in fury throwing it as far as she could into the thick brush behind him.

The man whirled around furiously raising his fist in rage at whoever dared interfere. He quickly dropped his arm in surprise when confronted with a deadly revolver pointed straight at him. He lifted his head and gazed into icy turquoise eyes, immediately recognizing who was facing him. He swore silently to himself in frustration.

Melissa stared at the sandy brown haired man in disbelief. He had dark blue eyes, and a brown handlebar moustache that he always kept neatly trimmed. He was slim, almost too thin, and shorter then Melissa by three inches at five feet eight. Her anger exploded as she recognized the only man other than her father that she had any respect for. That admiration disappeared from her eyes in a heartbeat!

Brian Adams winced then swore silently too himself again. As he watched the esteem he had so carefully nurtured over the years instantly fade from Melissa's eyes he knew he had made a grave error.

Melissa turned from Brian in loathing and disillusionment then put her revolver away. She looked at the frightened colt again...it was love at first sight. Brian saw that look as she turned towards him and knew what had to be done.

He looked at the grey thoroughbred for a moment in regret and thought of all the trouble and expense the stud had caused him. In the past, before he cared what Melissa thought, he would have trained his horses at his ranch. However, Melissa was so against people beating horses that he had to hide his true nature. Brian sighed in frustration at loosing such a valuable animal but he had no choice. He had to take that look of disgust off Melissa's face. It had taken him too long to get where he was with her, and he wasn't going to lose everything because of a horse, no matter how much it cost.

Brian shrugged in resignation turned back to Melissa and handed the halter rope to her. "Here, I give him to you as a gift with my apologies. I can't do anything with him anyway."

Melissa stared at Brian in disappointment, a scowl of disbelief still on her face. "I can't believe that you, of all people, would harm an animal. You know how I feel about any kind of abuse!"

Brian lowered his head in apparent shame, giving himself time to come up with a good excuse. He shrugged as he looked up at Melissa, pleading for understanding. "I didn't really want to beat him. I bought him from a rancher in South Dakota as a birthday gift for Mary. I've been working with him now for over a month in secret so she doesn't find out about him. I just can't seem to do anything with him. Every time I go near him he kicks and rears up, completely out of control. I got so frustrated I lost my temper and took out my whip and that's when he came after me like a mad dog. I had to use my whip to protect myself! When you got rid of the whip and started talking, he calmed down."

Brian watched her expressive face at his explanation, realizing he had her fooled. He gained momentum and continued his charade. "I just realized that the sound of your voice is what stopped him from attacking me further. Perhaps it was a man who beat him and that's why he has such a violent reaction when I go near him. So here you are, he's all yours and I hope you have more success with him then I did."

Since that time a close bond was formed between Melissa and Lightning. It had taken her a long time and a lot of patience to get him to trust her, but it had been worth it in the end.

Melissa's thoughts returned to the present as she faced the creek and began removing her boots and socks to wade in the inviting looking water. Melissa's face was slightly pensive as she reflected on the explanation Brian had given her for the cruel treatment towards the colt. It had made sense at the time, but reflecting on their conversation made her realize that his explanation had been lame and even laughable.

Why would Brian purchase such a valuable animal for his sister, when it appeared to Melissa that he didn't seem to like her? Was she a thorn in his side? Could it be possible that he even hated her? Melissa hadn't pressed the issue afterwards since she had no way of knowing what Brian had actually planned for the stud. After all, she couldn't call him a liar without proof, could she?

Not long after this incident Brian changed for the worst. Melissa had started avoiding him more and more, especially after he had asked for her hand in marriage and she refused him. The fury on his face took her by surprise, and left her feeling uneasy.

Suddenly, Lightning gave a warning snort just as Melissa heard the menacing growl of an animal. She looked up in surprise as a large black wolf sprang towards her unexpectedly and she heard hoof beats clattering on the ground behind her as Lightning sped towards the scene.

Melissa instinctively put her left arm up to protect her face and grabbed for her right revolver, which she hadn't tied down yet, while screaming at her horse to keep him out of harm's way. "Stand Lightning, stand!"

Her revolver came loose just as the big wolf surprisingly jumped past her. She almost fell backwards in astonishment, as he grabbed a large rattlesnake not more than a foot away from her back.

Lightning came to an abrupt halt at Melissa's sharp command. He stopped, quivering in fear at being so close to a wolf, but he stood his ground and refused to leave his mistress.

Melissa sat there bewildered and dazed with her revolver hanging limply in her hand, watching the wolf kill the deadly rattler. It was then she noticed that her horse had also been heading in the direction of the snake not towards her as she had first thought.

A sharp whistle sounded to her left, and Melissa watched in amazement as the wolf obediently dropped the dead rattler, and ran over to sit docilely beside a large man dressed in buckskin pants, moccasins, and a fringed doeskin shirt. The man stood at least six feet five or six inches tall, with large hands that appeared surprisingly gentle, as he stroked the wolf's head in praise for killing the snake.

Melissa felt a cold nose poke at her shoulder as Lightning nudged her, checking to see if his mistress was all right, but she ignored him. She hastily put her gun away but didn't tie it down in case she needed it.

Pulling her socks on before jamming her feet back into her boots, she jumped up as another man emerged from the trees further left of the first man. Melissa's hand automatically reached for her right revolver again but didn't draw it this time since they had just saved her from a nasty rattlesnake bite. She took small hesitant steps towards the two men for a closer look.

As she got closer she noticed the second man was Indian, or maybe part Indian since he was the largest Melissa had ever seen. As she approached the men cautiously she examined them more closely.

The white man's face was very rugged and masculine. His nose was straight and fit his face perfectly not too big or too long. His lips were full, almost too large. His chin jutted out giving him a slight appearance of arrogance, and long coal black hair hung down to his shoulders. As Melissa studied his eyes, she was surprised by their misty light blue colour. Gazing back at her he seemed to see right through her. His expression seemed sombre until he smiled, as he did now in reassurance. Tiny laugh lines appeared at the corner of his eyes and there was a small dimple beside his lower lip. The smile softened his face considerably, and when he smiled it was devastating!

Melissa shivered slightly as she felt the effect down to her toes. She could tell a lot about people by studying their faces. It was part of her job to assess a person quickly, and she was very good at it. What she saw in the white man's face relaxed her considerably as she removed her hand from the butt of her gun.

Melissa then turned her head to study the second man intently. She revised her thinking. He was definitely a full-blooded Indian, and Cheyenne to boot. There were a couple of scattered bands just over the border in Montana, but most had moved on and were settled further west. She could tell he was a leader or a chief just by the way he carried himself, and by the way he was dressed. Mell happened to know all the chiefs at the border but she didn't recognize this one, so he must be from Western Montana. What was he doing this far from home? And why was he traveling with a white man?

As Grey Wolf studied the woman approaching them, her beauty amazed him. He became annoyed at himself as he gazed into her deep turquoise eyes, feeling the first stirrings of desire since his family had been killed so many years ago. He gave a slight sigh of relief as she turned away from him to study Giant Bear.

As the white woman got closer, Giant Bear stepped into the background not wanting to cause trouble for his friend. He smiled slightly, impressed by what he saw in the woman's eyes, because she didn't hesitate to approach them and showed no fear as she studied them intently.

Melissa stopped suddenly, looking from one man to the other curiously but not afraid in the least. "Who are you?"

Grey Wolf stepped forward immediately wanting to put the woman at ease, and answered for both of them as he motioned first at himself then at Giant Bear in introduction. "My name is Jed Brown and my friend here is Chief Giant Bear."

He then pointed to the wolf. Looking down to make introductions he grinned fondly at the comical looking wolf as he sat there scratching an irritating itch behind his ear. "And this is Three Toes. We gave him this name because he only has three toes thanks to the trap we rescued him from as a pup."

As Jed looked back at the woman, it was then he noticed her clothing. He eyed her in displeasure as he studied her closely in distain. He could hardly believe his eyes! She was dressed in men's clothing and carried two lethal looking colt revolvers on her hips, and from the worn looks of them, both were well used. Were they hers or had she taken them from her brother or father? In spite of the odd attire she was a very beautiful woman and he frowned again in aggravation at himself as he felt that slight stirring in his loins once more.

Jed shook his head in exasperation trying to clear his thoughts. He waved towards the woman in invitation then smiled encouragement trying to put her at ease. "And who are you if I may be so bold as to ask? I'm sorry if we frightened you but I didn't have time to warn you about the danger you were in."

Giant Bear, who had watched the two with silent curiosity turned and melted soundlessly into the surrounding trees, heading for their camp nearby to get their horses, knowing they wouldn't be spending another night here.

Melissa hadn't noticed Giant Bear leaving, being too preoccupied with Jed. Suddenly she tensed in mistrust as she glanced to the left and realized he was absent. She quickly looked back at Jed threateningly as her hand automatically dropped to her gun. "Where'd your friend go?"

Jed noticed her quick reaction towards the gun on her right hip. He noticed immediately the speed of her hand and felt a touch of admiration. She might even be faster than he was as he wondered silently why she wore two guns when she only reached for the one. Perhaps she only used the one on her left as a back up or if there was more than one opponent. That also left him to speculate why she would feel the need of such protection unless there was trouble with outlaws in the area, which was always possible. So judging by her quick action the guns must be hers. Her movement was too quick and practiced for the guns to be someone else's.

He grinned disarmingly and held out his hands soothingly, showing that he wasn't a threat to her. "Giant Bear went back to camp to gather our belongings. We're looking for work in this area but so far we've had no luck."

"I could use a couple of new hands on my ranch."

Melissa scowled furiously at herself as she immediately lamented her thoughtless outburst, but it was too late to take back the offer now as she saw Jed nod quickly in acceptance not even hesitating.

Jed turned away quickly having noticed her grimace of regret. Before she could change her mind he spoke over his shoulder as he headed in the direction his friend had gone. "I'll go get Giant Bear and we'll follow you to your ranch."

With that comment he disappeared into the trees quickly before she could run off without them. His curiosity was definitely aroused now by her offer and by the woman herself. Not only did she carry two revolvers, she also had her own ranch. She had said 'my ranch', not our ranch. Was she widowed? Whatever the reason his interest was piqued and he knew there would be no leaving now until he found out all the answers to this mysterious woman. Giant Bear met him half way and they returned quickly to the creek.

* * *

Melissa led Lightning to the water for a drink then rested against him waiting for the two strangers. Her thoughts were on the man that she wanted to know more about, but still regretted her offer. As her thoughts went to Jed she felt that tingle once again. Shrugging in frustration unsure if what she was feeling was a warning or premonition, but she desperately needed to find out what was causing it.

When the two men appeared she sprang up on her horse to lead the way. Mell took the opportunity to study both men closely as they rode along and liked what she saw. You could tell a lot about men by the horses they rode and by the guns they used. The white man, Jed, rode a bay gelding that was larger than Lightning. He was obviously well cared for with no cruel spur marks on the horse's side, or a chaffed bleeding mouth from a cruel bit. His six-gun lay so low on his hip that it would take only a flip of his hand to grasp it.

The Indian rode a smaller paint mare. His saddle was a worn brown blanket and his halter and reins were made of homemade rope, with no bit in the horse's mouth. He wore no spurs or guns but he did have a rifle in a homemade beaded pouch hanging from his saddle blanket and she could see that it was well cared for as well.

Jed caught Melissa starring curiously at them and smirked enquiringly but didn't make any comment. Melissa flushed in embarrassment and quickly averted her head.

Jed's grin turned into a mischievous smile as she looked away. He allowed his own gaze to roam over her figure assessingly. When he'd first glanced into her expressive eyes he had seen honesty but also a stubborn resolve and determination in her look that made him think she was a widow, bound and determined to keep her ranch. However, the girlish flush at being caught staring baffled him slightly. It made him think of a young girl mortified at being caught looking at a man and he frowned confused. She was definitely a beautiful woman but not young, perhaps in her late twenties. She must have been married at one time.

He shrugged slightly to himself determined to understand what she meant by 'my' ranch. He lowered his gaze to her stallion in appreciation. He approved of the way she handled her horse but wondered how she managed to keep a stud under control. She almost seemed a part of him.

At that moment Melissa was wondering what Jed would think when she told him how she had acquired the ranch and what her profession was. She grimaced slightly in anxiety. What would he say? She was sure he wouldn't understand, as most outsiders didn't. Most of the town's people hadn't understood it at first either. Of course, they hadn't known she was a woman when she had first started working there, but over the years she had proven herself many times over to be more capable at the job than any man.

After riding south for most of the day they turned southeast for several hours before cresting a hill, just as the sun was slowly sinking. Melissa heard Jed draw in a deep breath of amazement and she smiled in satisfaction. The view before them was spectacular!

Nestled in a valley was a long two-story ranch house painted red and white, surrounded by trees on three sides. There were two large corrals neatly constructed and painted, with two-dozen mares and their foals that were sired by Lightning inside one. In the other corral were six horses, some for breeding and some for gelding. The barn on the right side of the corrals was also painted red.

On the left side of the corrals were two bunkhouses side by side, both painted white. Further back Jed could see a couple other small buildings probably for chickens, pigs, and milk cows. Surprisingly enough, nothing was built from logs. Everything was built with lumber, which was an unusual sight in Dakota. Another large building could be seen about two miles north, deeper into the forest.

Melissa heard a warning shout from the ranch yard and saw half a dozen of her men galloping towards them. She slowed her horse, frowning in disapproval, knowing now why she hadn't seen Joe at his post. He must have seen them coming and rushed ahead to forewarn the other men that strangers were with her. She stopped to wait for them with a scowl of annoyance. The others in her party stopped unquestioningly.

As the wolf growled a warning, Jed snapped his fingers sharply not wanting him to get shot by mistake. "Three Toes come here and lay down."

Three Toes obediently moved closer to Jed. The horse snorted irritably and sidled sideways slightly. The wolf lay down dutifully and watched the newcomers closely with no more show of hostility, his job of alerting his master now done.

Jed watched the man in front closely, guessing him to be the foreman of the ranch. He had dark brown hair and was clean-shaven. He estimated his age to be early forty's with hair slightly greying. The closer he got the more Jed could see of the man. He had leathery looking skin and obviously spent a lot of time outdoors. When he was close enough Jed could see honesty and straight forwardness in the man's brown eyes. Jed grunted slightly to himself in approval at Melissa's choice of foreman.

Melissa's men came to a halt a few yards in front of her. The foreman eyed the strangers suspiciously. Speaking for all the men waiting anxiously behind him, he looked at Melissa enquiringly, nodding towards the two men with a slight hint of command in his tone inquired. "Do you have a problem here?"

Melissa sighed in vexation and shook her head in incredulity at her foreman, waving slightly in furious reprimand at her men. "Of course not you know that I can take care of myself."

Her men looked abashed, smiling sheepishly at each other, but it was her foreman who spoke for them again as he smirked without any hint of guilt on his face. He shrugged in explanation at his angry boss. "We can't help it Mell, we worry about you, and so I guess you'll just have to put up with us!"

Mell grinned resignedly well aware that her men would never change. She chuckled slightly in humour at the look of amazement on her men's faces' as they looked the strangers over carefully. After introducing everyone she motioned to her foreman as she pointed at Giant Bear. "Wade, I want Giant Bear to work here and Jed will be working with me in town."

Jed frowned in surprise, nodding without question when Mell turned to him in forewarning. "Be ready to ride before sun up. Wade will show you where to bunk down."

Melissa glanced down at the wolf then looked back at Jed as she cocked an eyebrow in enquiry. Jed shrugged in apology then smiled at Mell's silent question concerning the wolf. "Three Toes chooses his own path."

Melissa looked down at the wolf nodding in acceptance as her expression softened considerably. "He can go anywhere he wants on my land. After all, it's the least I can do after he saved my life."

Wade gave Mell a quizzical look when she looked back at him but he didn't comment knowing that she would explain things to him at their customary meeting later that night. He beckoned for Jed to follow him and they turned their horses towards the ranch.

Mell felt that Jed's friend would be more comfortable with Dan, who was half Cheyenne, so waved him towards Giant Bear. "Take Giant Bear to the bunkhouse and help him settle in."

Giant Bear had eyed the half-breed Cheyenne in curiosity as Melissa and her foreman were speaking. He was in his early thirties with the typical light dusky skin of a half-breed. He had dark brown eyes and black shoulder length hair with a headband that showed he had once lived with the Cheyenne. His gaze was direct as he stared intriguingly at Giant Bear, without shame, for having chosen to live with the white man rather than his Cheyenne family. Giant Bear inclined his head slightly as he grinned in praise towards Mell, at her choice, when he past her but didn't comment.

Melissa nudged her horse into a trot as she headed for the ranch house after waving to the rest of her men to go about their business. She was glad to be home in familiar surroundings where she could get her bewildered thoughts together.

When she entered the yard and got closer to the barn her horse had to step up slightly as a sharp hollow sound came from the horse's hooves for a moment. Lightning was crossing planks that were laid along the ground in the form of a sidewalk going from the house, to a small door on the left hand side of the barn. More wooden planks went from the barn door and turned left towards the paddocks then went to a small gate that her father could open to go through with a ramp that allowed him to coast in his wheelchair to firm ground. This had been constructed to help him get to the barn and corrals without assistance when he needed to.

Melissa looked down and was surprised to see that Three Toes had followed her. Laughing down at him in permission she nodded in amusement. "Okay, you can come too if you want."

Melissa dismounted not far from the barn doors and immediately young Tommy appeared from the stables to care for her horse. When he saw the wolf he stopped short and trembled in shock and terror. Melissa smiled in encouragement at the young boy and held out her reins invitingly. "He won't hurt you Tommy I promise. He saved my life!"

Tommy was taking no chances as he grabbed the horse's reins and ran back into the stable without comment. Melissa laughed at the retreating boy and shook her head in humour. He was only ten after all, with light brown hair and blue sorrowful eyes with the high cheekbones of the half-breed Indians. He hadn't left the ranch since his mother brought him here at the age of six for Mell to look after.

She shook off her reflective mood and turned away from the stables as she raced across the yard to the veranda steps. She took the four steps two at a time and walked towards the front door. A little further to the right was a gently sloping ramp for her father's wheelchair that he used to get to the sidewalk that allowed him to move about more freely.

Three Toes slipped by Melissa when she opened the door and he trotted inside uninvited. Having completely forgotten about the wolf she made a grab for him but missed. "Oh no you don't!"

She was too late as Three Toes looked back at Melissa with what she could only describe as a wolfish grin and Mell chuckled in surrender as she let him have his way. "Okay, I said you could go anywhere you wanted so you can stay."

Melissa glanced around in pleasure as she slowly began removing her outer clothing. She was very proud of her home. It was much bigger than the others in the area and more open than most ranch houses around. It was made of lumber not logs and it even had a second floor. Only one other ranch could boast about having a second story and it belonged to Brian.

There was a large front entrance leading into a wide hallway. To the left was a stairway that led to the second floor. The banister was made of oak intricately carved at the top and bottom with a lion's head. Under the stairway was a room where linens and cleaning supplies were kept.

Upstairs there were five bedrooms. The one on the left was the master bedroom which had its own sitting room. Then there were two guest rooms tastefully decorated. Gloria and Tommy occupied the remaining two bedrooms at the end of the hallway. All the bedrooms had fireplaces in them for cold winter nights.

Melissa frowned as her thoughts returned to Tommy again. She just couldn't help herself. He was such a sad boy for his age but very intelligent and too mature for one so young. Tommy was Mary's son, and she was Brian's sister. Tommy was half Cheyenne and because of this, his uncle hated him. He had threatened to harm her son so Mary had brought him to Melissa and Tommy had been with Mell since. Melissa shook all thoughts of her adopted son from her mind as she continued disrobing.

Her reflection once again turned to her home. On the right side of the main entrance there was a large formal drawing room with a western décor. It boasted a piano, a huge fireplace along the far wall, and a large portrait of her mother hanging above the mantel. This room had seldom been used since Melissa and her father had moved in, only a couple of times for formal parties.

Past the drawing room was the dining room, which leads to the kitchen and then the back entrance with a door that leads into the cellar. Across the hallway from the kitchen was her father's living quarters, which included access to the library and den.

Since her father had come to live with her she had redesigned the downstairs of her home to accommodate him. She had added a comfortable leather couch and chair around the fireplace in the library. Shelves lined each wall, which held books of every description. Some had belonged to the previous owner and her dad had added all of his, which filled the bookshelves to capacity.

An archway connected the library to a den, which was large enough to hold a couch and several chairs, along with a cozy fireplace. A desk with chairs surrounding it was against the wall across from the archway, where Alec did the daily ranch business. The den's main entryway was almost directly across the hallway from the dining room.

Melissa hung her clothing and holster on pegs along the wall, before putting on her inside moccasins, as she turned and headed down the hallway calling out expectantly. "Dad, Gloria, where are you?"

She heard the squeak of wheels coming from the den as she hurried past the stairway then turned left and pushed the door further open since it was slightly ajar. As she entered the den she stopped short in surprise. There was Three Toes sitting on his haunches regarding her father fixedly with his head cocked slightly to the left. Her father was staring just as intently at the wolf in awe wondering if it was safe to move.

Melissa regarded her father while he was occupied studying the wolf. Her smile was both loving and sad. She had inherited his curly blonde hair but his eyes were crystal blue, while hers were turquoise like her mothers. Before the accident put him in the chair he had stood at six feet eight inches tall, which accounted for Melissa's height. Her mother had died in the same accident that put her father in the chair. Pain and worry lines filled his craggy face, which had once been filled with love and laughter. She pushed thoughts of her mother away. It was still too painful for her even after all this time.

She had learned about something called a wheelchair that was being used in the hospitals in Boston. When she went to investigate this new invention and saw the huge ugly high backed chairs they had, she knew there was no way that Alec could manoeuvre that cumbersome thing around by himself.

She eyed her father's chair in pride. She and the ranch hands had custom made it just for him, as well as his outside chair. The custom made wheelchair allowed him to keep his pride, making it possible for him to be independent.

When she returned from Boston Melissa and her men had taken a sturdy wooden chair and cut off the legs. They made two wheels similar to wagon wheels, but smaller, and riveted them into the center of the chair making sure that the wheels moved freely and that they were strong enough to hold her father's weight. It was only made of wood of course so wasn't sturdy enough for outside. But while she had been in Boston she had bought one of those new bicycles. Of course one of her men just had to come up with the idea of using that for an outside chair. It hadn't taken them long to figure out how to put it together and make it work. Melissa lost her bicycle but it had been well worth the loss to see the look of relief and contentment on her father's face.

Melissa shrugged off her thoughts then laughed at the sight of the two staring at each other so intently. She shook her head in amusement as she walked over to her father's chair and bent down to kiss him on the cheek. "Hi dad, how was your day?"

Alec Ray looked away from the wolf for a moment as he accepted his daughter's kiss then glanced at her in loving pride. "Mine was fine how was yours?"

Melissa grinned down at her father as she patted his shoulder in reassurance then she motioned towards the wolf and made introductions. "Just great dad, this is Three Toes."

Then she looked over at the wolf and snapped her fingers sharply in invitation. "Come here boy and meet my father."

Three Toes instantly dropped to his belly whining eagerly and crawled forward, as he approached Alec's chair ever so slowly. When he reached him Three Toe's raised his head until Alec's hand touched him, and then still unthreateningly, he sniffed the hand that Alec had turned over for him.

Alec beamed in delight then he leaned forward to touch the wolf fully when the wolf licked his hand in greeting, and introductions were complete. Alec looked up at Mell enquiringly as he continued to stroke the wolf's silky fur in enjoyment. "He's a fine looking animal. Where did you find him?"

Melissa smiled down in appreciation at the wolf's antics, and looked back at her father as she gestured casually. "I hired a couple of new hands today and Three Toes was with them. He decided that he liked me better and followed me into the house. He saved my life so I couldn't refuse to let him in."

Alec looked back down at the wolf to hide his concerned expression as he frowned slightly in surprise, but didn't ask any more questions. His face under control once again he looked up and waved towards the kitchen. "Gloria came in a few moments ago to call us for supper but I decided to wait for you. How about giving your old man a helping hand?"

Melissa chuckled in humour at his reference to himself, in calling himself 'old man', then walked around her father's chair and took hold of the handles while gladly pushing him into the kitchen where supper was waiting.

CHAPTER TWO

After supper Melissa and Alec went out on the veranda to watch the sunset as they did every evening to discuss the day's events. The days were getting noticeably longer and soon they would be able to take longer evening ride, which Alec thoroughly enjoyed.

Alec, unable to keep silent any longer, cleared his throat loudly as his curiosity got the best of him. He wanted to know about the two new men Melissa had hired. He was mystified at her decision to hire new hands without first discussing it with him, as was her usual custom. "How about telling me about your new hands and about the wolf saving your life?"

After thinking it over Melissa decided not to tell him about the three men who had chased her earlier. She realized that they couldn't have been her men because Wade would have teased her when she had arrived back at the ranch. So instead she told him about the rattlesnake and being rescued by her new companions.

Alec looked away to hide his hopeful expression then turned back once he had his face under control again and indicated hastily as soon as she finished her tale. "I want to meet them."

Melissa sighed in resignation already knowing what he was up to. She knew that he would check Jed out then decide whether or not he was marriage material then he would try to play matchmaker again. It happened every time new hands were hired. Melissa shook her head in irritation but couldn't refuse her father anything. She motioned enticingly hoping to distract him. "Do you want to ride tonight Dad?"

Alec beamed over at his daughter in pleasure giving her an innocent look. "Oh, that would be wonderful!"

Melissa sighed not fooled at all by her father's expressionless face then left and went to the barn to ask Tommy and Dan to saddle up Lightning and Lady for their evening ride, while Alec went to change.

Melissa saw Wade standing by the corral as she was leaving the barn and beckoned him over. "Wade, please bring Jed and Giant Bear over to meet my father."

Wade snickered knowingly guessing what Alec was up to then shook his head teasingly at Mell. "Are you sure you want me to do that?"

Mell grimaced in embarrassment then flushed slightly because at one time her father had tried matching her up with Wade. It was a standing joke in the bunkhouse as to whether Alec would ever succeed in finding her a husband.

Wade turned and walked away making sure Mell heard him as he mischievously whistled a wedding tune.

Melissa frowned in annoyance as she waited for her father thinking it would be all over the bunkhouse by tomorrow. Oh well she thought shrugging. There was nothing she could do about it. Her father would never change.

Alec wheeled his outside chair down the ramp and over to his daughter then smiled up at her still trying to look innocent. "Well, where are these men you were talking about?"

Just then Wade came around the corner with Jed and Giant Bear in tow. Alec whistled in appreciation at the size of the two men especially the Cheyenne. "Boy, you sure weren't exaggerating about their size."

Jed walked over to the boss and was surprised to see the older gentleman with her. It didn't take him long to realize that he was probably her father. He had the same thick slightly curly blonde hair as his daughter and he would surely be just as tall as Jed himself if it weren't for that chair he was in. That would account for Melissa's height but he had crystal blue eyes, therefore, Melissa must have inherited her mother's eyes. Jed waited for introductions then shook Alec's hand firmly.

Alec could see the interest in Jed's eyes and smirked in response. Smiling he turned his attention to Giant Bear. He was amazed at his enormous size, and there wasn't an ounce of fat to be seen. He reminded Alec of someone but he couldn't quite remember who the person was at this time. Alec was familiar with his language and began to converse with Giant Bear in his own tongue trying to make him feel more welcome.

Jed was taken aback at Alec's fluency in the Cheyenne language for very few white men could converse in the native tongues. Jed turned to Melissa inquisitively, or Mell as her ranch hands called her. Melissa looked at him and smiled broadly at the surprise on his face. "I can also speak in three native languages."

That surprised Jed even more and his regard for her went up a notch. Even he couldn't speak in three Indian languages, only two. He gazed around the homestead in admiration. It was definitely a beautiful place. Dan walked towards them leading two horses and Jed wondered who was riding the mare.

Wade moved Alec's wheelchair over to the mare and helped Dan lift Alec into the saddle. They strapped his legs against the horse's girth to hold them in place when his horse went faster than a walk.

Jed admired the way Alec sat on his horse even with his useless legs. Obviously Alec hadn't always been in a wheelchair. Jed was impressed that the old man didn't let his handicap stop him from riding.

Mell turned to Jed and nodded good-bye with a slight insistent note in her voice. "I'll see you at the barn by five o'clock sharp! I want to be out of here no later than six."

Mell turned to Giant Bear next without giving Jed a chance to comment and nodded farewell to him as well. "I hope you'll like working here."

Giant Bear grunted in acknowledgment as he watched Mell mount her horse then couldn't help mumbling to himself in a low tone. "I think it might be interesting."

Jed watched them ride away and noticed Three Toes loping along beside Alec's horse. He turned to Giant Bear and laughed good-naturedly, not in the least put out. "It looks like Three Toes has adopted Mell and her father."

Giant Bear smiled at his friend but made no reply. He turned towards the bunkhouse since he hadn't had any supper yet and left Jed standing there staring after Mell and her father.

Jed stood for a while longer and reflected pensively on the evening he had spent with Wade. He had talked a lot but really hadn't told him much about Melissa. All he had learned was that she had worked in town for about ten years. At first she had lived in the saloon since there had been no hotel in town at that time.

She had moved out to the ranch and had been here the last six years. That was all he could get out of Wade. Jed had asked about Mell's job in town but Wade had just smirked in humour and refused to answer, much to Jed's disappointment. He shrugged his shoulders resignedly then reminded himself that patience was a virtue. He would learn more in the days to come, he was sure.

Jed went into the bunkhouse for some dinner. He had been too busy settling in earlier to eat. The only men still at the table were Giant Bear and the stableman Dan who looked more Indian than white. Hopefully, Jed could find out some information from him about the woman he was looking for. He dished up some stew that had been left on the back of the cook stove, and went over to sit beside Giant Bear.

Jed stuck out his hand to Dan in introduction. "I'm Jed Brown to the whites, and Grey Wolf to the Indians."

Dan shook Jed's hand firmly then inclined his head slightly in greeting. "I'm Dan to the whites and Red Eagle to the Cheyenne."

Jed grinned in acknowledgment then dug into his stew ravenously. He was hungrier than he had realized. After eating in silence he pushed the bowl aside, and turned to Dan inquiringly. "How long have you lived in North Dakota?"

Dan eyed the inquisitive Jed thoughtfully wondering where this was going, but didn't see any harm in the questions so answered honestly. "Well, I've lived on this ranch for twelve years now and I was born and raised right in town although I did go stay with my Cheyenne family for awhile."

Jed sighed in relief maybe now he could finally get some answers. "Good! Maybe you can help me then; I'm looking for a white woman."

Dan chuckled knowingly then waved towards town. "I can introduce you to a few at Chelsie's Bar, although Chelsie doesn't like her girls getting that close to the men, but she does look the other way occasionally. Or Pam's Ladies', at the local fancy house in town, but I don't get any time off until next week."

Jed hooted in amusement then shook his head negatively at the misunderstanding. "No, no I'm not looking for that kind of woman. I'm looking for a specific woman. I can't tell you much about this one because I have no idea who she is. All I can tell you is that she should be in her forties or fifties, and she killed two men somewhere around fourteen or so years ago then turned three others into the authorities. These three men later escaped I can't tell you why she turned them in. All I can do is guess that either they tried to kill her, or were rustling her cattle, or maybe even both."

Dan sat for a few moments rubbing his chin thoughtfully then looked at Jed and shook his head negatively. "No, I've never heard about anything like that happening around here, and I definitely would have heard about it. North Dakota has only recently been civilized, and fourteen years ago there were very few women around. The town was just beginning then so there were only a couple of white women but non-outside of town. Another point to consider is that we have the only law in North Dakota. If something like that had happened anywhere nearby, the Sheriff would have taken the outlaws into custody and brought them in to hang."

Dan watched disappointment flicker over Jed's face for a moment then motioned intriguingly as he leaned forward enthusiastically sensing a good story. "Why are you looking for this woman if you don't mind me asking?"

Jed exhaled noisily in aggravation he had thought for a moment there that his search was over, but again he was thwarted. He shrugged gravely at Dan and answered honestly. "We're actually looking for the three men that got away. We think they're around here searching for the woman, if we find her we should be able to find the men."

Dan sat back then tapped his lower lip with his index finger reflectively for a long moment, knowing that Jed wasn't going to tell him anymore but wanting to help then motioned at Jed inquisitively. "Are you sure she lives in North Dakota?"

Jed shook his head negatively. "No, why do you ask?"

Dan smiled confidently figuring he had the answer, he waved towards the south dramatically. "Could she be from South Dakota? I ask because it was civilized longer than North Dakota."

Jed grumbled reluctantly not really having any clue. "We don't know for sure. All we have is the name, Dakota."

Dan heaved a sigh of disappointment then shrugged in regret. "Not much to go on. You can talk to some of the old timers tonight if you think it might help. We usually have a poker game going later in the evening. But I'm betting the woman you're looking for is living in South Dakota, or did at one time."

Jed scowled dejectedly and turned to Giant Bear resignedly as he motioned in frustration. "I guess we'll just have to keep looking. We will stay here until the end of the month or until those men kill again whichever comes first."

Dan pushed back his chair as he got up to leave. "I'm sorry I couldn't be more help to you."

Dan turned to Giant Bear inquiringly willing to please. "Are you sure you want to sleep in the barn?"

Giant Bear nodded his head that he did but didn't answer.

Dan frowned in disappointment, he had hoped to spend more time with Giant Bear, oh well tomorrow would do he supposed. He turned back to Jed then nodded expectantly at him. "I'll see you tonight at the poker game then."

He turned with a wave once Jed inclined his head slightly in confirmation that he was going to play poker with them. He left for the barn to finish up his chores, while he waited for Mell and her father to get back.

* * *

Mell led her father towards Devil's Rock they weren't going that far of course since it was a five day trip if you weren't in a hurry. She always tried to find different ways to travel so that her father wouldn't get bored.

As she rode along her thoughts kept returning to the three men who had shot at her earlier. Who were they and why were they on her land? She was definitely going to have to find out tomorrow when she went back to work. There was just no way was she going to allow anyone to trespass on her land shooting at people without trying to put a stop to it. If she had known it wasn't her men in the beginning she would have turned back and followed them to see where they were going, but unfortunately she hadn't known, and to go back now would be futile they could be miles away.

They were about an hour away from the ranch when Alec rode up beside Mell. He cleared his throat noisily to catch her attention as he motioned curiously in concern. "What's the matter Mell? You've been so quiet tonight it's not like you to be this quiet. Something must be troubling you?"

Mell turned to look at her father and grimaced in apology. "I'm sorry Dad. Do you mind if we cut this short? I have a few things to figure out and I'm just not in the mood for riding."

Alec inclined his head in understanding not even hesitating as he turned his horse around and headed towards home. "Did something happen at work that I should know about? Or does it have something to do with your new hands? I've never seen either one of them before and it's not like you to hire complete strangers without talking to me first."

Mell looked over at her father in reassurance then she smiled and shook her head negatively. "No Dad nothing happened at work everything was fairly quiet. As for the new hands, I don't really know why I hired them we don't really need anyone right now. It was just a spur of the moment decision made more out of curiosity than anything else. I've never seen an Indian Chief traveling around with a white man before, especially in white man's territory. I'm hoping to find out the answer tomorrow. I'm taking Jed to work with me and I'm hoping he's more open-minded than most men. If I get the typical reaction from him that I get from others I'll be very upset."

Alec nodded in understanding remembering how disappointed she was in the town men when they had first found out she was a woman. "You like Jed, don't you?"

Mell glared at her dad in dismay then frowned in forewarning as she gestured sharply in rebuke. "I don't even know the man! And don't you start your match making with him! For all we know he might be a killer, or a hired gun. Until I know more about him you just stay away from him!"

Alec smirked shrewdly at Mell. "I think you protest too much!"

He held up his hands in surrender and chortled in amusement as he saw Mell gearing up to give him another blast. "Okay Mell, I'm sorry. I'll stay out of it until you know more about him."

Mell heaved a sigh relieved as they came in sight of the stables not wanting to continue the conversation.

Dan and Tommy came out and helped Alec into his chair before tending to the horses.

Mell thanked them both then pushed her father to the house. Three Toes followed them into the house without even hesitating and trotted into the den without waiting for them.

Alec beamed up at his daughter in pleasure as he motioned after the retreating wolf. "It looks like Three Toes has adopted us. He even knows which is our favourite room already."

Mell smirk benevolently down at her father but made no comment. She pushed him into the den then through the archway into the library and over to the table where he kept his pipe, tobacco, and current book. Three Toes was already under the table sleeping.

Gloria, Mell's maid popped her head through the door to make sure it was Mell and Alec making all the noise. "You're back early. Do you want your tea and cakes now or do you want me to wait a bit?"

Alec eyed Mell's slightly plump middle-aged maid and couldn't help grinning. Gloria at four feet nine inches tall with light hazel laughing eyes always seemed to bring out a grin from Alec. But don't let her smiling eyes fool you, she had a strong will, and would take no back talk from anyone and she was absolutely loyal to them. Alec motioned plaintively over at Mell in explanation, but didn't look away from the maid as he beamed over at Gloria. "Mell didn't feel like riding anymore so we came back early. You can bring the tea anytime there's no rush."

Gloria nodded and ducked back out of the door.

Alec turned back to Mell as she sat down on the couch and his expression sobered in thought as he brought the subject back to their two new hands. "So you think the men are up to something?"

Mell shrugged indifferently not really sure what was causing her apprehension, and not wanting her father to read anything special in all this, so she kept her tone casual. "I don't know for sure. I'm hoping Jed will confide in me tomorrow."

Alec nodded thoughtfully not fooled by Mell's tone as he eyed her speculatively not wanting to give up talking about the men yet, so he continued. "Do you think there's anything at the Sheriff's office on them? Maybe you should look into that tomorrow."

Mell scowled in exasperation wanting to get off the subject of her unease then gestured placatingly. "I don't know Dad but I'll look into it tomorrow when I go into town I promise."

Gloria entered with a tray and set it on the table. She was just pouring tea for Alec and Mell when Wade came in, so she poured a cup for him and another for herself as they all found seats. This was an evening ritual and every night they gathered together to talk about their day.

Wade helped himself to a cake from the tray then turned to Mell and motioned in aggravation. "That new man of yours Jed, he's been asking a lot of questions about three men and a white woman in her forties or fifties. When he wasn't asking about them he tried to find out more information about you and your father."

Mell shrugged unperturbed that Jed was asking about them. "It's only natural for them to ask questions about us since now he will be working for us. I'll be taking Jed with me tomorrow so I'll find out what he's up to then I hope."

Wade nodded in satisfaction and changed the subject. "Mell, you only have about a week or two before you have to start riding your gelding instead of Lightning. It's that time of year again!"

Mell exhaled noisily in disappointment she hated leaving him behind but they had several horses that needed breeding. Everyone in the room could hear the disgruntlement in her voice as she concurred. "Let me know when you need him and I'll switch horses."

Wade chuckled at her tone but didn't say anything. He didn't really have anything interesting to report tonight so the four sat quietly drinking their tea.

Mell looked at the mantel where the clock sat and right on time she heard the hum of low voices as the rest of the hands entered the den first then the library. They milled around for a moment then everyone quieted respectfully as Mell rose from her chair and cleared her throat for quiet. "Anybody have anything interesting to report?"

Mell watched everyone shake their heads in denial and she frowned pensively, well obviously nobody else saw those three strangers she had seen earlier. It relieved her mind slightly they were probably just passing through fortunately.

Mell smirked mischievously as she looked over at Jed and decided to tell her men about her run in with the wolf and snake. She beckoned to Jed and Giant Bear to step forward. "As you're all aware by now we have two new hands Jed Brown and Chief Giant Bear of the Montana Cheyenne."

Both men stepped forward and nodded in acknowledgment of the introductions.

Mell looked under the table and smiled fondly at the sleeping wolf then waved down at him. "And this is there wolf; Three Toes even though he seems to have adopted us for the moment, let me tell you how he saved my life!"

The men all listened raptly as Mell told her story and Jed grinned in humour as he watched her embellish the story until all her men were jumping in reaction at all the right places. They gasped in surprise as she snarled like the wolf and jumped towards her men as if attacking them, even Three Toes looked up at that for a moment. Seeing no other animal around he laid his head back down and went back to sleep in disinterest.

Jed leaned towards Giant Bear then whispered so the others wouldn't hear him. "She's good isn't she?"

Giant Bear grunted as he indicated agreement. "She would make a good story teller."

Mell finished then smirked in satisfaction at her excited men as they talked among themselves appreciating her dramatics.

One by one the men started going to Mell to wish her a good night then each one stopped and shook Jed and Giant Bears hand then introduced themselves before leaving.

Jed and Giant Bear left after wishing Mell a good night and quiet descended for a moment as Alec, Wade, Gloria, and Mell finished their tea in silence.

Wade got up and turned to Alec before he left as he waved in farewell. "I'll see you in the morning to go over the supplies list instead of tonight I think I'll retire early."

Wade then turned to Mell after Alec nodded and tipped his hat respectfully in farewell before leaving.

Gloria got up hastily as soon as he left and looked down at Alec then bobbed her head goodnight before she turned to Mell anxiously and motioned expectantly. "I'll bring you the list of supplies I need tomorrow as well. So if there's nothing else, I'll take the tray to the kitchen, and call it an early night too."

Mell beamed up at Gloria wondering what all the rush was tonight then waved her out impatiently. "It's okay Gloria you go on ahead I'll take the tray to the kitchen on my way to bed."

Gloria mumbled her thanks hurriedly and scurried out of the room as if she had forgotten something.

Mell smiled over at her father then got up and walked over to his chair for a goodnight kiss. "I'm going to bed early as well I think I tuckered myself out with that story. Is there anything you need before I go another book perhaps or more tea before I take the tray?"

Alec shook his head in refusal before accepting a goodnight kiss. "No, I don't need anything. I'll probably go to bed late so my chair can sit by my bed for one night."

Mell leaned down further after giving her father a kiss to give Three Toes a goodnight pat under the table, before she picked up the tray, and left to deposit it in the kitchen sink before she went up to her room.

* * *

Out in the bunkhouse Jed sat down at the poker game and was introduced to everyone again. There was Dan the half-breed, of course he worked in the stables, and was dark like the Indians but fairly husky almost fat like the white man.

Then there was Cookie, the bunkhouse cook, Gloria wouldn't allow him anywhere near her kitchen so he only cooked for the hands. He looked like a cook to with chubby cheeks, a double chin, and he was just about as round as he was tall at five feet three inches. His character was plain to see in his face by the merry look in his grey blue eyes and the laugh lines visible all over his baby face.

Jerry was next with his typical cowboy look he was one of the horse breakers. He was painfully thin and wiry with honest hazel eyes, and light brown hair. He had a habit of slouching slightly so was taller then he looked at five foot eleven inches. Jed figured he had some Mexican in him he moved with a slow almost methodical grace, and Jed figured he'd be one tough hombre when riled.

Dwayne sat next to Jerry he had black hair, and blue green eyes. He was medium build and average in height at five feet five inches tall. He helped with the horse breeding but only reluctantly. He nodded dismissively at Jed not even bothering with any greeting. He was very good looking and knew it by the look of him. He was dressed like a fancy gambler but Jed figured he wasn't good enough for that, that's why he was breeding horses instead of gambling. He didn't look like much but Jed knew that looks could be deceiving sometimes.

There were two others at the table both older than the rest, but he didn't catch their names, Jed wasn't interested in them anyway except maybe for information he could tell just by looking at them that they were just ordinary cowpokes.

Wade wasn't among the players and two others were lying on their bunks sleeping so he didn't get a good look at them.

Dan smiled over at Jed and explained the rules. "We don't play for big stakes here, Mell doesn't allow us to. We open the game with a penny, and you can't go any higher than a dollar."

Jed threw a penny on the pile then while the cards were being dealt out he tried to bring the conversation around to what he wanted to talk about. He assumed a casual talkative tone pretending he wasn't really interested in the answers. "There seems to be a lot of men working here for such a small ranch."

Cookie frowned over at Jed pensively not sure if he should tell the new hand anything or not. Finally he decided to just give him vague answers if he wanted to know more he would have to ask Mell. "Well, most of us were working here before Mell and her father came. We worked for Bradley Henderson when he was alive; back then there were a lot of cattle here. When the town took it over they sold all the cattle but left us on anyway to look after the place. When Mell and her father took over they let us all stay on even though they don't really need all of us most of the time. They always seem to find something for us to do."

Jed nodded distractedly not really caring why there was so many men here, but wanting to keep the old cook talking as he threw another penny into the pot for two more cards. "What happened to Alec, how did he loose the use of his legs?"

Cookie shrugged not sure of the answer to that question. "All we know is that he was in a carriage accident that also killed his wife and the doctors said he would never walk again."

Jed scowled in disappointment then tried another question as he looked at his cards in interest he had a full house kings and three's, so he threw two bits into the pot. He assumed a casual tone trying not to let the others know just how interested he was. "And what job does Mell do in town?"

The other men exchanged looks and grins not fooled by Jed's tone at all. But it was Cookie who answered for all of them as he grinned mischievously at Jed then couldn't help the teasing note in his voice. "You'll have to ask Mell that question."

Jed nodded in dissatisfaction then dropped his cards on the table face up. "Read them and weep!"

All the men groaned in frustration and threw their cards into the center of the table as Jed raked in his winnings.

Cookie gathered up the cards and began shuffling them.

Jed sighed in exasperation still unable to get any answers about Mell so he thought it best to turn to a different subject of conversation. He would try again later to find out more about her. "How long ago was the town built?"

Cookie now the official spokesman continued to answer Jed's enquires as he dealt out the cards. "They started building the town about fourteen years ago, but there weren't many people here then. It wasn't until about ten years ago that we even had enough people here to call it a town, but it was pretty lawless at that time the Sheriff was pretty old, and we only had a few woman around mostly Ladies that you can't tell your wife about."

Jed grimaced and exhaled noisily in frustration already knowing the answer but he asked Cookie the same question he had asked Dan earlier anyway.

Cookie looked at the two older cowboys for conformation and saw them shake their heads negatively. Then he turned back to Jed and shook his head in denial as well. "Never heard of anything like that happening around here."

Jed scowled in disappointment at the expected answer then picked up his cards and began playing without asking any more questions.

CHAPTER THREE

Melissa woke while it was still dark outside as she usually did and wondered why she felt so peculiar this morning. Perhaps it was just nerves because she was taking Jed with her. She hoped that she wouldn't get the customary reaction from him that she got from other men. Mell shrugged to herself there was only one way to find out. She got up and lit a candle before dressing it was time to go to work!

* * *

In the bunkhouse, Jed finished getting dressed and had a few minutes to spare so sat back down on his bunk to think about last night's poker game. He had quizzed everyone about the three men he was tracking, and the woman who had killed two men then sent the other three to jail, but nobody seemed to know anything about the woman or the three men.

He was also frustrated because he couldn't get any information about Mell either or about what kind of work he was going to be doing, everyone just snickered it was really making him nervous. The worst of it was that he didn't know why he felt it was so important to find out what she did for a living. Maybe it was because he didn't want her to be a madam of a whorehouse, or a saloon owner that had ladies of questionable means. Jed shook his head irritably at himself then told himself to quit thinking about Mell, she is what she is, and it wasn't up to him to criticize. He needed to concentrate on finding out where the three men and that mysterious woman were, not on Mell.

He had tracked the three men slowly across Montana and into the Dakota Territory, but after that they just disappear again; it seemed that every time he got even remotely close to catching them. Unexpectedly they would disappear without a trace! There was no wanted poster out on them because they never left anyone alive to identify them. Unfortunately, Jed only had a vague description from his dying son. The Sheriff he had talked to in Montana said it wasn't enough to go by.

In Montana they were known as the Shadow Killers. They seemed to kill for no reason and they only hit women or children that were alone. That's why he was looking for the woman that his dying son had mentioned, but he had no description of her either. Every time he heard of the Shadow Killers, killing again, he would rush there but of course they were gone.

Well he'd just have to keep his eyes and ears open and sooner or later they would kill again then he would be able to continue the chase. Right now it was time to get moving, so he strapped on his gun then walked towards the door.

Cookie intercepted him at the door with a bowl of porridge and handed it to him with a merry twinkle in his eye, but he used a firm no nonsense tone as he shook a beefy finger at Jed warningly. "Eat before you go, I can't in all good consciousness let you go until then."

Jed nodded in thanks and ate obediently then handed back the bowl before rushing out, it was almost five o'clock. Jed hurried into the barn then slowed when he heard voices. He was just in time to see Mell slapping Wade on the back with a laugh of pleasure at something Wade said. Jed stopped abruptly and scowled at the pair, he had to restrain himself all of a sudden from marching over there and stepping in between them.

Mell caught sight of Jed suddenly and stopped what she was going to say to Wade. She smirked at Jed good-humouredly instead. "What took you so long?"

Jed's smile was a little strained as he fought the feelings of jealousy he couldn't help feeling. "I'll be with you in a moment."

Mell oblivious of the battle Jed was having with himself, turned back to Wade inquisitively. "You have your instructions for today. Do you or any of the other guys need anything from town?"

Wade smirked perceptively after Jed but unlike Mell he had caught the furious green-eyed look on Jed's face. He turned to Mell and put his arm around her. He just couldn't help himself that look on Jed's face made him do it "Yeah, Mark wants a plug of chewing tobacco and Dwayne wants a pack of his favourite cigars."

Mell moved away from Wade taken by surprise, but not before she elbowed him in the ribs in rebuke, as she continued. "Okay, I'll see you tonight if nothing unusual comes up."

A groan of agreement was all she got from Wade, as he messaged his sore ribs; he smirked devilishly at Jed as he walked passed hiding the fact that Mell had elbowed him hard in reproach.

Mell took a hold of her horse's reins and shook her head in puzzlement at how strange Wade was acting all of a sudden. She led her horse out of the barn with her packhorse already tied to her saddle, so he followed her out too.

She mounted as soon as she was clear of the barn. If she could have seen Jed's face as he led his own horse out of the barn she would have been even more bewildered.

Jed struggled to conceal his feelings of jealousy but was unsuccessful as he heard Wade laugh teasingly behind him. Finally succeeding in controlling his look of fury he swung into his saddle and turned to Mell then eyed her packhorse in surprise. Jed speculated again about her job but knew better than to ask.

About half way to Smyth's Crossing Jed's curiosity finally got the best of him. He looked towards Mell and motioned at the horse following Lightning. "Mell, what is the packhorse for?"

Mell grinned naughtily over at Jed and only gave a vague answer not wanting him to know yet. "I started taking a packhorse with me, because sometimes I have to be on the trail for days without notice."

Jed opened his mouth to ask her again what her job was then quickly snapped it shut audibly. He swore he wouldn't ask her again even if it killed him, and it just might.

Mell nudged her horse into a canter it effectively forestalled any more questions. She was running a bit late as it was since it took a good two hours of hard riding to reach Smyth's Crossing, but she had dawdled a little this morning. If she kept them at a leisurely pace it would take them half a day to get to town, and that was unacceptable.

When they rode into town it was just after eight o'clock in the morning. As they entered town Jed looked around speculatively. On the left side was the smithy, and barns. He could just here the whoosh of the forge as it was brought to life. A few horses milled around in the small paddock pawing and snorting in anticipation as a short black haired kid ran out with water and oats for the morning feed.

On the right was the general store with three wagons unloading supplies. There was a lot of groaning and complaining from the five youngsters struggling with sacks of flour, sugar, coffee, and other staples needed.

Jed chuckled in sympathy then turned to his left just in time to see the saloon sign which read Chelsie's Saloon. It was two stories so either had rooms to rent or fancy ladies. He shook his head to himself Dan had said Chelsie frowned on that sort of conduct, so it was probably rooms for rent and for her ladies. It was fairly quiet at this time of the morning. A drunk sleeping it off on the porch swing and he spotted movement in the alley where another drunk had fallen asleep against the building.

Jed nodded in approval to himself at having the barns and the saloon so close together it was a good idea. This way horses were taken there instead of left out in the street.

Next to the saloon was a hotel it was strange having a hotel and a saloon so close together. He could smell fresh bread backing and he sniffed appreciatively it was coming from the hotel. The sounds of people stirring inside caught his ear they probably smelt the bread too, it was making Jed's mouth water, as they went for breakfast.

Jed turned to the right again there was a dentist office, and doctor's office all in one. He chuckled probably the same man did both jobs. Next to that was a barbershop a short older gentleman was sweeping the porch getting ready for the day. A sign on the next building read Barrister Timothy Rowling at Law. Under that was, 'All your Lawyer's needs'.

When he turned left again there was a few houses, and Jed smiled a greeting at a young lady as they passed by. She stopped hanging cloths in order to wave hello. He tipped his hat respectfully, returning the greeting.

A courthouse was almost the last building, unless you looked further down. Jed could see a three-story house just a little ways out of town. It was dark and all by itself he figured it must be the whorehouse Dan had told him about last night.

The few people out at this hour called out good wishes to Mell. "Morning Mell have a good day!"

One even informed her that everything had been quiet since she left. Jed shook his head completely bewildered now obviously she wasn't a madam.

He continued looking around in interest as he turned to his right once more the sheriff's office was next and he could just see beyond that was the stage coach office with a stage just getting ready to leave as he heard the crack of a whip, the slap of the reins, and a loud giddy up from the burly driver.

Mell halted outside the sheriff's office and Jed looked .around anxiously. Although no posters were out on him that he knew of, he just had no use for sheriffs. He found most of them to be obnoxious bullies.

Mell dismounted and tied her horse to the hitching rail then walked into the building before stopping to wait for Jed. After removing her hat she hung it up then she walked around the desk and sat down in the chair then took out a sheriff's badge and pinned it on. Reaching in her desk once more she pulled out a deputy's badge and laid it in front of Jed on her desk.

Jed stood there gaping in astonishment for a moment. His mouth opened and closed several times as if to say something but nothing came out. He visibly pulled himself together as he sat down hard in the chair that was in front of her desk as he shook his head in incredulity then motioned in bewilderment. "How did you a woman get to be a Sheriff when most women can't get any job outside of the home without jeopardizing her reputation? Not to mention your father and the men in this town agreeing to all this to begin with."

Mell shrugged self-consciously. "It's a very long story so sit back and relax while I try to explain everything."

Jed settled back in the chair still having a hard time believing Mell was a sheriff. He watched as Mell get up and poured them both a cup of coffee that someone must have made for her earlier, probably a deputy.

Mell handed him the coffee cup then sat back in her own chair. Her face turned pensive as she thought back to the time before her mother's death then she began… *"I was born and raised in South Dakota in a town called Windy Creek. My father was foreman of the Triple Horse Ranch just a few miles out of town. Except for me all of the children out there were boys, so naturally I learned everything the boys did. I learned to ride before I could walk, and how to shoot a rifle at five. At the age of seven I was learning how to use a revolver as well as how to track people and game. By the time I was ten I could out draw, out shoot, and out track most of the boys I grew up with. When I was thirteen I could out wrestle, and out box most of the men. I was taught to speak three Indian languages mostly by the half-breeds that worked there and how to speak French by one of the cowboys that was from France. My mother taught me reading, writing, and arithmetic. She also tried her best to teach me the ways of a Lady although she despaired of me ever using that knowledge. I also learned how to survive off of the land winter or summer for weeks or months at a time, if necessary. After I had proven myself I was allowed to help the men with round ups and was a great help when problems arose. Most of the time the men forgot I was a girl. I was late in blooming so I resembled a young boy until I was older. My mother couldn't do anything about it I was a real tomboy. But I often wonder if things would have been different if my parents could have had another child, preferably a boy."*

Mell paused and got up to pour more coffee there was only half a cup left for each of them so she added some whisky to their cup. She knew she was going to need it to finish her story then she sat back down and tried to collect her thoughts before she continued.

Jed sat quiet and waited he wanted her to continue in her own time. He was beginning to understand what made Mell the person she was today and he was totally engrossed in her remarkable story.

Mell took a fortifying sip of her whisky laden coffee then continued as her brow became furrowed in pain remembering the day her world was shattered and changed forever… *"Everything was going great until I was fifteen. We were out tracking some rustlers with a few of the ranch hands and managed to find them at the fork in the road not far from the ranch. There were five rustlers all together and four of us. After the smoke settled we had managed to kill two of them and we took the other three to the Sheriff in town. You should have seen their faces when I took my hat off to wipe the sweat off my forehead and they realized that I was a girl. They started shouting insults and loud comments that I didn't understand at that time then they talked about revenge. My parents had gone to town earlier in the day so after we dropped off the rustlers I went looking for them. I asked around town but they had already left which I figured was odd because we should have met them somewhere along the way. After we left town I started looked for their wagon tracks and when I found them I followed. I just had this gut feeling that something was wrong. When we came to the fork in the road that we had used to capture the outlaws I noticed some odd marks. It looked like the horses pulling the carriage had reared. We followed the tracks along the road going east and I knew for sure then that something was definitely wrong because that road led to a dead end with a ravine at the bottom. When we got to the top I could hear a horse screaming in pain and fear down below. We climbed down and the first thing I saw was one of our horse's half sitting attempting to stand up. He was covered with blood and I knew by the look of him he wouldn't make it, the other one was already dead. Then I looked to the left and I saw my mother lying there. I knew before I even got to her that she was dead. Her head, arms, and legs were at unnatural angles obviously broken. Then I heard a groan coming from underneath the carriage when we lifted it my father was laying there breathing heavily, but still alive. I wrapped my mother up in a blanket and put her on my horse then we made a stretcher out of the broken wagon and took them both to town. At first the doctor couldn't find anything wrong with my father except for a large lump on the back of his head. But when they turned him over we noticed a lot of swelling at the base of his spine. The doctor figured that his back was broken and he said that my father would never walk again. I hoped he was wrong at first especially since he was really a vet doctor and only knew a little bit about doctoring humans since he had been forced into it a few times, but unfortunately he had been right. We buried my mother the next day because it would be impossible to know when my father would regain consciousness. It was six months before he came out of the coma and the first thing he did was to ask for my mother. When I broke the news to him he was devastated. The only thing he said was that it should have been him who had died. Later he told me the details of the accident. When they had came around the bend in the fork some of the bullets that were flying around hit the dirt in front of the horses, which made them, rear up in fright. They jerked the reins from my father's hands and bolted. The last thing he remembered is going over the lip of the ravine. It took my father a year to recover enough to get out of bed. Although he rarely smiled after that or hardly ever spoke of my mother again for many years he finally did recover except for the use of his legs. He's had to make use of a wheelchair to get around ever since. My father's partner had been a real help to us the first six months but then he began to notice that I was finally developing into a woman."*

Mell blushed at this point then turned her head and gazed out of the window as she continued in embarrassment… *"He started trying to touch me all the time or he would try to corner me at different times of the day. Most of the time I was too fast for him and managed to get away but there was those times when I had to use my wrestling tricks on him to keep him at bay. It was a year after the accident that I felt my father was recovered enough to enable me to pack up my gear, and leave the ranch. I decided to leave South Dakota entirely, because I knew that I'd never get another job on a ranch out there since everyone knew I was a girl. So I left and headed to North Dakota where nobody would know me. I traveled from town to town picking up odd jobs here and there, but never staying long searching for something but I didn't know what. Finally I hit this town just after my seventeenth birthday they were having a lot of trouble with a group of outlaws terrorizing the area. The Sheriff at the time was trying to organize a posse of men to try to stop the outlaws, but nobody would help him they were all too afraid. So I offered to help him and that is how I became a Deputy. When we left to track the outlaws there was only the old Sheriff, his original Deputy, two volunteers, and myself that is all the help we could manage. We tracked the outlaws for about three days then finally cornered the leader and three others. It was a bitter fight but we managed to kill the leader and captured the other three. The original Deputy and the two volunteers took the three men back to town to stand trial. While the Sheriff and I took off after the rest of the gang, it took another three days to track them down but finally we managed to capture them all. When we got back to town we were treated like heroes and they convinced me to stay on as a Deputy. The old Sheriff taught me everything he knew about the law and everything he didn't know I learned on my own. It took a year of acting as his Deputy before the Sheriff discovered that I was a woman. At first the Sheriff was going to fire me, but then his other Deputy got shot. So I managed to talk him into keeping me on for another year as long as I didn't let anyone else know that I was a girl. Then the old bugger got himself shot by an outlaw he was chasing. I was away visiting my father at the time and when I got back the townspeople had already elected me as Sheriff. Everything was relatively quiet for about a year, except for a few drunks and hot heads. Then I got found out by the rest of the town because of a boy I didn't even know."*

Mell slapped the desk unexpectedly and made Jed jump slightly in surprise as she chuckled in humour remembering the black haired boy's reaction then continued on with her story… *"I had gone to a private pond where I knew that no one went. It was quite a ways back in the woods, completely isolated or so I thought. I had found it when I was out tracking an outlaw the year before. I took my hat off and began removing my clothes when suddenly I heard an indrawn breath of shock. I spun around quickly gun in hand and spotted this black haired boy resting beneath a tree. He had obviously skipped school to sit by the water and fish. I didn't know the boy so I didn't think he recognized me. I yelled at him to get on home and he took off like a scared rabbit. It was really funny watching him peek over his shoulder to see if I was in pursuit. It never occurred to me to worry. I was so confident of my disguise that I leisurely finished my bath and headed back to town. As I rode down the street towards my office I noticed everyone staring at me funny. I checked my hat to make sure my hair wasn't showing and that my hat was on properly. Everything seemed to be in order so I continued on my way. As I got closer to the hitching post by my office, I noticed a crowd gathering. As I slid off my horse the Mayor approached me and asked me to remove my hat. That's when I noticed the black haired boy standing there gawking at me. I knew then that the game was up so I gave a resigned sigh and took off my hat reluctantly. You should have seen their faces, when my blonde hair fell down my back. You see that was the only vanity I allowed myself. I promised myself that I would never cut my hair especially after my mother died. My fondest memory was of her combing my long hair at night before bed."*

Mell grinned in humour then smirked as she remembered the townspeople's reaction to her long hair as she leaned back, and continued once more… *"Some of the men and women gave outraged cries while some of the men gave wolf whistles. Others just stood there gaping in astonishment not sure what to do or say. The Mayor told me that because I'm a woman it wouldn't be proper to allow me to continue on as Sheriff. I tried everything to make him change his mind. I pointed out all the ways I had made this town a safer place to live in. I even used some feminine wiles and pleaded very prettily. But he was adamant and insisted on paying my salary immediately. He even paid me extra to keep me quiet about being a woman so he could save face. So once again I packed up my gear and headed out of town. I didn't go far because I knew the young kid they planned to hire wouldn't last two months. Besides, I had come to think of this place as home. So I decided to look for a ranch and use the money I had saved up to buy it. I found my ranch about a month later, but the price was more than I could afford. I found out that the town owned it because the previous owner had died and left no heirs. Soon after this my prediction proved true as the new Sheriff picked a fight with the wrong guy and died. I went after the Sheriff's killer and brought him in. With the reward I still didn't have enough to buy the ranch, so I just kept on hanging around waiting for an opportunity to make some more money. I picked up odd jobs here and there for the next few months. Then one day while traveling along the trail to town I came upon three men holding up a coach. I managed to take them by surprise and shot all three of them. They had been in the process of dragging a lady out of the coach and were ripping off her clothes when I appeared on the scene, so they didn't notice me. The man who had accompanied her was tied up already so couldn't help her. It wasn't until I got closer and recognized the man that I started thinking of a way to use the situation to my advantage. It was the Mayor who had treated me so unfairly, and his wife. I quickly untied him and he hurried over to comfort his sobbing wife. He described how the town had turned lawless after my dismissal then went on to ask if I would take my job back. It would be my reward for saving his wife, and unborn child. I told the Mayor that much as I would like my old job back they didn't pay enough money. I explained that I was saving my money to buy the old Henderson place. The Mayor's wife had quit crying finally and was quiet up to that point but then she winked at me before whispering something in her husband's ear. He visibly brightened then said that he would throw in the property with the job offer. After thinking it over, I said that I would accept the offer on the condition that the ranch would still be mine if sometime in the future I should quit my job, or get married. The Mayor stuck out his hand and said it was a deal. I went back to my office the next day then I proceeded to clean up the town. I moved out to the ranch as soon as I could and got everything organized then sent for my father. We've been here ever since."*

Jed sat quietly for a while then mulling over what she had said, and what she hadn't said. It was obvious that she had been deeply affected by her mother's death even though she tried to hide it.

Jed also started wondering if this was the woman he had been searching for all this time. If so, it was no wonder he could never find her. When he had asked his questions they were always about an older woman it had never occurred to him that she could be so young, but the time frame matched. He sat forward anxiously as he motioned inquisitively. "Mell what happened to the three rustlers you first captured?"

Mell eyed Jed in surprise for a moment at his enquiry what was so important about that incident then sighed in irritation, seeing no harm in the question, she shrugged unknowingly. "They got away shortly after we handed them over to the Sheriff. At first I was always looking over my shoulder thinking they would come looking for me, but they disappeared after escaping from jail."

Jed leaned forward fervently now he was so close to the desk that he had to put his hand on it to hold himself upright and the urgency was plain in his voice. "Can you describe them to me?"

Mell eyed Jed in speculation of all the things he could have asked about her profession she couldn't figure out why he should ask about the rustlers. But since he seemed so intense about it she decided to continue telling him, more out of curiosity now though. At least he hadn't put her down like most men did when they found out that she was a sheriff.

Mell gazed into the distance thoughtfully trying to recall that long ago day she looked at Jed as the image of the three men formed in her mind. "From what I saw and heard they were either brothers, or related in some way. They all had the same blue eyes, but different hair colour. One had black hair, one had brown hair, and the other one had blonde hair. Their names are even etched in my memory although I'm not sure which one is which Marty, Jimmy, and Sam."

After she told Jed the names she could see the fury in his face, and she jumped slightly in shock as he drove his fist into her desk then jumped up unexpectedly.

Jed stood there angrily for a moment as he began pounding on his leg with a balled up impotent fist then started pacing and muttering to himself in agitation. "You should have killed them all!"

Mell frowned as Jed paced frantically obviously he knew who these men were then she scowled in surprise at what she heard him saying. She leaned forward in cautious concern, now getting just a little upset at Jed's words. "What is it, Jed?"

Jed spun around and looked back at her in shock as if he had just remembered her presence in the room. He gave a weary sigh then sat back down and began to tell her about the massacre of his family and Giant Bears. After he finished he frowned in apprehension. "They are known as the Shadow Killers and we've slowly tracked them across Montana then finally here into North Dakota. We were also looking for you, but we didn't know who you were. You see, before my son died he told me that he could remember them saying something about going to Dakota to find the woman who had killed their brothers. They didn't describe you at all so we didn't know who we were looking for, or what you looked like."

Mell sat for a moment contemplating all that Jed had told her. She had heard of the Shadow Killers of course, but with no description of them she hadn't linked them with the outlaws of her past. Suddenly she sat up straighter in her chair in excitement as she remembered yesterday. "Jed! There were three men who chased me yesterday just before I met you. I thought they were my men because once or twice a month some of my men try to sneak up on me. They do this to keep me on my toes and it's saved my life more than once. It looks like it's saved my life again."

Mell picked up the deputy's badge and handed it to Jed. He pinned the badge on without any hesitation then got up in excitement. As he turned for the door he threw an urgent comment over his shoulder, as he walked not even waiting for Mell. "Let's go, Boss!"

Mell hurriedly grabbed something out of her desk drawer before jumping up taken by surprise at Jed's rush then dashed around her desk after Jed. She quickly grabbed her hat off the rack where she had put it. But before either of them could reach the door her regular deputy walked in and smiled in greeting. "Hi, Mell…"

Her deputy stopped what he was going to say suddenly in anxiety as his gaze fell on Jed who had jumped back behind Mell quickly to avoid the door. He stared in shock at the deputy's badge pinned to Jed's shirt and the smile left his face instantly.

Mell nodded at her deputy in greeting unaware of her deputy's feelings as she motioned in apology. "Good morning Greg thanks for the coffee this morning. I also have to ask you even though I hate to, since I just got back, but I need you to make the rounds for me this morning and to keep everything quiet while I'm gone."

Her brows drew together in a troubled frown when Greg didn't answer, but just kept staring at something over her shoulder. She turned to see what he was staring at and finally remembered her manners. Mell moved to the side so the two men were facing each other and belatedly she introduced them. "Greg, meet Jed Brown he'll be working with us from now on. Jed, this is Greg Warren he acts as my Deputy in the evenings and when he's needed usually when I'm on the trail. He keeps everything here quiet for me."

Jed stared hard at Greg assessing him, he had dirty blonde hair and misty light blue eyes he stood just under six feet so was a little taller than Mell but not as tall as Jed he was hefty but not fat. Jed frowned thoughtfully in surprise there was something that flickered in Greg's eyes for a moment, panic perhaps, that disturbed Jed then it was gone.

The two men shook hands as they both mumbled greetings. You could tell right from the start that they didn't like each other. Mell scowled in bewilderment at the two men then turned to Jed without commenting on the dislike plain on both men's faces. "I have to make a stop at the general store and another at the ranch before we hit the trail."

She turned back to Greg as she sighed apologetically at having to leave him again to look after things. "I don't know how long we'll be gone so you might have to look after things for at least a day or two."

Greg frowned perplexed as he motioned in confusion. "What's up Mell? And where are you headed? You just got back the other day!"

Mell told him about the three men who had shot at her yesterday, and the fact that they were outlaws wanted for robbery and murder, but not that they were the Shadow Killers. For some unknown reason she didn't tell him about Jed's involvement in the case or her own either not really wanting to take the time.

Mell waved for Greg to move out of their way.

Greg stood for a moment more blocking the doorway then sighed in surrender as he moved. Greg walked outside frowning anxiously as he watched the two leave that new deputy was going to cause them grief he just knew it. He shrugged nothing he could do about it. He turned and went back inside mumbling irritably to himself wondering if he should warn his cousin then decided against it he would find out sooner or later.

* * *

Jed followed Mell out to where their horses waited and they mounted then rode down the main street headed out of town. She made a quick stop at the store where she picked up cigars, and chewing tobacco for her men as promised. She also added extra supplies for the trail in case they were needed and seeing a hunting knife she liked bought it as well, and tucked into the back of her shirt as an afterthought.

Jed purchased some bullets, tobacco, and rolling papers. Mell had the clerk add Jed's bullets to the town's tab as well as her own and the hunting knife.

They finished and left for the ranch to go speak with her father. As they rode along Mell turned to Jed then pulled out the extra deputy's badge to show him. "I brought along another Deputy's badge for Giant Bear since he's just as involved in this as we are I thought he might like to join us in our search."

Jed turned and looked at Mell in amazement for a moment as she held out the badge to show him. "You would deputize an Indian?"

Mell instantly stiffened thinking that he was criticizing her. But the thought quickly vanished as she realized that he was probably thinking that most sheriffs were prejudiced he didn't know her very well if he thought she was one of them. She smirked over at him then put the badge back in her pocket as she nodded decisively. "Yes, I would deputize an Indian. Actually, he won't be the first one I've deputized."

Mell looked up at the cloudless sky in relief as long as it didn't rain their trail would be very easy to follow, if the three men who had chased her yesterday were the same three that Jed was looking for she hoped to find them fairly quickly before they found her or killed again.

Mell turned to watch Jed, he was obviously thinking about his dead wife and child, his jaw was clenched as if in pain and he had a hard resolute expression on his face. Mell cleared her throat loudly to get his attention to try and distract him. "See that line of trees just ahead?"

Mell pointed to a slight hill just ahead of them. Jed looked towards where she was pointing and nodded that he did. Mell smiled as he turned back to her inquiringly as she continued. "That's the border to my land it extends east for about two and a half day's ride then west for another two days. If you decided to do a full circle you would have to turn east from here for two and a half days then turn north again, and follow the trees all the way up until you get to the bottom of those mountains that would be the end of my land. We call those mountains Devil's Rock, and they're about five days ride from here. You then turn west and follow the edge of the mountains. It would take you about five days to reach the end then you would have to turn south which would bring you back towards town. On your way south you would pass the spot where we met it's a four day journey south, before you would turn east for two days to reach this point. Of course those lines aren't totally straight. We only use a small portion of the land at the moment. I have thought of selling some, but then again I might decide to use more later on. Right now I only raise horses, and harvest lumber but later when I retire I might get into raising cattle. It was lucky for us that the town grew northward so now they are only two hours of hard riding away from the border of my land once you get here I'm only another hour and a half away so when the town needs me for any reason I can get there pretty quick."

Jed nodded as he looked around speculatively. He was pondering that if he were running things he would definitely put cattle here. He turned to Mell and gestured around him. "From what I've seen so far you have very good land for cattle. If I owned this that's one of the options I would look at."

Mell congratulated herself on distracting Jed then she nudged her horse into a canter and they rode the rest of the way in silence content in each other's company.

CHAPTER FOUR

Mell and Jed slowed their horses, as they got close to the ranch yard to let them cool down both horses were sweaty but not foaming or blowing hard. As they got close to the bunkhouse they could see that the door was open so Mell called out loudly hoping Wade or Giant Bear were inside. "Wade, Giant Bear come on out I need to talk to you."

Wade appeared in the door of the bunkhouse then jumped of the veranda and followed them to the barn as he looked up at Mell in concern. "What are you guys doing back so early it's not even noon?"

Mell slid out of her saddle then walked around her packhorse and rummaged around in the saddlebags for the cigars and chewing tobacco. She handed them to Wade as she turned to him. "Where's Giant Bear I need to see him too? When I was out riding yesterday three men rode out of the woods shooting at me. I managed to out ride them but we're going after them now."

Wade scowled irritably at Mell as he waved in bewilderment. "Why didn't you mention this before? It wasn't us this time!"

Mell grinned confidently as she motioned soothingly. "I know that Wade. If it had been you guys I would have been teased unmercifully yesterday."

Giant Bear appeared around the corner and stopped short in surprise when he saw Mell and Jed. Mell turned her horse over to Wade then turned to leave for the ranch house. She threw clarification over her shoulder to Giant Bear. "Jed will explain everything to you Giant Bear while I go up to the house, and talk to my father."

Giant Bear nodded after her in uncertainty even though she didn't see him and turned to Jed inquisitively.

Mell ran to the house and entered in haste she didn't even bother to remove her outer clothes this time or her guns as she called out immediately. "Dad, where are you?"

Not even taking the time to remove her boots she walked down the hallway quickly at her father's distant call. "I'm in the den Mell."

Mell stepped into the den and the first thing she saw was Three Toes stretched out watching her father. She giggled in amusement as she motioned towards the wolf in humour. "I guess Three Toes has become your guardian for the time being."

Alec gazed down at Three Toes with affection before looking back at Mell. "Yes, he's hardly left my side all day. He even follows me when I go outside and sleeps beside my bed. You're home early Mell what's up?"

Mell sat down in a chair as she reported everything to her father that she had learned today and apprehensively waited for his reaction.

Alec frowned anxiously as he leaned forward then gestured fearfully. "Mell, I know you've been a Deputy since you were seventeen then a Sheriff for the last seven years, but are you sure you can handle this?"

Alec noticed the frown of hurt and disbelief on Mell's face so added quickly as he reached out to take her hand. "I don't mean that you are incompetent or anything, but think about it. Whenever you've had to go after anyone or put them in jail, it's always been someone or circumstances that don't concern you personally. This time you're directly involved these men are out to kill you, not just because you're the Sheriff, because you hurt them by killing two of their brothers. Can you keep your emotions out of it this time, or would it be better to let someone else handle it. I've already lost your mother to these killers I couldn't handle losing you too."

Mell carefully contemplated all that her father had said then analyzed her feelings cautiously. She stared at her father pensively as she squeezed his hand in assurance then gestured resolutely with her free hand as she spoke calmly. "I know this hit's closer to home than any other job I've done and I do realize how deeply my emotions are involved. But dad if I didn't do everything in my power to stop these men from hurting anyone else I could never forgive myself. I might as well give up my badge right now because indirectly it's my fault that these men have murdered innocent women and children. If I had killed them or at least made sure they hung when this first started all those innocent people would still be alive. So please understand that I have to do this for myself as well as for every woman and child they have put to death."

Alec's chest puffed up in pride as he gazed on this only child of his. How well she had turned out even though she hardly ever acted like a woman! He also understood that nothing he could say now would dissuade her but he had to try one more time. "You were only fifteen at that time, so how can you blame yourself for not destroying them I didn't raise you to be a killer."

Mell motioned pleadingly with her free hand hoping for her father's understanding. She heaved a sigh forlornly as she shook her head remorsefully. "I know that! But I still feel responsible!"

Alec smiled in sympathy and conceded as he let go of Mell's hand. "I understand how you feel Mell so do what you think is best. Are you taking Jed with you?"

Mell grinned in relief as she got up to leave. "Yes, and I'm also taking Giant Bear."

Alec visibly relaxed as he received that information, at least she won't be alone.

Mell left the den and ran upstairs to grab a few things from her room before she said a final good-bye to her father.

Alec sat there with an apprehensive look on his face and cursed the fact that his legs were useless as he pounded on them in a powerless fit of pique. A shiver rippled down his spine as a premonition hit him that nothing would ever be the same when Mell returned. He also felt strongly that someone would die, but he didn't know who it would be.

Three Toes sensing Alec's panic walked over to his chair and put his head on Alec's lap then whined in concern. Alec absently stroked the wolf's head. The wolf calmed him down enough so that by the time Mell came in to say good-bye, Alec had managed a calmer expression and Mell didn't see how distress he really was.

Mell dropped a light kiss on her father's forehead then looked down at Three Toes in command. "You take good care of Dad, Three Toes!"

Three Toes whined up at Mell then as if he understood what was going on he lay down beside Alec's chair and continued to watch his every move.

Mell chuckled in amusement at the wolf then turned back to her father as she patted his shoulder in farewell. "I'll see you when I get back. You're in good hands with Three Toes on guard."

Mell left the den and headed for the door but she paused then turned back as she heard her father call out to her. Alec wheeled himself into the hallway and gestured solemnly at Mell. "No matter what happens Mell, remember that I will always love you!"

Mell beamed encouragement at her father as she waved a final good-bye then turned and left without comment as she closed the door after herself. She didn't hear her father's whispered prayer to his dead wife to keep their daughter safe.

Mell rushed over to the barn where Jed and Giant Bear were waiting. When she reached them she dug in her pocket and took out the extra deputy's badge she had grabbed on her way out of the office, and handed it to Giant Bear.

Giant Bear accepted it without hesitation and immediately pinned it to his buckskin shirt.

Mell looked at the two men gravely and with a deadly profound tone she recited the deputy's oath that she had once made herself. "I want you both to raise your right hand and repeat these words after me. I say your full name, solemnly pledge my oath to uphold the laws and protect the innocent even unto death, as long as I shall live."

Jed and Giant Bear both repeated the vow there expressions absolutely serious well aware of the significance of such an oath then they turned and readied their horses.

Mell hurried over to Wade and gathered her reins from him as she frowned in edginess. "Who's on watch tonight?"

Wade smiled soothingly as he backed away so Mell could mount. "Joe is on watch until twelve fifty then Dwayne takes over before one o'clock."

Mell nodded relieved Joe was one of the older hands and quite capable. She mounted quickly and looked down at Wade intently. "Please ask them to keep a particularly vigilant watch tonight just in case. There's something in the air that disturbs me!"

Wade frowned nervously as he watched Mell leave with her two new deputies following her. Usually when Mell gets one of her feelings it doesn't bode well for any of them. He shrugged no use fretting about it, all they could do was take a few extra precautions and hope for the best. He turned to go inform Joe.

Mell and her deputies left to find the trail of the three outlaws. After several hours of hard riding Mell finally found the spot where she had last seen the three men coming out of the trees. She turned to Jed and pointed towards the forest headed west. "They came out of those trees and fired a shot at me, I didn't get a good look at them, so I'm not even sure they are the ones your after."

Giant Bear threw an inquiring look at Mell but didn't speak.

Mell nodded in consent aware of what he wanted and he took the lead in the direction she had pointed out. Mell followed and Jed brought up the rear with the packhorse.

It took them the rest of the day to find the outlaws abandoned camp. When they did find it they decided to stop and make camp as well, since there was still firewood left over from the last occupants and dusk was falling fast. In less than an hour you wouldn't be able to see anything because of the thick trees.

As they got settled Mell frowned in apprehension as she hunkered down beside the fire then looked at the two men for confirmation of her opinion. "It looks like they're headed for town."

Jed nodded but didn't look up as he continued to feed the fire to get a good blaze going. Mell's frown deepened as she held her hands out to the warmth of the small crackling fire it was still a little cool out in the early spring evenings, especially in the forest, out in the open where the sun reached the ground it was a lot warmer. But the fire wasn't big enough yet to cook their food or to warm her up much.

Her thoughts were in turmoil as her mind turned back to the outlaws and she began to fret even more as she rubbed her hands together. She finally turned to Giant Bear inquisitively. "What do you think?"

Giant Bear waved at all the tracks he had studied when they had first arrived. "I agree, and I am sure they camped here again after they chased you yesterday then they headed to town they have not returned here since."

Giant Bear got up then walked to the opposite side of the camp and disappeared for a short time. When he returned he beckoned them to follow him and the two obediently got up then hurried after him as he showed them all the signs he had discovered. This was where they had picketed their horses and he squatted down as his hand followed the trail so Mell could see what he saw. "This is the way they left later in the afternoon and their trail definitely leads southeast towards town."

Mell looked around at all the signs trying to figure out what the outlaws were up to unless they were just looking for information. But if that was the case why did they disappear they couldn't have been in town or Greg would have mentioned strangers around before they left. They wouldn't need to go to town in any case to find her since everyone around here knew where she lived. Unless they had also found out that she was now a sheriff and that had scared them off. She shook her head to herself, nah, highly unlikely that they would scare off that easily so where did they go.

Giant Bear decided to do a little hunting and find some fresh meat for their supper instead of using their supplies. He stood up then motioned to Mell and pointed to his left. "I am going hunting if you have no objections. I also noticed a creek over there if you are interested Mell."

Mell grinned in relish at the thought of a bath. "No I don't mind if you go hunting and I would love to have a bath if the creek is deep enough."

Mell turned back to their camp then went to the packhorse and grabbed her soap as well as a small towel she always carried. Before quickly turning back towards the promised creek in anticipation and disappeared through the break in the trees that Giant Bear had indicated.

The creek she was heading towards was the same one that ran through her favourite spot she could see quite a ways down the path that the water took and it headed straight towards her haven. Only this part was a little deeper by the looks of it. So she shouldn't have any trouble bathing completely in it. Lucky for her it was warmer once she left the trees and strolled out into the open, but she knew it would still be a cold bath.

She leisurely walked towards it with a pensive frown as a million questions ran through her mind. How did these men happen to be in this area? Had they actually known she was here or was it just a coincidence that had brought them here at the same time that she was passing by? Did they realize it was her, when they took that shot, if so why didn't they pursue her further? She shook off her feelings of agitation then dropped the soap and her towel on the ground so she could undress and reached for the buttons on her shirt first.

* * *

Jed went back to camp and noticed his fire had almost gone out so he squatted down as he stirred up the ashes then added more wood. He had watched Mell depart with a preoccupied frown and hadn't even noticed Giant Bear leaving to go hunting. He had finally wandered back to camp on his own.

Once the fire was crackling he sat down on a large rock to think. What was there about Mell that caused him to have thoughts of settling down again? Every time he was near her he couldn't help speculating, wondering what she hiding underneath that strange assortment of clothing she wore. Just thinking about the first time he had seen her without her hat on, a riot of golden curls fanning about her shoulders caused his manhood to instantly harden in desire.

Before he could stop to reconsider his actions he rose from where he had sat down and strode purposely towards the creek where Mell had gone to bathe. When he arrived she was just removing her shirt. Beneath which she wore a white binding wound about her in layers. She used this to flatten her chest so no one would guess at the abundant flesh it hid.

* * *

Mell's thoughts had turned to Jed wondering why she felt warm and shivery every time she was near him. Was there something wrong with her?

Mell unwound the tight binding from around her chest then took a deep breath of air as she felt a surge of relief as her large full breasts sprang free. She gently touched one and felt that peculiar sensation again then instantly her nipple hardened and she frowned perplexed. Usually her nipples only hardened when it was very cold out and it was definitely not that cold yet.

Suddenly she heard an indrawn breath, instantly she spun around in disbelief and saw Jed studying her from a distance. All of a sudden she was filled with a sense of anticipation and that strange tingling sensation came over her again. Not thinking about what she was doing or the consequences involved, it was almost as if she was dreaming, as she kept her eyes locked on Jed's she reached for the buttons on her trousers.

Jed tensed in surprise and desire as he watched Mell in fascination as her long tanned fingers started slowly undoing the buttons on her trousers. Then she slowly lowered her pants until they were pooled around her feet and she step out of them slowly. Finally she stood before him naked.

Jed moved towards her cautiously afraid she would bolt before he could get to her, but she didn't move an inch. Not wanting to frighten her away but a little more confident of himself now, Jed whispered caressingly as he reached for Mell. "You're even more beautiful than I imagined."

He hauled her to him roughly as he leisurely lowered his head. It was almost as if he was giving her a chance to pull away but she remained and he moaned in pleasure as their lips met.

Mell immediately melted against him in surrender as he deepened the kiss, unsure of what was happening to her, but knowing she needed more of something.

Jed became more insistent as he whimpered in desire. He slid his hands up and down her arms then paused in anticipation for a moment as the back of his hands brushed against the curve of her breast. He took his right hand away from her arm and trailed a tentative finger across her breast until he touched one of Mell's tender swollen nipples.

Mell cried out in pleasure and uncertainty but didn't move away.

Jed took this as a sign that she wanted more so his caresses became more needy and persistent. Suddenly, his ears caught the sound of someone walking through the tree's some distance away making an awful lot of noise. He stiffened instantly and groaned in reluctance as he pulled away unwillingly already guessing who was making so much noise making sure that he was heard.

Jed tenderly stroked Mell's face as he stared down at her in regret with a look of thwarted need plain on his face. "Giant Bear is back. I better leave before he comes this way."

Mell nodded incoherently as she watched him walk away in silent frustration. She turned and waded into the creek to cool off her over heated skin. She shivered as the icy cold-water hit her full force and she finally woke up. She shook her head in incredulity and humiliation. She couldn't understand what had come over her. She felt ashamed of the way she had practically thrown herself at Jed never had she ever had such strange feelings towards a man. At the same time, she wondered how far they would have gone if Giant Bear hadn't returned.

She finished her bath in record time and got dressed quickly as she headed back towards camp her emotions in check, or so she thought.

* * *

Jed skinned the three rabbits Giant Bear had gotten for their meal, while Giant Bear fashioned a spit to cook them on. He skewered the rabbits as soon as Giant Bear handed him the spit then put them over the fire before Jed turned and looked intently at his friend. "What do you think of Mell Giant Bear?"

Giant Bear looked at his friend and long time companion steadily. He could see that Jed was falling in love with Mell, he had made sure to make a lot of noise on his way back to camp well aware that Jed had went to the creek after he left. "She is very beautiful and spirited. But my friend you do realize that you would never be able to change her, do you not?"

Jed frowned at Giant Bear in surprise as he motioned in confusion. "What do you mean change her?"

Giant Bear chose his words with care not wanting to offend Jed or have his meaning mistaken in any way. "Mell is very attractive but she is also very strong willed. She will never give up her job as Sheriff nor will she give up her ranch to go roaming around the countryside with you. She is also very honourable for a woman I can see it in her eyes. If you think you can love her then leave her you will hurt her very badly. She is more the marrying kind you will need to remember that if you plan to get involved with her."

Jed stared at Giant Bear in amazement. That was the longest speech Giant Bear had ever given in all their years together, sometimes it was even easy to forget that he could speak English so well now. Giant Bears English had improved immensely compared to when Jed had first met him but usually all he did was grunt, or nod his head, or he didn't say anything at all. That made his words all the more worth taking heed of. Jed knew that Giant Bear had spoken from the heart as well as through his many years of wisdom and he was right that Mell was the marrying kind.

Mell walked into the clearing, as her eyes met Jed's she turned scarlet with embarrassment and suppressed desire. They stared at each other for a long moment until Giant Bear cleared his throat noisily to remind them of his presence.

Mell turned away from Jed immediately and her face became an even darker red, but this time from mortification as her gaze met Giant Bear's.

Giant Bear heaved a resignedly sigh he knew by her expression that she was already in love with Jed. He just hoped for her sake that Jed would get over his dead wife, and settle down. He knew that these two friends of his would be good for each other, but he also knew that their relationship would be anything but smooth. If they did get together and got married it would be a constant struggle between two strong willed and forceful people.

Mell finally wrenched her gaze away from Giant Bears and walked over to the fire then sat down with her eyes lowered quietly thinking.

Eating was a quiet affair and only Giant Bear seemed to be able to eat, not letting the atmosphere between his two friends get to him. After they finished eating Jed rolled three cigarettes he lit them then handed one to Mell, and one to Giant Bear. Then sat with his back to a tree and puffed on his own contemplatively still thinking about Mell and Giant Bears words of warning.

Mell inhaled deeply on her cigarette then heaved a sigh and broke the silence as she looked at the two men gravely. "I'll take the first watch it's about nine o'clock now then I'll wake you up at midnight Jed, and you can wake Giant Bear for the last watch at three o'clock."

The two men nodded as they threw their cigarettes into the fire and got up obediently as they walked over to their bedrolls that they had put out earlier.

Mell went to her saddle and unhooked her whip then moved into the shadows for a good view of the camp but hidden enough so that anybody approaching them wouldn't see her, and she could surprise them if need be.

She had decided to take the first watch because she knew that she wouldn't be able to sleep anyway. She needed to sort out her thoughts then decide what to do about Jed and her confused feelings over him. She spent the next three hours trying to figure things out but it was no use she just couldn't resolve anything. She finally came to the conclusion that she was just going to have to ignore this unwanted attraction until the outlaws were caught. For now, she would just pretend that Jed was one of her men. With that resolution in mind she went to wake Jed up for his watch.

Jed stretched as he watched Mell leave he yawned then walked over to take Mell's place. When he had looked directly at Mell as she woke him he had seen the look of grim resolve in her eyes. He knew instinctively that Mell had decided to ignore her feelings and he silently agreed with her. Neither of them could afford to be distracted right now or someone could die. Just the thought that it could be Mell made him flinch in fear.

He also knew that what Giant Bear had said was right. If he wanted her he would have to marry her and settle down. But after the trauma of losing his family did he really want to go through the pain of loving someone and possibly losing them again? Mell's job was very dangerous and there was always the possibility that one of them, or even both of them could die.

Giant Bear had also been right in saying that she wouldn't give up her job as sheriff, could he live with that? And another thing could he love someone so opposite to his dead wife?

Victoria had also been a beauty she was soft and sweet but very timid and never argue with him. She had always given in to his judgment right

71

or wrong, but it would have been nice if she had stood up for herself more. It was too late now to regret making his wife and son come out here with him, but there was no way of knowing what would happen. If she had refused to come with him to Montana this time as she had done every other time, maybe Victoria and his son would still be alive now.

Jed chided himself for this thoughts it was no use beating himself up over what was done and over with, he had done enough of that in the beginning. If it hadn't been for Giant Bear taking the bottle of whisky away from him he would still be drunk in that first town they had stopped at. Then there was his promise to his dead wife he must not think of a future love until he had avenged his wife, unborn child, and son.

Love! That thought slammed through his brain like a hammer and unlike the confused Mell he knew what love felt like. Jed sighed in frustration and irritation it all depended on finding the killers of his family until then his life was on hold. And he was certainly getting tired of chasing those men with never any success in getting even close to them in all this time. It's definitely been a long nine years, but finally the end was getting closer. Those men were so close now he could almost feel them and now that Mell was in the picture he was even more anxious to put the past to rest and get on with his life.

Jed stood up and stretched tiredly then decided to walk around the camp before waking Giant Bear. He made a full circle then found himself standing over Mell watching her sleep he hadn't planned on going anywhere near her, but here he stood unwillingly. He turned away and strolled over to sit in the same place, so that he could continue watching the camp.

He tried hard to ignore the need to go over and continue watching Mell sleep. The urge got so bad that he finally got up to march over there again unable to help himself.

Jed turned in surprise at a noise behind him and was relieved to see Giant Bear coming towards him to take over guard duty. Jed smiled in relief before mumbling hastily. "Goodnight!"

Jed rushed quickly to his own bedroll without saying another word and fell on top of his bed staring upwards sleeplessly.

Giant Bear watched Jed walk away without comment and shook his head in disapproval. He had watched Jed earlier and had decided he had better take over the watch. Jed was in no condition for guard duty tonight. He probably wouldn't even notice how early it was. Giant Bear sighed resignedly and sat down in the shadows of the big tree.

He listened to the chirping of the crickets and heard the deep croaking of the frogs then suddenly everything went deathly quiet as he heard the hoot of an owl right above him. He looked up in surprise at the owl that was staring down at him intently. For a full two minutes the owl gazed at him without moving an inch then suddenly he opened his huge wings and flew up above the trees. Giant Bear watched him circle above them before the owl disappeared from view. He frowned troubled usually the sight of an owl during the day was a forewarning, but not usually at night.

The strange behaviour of that owl made him nervous and he got up then hurried over to his saddle blanket and took out his rifle just in case. He settled back to watch over his two confused friends then made himself comfortable; it was going to be a long night.

He felt a little better once the crickets and frogs continued their songs but the apprehension continued throughout the rest of the night.

CHAPTER FIVE

Back at the ranch the quiet was shattered suddenly as two men galloped in with guns blazing. The men that were sleeping in the bunkhouse staggered outside in confusion more asleep than awake. Most of them died before they even realized what was going on, or even where all the bullets were coming from.

There was a third man shooting as well, but nobody could see him since he was hidden strategically up in the barn facing the bunkhouse, and he was shooting at anyone who stumbled outside.

Alec sat up in bed with a stunned jolt at the sound of gunfire exploding outside and Three Toes warning growl. He reached for the loaded pistol he kept in his bedside drawer, but didn't quite make it before a strange man burst into his room.

Three Toes snarled savagely then jumped at the intruder instantaneously but he was too late as the man fired a shot at him. He fell to the floor twitching.

The distraction the wolf caused gave Alec time to grab a knife hidden under his pillow and he shoved it into his long johns quickly then removed his hand before the black haired outlaw could see him.

"Hold it right there!"

Alec immediately put his hands up at the man's ominous shout. He grimaced in rage impotently. "What do you want?" •

The man grinned forebodingly over at Alec without a hint of remorse, as he kicked the wolf in pleasure on his way around the bed. "You're coming with me!"

The stranger turned towards the closet without even a hesitation and pulled out the wheelchair that was stored there. Alec was astounded to see the man retrieve his chair and wheel it over to the bed. The man then went back to the closet and threw Alec a pair of pants as well as a shirt.

The stranger waited impatiently as Alec struggled to get dressed as fast as he could. The man grunted in satisfaction when Alec finished then turned back to the closet and pulled out a pair of spare boots that Alec always kept in there. Still without saying a word he checked for hidden knives as he walked over to the bed and helped Alec put them on hurriedly.

The man pointed to the wheelchair in command. "Get in! NOW!"

Alec didn't dare argue well aware of his inadequacies in defending himself with useless legs as he eased himself off the bed and into the wheelchair.

As the man wheeled him around the bed Alec caught sight of the wolf lying on the floor dead. He began to shake uncontrollably and had to force control over his emotions. Alec shook his head in bewilderment and fury as he muttered to himself quietly, so that the stranger couldn't hear him. Someone must have betrayed them, but who would do such a thing. There had to have been somebody because this man knew exactly where his chair was kept. Very few people had access to his private living quarters.

It couldn't have been anyone from the ranch because the outlaw hadn't been prepared for Three Toes. The astonishment on the man's face just before he shot the wolf attested to that.

Alec was so deep in thought he didn't even realize that they had reached the barnyard area, but when he did, Alec's face paled in shock as his gaze fell on the dead bodies of his friends and hired men littered all over the ground. The only one left alive was Wade and he was holding his left arm close to his side obviously wounded.

Alec and Wade gazed at each other intently for a moment as a silent message passed between them. They both knew who the men were, but they were unsure of why Wade was the only one left alive besides Alec.

The black haired man pushing Alec walked around the wheelchair and up to Wade then handed him a letter remorselessly as he pointed in the direction Mell had gone yesterday. "Take this to the woman! Tell her she has five days to produce herself or her father is dead!"

Wade took the letter grudgingly from the obvious older brother and leader of the three outlaws then inclined his head unpleasantly but didn't say anything. His thoughts were churning as he contemplated furiously, who had betrayed them, there had to have been someone how else would they know to hit the ranch at ten to one just before shift change?

Wade was unaware that Alec also figured it was an inside job.

The blonde skinny gawky looking cowboy brought two horses from the barn. He wasn't as tall as his brother's not quite reaching six feet. He handed the reins of Wade's horse to him then brought Alec's mare over to Alec without any hesitation.

Wade and Alec quickly shared another quick glance both aware now that the other knew it was an inside job.

Wade mounted his horse slowly in obvious agony then almost blacked out from the pain shooting up his arm. He shut his eyes and leaned against the pummel of his saddle to steady himself before he was finally able to ride away.

The largest outlaw among them stomped over to Alec. He had greasy brown hair, and black rotten teeth, as he grinned down at Alec evilly. Alec figured he was pretty close to his own height at six feet eight inches. He was huge and beefy unlike Alec's tall slender frame. He had a blank cruel look on his face and Alec shuddered in revulsion, figuring the man was simple. He was obviously younger than his other two brothers. The man was extraordinarily strong as he easily hoisted Alec into his saddle by himself without any help from his brothers before strapping Alec's legs in.

Alec remained silent even though he was having a hard time keeping quiet wanting to find out what was going on, but he didn't want to antagonize the outlaws either.

He heard the blonde skinny outlaw mutter to his older black haired brother. "Smart man! He knows when to keep his mouth shut. Better put that blindfold on him, he doesn't want the old man to know who he is, just in case anything goes wrong."

Alec sat quietly as they tied a bandanna around his eyes and wondered who the person they referred to as, 'he', was. As they rode out Alec realized that his earlier premonition that someone would die had proven true. He prayed to God that no one else would die before this was all over.

Alec felt the knife that he had hidden in his underwear earlier and was comforted a little. At least he wasn't completely vulnerable, what he could do with a pitiful knife against all these killers he didn't know, but it did help him to stay calm and that was the most vital thing right now.

Alec heard another horse racing to catch up to them. There was a mumbled discussion then the horse was racing away again. The exchange of words had been too low for him to hear, but Alec was sure that whoever it was had betrayed them all.

Alec hadn't had time to see if anyone from the ranch was missing even though he was still positive it wasn't one of their own men who had betrayed them, but he couldn't be totally sure either. He just hoped that Mell would be able to get to him in time.

* * *

Wade rode hard for several hours as he followed Mell's tracks. Good thing there was a full moon out to see by and Mell hadn't felt the need to hide her trail. Even with the glow from the full moon he still managed to ride right past where Mell and her two deputies had turned off. It took him a good half hour to finally decide he had lost the trail. He turned back and picked up the trail once more then turned into the forest going west.

As he entered the trees all the illumination from the moon vanished unexpectedly and Wade had to close his eyes to adjust to the darkness. When he opened them again he become conscious of the fact that there was no way he could track any further. It was just too damn dark. He decided to ride west in the hopes that he would stumble into Mell's camp. Wade tried to go as straight as he possibly could but ended up going more northwest.

As he rode along his thoughts were busy. Still trying to figure out who had betrayed them and why? There were only a handful of people who knew the routine of the ranch. Only four of them, other than the ranch hands, knew that the watch changed at ten minutes to one. It was too coincidental that the outlaws had hit the ranch at twelve forty five when the first sentry was getting drowsy and just before the new sentry who would be fully alert arrived. They also knew where the watch was posted because he had passed Joe's dead body.

Wade stumbled across Mell's camp just after six in the morning. To let them know it was him approaching he called out Mell's name as loud as he could so that he wouldn't get himself shot again.

Mell rushed anxiously towards Wade as he finally wavered and fell weakly to the ground having lost way too much blood to hold himself up any longer. She gasped in disbelief as she saw the blood trickling down his arm and knelt beside him in fear as her voice trembled in panic. "Wade oh my God, what happened? Why did you leave the ranch untended?"

Jed hurried over and knelt beside Mell in concern. "Mell let me patch him up while he answers your questions or he's liable to die from loss of blood before he can tell us anything!"

Jed looked for Giant Bear, but he was already heading to his pack to get his medicine bag. Jed nodded in relief as he sent Mell for the warm water that they had heating for coffee. He ripped open Wade's shirt to examine the wound.

Jed nodded thanks distractedly, at Mell, as she knelt beside him again with the pot of warm water and a bottle of whisky she always carried for emergencies. Jed ripped a strip of cloth from Wade's shirt then wet it as he cleaned the bullet hole in Wade's shoulder as best he could then poured a generous amount of whisky directly on the injury.

Wade bellowed in agony as the whiskey hit his opened wound unexpectedly. He managed to tell them about the terrible events that had taken place at the ranch once he got his breath back. Then he handed the note to Mell, as she read it her face became bloodless and she swayed slightly on her knees.

At first Jed thought she was going to pass out, but she visibly pulled herself together. Giant Bear brought him the medicine bag even though he really didn't need it the whiskey would have been sufficient. Lucky for Wade the bullet had went clean through his arm, so it didn't need to be dug out. Jed searched through the bag and found the roots he was looking for then turned back to Wade to dress the wound.

Mell finally spoke but her voice cracked in strain as she fought for control of her emotions. "They have my father and they're taking him to Devil's Rock. There's a trail leading up to a miners shack up there. They want me to meet them there within five days or Dad's dead! They warn me not to bring anyone with me or they'll kill him instantly!"

Wade interrupted her as he grimaced painfully as Jed packed his wound with herbs. He gritted his teeth trying to talk through the agony. "Me and your father think it's an inside job."

Mell looked at him in astonishment. "When did they let you talk to my father?"

Wade shook his head negatively at the misunderstanding. "They didn't let us talk it was just obvious to both of us when they knew which horses we rode. I knew we were right when I passed Joe dead at his post only four men know when each shift changes Greg, Brian, Daniel Grey, and the Mayor. They're the only ones who would have that information except the ranch hands and I'm pretty sure they're all dead."

Jed scowled angrily as he thought sadly of all those men he had just come to know. He gestured anxiously at the thought of his wolf. "Is there anyone else alive at the ranch? What about Three Toes, the housekeeper, and the boy Tommy?"

Wade shook his head sadly as he thought of Tommy and Gloria it had been an excruciating decision for him to make to leave without checking on them. He had wanted to go back and after seeing Joe dead he had even turned his horse around to do so. He had changed his mind though knowing he wouldn't make it to Mell's camp if he went back to the ranch. So he had gritted his teeth enraged then reluctantly turned away. "I don't know Jed. They made me leave right away and I was afraid I wouldn't have been able to make it this far. I figured Mell would want to stop at the ranch first anyway to check for survivors and to bury the dead, so I never went back."

Mell nodded decisively as she wiped her tears away and grimaced grimly at the idea of having to bury her men. "Yes you did the right thing coming to get me right away, we'll go to the ranch first then we can find out which trail they took to Devil's Rock. Nobody's aware of the fact that

I used to go up to Devil's Rock when I had time off and explore, so I know the area pretty good. That's the only advantage we have right now."

Mell and Giant Bear quickly broke camp while Jed finished tending to Wade. Jed helped Wade stand after bandaging the wound then guided the still wobbly Wade over to Mell's horse and assisted him in mount behind her. Then he jumped onto his horse and they took off with Giant Bear in the lead. Mell followed with Wade holding onto her from behind, since he was too weak to ride on his own. Jed brought up the rear leading Wade's horse with the packhorse tied to the back of Wade's saddle.

Their progress was painstakingly slow because they didn't want to jostle Wade's wound too much and have it start bleeding again before they could get to the ranch and tend to it properly. They were all very quiet as they tried to prepare themselves for what awaited them at the ranch.

Several hours later the four riders approached the ranch yard solemnly certain that they were prepared for what was to come, but they weren't.

Mell gazed around in horror, all her men and friends were dead, lying exactly where they had fallen.

In silent dread Jed and Giant Bear dismounted then helped Wade off Mell's horse before walking around checking all the bodies for possible survivors, or for anyone missing.

As soon as Wade dismounted Mell raced to the ranch house as fast as her horse could go. She jumped off him in a panic, before he could even stop, as she ran towards the stairs. Mell took them two at a time before running into the house to look for Gloria, Tommy, and Three Toes. She entered and didn't even bother closing the door as she ran down the hallway urgently searching as she called out for Gloria and Tommy in anguish fearing the worst. "Gloria, Tommy! Where are you?"

Mell received no answer so she ran back to the stairs in the hallway then up to the bedrooms in dread. She paused in front of the door at Tommy's room not sure if she could go in. She looked up at the ceiling praying to God for all she was worth. "Please God no! I don't think I could bare it!"

She finally opened the door looking around frantically but no one was there and her hopes lifted slightly. Mell went to Gloria's room next wondering if Tommy had ran to her for protection and that's where she would find them. Again she looked up imploringly!

Her heart was in her throat as she slowly opened the door fearing the worst. She cried out then slumped in relief unable to move for a moment as she stared at the empty room then turned ecstatically as she hurried back downstairs.

Mell ran down the hallway and into the kitchen it was the only way to get to the back entry where the cellar door was located. She tried the handle once she reached the door but it was locked from the inside. Mell exhaled noisily relieved. She banged on the door repeatedly and kept calling Gloria's name desperately. Finally the door creaked open.

Gloria opened the door a smidgen as she peeked out cautiously. When she saw Mell she swung open the door all the way, but was unable to move any further. Gloria stood in the doorway quivering in fear as tears streamed down her chubby cheeks. Her voice was barely coherent as she whispered in terror and grief. "We were so scared Mell. When we heard the shooting we crept down the upstairs hallway then slipped down the stairs. We were planning on getting your father and barricading the three of us in the cellar, but just as we got to the bottom of the stairs we heard a shot coming from your father's room. I grabbed Tommy and we ran to the cellar then I locked us in. I'm so sorry Mell I think your father is dead. I really didn't know what to do, I had no way of protecting us."

Gloria burst into fresh tears then finally able to move she threw herself bodily at Mell crying hysterically.

Mell held her for a moment and murmured soothingly slightly shocked to see her break down so completely, usually nothing fazed the formable Gloria. She tried pushing her at arm's length to explain that her father wasn't dead, but Gloria clung to her desperately refusing to let her go as she sobbed feverishly.

Gloria continued babbling hysterically not listening to anything Mell had to say. "Oh Mell it was terrible we were so frightened but I didn't know what to do!"

Mell's patience gone she tried again to break loose from the clinging inconsolable Gloria and had to finally resort to shaking her slightly in order to get her to listen. "Gloria enough! Please go and make us something to eat there are still four of us alive Jed, Giant Bear, Wade, and me. My father is also still alive they took him prisoner that's why they raided the ranch."

Gloria visibly brightened then quit crying instantly as she stepped back. She stared up at Mell with anticipation. "Wade is still alive?"

Mell nodded mutely in confusion when Gloria's frantic crying stopped suddenly. "Yes. He caught a bullet in his arm that went clean through. He lost a lot of blood before he found us, but otherwise he is unhurt."

Gloria quickly wiped her tear stained face with the back of her hand then reached down calmly and smoothed her dress as she turned slightly. She gestured impatiently behind her to Tommy who was still slightly inside the cellar unable to get out with Gloria blocking the doorway. "Good I'll make lunch come out now Tommy you can help me."

Mell stared after the two retreating figures completely bewildered. She watched Gloria walk away very much in control, as if a few minutes ago she hadn't been hysterical. Mell shook her head perplexed, she would never understand women, even though she herself was a woman she had never been prone to such mood swings so had no idea how to deal with a woman who had them.

Mell finally shrugged baffled then turned and followed Gloria into the kitchen. She went through it, into the hallway, and across to her father's rooms looking for Three Toes. Mell walked into the room and found Three Toes lying on the floor beside her father's bed dead. As she turned away to go give the sad news to Jed, she saw one of the wolf's legs twitching unexpectedly, Mell heard a painful low whine came from deep in his throat.

Mell instantly ran back to the doorway and yelled across the hallway at Gloria. "Gloria, send Tommy to get Jed! Three Toes is still alive in here!"

Mell rushed back over to the wolf then knelt beside him talking soothingly to keep him calm and still. She stroked his head in encouragement and waited impatiently for Jed. She finally heard footsteps behind her and turned to Jed with tears in her eyes as she looked pleadingly at him. "Oh Jed, please tell me he's going to be all right!"

Jed knelt on the other side of Three Toes and examined him for injuries. He looked over at Mell and smiled thankfully as he sat back. He grinned relieved as he nodded reassurance. "Yes, it looks like his head was just grazed by a bullet leaving him more stunned then anything. Good thing he has so much fur it slowed the bullet enough that it didn't cause too much damage only knocked him out cold. He should come around soon since he's been out for a while. I can't find any other wounds thank God!"

Three Toes opened his eyes a few minutes later and licked Mell's hand as she stroked his nose gently. The wolf managed to stagger to his feet on his own then wobbled over to Jed. He licked Jed's face in greeting as he whined slightly in pain. He finally turned away after getting a reassuring pat. Three Toes went over to the bed and smelt it, before sniffing around the floor searchingly. When he found the scent he was looking for, he turned and followed it out of the room. Down the hallway and out the still open front door before going down the ramp into the yard.

Mell and Jed followed Three Toes outside intriguingly and watched him sniff around the yard. Wade and Giant Bear came over to stand beside them and they too surveyed the wolf wondering where he was going.

He staggered a few times but continued on doggedly as he followed the tracks out of the ranch yard. He trotted faster when he came to the trail leading to the north approach to Devil's Rock then he finally stopped. The wolf turned expectantly as he looked back at Jed as if asking permission.

Jed nodded in consent then called out loudly to the wolf. "Okay Three Toes go and find Alec!"

Three Toes lifted his nose in the air and howled his intention then turned back towards the mountains and started loping drunkenly towards Devil's Rock. He was still very unsteady from his head wound but that didn't stop the determined wolf, as he put his nose to the ground and he never looked back.

Mell frowned in apprehension, as she turned then looked at Jed in concern. "Will he be okay Jed?"

Jed smiled in reassurance as he looked at Mell's concerned expression. "Yes he'll find your father and watch out for him until we catch up to him."

After watching the wolf disappear the four returned to the house to decide on a plan. As they gathered around the table Gloria entered and started setting out lunch.

Mell noticed the look of adoration in Gloria's glance as it rested on Wade. Mell couldn't help but smile in pleasant surprise when she saw Wade return the look. Gloria turned away with a gratified look on her face. As she turned she saw Mell watching her and she blushed deeply then hurried out as Mell's grin widened. Now Gloria's hysterical actions earlier made a little more sense.

When lunch was finished Mell turned to the three men resolutely already having a plan in mind. She waited until Gloria came back into the room before she began. "There are three entrances to Devil's Rock. Two are hidden so unless you're very familiar with the area you wouldn't know about them. I'll take Giant Bear to the one that leads up to a cabin where they're holding my father and Jed to the other one."

Mell took a fortifying breath then her face became hard and expressionless because she knew the men wouldn't like her plan. But that didn't matter her father's life was at stake and she would do anything she had too to save him, even give up her own life if need be. "If we ride hard we should be able to get to Devil's Rock in three days, four at the most. Once I show you where the hidden trails are I'll give you both until dark to find your positions. Then I'll ride up to the bend just before the main pass and make camp there, that will give you both time to find a good location before first light of the fifth day, so we can all see clearly. Then I'll ride up the main trail to take attention away from your goal, which is a miner's shack where they're holding my father."

Mell turned to her foreman next and waved towards the southeast. "Wade I want you to stay here and send Tommy to the Johnson's place to get someone here to help dig the graves for the men who died and lay them to rest. We'll have a service when we return with my father. Gloria, I want you to have food ready for us hopefully within ten days make sure you gather bandages and have the material on hand in case anyone is hurt bad enough that we can't fix it on the trail."

Wade nodded but just as she had known Jed and Giant Bear didn't like her plan at all.

Jed frowned angrily and gestured sharply in denial as he argued vehemently. "Mell you can't sacrifice yourself your father wouldn't want that!"

Mell sighed in aggravation as Jed questioned her authority as sheriff but she had known he would sooner or later. It was good to get him to do so now. This way he would see that she did know what she was doing, even if it didn't seem like it.

She smiled reassuringly over at the disgruntled Jed as she motioned consolingly. Mell explained her motives even though she didn't think she should have to. "Jed, think about it they waited until I was away from home before they grabbed my father. If they had wanted to kill me outright they could have come in the other night and ambushed us, since they obviously already knew where I lived. I think that's why they chased me the other day without really trying to kill me. They must have known I would go searching for them and that would get me out of the way. So obviously they want me to suffer before they kill me, they're not going to kill me on sight, if that's what you're worried about. This will give you plenty of time to rescue my father and to help me out afterwards."

Giant Bear frowned thoughtfully as he nodded towards Mell. "I think you are right about them wanting you to suffer. But what if you're wrong and they have your father with them when they go to meet you? What would we do then?"

Mell shrugged dismissively as she waved towards both of them, not worried in the least. "Then I guess you both will have to rescue us. It's the only way I can see to keep you two hidden until it's too late for the outlaws to retaliate."

Jed growled angrily as he smashed the table with his fist to emphasis his point. "I don't think we should take that kind of risk!"

Mell's face became expressionless as she leaned forward irritably, not wanting to argue any more. She pointed a finger towards Jed in forewarning. "It's a good plan, if for some reason it doesn't go like I think it will, I trust you both to help my father first! I can look after myself but he can't! Is that understood?"

Jed opened his mouth to refuse but snapped it shut sullenly as Giant Bear touched his arm to get his attention. Afraid Jed was going to say something he would regret. Jed turned to his friend and saw him shake his head in warning, Giant Bear knew Jed was scared for Mell but they didn't need her disappearing on them and he figured she was right anyway.

Wade motioned to Tommy and they left to go saddle the horses since he couldn't handle it himself, while Gloria cleaned up lunch.

Jed threw up his hands in surrender giving up. Obviously trying to talk Mell out of sacrificing herself was not permissible. They all left the table then went to change and prepare to ride out again.

* * *

Mell took them in a different direction from the one Three Toes had taken. It would take them a few hours longer but she wanted to make sure that the outlaws wouldn't spot them if they happened to have someone watching for her.

Jed looked around him in pleasure as they rode along then turned to Mell in definite approval. "This is all yours?"

Mell nodded over at Jed as she smiled in pride at his obvious pleasure in her ranch. "Yes I not only look after the town but once a month I ride to all the smaller settlements. When I rescued the Mayor and his wife they gave me the ranch on two condition, one that I wouldn't draw anymore wages, and two I'd have to administer the law to all the out of the way places that have no Sheriff. The town pays my Deputy's and all my expenses for traveling around."

Jed stared at Mell in astonishment. "How do you find the time?"

Mell beamed in pleasure at Jed's interest in her then shrugged dismissively. "Well, it's not that hard. I have one Deputy in each small settlement and when there's a problem they send someone for me. My own town is fairly quiet now except for a few drunks getting out of hand once in awhile. I'm not there very often usually Greg look's after things for me. Actually I just got back a couple of days before I met you. I just finished my rounds so I don't have to go again for another three weeks or so."

Jed thought about it for a moment before motioning in understanding, as he turned back at her. "Okay I see how it might work but what do you do for money when you get no wages?"

Mell shrugged in unconcern the money had never really mattered to her, but of course Jed wouldn't know that. "Well of course when I'm on the trail all of my expenses are paid for. The supplies such as I acquired from the store yesterday is billed directly to the town even yours. Did you notice a building in the trees about two miles from the ranch house?"

Jed nodded that he had. "Well yes but I figured it was somebody else's or abandoned."

Mell smiled teasingly then shook her head negatively. "No it's not. You did notice that the ranch house, barns, corrals, and both bunk houses are made out of lumber not logs didn't you?"

Jed frowned considering then caught on as he grinned back at Mell perceptively. "Oh I see, you have a saw mill that's why I saw such small trees when we first met."

Mell chuckled as she winked playfully. "Why do you think the town is so large already, they don't have to wait for lumber, they just put in an order from me? We will haul lumber anywhere mostly into Montana it's our biggest market right now. I have about a dozen wagons out now selling as they go, when they get back I'll start cutting again. We don't cut wood continuously because we don't want to deplete our supply and we always make sure to plant more trees as we cut them down. We also do okay selling, breeding, and breaking horses. Most people who see my stud fall in love with him and want their mares bred to him."

Jed shook his head in amazement. "Haven't you ever thought about settling down with a man, getting married, you know maybe raise a couple of kids?"

Mell shrugged self-consciously as she nodded wishfully. "A few times but I've never met anyone who could accept me the way I am. I'm not the stay-at-home; look after the kid's kind of woman. I love my job and everything that goes with it. Few men would accept that."

Jed sighed in understanding and recalled Giant Bear's words on the same subject. He lapsed into silence as they finally urged their horses into a full gallop, now that the horses were warmed up, and raced towards the mountains urgently. It would be a gruelling three days with very little sleep.

CHAPTER SIX

Alec held on tightly to his saddle horn so that he wouldn't be tempted to lift the blindfold. He had a feeling that if he tried it they wouldn't hesitate to kill him no matter what the consequences.

It was late the evening of the fourth day and he was half asleep when suddenly they started climbing a steep hill. He woke instantly as he realized where they were taking him. According to the time that had past and the change in terrain they must be going up Devil's Rock.

Alec heard a horse galloping towards them unexpectedly and he tensed then his ears picked up another sound and he frowned pensively or maybe there were two horses. He couldn't tell for sure and his optimism rose hoping it was Mell and Jed coming to rescue him. He waited anxiously ready to urge his horse into a run immediately but then his hopes plummeted as the call to run never materialized.

There was a hurried conference, which dashed Alec's thoughts of a quick rescue, with a lot of arguing that Alec strained to hear but couldn't then a horse was galloping away again. He was sure this time that there was only one horse.

They started riding again and after a couple of hours of riding up some steep terrain they finally reached their destination. Alec was lifted off his horse by someone, probably by the same one who had put him on his horse each time they had stopped for a rest, and he was carried into a building then put down roughly on a bed or cot maybe by the hard lumpy feel of it.

His hands were tied together behind his back before the blindfold was finally removed, after almost four long days of wearing it. Alec cursed silently in disappointment as they tied his hands, now he wouldn't be able to get to his knife. He had hoped to retrieve his knife and if the worst happened, to take at least one of the outlaws to the grave with him.

He looked around inquisitively and saw the same three outlaws that had hit the ranch lounging around in chairs then he noticed another man standing in the shadows. Alec's eyes widened in shocked surprise and recognition he exhaled in incredibility stunned for a moment! He knew now he was a dead man as the outlaws let him see the traitor!

* * *

The three rescuers were totally exhausted and so were their horses by the time they reached the bottom of Devil's Rock. They had stopped only when their horses were too weary to go any further and they would sleep for a couple of hours before racing on again. But tonight they all knew they would be able to get a good night's sleep.

It had taken them three and a half gruelling days to get there. It was very late almost midnight by the time they arrived. Mell was silently thanking God at that moment for the fact that they should only be one day behind the outlaws, but unknown to all of them was that they had almost caught up to the kidnappers. If they would have went on the main trail instead of around they would have caught the outlaws in the pass at Devil's Rock. It was only two hours ago that her father had disappeared up the main pass.

Devil's Rock wasn't really a huge mountain it was more like a mountain range with cliffs protruding everywhere a main pass ran almost in the center up to an old miner's cabin.

On the west end there was a thick forest with a back entrance up the steep cliffs that Mell had found years ago when out exploring on one of her rare occasions off.

The old miner that use to live up there would come to town once and a while mumbling about devils stealing his things, so it became known as Devil's Rock. Once you reached the cabin there was a small valley with lots of trees behind it, that's where she had found one of the secret passes, there was even a fresh water spring that gave the sweetest tasting water she had ever tasted. She had tried to find the source of the water but search as she might she couldn't find it.

When she had time off, which was rarely, and she was tired of the little valley she had visited the other day this was where she would come to hide out.

Mell guided Giant Bear to the trail he would take alone it would bring him directly behind the cabin that Mell knew her father was being held in. Just before leaving Giant Bear she gave him some extra instructions. "You will be closest to the cabin and in the best position to rescue my father. I want you to go in and get my father out while the other men are occupied with me. Jed will watch your back and he'll also have a clear view of what goes on when I ride up. That way if anything goes wrong both of us have back up."

Giant Bear nodded without hesitation then horse and rider melted into the forest without a sound.

Mell turned her horse away then urged him into a canter going east, closer to the main pass that she would be taking. The two remaining rescuers continued on for two more hours before they left the forest behind and scraggly bush took the place of the forest. Behind the bush Jed could see huge rocks and boulders protruding everywhere, how he was suppose to get up them he had no idea, but Mell seemed so sure he would just have to trust her.

Mell took Jed around a sharp turn and she halted her horses then dismounted in silence. Jed followed her lead then looked towards where she was pointing. He inclined his head in acknowledgment as he saw an opening behind the bushes then dropped his horse's reins and walked towards Mell. He stopped in front of her and motioned anxiously in demand. "Are you sure your plan will work Mell."

Before she could even answer Jed clasped her by the upper arms and pulled her towards him roughly, as he pleaded urgently. "Don't do anything rash! I don't think I could bare to lose you too! I want to finish what we started at the creek!"

Once again Mell tried to speak but her words were cut off as Jed's lips covered hers unrelentingly, in a searing kiss full of unleashed passion and promise. He pushed her away suddenly without speaking or even giving her a chance to speak, and he quickly grabbed his horse's reins before disappearing into the bushes.

The path he followed wound up a cliff then ended in a flat shelf that gave the best view of both the cabin and the main trail leading up to the cabin, so he could see everything that would be going on tomorrow. Satisfied he climbed back down to his horse then grabbed his bedroll. He rolled himself into it and was fast asleep almost immediately too exhausted to even think about the kiss he had just shared with Mell.

* * *

Mell stared after him in amazement as she softly touched her bruised lips. She turned away and remounted her horse before riding further east several miles to the main trail leading up Devil's Rock. She hid behind a wall of rocks and waited until a dark cloud covered the three quarter moon. Giving her more cover just in case they had someone this far watching for her.

This was the first part of the pass it was fairly wide and she was sure they would wait further up closer to the cabin. Besides there was a little spot just up ahead a ways that branched off into a kind of deep nook almost a cave but not quite that she could sleep comfortably in. It was even large enough to put her horse behind her.

Mell turned to her saddlebags then rummaged inside and pulled out four sheets of cloth with rawhide threaded through going all the way around the cloth. She put three on the ground then clucked softly to her horse and he obediently lifted his front foot familiar with this indignity as he snorted softly in rebuke. She chuckled quietly as she slipped the cloth over his hoof then tied it to keep it in place. She patted her horse in apology before going to his other hoof until all four hooves were covered. Mell led her horse quietly up the trail as she whispered a prayer for everyone's safe return tomorrow.

* * *

Alec stared in absolute shock at the man standing in the shadows. Of all the men he had thought of and discarded, as the traitor Mell's trusted deputy from town was not one of them.

Greg stepped into the light as he sneered viciously and cackled in satisfaction at Alec's shocked stare. "Surprised to see me old man?"

Alec nodded in furious disbelief as he eyed Greg wearily. "Now I know how they knew so much about the routine of the ranch. But how did you know where I keep my chair?"

Greg shrugged dismissively as he waved negligently. "Not hard to find out if you ask the right questions."

Sam the black haired oldest brother and leader walked over then turned his back to Alec to block his view of Greg. He spoke harshly to Greg but to low for Alec to hear what was being said.

Greg bobbed his head in frustration at Sam without saying a word then glared down at Alec as Sam moved aside to let Greg pass, as if it was his fault, before stalked out in obvious rage. Sam and Jimmy followed him, and only Marty the blonde gawky cowboy was left on guard duty.

Alec lay down as best he could with his hands bound behind his back thinking furiously as he frowned perplexed. If Greg was here who had left on horseback, was there someone else involved, or did Greg ride ahead of them? He finally dozed too exhausted to stay awake any longer. At one point he jerked awake, thinking he heard a different voice in the background. But when Alec turned his head only Marty was there, standing staring fixedly at the door. No one else seemed to be about.

Alec finally managed to go back to sleep still wondering if someone else had really been there or if it was just his imagination playing tricks on him.

Sometime later Alec woke again. He cocked his head listening; trying to discover what had woke him this time. He looked around guardedly and saw Marty sleeping in a chair once more. He was snoring softly but not loud enough to wake Alec up.

Suddenly he heard scratching against the wall outside and a low pleading whine. Alec smiled widely in joy, Three Toes hadn't died after all, and Alec whispered as quietly as possible. "I'm okay boy go find Jed Three Toes."

Three Toes whined plaintively once more at not being able to reach Alec. He had caught up to Alec the second day of the kidnapping but couldn't get close enough to him to help. Alec heard the wolf scratching at the dirt under the cabin for a moment longer then he gave up and Alec didn't hear him again.

Alec looked towards Marty but the man hadn't moved. Alec sighed relieved then wriggled around trying to get more comfortable. He sighed thankfully, finally able to sleep, knowing help was on the way.

* * *

Mell arrived at a large opening further up the trail with huge rocks rising high on both sides this was the actual entrance to Devil's Rock that's why the old miner had added rock to the name instead of mountain, she had guessed long ago. It was around eight o'clock in the morning now and full daylight already.

She had camped in her hiding place around three o'clock this morning further down the trail and while she was making a quick supper she had noticed Three Toes skulking around the opening of her little nook. She had called out to him but he had turned and headed down the trail probably looking for Jed and Giant Bear.

As Mell entered she saw three men coming towards her. She lifted her arms unthreateningly to show that she wasn't holding any guns. At first she didn't recognize any of them, but as they got closer Mell drew in an outraged intake of breath. As she identify one of them it was Greg her deputy at Smyth's Crossing! Mell was seething by the time the three men got close enough and her voice trembled in fury as she fought to control her rage. "You sold me out you son of a bitch!"

Greg sneered maliciously as he waved to his companions in introduction. "Now Mell let me introduce you to my cousins."

Greg chortled in mockery at the stunned look on her face. "That's right Mell you killed two of my cousins and now you will pay for it with your life. Get down off of that horse! NOW!"

Greg turned to the huge man on his right as he motioned in caution. "Jimmy, she carries a knife in each boot. She also carries two revolvers. Don't overlook the whip behind her saddle either. She can be lethal with it."

Mell and the man called Jimmy both dismounted then she stood stiffly while he stripped her of her weapons. Mell looked up into his face, he was a lot taller than she was, hoping to see some sign of compassion then she stepped back hurriedly in revulsion at the cruel hateful look on his face.

Mell thanked her lucky stars that Greg didn't know about the knife she had purchased when she had left town with Jed. It was well hidden under her shirt as well as a small pistol that she always kept out of sight, unknown to anyone, even her father.

Greg pointed to Mell's horse remorselessly. "Mount up Mell and behave yourself, or your father is dead!"

Mell glared up at Greg intently, before mounting, her voice was whisper soft in lethal promise as she gestured unflinchingly. "Did you hurt him Greg? If you did, you're a dead man!"

Mell's tone was ominous and she saw Greg's hand shake slightly in reaction a little, as he lifted his hat to wipe the sweat of his brow. He tried to hide his momentary panic from his cousins then he sniggered at her threat before sneering in derision as he jammed his hat back on. "Mighty big threat for someone who is going to die soon!"

Mell wasn't fooled for a moment and she could tell Greg knew it as she turned then mounted silently with no further comment her pledge already given.

Jimmy giggled with his cousin unaware of Greg's apprehension then he rode ahead with his older brother letting Greg and Mell ride together.

* * *

Meanwhile Giant Bear cautiously approached the cabin looking for a sentry, but the outlaws were so confident in Mell's doing what she was told that they had left only the one man inside alone. He peered into a side window of the cabin to see how many men were inside. The first person he noticed was Alec sitting quietly on a cot in the corner. His hands were tied behind him and he was staring at someone standing not far from the front door.

Giant Bear's glance flew in that direction then he became very cold and motionless as he looked at the man his sister had called Marty. He was exactly as she had described him his sister had even described how the man had gotten his broken nose. Giant Bear's wife had hit him in the face with a rock during the struggle as he was raping and strangled her. They had gone on to rape Giant Bears sister repeatedly that's why she had taken her own life, after she had told her brother what had happened to them. The dishonour had been too much for her to bare now there he stood with his back to the door taunting Alec.

Giant Bear crept around to the door then slowly pushed it open hoping the door wouldn't creak and his silent hope was answered as the door opened soundlessly.

Giant Bear grabbed Marty from behind then turned him around quickly before locking the unfortunate Marty in a bear hug. Marty was completely taken by surprise and didn't even have a chance to call out as he stared at the huge Indian in shocked alarm.

Giant Bear's eyes narrowed remorselessly at the dumbfounded Marty as he stared him right in the eye. Not once did he look away and with no hint of repentance for what he was about to do, as his voice echoed through the cabin eerily. It was void of all feeling except for satisfaction. "You raped and killed my wife then raped my sister and left her to die. Now I will kill you slowly! I will crush the life out of you and you will die looking into my eyes so that you will know that my wife and sister have been avenged. They will haunt your after life forever as you see them reflected in my eyes."

Marty groaned agonizingly and strained against the arms holding him, but he was caught like an animal in a trap, he couldn't break free or even look away from the enraged Cheyenne Chief even though he tried desperately to. Marty shuddered in excruciating torture as he felt his ribs finally break slowly one by one. The jagged pieces started piercing his lungs and he could feel them as they entered the soft lining then finally penetrated completely. He let out a stifled scream as the blood gushed into his mouth choking and gagging him slowly. The blood finally overflowed his lips and dribbled down his chin faster and faster.

Giant Bear kept his merciless gaze locked on Marty's face relishing every moment of agony the outlaw suffered. He knew the moment death found its mark and he dropped the limp body to the floor without one show of emotion. Taking out his hunting knife Giant Bear bent down then grabbing a hold of the outlaw's hair then scalped him. Giant Bear stood up slowly then raised the scalp towards the ceiling as if to show his sister and wife that he had avenged them. He let out a blood-curdling shriek of satisfaction!

Giant Bear quieted then muttered under his breath as if saying a prayer as he dropped his arm then tucked his grizzly trophy in his belt before going over to a bucket of water to wash his hands and the knife. He turned finally and went over to Alec to release him.

Alec had sat silently shuddering as he witnessed Giant Bear's revenge but he said nothing respecting his friend's Indian ways and not judging him.

Giant Bear sliced the ropes binding Alec's hands. Alec sighed in relief as the tingle of circulation slowly returned. He beamed up at Giant Bear in gratitude as he brought his hands out in front of him then massaged his wrists hoping to return some circulation to them. "Thank you Giant Bear."

Alec cast an apprehensive look at the door searchingly but he didn't see Mell. He looked up at the Indian Chief anxiously. "Is Mell nearby Giant Bear?"

Giant Bear eyed Alec respectfully. He hadn't shied away from him, even after witnessing the killing of the white man. Although he probably would have done it differently his only sigh had been one of relief, when Giant Bear had washed his hands before releasing him. Giant Bear nodded in admiration down at this crippled white man that he was proud to call his friend. His voice clearly reflected his approval as he waved towards the door of the cabin. "Yes, she is with the other outlaws. Hold on to me tight while I take you to your horse. I must leave you in a safe place while I go to help the others."

Alec acquiesced as he put his arms around Giant Bear's neck trustingly without any qualms as the huge Indian bent down to scoop him up. Giant Bear tenderly enfold Alec in his huge beefy arms as he stood up then carried him out of the cabin. He had to step over the body of the outlaw but neither man spared the dead man a glance.

Giant Bear looked down at Alec when they got outside and he motioned with his head towards the cliffs on their right. "Alec wave your hand toward those cliffs so that Jed will know that you are all right."

Alec obediently did as he was told even though he couldn't see Jed way up there.

* * *

Up on a ledge overlooking the cabin Jed had watched Giant Bear disappear inside and emerge later with Alec in his arms. Giant Bear's head was lowered and he appeared to be saying something to Alec. Alec waved his hand in Jed's direction. Jed sighed in relief Mell's father was okay.

Jed didn't wave back in acknowledgment afraid the outlaws would see him. He turned away then climbing down the ledge cautiously so that he was kneeling over the lip ready to jump down and ambush the outlaws but they weren't even close to that spot yet.

Jed heard a rustling in the bush behind him he stopped short and quickly went for his gun. He dropped his hand with a sigh of relief as Three Toes appeared beside him. He stroked the wolf's head tenderly and whispered softly so only he would hear him. "Good boy follow me now."

The pair carefully followed the edge of the cliff until Mell and the remaining outlaws came into view on the trail below. Jed crept into position as he directed the wolf to take down the simple Jimmy. Then he looked down at the black haired Sam and felt the rage he had kept bottled up for so long seep back to the surface in a heartbeat. He remembered his son saying that it was Sam who had finally killed his wife and unborn child after everyone had finished raping her. Sam had then plunged his knife into her belly viciously before turning and plunged the same knife into his son leaving him to die as well.

Jed gave the wolf the signal to attack then jumped down and knocked Sam out of his saddle. They both fell hard to the ground as Sam's horse spooked by the smell of the wolf bolted up the trail leaving his master defenceless.

Three Toes jumped of the cliff knocking a shocked and bewildered Jimmy out of his saddle. Jimmy landed hard on the ground and the air was knocked out of him as his horse screamed in fear then bolted. The wolf landed lightly on his feet then turned quickly and grabbed the disorientated Jimmy by the arm unable to get close to the huge mans beefy throat.

Jed got to his feet quickly and drew his knife out of its sheath not even bothering with his gun, wanting Sam to die the same way his Victoria had. He prepared himself for a fight to the death.

Sam growled in furious disbelief as he glared up in astonishment at the stranger towering over him. "Who the hell are you?"

Jed opened his mouth to answer but snapped it shut again in fear as the sound of a horse screaming in pain behind him made him jerk around in panic. He glanced quickly in that direction to make sure it wasn't Mell's horse that was hurt. He realized that Mell was attacking the fourth outlaw and she wasn't hurt so he brought his attention back to Sam quickly. He was only distracted for a moment but he cursed at himself for his lost opportunity as he stared at Sam now standing in front of him holding his own knife.

Sam had taken the opportunity of Jed's distraction to get to his feet and take out his own knife but he didn't attack, usually he would have if someone was stupid enough to give him his back, but he wanted to know who the stranger was first.

Jed smirked threateningly as he pointed at himself in introduction answering Sam's earlier question. "My name is Jed Brown and I've been tracking you and your brothers all across Montana. My search started in western Montana where you raped and killed my pregnant wife then stabbed my ten-year-old son and left him to die. At long last I will destroy you for it and avenge their deaths."

Sam inclined his head thoughtfully as he remembered that day then he beamed in satisfaction evilly as he teased Jed playfully. "Oh, yes. The beautiful brunette the best whore I ever had as I felt the blood of her child gushed out of her body and enveloped me with blood!"

Jed attacked him in frenzy as he lifted his arm to plunge the knife into the man's throat, unable to hear him give further description of the horrible massacre of his wife and children. But he didn't quite make it there as he stumbled backwards in grief instead, as he heard a gunshot followed by the howl of an animal in pain. Then out of the corner of his eye, not daring to look away from Sam completely, he saw the huge wolf fall to the ground and he groaned in regret.

Giant Bear emerged from the hills just moments too late to save Three Toes and he tackled Jimmy with a vengeance livid at losing one of his friends.

Sam had also turned and his mouth dropped open in stunned disbelief when Giant Bear emerged from behind Jimmy wondering where the Indian had come from. Sam could hardly believe his eyes. That was the biggest Indian he had ever seen, that moment of distraction cost the outlaw his life, Jed's knife struck deeply into his chest.

Jed kept his gaze locked on Sam's face as he smiled in pleasure. "I would have done this more slowly but I have friends to help out."

With that Jed savagely twisted the knife deeper into Sam's chest and ripped it upwards through the outlaws black heart. Jed felt the deepest satisfaction as he watched the life drain out of Sam's eyes. He dropped the lifeless body in contempt.

Jed looked in Giant Bear's direction just in time to see him scalp his victim. So Jed walked over and knelt down beside the dead wolf sadly as he gently patted the stiffening body in farewell.

* * *

Mell was listening to the conversation of the men riding ahead of her they were describing in detail how they were going to kill her. It was going to be a long slow process according to them. Suddenly the voices in front of her stopped in stunned shock as the two horses reared and screamed in fright then they both fled as their riders were knocked from their saddles.

Mell saw Three Toes and Jed leaping from the cliff edge. This was what she had been waiting for and she didn't waste any time as she shouted a command to her horse and he reared at the horse Greg was riding.

Greg barely had time to register his surprise at the turn of events when Mell's stallion's hooves landed on the back of his horse's neck. He would have been crushed under his horse if Mell hadn't jumped at him and they both fell out of their saddles onto the hard ground.

Mell jerked the knife from its hiding place behind her back as she stood up slowly and with deadly assurance plain in her voice she stared down at Greg threateningly. "You will die now Greg like the dog you are. You will pay for your betrayal!"

Greg pulled a knife from his boot top then got up as well. They circled each other both looking for an opportunity or an indication of weakness.

Mell heard a shot and a howl but kept her concentration focused on her prey. Out of the corner of her eye she saw Giant Bear racing to help and she heaved a sigh in relief.

That split second of distraction almost cost her life as Greg took the opportunity to attack her without warning. She managed to side step him neatly then she aimed a swift kick that connected solidly in his stomach and Mell smirked in satisfaction. Glad now for all the wrestling and boxing she had done as a kid at the ranch her father looked after, even though her mother had been horrified when she caught her fighting with the boys behind the barn.

Greg doubled over in pain holding his abdomen in disbelief not having expected that at all as Mell ridiculed him in gratification. "What's the matter Greg getting old?"

Greg roared in rage and frustration as he stood up straight then charged at her again.

This time Mell slipped under his left arm then came up behind him and for a split second they were standing back to back but the agile Mell turned quickly before Greg even figured out what she was up too and stabbed him in the back in the right shoulder just below his collar bone as she taunted. "That's for killing my friend Joe!"

Greg groaned in agony as he realized that Mell planned on cutting him to ribbons before she finished him off. He became desperate as he spun around to face her and lunged for her again.

This time she took a step to the right, and sidestepped him as he charged right past her. She spun around quickly once he was clear of her and brought her knife up then plunge it into his back in the left shoulder this time, again just below his collar bone. "That's for Dan my stableman."

Mell caught movement out of the corner of her eye and become conscious that Jed and Giant Bear had arrived to watch the knife fight. She couldn't chance acknowledging them and possibly risk losing her concentration. But just that second of hesitation gave Greg time to leap at her again as he turned around unexpectedly this time he managed to get under her guard, Mell falter slightly as she felt his knife pierce her left shoulder.

Jed was admiring Mell's expertise in handling her knife but when Greg wounded her he couldn't stand by any longer and he stepped forward to help her.

Giant Bear put a restraining hand on Jed's shoulder then pulled him back to stand beside him as he shook his head at Jed compassionately when Jed looked at him infuriate. "I am sorry my friend but this is her fight you must let her deal with him."

Giant Bear watched Jed's face patiently waiting for him to agree. There were actually two reasons why Giant Bear refused to let Jed go. One was because Jed needed to see Mell in action in order to understand her better, and it would also build his trust in her when he needed her in the future. The second reason was because Jed's first wife had been a wealthy debutant in Boston. When Jed had described his wife to Giant Bear after they first met he had always described her as fragile and delicate unable to even look after herself when left alone. He needed to see that Mell was completely opposite to his dead wife and could look after herself without his help. Or Jed would forever be racing to save her when she didn't really need saving and that would make Mell resent him.

Jed's angry frown eased as he nodded in reluctant agreement then he turned back to the fight in time to see Mell rally back. He could hardly believe what he was seeing! She was cutting Greg to ribbons and every time she cut him she named someone else from the ranch that had died. Jed could see that Greg was tiring from the many wounds he had taken already as he desperately tried again to get under Mell's guard but was outwitted at every turn.

Jed watched Mell in stunned fascination her moves were cleverly executed she didn't rush in then stab, but used her feet and body in perfect symmetry almost like a dancer. Greg outweighed her by quite a bit but she was slightly taller and had a longer reach, which she used to her advantage.

Greg was becoming more frantic as he charged wildly for Mell but she evaded him again then kicked out with her long legs and went in for the kill. Greg's eyes bulged in surprise and shock as he felt the twinge in his chest even before he realized that she had struck.

Mell twisted her knife viciously then ripped it upwards making sure that he was dead as she painfully gasped out in exhaustion. "And this is for my father!"

Mell thought she whispered her final words to her deputy but it was more of a shout and both the men watching heard her last words to Greg as the fatally wounded man fell dead at her feet.

Breathing heavily Mell stood for a few moments gazing down at the dead man almost in disbelief. Then she swayed in weakness as the loss of blood caught up to her. She slowly sank to her knees, as she dropped she felt someone put their arms around her then thankfully pull her away from the dead Greg so she wouldn't fall on top of him. She trembled in relief as she stared up into Jed's eyes and he drew her closer tenderly.

Giant Bear left without a sound to go get Alec and his horse as soon as he was sure Mell was okay.

Mell glanced around still a little dazed then saw Giant Bear returning leading two horses one was carrying someone. She sighed reassured as she recognized her father apparently safe and unhurt. At this point her eyes closed wearily then everything went black as she crumbled in Jed's arms without uttering a sound.

Jed was frantic as he called Mell's name desperately and he shook her slightly in panic. "Mell wake up! Don't you die on me now!"

Mell slowly opened her eyes and stared up at Jed pleadingly as she whispered weakly. "You can quite shaking me you know I'm not dying only very tired. Is everyone all right?"

Jed beamed thankfully as he gazed down at her in assurance then he nodded. "Yes except for Three Toes. He was shot before Giant Bear was able to get close to the man he was struggling with."

Mell was relieved that they had only lost one then closed her eyes weakly as she whispered softly. "Jed I love you."

Mell faintly heard his soft reply as she once again lapsed into unconsciousness. "I love you too Mell!"

* * *

The man watching from the cliff above them moved back slowly, so he wouldn't be seen. The fury and anguish on his face gave him a menacing and evil appearance. When he was far enough back that he was sure he couldn't be seen he turned to leave. He only went a few steps when he turned back suddenly once more and raised a furious fist as he spoke under his breath so nobody below could hear him. "I will get you for this! All of you!"

* * *

Camp was set for the night at the same place Mell had used the night before it was a little cramped but big enough without the horses inside for injures to be seen too. Mell's wound wasn't serious but she had lost a lot of blood and was exhausted both physically and mentally. Giant Bear had sustained knife wounds in his right leg and left shoulder from his struggle with Jimmy.

Jed gently cleaned both their wounds and packed them with a poultice of dried raspberry and oak leaves that he had found in Giant Bears medicine bag then he boiled the rest for tea and made them drink it for good measures to draw out any poisons.

Jed and Alec decided to let Mell rest for one night to get some of her strength back before allowing her to undertake the long trek back to the ranch.

CHAPTER SEVEN

Mell's party arrived at the ranch around noon of the ninth day. It was a weary and sober group that dismounted from their horses. Jed had to fight the whole way because of the extra burden he carried, so it had taken them an extra day to get back to the ranch. Jed had insisted on bringing back the body of the wolf he had felt that Three Toes deserved a decent burial with the rest of the dead men at the ranch.

Jed helped lift Alec off his horse they carried him up onto the porch and gently put him in his outside wheelchair. He then left the others, as they went inside, and he returned to his horse to carry the wolf over to the burial site.

Jed walked to the far end of the graves and tenderly lowered the wolf to the ground. He knelt down beside him and stayed there for several long moments as he gently stoked Three Toes soft fur, while the tears ran down his cheeks and dripped onto the wolf's thick coat. He wasn't only saying good-bye to his companion, but he was also putting away the ghosts of his first wife and child.

Jed stood up and grabbed the shovel lying on the ground then started digging a grave. As he was digging flashes of the past with his wife, son, and the wolf came and went. As they left he tucked them into a part of his heart to be closed away until such a time came when they could be shared with new loved ones.

When he was finished laying his family and friend to rest, he was only half finished with digging the small grave. He spent the balance of the time exorcising the feelings of rage, despair, and grief that he had carried around for so long.

When he decided that the grave was deep enough he picked up the wolf then knelt down and laid him inside tenderly. He paused and put his hand on the wolf's soft fur one last time before sitting back as he stared down sadly then murmured quietly. "Good-bye my friend."

He stood up and rapidly shovelled the dirt back into the gaping hole until it was completely filled and all that was left was a small mound of dirt over the grave. Jed dropped the shovel and stood up straight then looked up at the sky and smiled completely free for the first time in a long time. At that moment the sun came out from behind a small fluffy cloud and shone directly on him, as if God was pleased.

Jed felt like a new man and for the first time in years he laughed out loud for no apparent reason. Then he turned and hurried up to the ranch house to join the others.

* * *

Gloria and Wade met Mell and her party in the hallway prepared to give them any help they needed. She ushered Mell and Giant Bear into the den to examine their wounds. Gloria worked on Giant Bear first, but after unwrapping the bandages she nodded in approval at Jed's expertise in treating injuries. She left the bandage off satisfied that it was healed enough.

Mell filled Gloria and Wade in on the gory details as the housekeeper turned to her next. She listened to Mell absently as she cleaned the wound then nodded in relief at the scab that had already formed. It would leave a nasty scare, but Mell wouldn't care about that, she had several now one more wouldn't hurt her. Again she threw the bandage in a corner still listening absently.

Just as Mell finished her account of events Jed entered the room and told his story. Later a very quiet group sat around the table trying to force food into their mouths. Finally they gave up and pushed their plates aside. As if of one mind they all rose together and headed for the door.

Jed stopped to help Alec into his outside chair. As they walked along Wade turned to Mell in explanation. "I sent Tommy over to the neighbour's like you said and they sent Franklin to help us dig the ten graves. I didn't say anything in the way of a memorial, 'cause I knew you would want to be here for that, oh by the way Tommy helped us out too."

Mell nodded soberly. "Good work Wade and Tommy thank you!"

They gathered around the graves solemnly and Mell began by singing amazing grace. The others all joined in then at the closing of the hymn Mell asked her father to say a few words in prayer. When Alec finished there wasn't a dry eye in the group as they headed back to the ranch house.

Mell was hit the hardest by this senseless massacre the men had been with her since the day she had moved to the ranch. They weren't just her ranch hands they had been friends too. Most of her grief she kept bottled up inside, for now, since she needed to be strong for the others.

Once inside they all walked down to the den then found seats so they could discuss what happened and what they should do next. Mell turned to her father first inquisitively. "Dad, will you give us a run down on what happened to you?"

Alec reflectively thought back still mystified by a few things. He motioned in bewilderment as he scowled confused. "Two things puzzled me. First, after Wade left they put me on my horse and blindfolded me. One of those men Marty I think it was, the skinny blonde one, said that he didn't want me to know who he was. I figured that he meant the traitor. But when we got to the cabin they took my blindfold off and there was Greg standing in the shadows watching me. Why would they do that? I knew as soon as they let me see Greg that they were going to kill me in the end. The second thing is that when I woke up during the night at the cabin I thought I heard someone else and the voice sounded vaguely familiar, but I couldn't place it. I'm not really sure about that though."

Mell frowned pensively for a few moments then looked at Jed and Giant Bear to see if they had seen anyone else. They both shook their heads in disagreement then Jed spoke for both of them. "Nobody else was there!"

Mell nodded at the two men agreeing with them then she turned to her father and gestured in reassurance. "I agree with Jed and Giant Bear. It would have been easy for Greg to find out about your horse since he's been at the ranch several times unsupervised. I've never kept it a secret from him where you sleep or where you keep your chair. I doubt very much that anyone else was involved. I'm pretty sure we got them all."

Alec sighed comforted, but he shifted slightly still a little uneasy, he finally deferred to their judgment. "Like I said I'm not sure but if you think we got them all I'll not worry about it."

Mell eyed her father's troubled expression pensively then shrugged off his apprehension. "Well, I think that's about it. I want everyone to get a good night sleep tonight. Tomorrow Jed and I will head to town to give a report to the Mayor, who also happens to be our judge, and inform him where the outlaw's bodies are to be located in case he wants to send someone to bury them. As far as I'm concerned they can rot there! We will also go to the ranch hand's families and let them know what happened. I also need to send them the wages owing to the men along with a bonus. Jed, I'll need help recruiting more men. I don't want to leave the ranch untended for any longer than I have to. I still have men out selling lumber but who knows when they will be back."

Then she turned to Wade and waved towards Tommy. "I want you to take Tommy home to his Uncle Brian's to stay with his mother for a few days. Tommy, I want you to stay there until things settle down here."

Tommy frowned fearfully then interrupted her heatedly. "But Mell, Uncle Brian doesn't want me there. He hates me!"

Mell walked over to Tommy and put her arm around him comfortingly. "I know Tommy but it's the only thing I can do for now. I promise it will only be for a few days."

Tommy stomped off furiously to pack his clothes muttering beneath his breath as he left. Mell sighed sadly then shook her head regretfully.

Jed and Giant Bear exchanged concerned glances mystified at the obvious hostility on Tommy's part towards his Uncle. With silent understanding Giant Bear got up to follow Tommy. All of a sudden for some unknown reason changed his mind and stepped into the shadows to listen. While Jed went over to talk to Mell anxious about Tommy's safety, if his uncle really hated him as Tommy said. "Mell what's this about Tommy's uncle?"

Mell frowned unsure for a moment whether it was her place to tell Tommy's story or not. She sighed sadly and decided to tell Jed not seeing any harm in it. "Tommy's mother got married to a Montana rancher about twelve years ago before I moved up here. They were on their way back to his ranch when a Cheyenne war party came across them. Mary's new husband was killed along with the two ranch hands that were with them. Mary was captured and taken back to the Indian village, according to Mary the Chief was on a rampage looking for three white men that had murdered his wife. After a time Mary and the Indian Chief fell in love then were married in an Indian ceremony. They had only been married a short time when the Chief left to hunt for the white killers again, leaving Mary and his young daughter from his first wife, behind. Soon after he left Mary realized that she was pregnant. When her husband still hadn't returned after four months time, Mary decided to leave and go home to have her baby there. When she reached home and it became known that she had married a Cheyenne Indian her brother was furious. He constantly shunned her and when Tommy was born her brother Brian treated him cruelly. The older Tommy became the more Brian abused him. It got so bad that Mary asked me to take Tommy. Mary is still pining for her lost husband and that makes Brian even angrier."

Jed had been listening very carefully and when Mell paused he interrupted her pensively. "You know Mell that Indian Chief sounds a lot like…"

"Me!" Came the voice of Giant Bear as he stepped out of the shadows unexpectedly.

Everyone turned to look at him in amazement. No one had heard him leave the room so obviously he had never left. Giant Bear thought of his beautiful blonde wife that he had thought was still in his Indian village then motioned sharply infuriated. "So, my Golden Dove is here. All this time I thought she was safe with my tribe that is all that kept me going for so long. And now you say I have a son who I did not know about. I must go to her and bring her home, my son as well!"

Mell was frantic as she rushed after Giant Bear as he turned to leave. She grabbed a hold of his arm desperately holding on to him before he could escape out the door. "No! Wait Giant Bear! You can't go to Brian's ranch. He will kill you without blinking an eye no questions asked. He's already killed one Indian that has always been a bone of contention between us. He's been after me to marry him for years it would be a good match because our land borders each other. But I would never marry anyone that has such hatred for a people just because they are different. If you will just sit down for a moment I think I have a plan that will work."

Mell turned to Gloria hastily but didn't dare release Giant Bear afraid he would leave anyway. "Go tell Tommy that we talked it over and decided to keep him here. But don't tell him that Giant Bear is his father, his mother should be the one to tell him that."

Gloria nodded relieved, she had been afraid for Tommy not liking Brian at all. She left the room quickly with the good news.

Mell turned her attention to Wade next. "Wade, I want you to go to the creek at ten o'clock tomorrow morning that's when Mary usually takes her daily ride. Bring her here but don't tell her anything about what's going on yet!"

Mell turned back to Giant Bear and squeezed his arm gently in support. "I want you to stay out of sight until I have a chance to talk to Mary. I don't want her to pass out from shock."

Mell glanced around and it seemed that everyone was in agreement except Giant Bear. He stood undecided for a moment then slowly nodded his head in consent.

Mell sighed thankfully and let out a breath she hadn't even realized she was holding.

* * *

Later that night Mell lay in her bed exhausted after allowing her emotions to come to the surface and crying for about two hours nonstop, until she had no tears left. Now she couldn't sleep as her mind kept running over the events of the past two weeks, could she have done anything differently? Maybe she should have taken the outlaws into custody to be hung. But no she had done that once and she regretted that she hadn't killed them at the start. They had escaped and massacre innocent woman and children. She had been right to end it as she did and second guessing herself now did no good.

She put the memories of the outlaws away and brought her thoughts to what happened afterwards. She recalled how she had passed out in

Jed's arms after she killed Greg. She also remembered whispering to Jed that she loved him. Did she really tell him that, or was it just a dream? No, she was sure that she had said it out loud and also that Jed had replied that he loved her too. But if that was true why did he ignore her the next morning? All the way back to the ranch, for four days he hadn't even glanced at her, maybe she had just wanted him to say it so badly that she had imagined it.

She sighed in aggravation then turned over again and tried to go to sleep. Just as she started to doze off she heard a faint knock on her door. Thinking it must be her father she smiled slightly remembering about all the times her father would get two of the ranch hands to carry him and his chair upstairs to surprise her. She sat up slightly and called out softly in anticipation forgetting for a moment that all her men were dead. "Come in!"

Mell's smile slowly died as Jed entered her room. She sat further up quickly her first thought was concern for her father. "Is something wrong Jed?"

Jed shook his head quickly in reassurance. "No, I just wanted to talk to you for a moment privately."

He walked over and sat on the side of her bed. Noticing her tear ravaged face he gently reached over then brushed a tear away. "Is your shoulder hurting you Mell?"

Mell shook her head negatively and smiled slightly in surprise at his tender touch. "No not as much now it's more of a dull throb."

Jed nodded in relief and sympathy then explained why he was there. "I didn't come up here earlier because I knew you needed some time to grieve and collect your thoughts I must admit I also needed time for grieving and putting away some ghosts before I could come to you. But I couldn't wait any longer to confess how much I love you. I want to marry you Mell, tomorrow or whenever you want!"

Mell beamed comforted, at least now she knew that she hadn't imagined him saying he loved her before. "I love you too Jed, but…."

Jed grinned encouraged and gently covered her lips with his fingertip to keep her from saying anything more until he was finished. "Hush, do not say anything yet let me finish first."

He removed his finger slowly confident that she would let him continue. "I know you have some concerns, like your job."

Mell tried to interrupt again, but Jed held up his hand to silence her. Mell closed her mouth sullenly with an audible snap that Jed heard plainly, and she sat there with a stubborn look on her face fearing the worst. She expected him to ask her to quit her job and if that was the case he could forget it!

Jed just smirked indulgently as she sat there in a huff because he could guess at her thoughts and she was wrong. "Now about your job I doubt very much that you want to give it up. However, I do require some stipulations. First I wish to remain as your Deputy. Secondly when we decide to start a family you will have to put them first. Your job as Sheriff will have to be put on hold until each child finishes suckling. I'll act as Sheriff at those times until you can resume your job at the appropriate occasion. As to the ranch I think you manage it beautifully I'm not much of a rancher so I'll leave you and your father to deal with that. However I might want to buy up some land later then maybe bring in some cattle if you and your father agree. So Mell what do you say? Can I go to your father tomorrow and ask for your hand in marriage?"

Mell watched him closely fearing to ask this question, but needing to know, so studying his face closely to see his reaction. "Jed, are you sure you can handle having your wife as your boss? It would require taking constant orders from me. Do you think it could work? That might be pretty much to handle even for you!"

Mell held her breath in anticipation and dread as she waited tensely for Jed's reply. Jed frowned thoughtfully as he stared intently at Mell and tried to be as honest as he possibly could. "Well I've thought about it long and hard, I'm not saying that I'll always agree with your methods and decisions. We might even get into a few fights about it, but I'll never dispute you in front of others ever. I do expect you to listen to me when I have an opinion and give me a fair hearing. But in the end it will always be your decision. I do not say these things because you are a woman or my wife. If I worked for a man I would expect the same consideration boss or no boss."

Mell was very delighted with Jed's answer and her wide smile of approval showed her pleasure. Then she nodded her permission to his all-important question with no more hesitations. "Yes Jed I'll marry you! You can talk to my father tomorrow if you want."

Jed whooped in joy then enfolded Mell in his arms but she continued speaking not wanting any misunderstanding between them as she went on to explain a few things. "I must tell you that although I make some of the decisions about the ranch, I leave them mostly in my father's hands. So you'll have to discuss buying cattle with him. He takes care of the buying and breeding he has never allowed me anywhere near the horses during their season. Even my stud is off limits to me at that time, I have to use a gelding for a month."

Jed was puzzled by Mell's father's old-fashioned views. Considering how open-minded he was about letting his daughter do a man's job without any protest. But he had other things on his mind so changed the subject as he held Mell tighter. "Mell I've waited for you for so long, and I need you so badly, please let me love you tonight. I don't think I can wait another moment."

Mell saw the love and passion in Jed's eyes as she moved back slightly and looked up at him. She whispered softly in joyful as she reached up then stroked his cheek in permission. "Yes, oh yes!"

Jed slowly lowered his mouth to hers nibbling and tasting her lips. He didn't want to scare her because he knew that she was innocent. He had known it that day at the creek as he kissed and touched her. Her untutored responses had been blazingly apparent and he wanted her first time to be one of joy, not pain. He planned to take it slowly even if it killed him. He continued suckling on her lips and tongue as his hands slowly drifted to the hem of her nightgown and lifted it upwards before removing it altogether. At this point he sat up straighter to get a better view then murmured caressingly. "Let me look at you! You're so beautiful!"

Then he reached for her hand and laid it in his lap so her palm was pressed against the bulge in his pants. "Here feel how much I need you."

Hesitantly Mell touched Jed's manhood through his trousers and felt it quiver in reaction. As Jed moaned in pleasure Mell jerked her hand back in fright thinking that she had hurt him.

Jed chuckled at her hesitant response then smiled encouragement. "It doesn't really hurt Mell it just feels good. I want you to explore and get to know my body so that you won't be frightened."   •

Jed opened the buttons on his trousers so that his manhood would be free and Mell could explore him more fully. Mell gingerly felt the bare flesh then became bolder as she applied more pressure and put her hand totally around it. She was surprised that it felt so soft and velvety, but at the same time strong and hard. This time she didn't flinch at the twitching reaction.

Jed moaned in pleasant torture as Mell continued her exploration. He began stroking and investigating her body as well. He paused at her breasts and worked his fingers around her nipples then bending his head he began to suckle first one then the other one gently.

Mell moaned and shuddered then arched her body upwards to give him better access. Jed took her hand away and got up. Mell moaned in denial thinking he was leaving her. Jed just smiled and removed his clothing.

Mell gazed at him in awe and a little fear. He was so huge! His chest was corded with muscles and dark curly hair. Then she caught sight of his arm muscles and she shuddered with a mixture of panic and pleasure, thinking that he could probably break her in two with one tight squeeze. She felt tiny and delicate for the first time in her life and she wasn't sure if she liked it. She lowered her gaze to his hands they were also large and roughly callused, but had been ever so gentle as he touched her breasts. Traveling still further downward her eyes came into contact with his slim belly with black hair tapering down to the juncture of his thighs. Then her eyes became huge at the sight of his fully erect manhood with the sac below.

Mell's cheeks flushed heatedly and she looked up at Jed for a few moments, not sure if she wanted to continue. Taking a deep breath of courage she lowered her eyes then finished her exploration. His thighs were well muscled and his long legs were covered with hair. He was so beautiful to look at, but also alarming. Mell had never seen a man unclothed before. She wrenched her eyes up to Jed's again. Her gaze a mixture of terror and desire!

Jed realized that this was going to be more difficult than he had thought. Obviously no one had ever explained to Mell what took place between a man and a woman after they were married. The first thing that he had to do was to take that look of distress out of her eyes. He wanted this marriage to be different then his first marriage. There was no way he was going to hide himself this time, do his duty then turn away unsatisfied.

He had tried to make his first marriage better but every time he attempted to get rid of the blanket, his wife held in a death grip, she would scream and scream until he would relent. After a year of this, lovemaking had become an unpleasant task, with a blanket between them that he just couldn't seem to get rid of.

He decided to try something different this time, in the hopes of making this marriage better. He sat on the side of the bed and felt Mell scoot to the other side quickly. He laid down facing her and pulled the covers over both of them, making sure that his lower body was hidden. He sighed in frustration as Mell curled up in a ball keeping away from him as far as possible. Jed reached out and took her hand then held on to it gently. "Mell do you trust me?"

He watched closely as she nodded her head that she did. "Okay, I'm going to make you a promise. We will plan to marry a week from today and we won't consummate our relationship until our wedding night."

Mell visibly relaxed as she listened. Jed smiled in triumph as the tension noticeably eased on her face. He continued even more confident now that his plan might work. "But we will sleep together every night. I'll touch you and taste you then you'll do the same to me. I'm doing this to allow you to become more comfortable with me. Hopefully by our wedding night you will be ready to become my wife in every way."

Mell was filled with relief and confusion. Her body wanted him so bad but he scared her too, which bewildered her even more. She had never been scared of anything in her life. But he made her feel small and delicate for the first time and definitely out of her element. She needed time to get used to Jed's naked body and also the idea of an intimate relationship without any undue stress. "Thank you Jed but are you sure you can wait that long? You look like you're ready to burst or something?"

Jed chuckled at her naïve question then shook his head in amazement. "Do I ever have a lot to teach you? Your first lesson of the night is that both of us will burst, as you put it, tonight and every night. There are so many ways of making love without consummating our relationship. Come here and cuddle for awhile then I'll show you."

Mell obediently scooted closer then rolled over onto her back, and waited tensely for whatever was going to happen next. Jed leaned over her with a pleasurable snort. "Okay I'll go first but everything I do to you, you will have to do to me is it a deal?"

Mell nodded hesitantly then waited anxiously. Jed very slowly bent his head making her wait in anticipation then touched his lips to hers almost in a butterfly kiss it was so light and delicate. Mell hardly felt it and her lips quivered in response wanting more. Then he flicked his tongue out and daintily ever so gently, traced first her top lip then moved down to her lower lip.

When she moaned and lifted her head for a deeper kiss Jed chuckled in satisfaction then backed away slightly. He kissed her cheek with the same velvety touch he had given her lips. He then moved to her ear next and flicked her ear lobe with a very, very light stroke of his tongue before trailing it delicately and slowly down her neck. Every few minutes he would lightly nibble as he went further. Still as gently as he possibly could so she would only feel it faintly.

Mell felt tremors running up and down her spine as he suckled then gently bit her neck unexpectedly. He then proceeded to soothe the bite by licking it before blowing on the wet spot. Mell shuddered in shocked pleasure as the cold air of his breath hit the warm saliva on her hot skin.

Mell shivered again in delight as Jed's hands lightly skimmed down to her breasts and traced her nipples teasingly, with his fingertips. He brought his right hand up slowly and put his first two fingers into her mouth to moisten them, before returning his fingers to her breast. Deep moans of ecstasy came from Mell's throat as her nipples hardened instantly into erect buds of desire. They were so hard now they almost hurt.

Jed lifted his head and watched the expression on her face expectantly as she responded to his caresses. He brought his head back down content that she was feeling everything he wanted her to feel. He flicked her hardened nipple with his tongue then blew on it lightly.

Mell gasp for air in amazement as goose bumps intensified all over her body and she arched up in excitement and torture. It was pure torment with all of her nerve ends screaming and she felt moisture seeping from her secret place. Mell clamped her legs together in alarm hoping to stop the excretion but it was no use.

Jed felt Mell's responsive shivers and he knew that it was time to advance further. He slowly slid his hand down her belly his touch was so light it tickled. Mell gasped in pleasure then giggled slightly in surprise, she just couldn't help herself. Jed felt her muscles bunch and tighten at his fingertips then he smiled knowingly to himself.

He reached his goal then played with Mell's triangle of curls teasingly, at the apex of her thighs. Enticing her hoping she would open for him but she had them tightly squeeze together. Jed brought his mouth back up to Mell's lips and whispered softly against them almost pleadingly. "Mell open your legs for me and let me touch you there."

Mell heard the entreaty in his voice and instantly responded to it as she did what she was told without knowing why. Jed parted her petals to reach her inner core before she could change her mind then he began lightly stroking her silky bud.

Mell felt pressure building up in her loins and she fought the feeling at first, unsure what was happening to her. As his strokes increased in pace the pressure became so strong she felt a sensation partly of pain and partly of intense pleasure. Mell continued to fight the phenomenon but couldn't hold out for long as she groaned in denial.

Jed could feel her fighting the passion and finally brought his mouth back to her lips then whispered desperately. "Mell, let yourself go, don't hold back sweetheart. I promise it will be the greatest pleasure you've ever felt."

Jed continued stroking her enticingly then pressed slightly harder against her bud. Mell groaned in surrender as she felt the pressure build up so high that she erupted against her will. Bright lights and stars seemed to explode in her brain. As she opened her mouth to scream in pleasure and shock Jed quickly fused their mouths in a searing kiss that effectively cut off her cries of gratification.

Jed pulled Mell up against him tenderly and just held her as she slowly came back down to earth. Mell curled herself around Jed contentedly hardly able to move or speak finally she couldn't help asking him drowsily. "Is it like that all the time or is it just the first time?"

Jed chuckled mysteriously. "It just gets better Mell you've only just tasted part of the pleasure."

Mell sat up instantly and she grimaced in simulated fear. "Damn! If it gets better than tonight I might not live through it!"

Jed's eyebrow rose in surprise as Mell used a curse word but he didn't comment on it. He chuckled again at her expression as he teased. "Oh it does get better and I promise you that you will live through it. Now it's time for you to explore me like I did you."

Mell turned slightly then eyed Jed shyly. "What do I do?"

Jed smiled innocently up at Mell with great anticipation at what was to come. "Whatever your heart desires, but to get you started you can kiss me first."

Mell leaned down so that she could reach Jed's mouth then tentatively touched her lips to his. Jed opened his mouth a little to entice her as she forced her tongue inside and began moving it around experimentally. She then poured little kisses all over his face around his eyes and down to his arrogant chin. Then she began nibbling on his neck before blowing on the wet spot she left. She smiled in delight as she tried his stunt and it worked on him too, as she heard him moan then felt him tremble at the contact of the cold air against his hot skin.

She shifted so that she was kneeling slightly so she could free up her hands. Mell brought both her hands up to his chest and ran her fingers through his springy black curls they tickled her palms and she giggled slightly at the erotic feeling. Her hands slipped lower and touched his nipples hoping it was as sensitive as hers.

Jed moaned in pleasure as Mell became a little bolder and brought her mouth down to his nipple then started sucking on one as he had done to her. He squirmed a little and moaned in pleasure as he felt Mell copy his method of wetting the nipple then blowing on it. He didn't know how much longer he could hold on as he felt the pressure building up in his loins. He gritted his teeth and fought the sensation trying to give her more time to explore.

As Mell's hands moved slowly downwards he gritted his teeth harder as she tentatively touched his engorged manhood and he prayed that he could hold on until she finished, but he doubted he could, it had been a long time since he had been with a woman.

Mell ran her curious fingers up and down his manhood then went a little further and picked up his sac. Mell felt two hard round pebbles inside and made a mental note to ask Jed later what they were for.

If Jed could have heard her thoughts at that moment he would have laughed at her naive curiosity. But instead Jed was emitting gasps of pleasure mixed with pain still fighting to hold on as Mell reached again for his manhood. She touched the head with the tip of her finger curiously. Mell frowned in surprise as she felt a sticky substance, and she jerked her hand back quickly thinking something was wrong.

Jed grabbed her hand tenderly then put it back demandingly as he managed to gasp out past his constricted throat. "It's all right Mell. It's the same thing that happened to you before you reach your peak. The moisture is natural."

Mell looked at Jed anxiously. "I don't know what to do!"

Jed beamed encouragement. "Just keep stroking and squeezing, every once in a while pump your hand up then down. It will make me explode like you did."

Mell did as she was told and held on tightly to him, using both hands, as she knelt above him since one hand didn't seem to be enough. Jed pushed upwards against her until he finally felt his control disappear and he found his own release.

Mell caught her breath startled as her hand became coated with a white gooey substance as Jed's manhood jerked in her hand. She felt his manhood slowly shrink and she dropped it in amazement as she watched it shrivel up to about a quarter of its previous size. At the perturbed look on Mell's face Jed couldn't help bursting into uncontrollable laughter.

Mell scowled down at Jed in mock anger at his laughter then planted her balled up fists against her waist waiting for him to finish wondering what she had done to cause him so much laughter. He was laughing so hard that tears were leaking from his eyes.

Her curiosity got the better of her and she ignored his laughter to demand indignantly. "Why did it shrink like that and what is that white stuff? I thought it would always stay the same size."

Jed got himself under control enough to answer her as he reached out and pulled her down beside him. They cuddle while he tried to answer her as best he could. "No the size you see now is its normal size. It only becomes enlarged when I get excited or first thing in the morning when I have to go to the bathroom. The white stuff is my seed it's what makes babies."

Mell nodded pensively in understanding. But then she thought of something else and the concern was obvious in her voice. "Oh that makes sense but doesn't it hurt when it grows?"

Jed smiled indulgently at Mell's curiosity and tried to answer as honestly as possible, it was a little difficult trying to explain how it felt to a woman. "No after it reaches full erection there's pressure but it doesn't really hurt."

Mell's expression became sceptical as she thought of Jed's earlier remark about lovemaking getting better she didn't know how that was possible. "Are you sure that lovemaking gets better?"

Jed smiled mischievously then nodded emphatically as Mell looked up at him curiously. "Yes it does, and tomorrow night I'll use my mouth down there instead of my hand."

Mell mulled this over for a few moments in surprise then shook her head in shocked denial. "I don't think I'll like that at all."

Jed chuckled in delight at Mell's horrified expression then he winked at her teasingly with the utmost confidence. "Trust me you'll like it. Now lie down and go to sleep we have a big day ahead of us tomorrow."

Mell yawned, too tired to argue with him one way or the other, then laid her head on his chest in contentment as she stretched out into a more comfortable position. "Oh I forgot to tell you tomorrow we have to stop at Brian's and let him know that Mary's husband is here. When we do, get ready for an explosion because he's going to be furious."

Jed nodded already guessing from what he had heard about Brian so far that he was going to be upset. He yawned worn-out then turned and snuffed out the light. Jed turned to Mell once more for a goodnight kiss before falling asleep contentedly.

For the first time in years Jed slept through the night with no nightmares about his wife and son's brutal murder. Now his dreams were filled with a life with Mell and the children to come.

CHAPTER EIGHT

Mell woke first she could feel Jed breathing against her neck and she felt a shiver of desire as well as embarrassment as she recalled their actions of the night before, was this how married people acted? She didn't know for sure but knew that she would have to ask her father. She remembered Jed saying that he was going to use his mouth, 'down there'. She felt her face burning at the thought. Maybe asking her father wasn't such a good idea after all.

Jed woke with a sensation of freedom, hope, and contentment. He felt Mell curled up against him and smiled. It was the first time in years that he felt anything but hate and despair when he first woke in the morning it felt good.

He hoped that Mell didn't have any feelings of regret about what had transpired the night before. He knew that she was awake so he brought his hand up to her breast and began fondling her nipple playfully. Mell rolled away quickly and took the top bed cover with her as she frantically searched the floor for the nightgown that Jed had stripped off her last night. She had forgotten to put it back on before she fell asleep.

Jed grimaced anxiously as he saw Mell's acute embarrassment. He knew that he would have to act quickly before she had time to think. He rolled after her then grabbed her around the waist and threw her back on the bed then jumped on top of her as he pinned her beneath him. He made sure though to keep his weight on her left side because of her sore right shoulder.

Mell was taken completely by surprise and lost her blanket as her arms flailed around shocked then found herself flat on her back pinned down by the grinning Jed.

Jed smiled teasingly down at her, once he figured she was subdued, then lowered his head and gave her a quick thorough kiss. He lifted up panting slightly as he too became excited and his manhood instantly hardened in desire. He watched in satisfaction as passion returned to Mell's expressive face. "A wife-to-be gives her husband-to-be at least a good morning kiss before she jumps out of bed Mell."

Mell looked up at Jed's smug face and smiled slyly up at him. Her grin turned devilish suddenly and that's all the warning he got. "Oh she does, does she?"

With no further forewarning Jed found himself laying flat on his back with Mell lying on top of him holding him down with a smirk of satisfaction. She then proceeded to kiss him thoroughly in return. When she ended the kiss she lifted up slightly as she gazed down at his flushed cheeks and passion filled eyes. She had to clear her voice slightly in order to tease him roguishly in return. "Good morning husband-to-be!"

Mell quickly jumped off Jed and scampered away but didn't escape quite unscathed as Jed leaped up and smacked her bare bottom for her impertinence, before she could get away fully. Mell squealed in surprise, but managed to get across the room relatively unhindered. She happened to glance out the window as she was passing by and she swore in surprise. "Oh darn it must be eight or nine o'clock. I've never slept this late!"

Mell hurriedly scurried into her clothing.

Jed winked over at Mell suggestively as he put on his pants and finished doing them up. "We could shock everyone even more by not going down until ten o'clock. I can think of a few things to keep us busy for another hour."

Before he got the last word out Jed felt something soft hit him in the face and he sputtered in indignation. Mell burst out laughing as her nightgown fell to the floor in a heap at his feet. She turned instantly and ran for the door as Jed started running after her. She quickly yanked it open then disappeared down the hallway.

Jed stopped quickly then turned back into the room as he realized he wasn't done dressing and grabbed his shirt before following her out. He smiled in relief and pleasure at Mell's teasing then he congratulated himself on getting Mell to forget her embarrassment as he followed her down more slowly.

* * *

Everyone was already seated around the kitchen table when Mell then finally Jed came into the room.

Alec glanced intently at his daughter in concern at her flushed face and wondered if she was getting a fever as she took the seat beside him. "How's your shoulder Mell?"

Mell shrugged in unconcern and tried to hide her flushed face. "Oh it's fine Dad, just a twinge now and again."

Gloria brought Jed and Mell a coffee then began serving breakfast since they had all decided to wait for the latecomers. At the end of the meal while everyone was relaxing with a cup of coffee it became apparent that Wade was uncomfortable and sort of squirming around in his seat.

Just as Alec was about to ask Wade if there was a problem he stood up and cleared his throat in embarrassment. "I have an announcement to make. Gloria and I have decided to get married as soon as possible."

With that statement finally out he sat down quickly took out his handkerchief and wiped his face in relief at getting that over with.

Mell jumped up in surprise and pleasure then rushed over and hugged Gloria ecstatically. "Great news Gloria I'm so happy for you. We can have the wedding a week from tomorrow. That will give you time to get used to Wade."

Gloria gave Mell a strange disgruntled look as Mell stepped back then waved in bewilderment. "What do you mean…. get used to him? I think I'm already used to him!"

Mell frowned in puzzlement as her face flushed this time in discomfiture. "Oh I thought all brides and grooms had to get used to each other before they wed."

Mell blushed even deeper as she saw that everyone was staring at her in amazement. She heard Jed start to chuckle behind her and she spun around then put her hands on her hips demandingly as she glared at him heatedly. "What do you find so funny?"

Jed held up his hands palms outward in a placating gesture and ignored her question but still he couldn't help another snicker from escaping as he turned to congratulate Wade.

Jed turned to Alec when he was finished with Wade and his expression became very serious. He had planned on asking Alec later for permission to marry his daughter but since they were already on the subject of marriage he decided to leap in with both feet, so to speak. "Alec while we're on the subject. Your daughter has consented to marry me and now I'd like to ask for your blessings."

Alec looked up at his daughters flushed face in surprise then looked over at Jed and beaming in satisfaction as he raised his hand to shake Jed's in glee and best wishes. "I couldn't be happier. Of course you have my approval looks like we'll be having a double wedding!"

Alec turned and looked over at Giant Bear intently as an idea surfaced and he smiled enticingly over at him. "Unless you and your wife would like to renew your vows then we could have a great celebration a triple wedding! What do you say?"

Giant Bear's stoic expression softened somewhat as he thought of his wife then he nodded. "I think my Golden Dove would like to get married in the white man's way then no one can ever take her away from me again."

Gloria started clearing off the table then grinned as she got an idea and looked over at Alec for consent. "How about an engagement supper tonight so that we can all celebrate?"

Everyone nodded in excitement and Gloria left the room, humming happily to herself, as she planned what she could make for such a happy occasion.

Wade jumped up and followed his fiancé into the back entryway to say good-bye to her privately. Gloria turned when he entered then rushed over to him for a passionate kiss, the supper forgotten for the moment.

Wade lifted his head after several minutes of passion and looked down at her flushed cheeks in pleasure then he chuckled at Gloria's eager expression and kissed her again for good measure. He stepped back reluctantly then tweaked her nose playfully. "I'll see you in a few hours, be good while I'm gone!"

Gloria's expression turned sober and her expressive face showed her fear for a moment. "You be careful out there I thought I lost you once and I don't want to ever have that feeling again."

Wade nodded in sorrow as he thought about the tragedy they had all endured the last couple of weeks. "I'll be careful. I promise."

Wade turned away from Gloria and slipped out the side door before walking around the house.

Tommy was already trotting out of the barn with his horse and when Wade got close to him, Tommy handed him his reins. Wade grinned down at Tommy in thanks although he didn't have to look down far already the young Tommy was close to his own height. "Well thank you Tommy do you have Mell and Jed's horses ready as well?"

Tommy's face lit up with a huge smile as he beamed up at Wade proudly. "Almost, Giant Bear came out a few minutes ago and is helping me. I was watching at the barn door and saw you coming. When I see Aunt Mell and Uncle Jed coming all I have to do is grab the reins and they're on their way."

Wade chuckled at the boy's enthusiasm then swung up onto his horse. He looked down at Tommy curiously. "You're calling Jed, 'Uncle' already?"

Tommy smiled shyly up at Wade then nodded matter of factually. "Of course I knew right from the start that Aunt Mell would marry Jed so when Giant Bear told me a few moments ago, I wasn't surprised at all!"

Wade looked down at Tommy in dumbfounded surprise then shook his head in wonder. Sometimes it really surprised him how perceptive Tommy was. That uncle of his was sure stupid to give up such a fine boy like Tommy, just because he was part Indian.

Tommy turned after waving good-bye then raced back to the barn to finish getting ready for Mell and Jed's arrival.

Wade kicked his horse into a trot for a few minutes to warm him up then urged him into a flat out run and headed straight for the creek where Mary always went. It took him several hours to get there and he slowed his horse in appreciation for the speed then patted his neck in gratitude.

"Sorry about that old boy but we can slow down now we made good time."

His horse whiffed at him as he blew hard at the demanding ride as if he appreciated the pat of gratitude and understood what his master was saying. Wade chuckled at his horse's attentiveness.

Wade got to the creek just as Mary was mounting her horse to leave and he sighed thankful that he hadn't missed her.

Mary tensed in surprise and suspicion when she heard a horse coming. She was ready to kick her own horse into a run if she had too. She didn't relax again until she recognized Wade. She waited until he was beside her then beamed warmly up at him and nodded pleasantly in greeting. "Good morning Wade what are you doing here at this time of the day?"

Wade grinned cordially then his expression sobered as he told her about the tragedy at the ranch. Mary was shuddering in horror by the time Wade finished and she shook her head in disbelief. "I can hardly believe that Greg could do such a terrible thing, are you sure my son is unhurt?"

Wade nodded sadly none of them had suspected that Greg was capable of such treachery. He smiled reassuringly then reached over and patted Mary's hand soothingly, that was sitting on the pummel of her saddle. "Your son isn't hurt physically but Mell figured you'd better come to the ranch anyway. Who knows how this could affect him mentally, we figured you should come and stay for a couple of days, just to make sure he's okay. Plus the Ladies will probably need some help until more hands can be found."

Mary nodded instantly concerned for her son and turned her horse towards Mell's place, not even questioning why she was needed, when Mell being a sheriff would have a better understanding of how to deal with such a tragedy.

* * *

Mell and Jed walked out of the house and headed for the barn. They were about half way there when Tommy came trotting out with both their horses and the customary packhorse, even though they wouldn't need him today. Still it was better to be safe than sorry.

Mell smiled knowingly at Jed and he nodded pleased as well that Tommy was thinking ahead of them then they both stopped to wait for

Tommy to get to them. Mell smiled in approval and thanks down at Tommy then took her reins from him. "Why, thank you Tommy! Did you saddle the horses by yourself?"

Tommy shook his head negatively then beamed up at Mell in pleasure. "No, Giant Bear helped me out then I waited until I saw you coming."

Jed grinned in appreciation as well and took the reins from Tommy. "Thank you and tell Giant Bear we said thank you also."

Tommy nodded that he would tell Giant Bear thanks from Jed. He was ecstatic at their appreciation wanting to be as useful as he possible could so that his aunt Mell wouldn't send him away.

Mell squatted down and her tone became deadly serious, as she looked Tommy straight in the eye, so her words would carry their serious nature to the young Tommy. "I have a big favour I want to ask you. This is very important and you won't understand right now, but I promise to explain it to you later."

Tommy nodded soberly and attentively, well aware that when his aunt talked to him like this it meant change of some kind in his life. "Aunt Mell, I love you and you can ask me anything. And you don't need to explain it to me, if you don't want to I'll still do whatever you want me to without asking why."

Mell looked at Tommy sadly for a moment thinking that soon she would lose him then gathered him into her arms impulsively to hide her tears as she whispered brokenly. "I love you too Tommy and I promise I'd never ask you to do anything that would hurt you, or anyone else."

Tommy indicated agreement trustingly then smiled shyly at Mell when she finally let him go. "I know Aunt Mell I trust you with all my heart."

Mell smiled back in pride at the trust this young boy gave her. She cleared her throat noisily so she could speak past the lump of emotion choking her up slightly. "Wade is going to bring your mother here today and I don't want her to go to the barn. So you will have to come and get her horse before she goes there. I also don't want you to talk about Giant Bear or Jed in front of her. Don't even mention their names when she's around. I want to tell her myself when I get back what happened and about my upcoming marriage okay. Can you remember this it's very important to me?"

Tommy nodded happily at such an easy request then beamed in delight at having a secret that his mother wasn't to know yet. He looked at Mell seriously then made a solemn vow as he put his finger over his heart and made the sign of the cross over it. "That's easy I promise not to say anything to her. Cross my heart."

Mell smiled in relief and gave him another big hug in praise. Then she pushed him away slightly so she could tell him her last request, but held onto his shoulders. "Thank you Tommy. I have one more favour to ask. I need the barn and bunkhouse cleaned out can you ask Giant Bear to do this for me?"

Tommy nodded then stood back as Mell got up off her knees. He watched his aunt mount her horses before voicing his own request as he looked up at her earnestly. "Aunt Mell, do you mind if I help Giant Bear clean up in the barn and bunkhouse."

Mell grinned down at Tommy then nodded her consent. "Sure you can help him. There are several burlap sacks in the tack room of the barn so ask Giant Bear to put all the articles of the ranch hands in them, so I can send it to their families later."

Tommy nodded without further comment then turned and ran back to the barn to give Giant Bear all the messages before he forgot any.

Mell and Jed rode in silence for a few moments then Jed turned to Mell and smiled in admiration as he thought of Tommy. "That boy loves you very much I was very impressed. You and Mary did a good job raising him."

Mell sighed sadly. "I hadn't realized how much Tommy had grown up, until today, with no other children around I suppose he couldn't help but grow up faster. I'll be sorry to lose him when he goes to Montana with Mary and Giant Bear. He's like my own son and I had always pictured him staying with me then taking over my ranch if I never have any children. You do realize I'm almost thirty years old I might be too old to have children."

Jed laughed in delight then shook his head negatively in reassurance. "Believe me you're not too old. My mother was pregnant with me when she was about thirty and I wasn't her last child."

Mell smiled in relief then motioned anxiously. "Good I was worried about that I was hoping to have at least two children."

Jed chuckled teasingly then his voice became serious and he waved for emphases. "As many as you'd like. I miss my son very much and I'm hoping to have at least one boy and one girl. But I want you to know that if it never happens, that's okay too, as long as we're together that's all I need to make me happy."

After a few minutes of silence Jed looked back at Mell and changed the subject. "What are we going to do first when we hit town?"

Mell sighed slightly in aggravation as she shook off her happy thoughts of a life with Jed and possibly children. She turned to him and the business at hand. "Well I want you to go to Chelsie's Saloon and Pam's Place, and let everybody know where looking to recruit five men to work and live at the ranch. When you pick the five you want make sure you take them aside and let them know what happened there. That way if any of them decide they don't want to take the job because it's too dangerous to work for me, you will know right away and can pick someone else in his place. I'll go to the families of all the ranch hands that live around here, and let them know what happened then give them the money I owed the men. Then I'll meet you in front of the Mayor's office and we'll go in together."

Jed nodded thoughtfully then looked over at Mell. "It's a good plan but I'd like to make a suggestion."

Mell laughed at Jed teasingly as she gestured jokingly at him. "Disagreeing with me already are you."

Jed smirked good-humouredly then shrugged negatively. "No but since neither of us knows how long the other person is going to be. Why don't we meet at the hotel instead for lunch I'll bring the men I pick with me, and you can meet them there. That way if you don't like some of my choices I can look for others."

Mell nodded then smiled over at Jed in approval. "Meeting at the hotel is a good idea, as for meeting the men you pick, I trust you."

Jed beamed in pleasure at her trust in him then waved placatingly. "I'm glad you trust me but I wasn't thinking in terms of trust. I was thinking more along the lines of you know these people and I don't. Besides we're all going to have to get along and just because I like a person doesn't mean you will."

Mell sighed pensively as she inclined her head slightly. "That's true enough okay we'll do it your way."

Jed laughed in devilish delight then grabbed his chest as if in total shock. "Oh my first victory I should probably mark this occasion down. I have a feeling you won't be this easy to convince by all my suggestions."

Mell smirked in amusement at Jed's antics and leaned over her horse for a quick kiss. Jed nudged his horse over and tried to meet her half way, but Mell almost fell out of her saddle, so she quickly straightened with a fiery blush at her boldness.

Jed laughed uproarsly at Mell's surprised expression and inflamed face. When he got himself under control he tried for a more serious appearance. But wrecked it by chuckling again, he got himself under control and sighed all business once more. "Now these men you want me to hire. Do you want all single men or family men?"

Mell sighed in disappointment at having the moment spoiled by business. This was only the second time she heard his unrestrained laughter and she enjoyed hearing it. She only hoped that he would do it more often. She shrugged thoughtfully and sighed sadly as she thought of what had happened to her ranch hands again. "I think single men would be better especially with what happened."

Jed frowned wistfully as he thought of his son. "But I would like to hire at least one family if you don't mind. It wouldn't take long to build them a cabin that way when you and Gloria are ready to have children there will be another woman around to help out."

Mell exhaled noisily aware suddenly of Jed's sadness then tried to lighten the mood. "Good idea I never even thought of that, come to think of it Wade and Gloria will probably want their own cabin now as well."

Jed shook of his thoughts then winked over at Mell. "I'm sure they would love to have their own private place. I don't think they want to stay in the bunkhouse with all the men."

Mell nodded contemplatively. "We have plenty of lumber on hand, it will deplete our reserves but once we have more men to help at the saw mill we can cut more this fall."

Jed sighed irritably as they rode into town he wanted to continue the conversation, he shrugged, oh well there was always later. He waved good-bye to Mell as he turned towards Chelsie's Saloon without further comment. While Mell headed for her office first to make out a report.

Jed dismounted at the hitching rail of the saloon and tied up his horse loosely. He checked to make sure his badge was in plain sight before entering so that everyone would know who he was.

Jed sauntered into Chelsie's and looked around curiously before he walked up to the bar. He smiled in greeting at the slightly hefty five foot one red headed woman standing behind the bar. "You must be Chelsie my name is Jed Brown and I'm the new Deputy in town."

Chelsie stuck out her rough calloused hand in greeting then smiled in pleasure, as she eyed the rugged muscular man standing in front of her. Her smile became slightly enticing as her Irish drawl thickened slightly in invitation. Normally she didn't allow for such going ons but once in awhile she made an exception. "Hi I heard Mell had hired a new Deputy."

Jed shook her hand firmly and ignored Chelsie's obvious enticement as he leaned over the counter to whisper in conspiracy, so there would be no more advancement's. "I'm also her fiancé do you know where I might pick up a nice wedding ring?"

Jed's wife's ring was gone when he had found them, which was unfortunate because it had been his grandmother's ring as well, but he preferred to give Mell her own ring anyway.

Chelsie's expression instantly lost the flirtiest look in surprise as she eyed the new deputy in disappointment. Until as she thought about what he had said then her smile lit up her whole face in congratulations as she slapped the bar and chortled loudly in delight. "Drinks are on the house! Mell is getting hitched."

Everyone there cheered at the news of free drinks then came over to Jed one by one and shook his hand, before introducing themselves as they offered best wishes.

Chelsie beckoned one of her girls over to tend bar then she turned and waved for Jed to follow her. "Come with me I might have what you're looking for."

Jed nodded perplexed but obediently followed the slightly heavyset but beautiful red head. He would guess she was Irish by her red hair and thick bur when she was excited. She seemed open and friendly but he could well imagine the temper this one could display. She kind of reminded him of his dead wife, a little heftier and more outgoing then his wife had been though.

He followed Chelsie to her office in the back and he watched her curiously as she open a safe hidden behind a cabinet then brought out a large jewelled box.

She brought it over proudly and set it on her desk carefully as she looked up at him. "Not too many people buy jewellery from me yet but I have quite a collection. I make my own of course. I get my gold mostly from gold miners wanting a few drinks. I also hunt the creek bed just outside of town for special rocks, or crystals if I can find them they work the best. My father was a goldsmith in Ireland and even made jewellery for the Lord's and Lady's when the King would come visit his estates. My father never had a boy so he passed it on to me, but then he remarried when my mother died, and I had to leave so I came to the new world hoping things would be different out here for a woman. Most of the stuff I have is just plain gold bands that I sell from one to ten dollars, but I do have a few unusual ones that I only show to special customers."

She opened the box lovingly and showed Jed shyly.

Jed caught his breath in wonder and surprise as he stared at the beautiful jewellery inside then he looked at Chelsie in speculation. "Why do you own a Saloon when you do such exquisite work with gold?"

Chelsie smiled in pleasure and pride at the praise then shrugged sadly. "The Saloon is just a side line there's not enough business in this small town for an actual goldsmith shop yet, so I do business here. I'm hoping to open a shop one day but until then the Saloon puts food on the table. Most off the work I do now are commissions. Actually if you're going out to Mell's place will you take a package to Alec for me?"

Jed nodded then watched her walk back to the safe to get Alec's parcel. She came back then handed it to him and he put it in his shirt pocket under his vest so he wouldn't lose it. He went back to studying the rings, necklaces, pocket watches, and other jewellery displayed inside the box. He picked up a ring that just seemed to jump out at him suddenly.

Chelsie chuckled in delight and admiration when she saw which one Jed was holding then nodded. "That one would be perfect for Mell luckily I had just finished it yesterday. Actually the inspiration for that ring came from Alec's commission. It would go perfectly with the bracelet and earrings I made for Mell at Alec's request. Alec had the stones shipped to me so I could make them for him and there was a little sliver of the gem left so I made that ring. If you hadn't picked it out yourself I would have showed it to you and recommended it."

Jed smiled up in thanks for the advice then looked back down and pushed a few rings around but didn't find what he was looking for. He looked back up at Chelsie inquiringly. "Is there another ring that goes with it?"

Chelsie shook her head slightly in disappointment she hadn't gotten around to one yet. "No, I haven't had time to make one but that's okay because you wouldn't want to spoil the looks of the ring anyway. I think the one is sufficient for most women especially Mell she's not into fancy jewellery."

Jed nodded well aware that his future wife was plain and simple not prone to elaborate things. He agreed with Chelsie's character description of his fiancée. "Okay I can run across to the bank while you wrap it up for me. Oh I suppose I should ask you what you want for the ring."

Chelsie laughed in delight at his flustered question. "Well I want a hundred dollars for the ring because of the special stone it contains."

Jed nodded then smiled slightly in embarrassment as Chelsie laughed at him. His grin widened as he thought of a perfect wedding gift for Giant Bear and Mary. "Fair enough but before I go to the bank I need two more rings just plain wedding bands though one for a man and one for a woman. My friends are getting married with us and it would be a perfect gift for them. Then I have business to discuss with the men in your Saloon actually maybe you can help me. I need to hire five men for the ranch preferably single, as well as one family to come out and live there too."

Chelsie frowned in concern then went back to her safe and brought out a plain box. She set it on her desk then looked down as she rummaged inside for two plain matching bands for his friends. "What happened to the men that are already out there have they been fired for some reason?"

Jed sadly shook his head as Chelsie looked up and held out two rings for his inspection. Jed took the bands in approval then he told her everything that had happened the last two weeks.

When he finished Chelsie sighed sadly and wiped tears away she had known them all of course and had even been bed partners with one of them. She shuddered in sympathy as she thought of Mell. "Oh how terrible, Mell must be devastated!"

Jed nodded then frowned in worry as he wondered how Mell was holding up right now. "Yes she is and while I'm recruiting more men she went to tell the families what happened."

Chelsie sighed sadly as she wiped more tears away and eyed his worried frown then fidgeted with her box in concern. "That will be hard on her, now I see why you want single men, but why do you want one family out there if you don't mind my asking?"

Jed expression lightened considerably and he beamed hopefully. "Well with both of us getting married and Gloria and Wade will also be getting married we're hoping to have children running around soon so the women will need extra help around the house."

Chelsie grinned mischievously as she asked slyly. "Will Mell be quitting as the Sheriff now, or are you man enough to handle having a Sheriff for a wife?"

Jed laughed in delight at Chelsie as she challenged his manhood then shrugged dismissively as he became serious and shook his head resignedly. "Do you really think I could get away with telling Mell she has to quit her job? Not on your life would she even consider marrying me, if I had even asked, she loves her job too much. No she will remain the Sheriff until we decide to have children then I'll take over her duties until she is ready to come back."

Chelsie sighed in relief at his wise decision. "Good, come on and I'll help you pick out the men you need. I also have the perfect family that would love to go work for Mell."

Jed pocketed the three rings and followed Chelsie out of her office, after she put her box back in the safe, as they discussed the price of the other two rings Jed wanted.

* * *

Mell walked out of the bank with eight bank notes made out to each family of the deceased. The bank manager almost had a heart attack when she had asked for each one to be made out for one thousand dollars.

Mell frowned thoughtfully then looked up and down the main street undecided who to see first but finally decided to go to Cookie's sisters. She walked to the hitching rail and mounted her horse then turned south before riding out of town. She finally turned into a farmyard and dismounted then dropped the reins on the ground so that her horse could wander slightly to eat but would stay close by if she needed him.

She went to the porch slowly dragging her feet slightly not looking forward to this at all. She walked up the steps then approached the door and couldn't put it off any longer as she finally raised her hand then knocked on it hesitantly.

A petite brunette opened the door instantly having seen Mell coming and she smiled in pleasure at the unexpected visit. "Well hi Mell how're you doing. Come in and I'll make us some tea."

Mell went in slowly then removed her hat respectfully as she walked over to the kitchen table and sat watching Ruby fuss over arranging pieces of cake on a plate. It gave Mell the time she needed to muster up the courage to tell her friend that her brother was dead, and it was her fault.

Mell sighed sadly as she watched the tiny mousy brown haired woman thoughtfully. Ruby was slimmer then her brother and shorter as well at four foot seven inches tall but she did have the same hazel eyes. Mell waited until tea and cakes were served and Ruby sat down across from her before Mell looked at Ruby straight in the eyes searchingly.

Ruby stared at Mell in concern as she took notice of Mell's upset expression then eyed Mell's sheriff's badge and she frowned knowingly as she sat forward anxiously. "This isn't a social call is it?"

Mell shook her head sadly and reached out for Ruby's hand in support. "No, I'm sorry but Cookie was gunned down over two weeks ago at the ranch as well as all the other men except Wade and my father."

Mell told the whole story first then held Ruby consolingly while she cried on Mell's shoulder. Ruby got herself under control and sat back as she wiped her tear stained face on her apron then looked up at Mell in gratitude. "Thank you Mell for coming to tell me personally and I also want to thank you for burying him out at the ranch. Cookie loved you and that ranch very much."

Mell sighed in relief she had been slightly worried about that wondering if she had done the right thing in burying her men out at her place, instead of in town at the church grave yard. She frowned sadly before reaching out once more and patting Ruby's hand in sympathy. "It was the least I could do. I have something for you as well."

Mell took out the bank note with Ruby's name on it then passed it across the table to her. Ruby stared at it then gasped as she looked up in shocked surprise at Mell but didn't touch the banknote. She had never seen that kind of money before. "Mell you don't have to do this Cookie knew when he decided to work for you that it was dangerous. We talked about it many times he was always aware that because you were the Sheriff that you would have enemies that might come after you at any time."

Mell took Ruby's hand again then squeezed it gently in reassurance and support. "I know I don't need to do this but all the men earned this money and more just for sticking with me all these years. Even though I couldn't pay them much at the beginning I now have more than enough money to look after their families now that they cannot. I have a suggestion for you though if you have no objections. As you can see the bank note is made out to you specifically. This is your inheritance from your brother, put some money in the bank for each of your children, take the rest and spend it on yourself. I'll also send you all his belongings that are still at the ranch once we have them all sorted out okay."

Ruby stood up slightly then reached across the table and hugged Mell in gratitude. "Thank you so very much for your thoughtfulness and I'll take your good advice."

Mell returned the hug enthusiastically and she smiled in pleasure as she sat back. She waited for Ruby to sit back down before continuing. "Good, now to change the subject, I do have another reason for being here. I would like to invite you out to the ranch next week for my wedding. I'll bring you a proper invitation later. It'll also be a good opportunity for you to see where we buried your brother."

Ruby's eyes enlarged in shocked surprise at the news of Mell's marriage. She grinned in delight and congratulations at this turn of events, before smiling in pure joy knowingly. "I'm so happy for you let me guess you're marrying that new Deputy you hired not too long ago."

It was Mell's turn to be flabbergasted and taken aback then her eyebrows rose in baffled inquiry. "How do you know I hired a new Deputy?"

Ruby laughed teasingly not sure if she should tell her or not then she gave in not able to keep a secret for long and shrugged good naturedly. "Greg went to Chelsie's the day you brought the new Deputy to town and was complaining to everybody who would listen about him. My James happened to be at Chelsie's at the time and he rushed home to tell me."

Mell smiled in humour at the picture of the black haired fat James rushing home, because James never rushed, ever. He was too fat to hurry anywhere, but she nodded in understanding before standing up to leave. "You're right it is my new Deputy that I'm marrying. I also want to tell you before I go that you can come out to the ranch anytime you like to visit Cookie's grave."

Ruby nodded in thanks as she got up and gave Mell a farewell hug before she left.

Mell went out the door and whistled for her horse he had wandered a little too far. She jumped of the porch and mounted when he obediently came to her then she turned back to town and headed for Dan's mother's next.

CHAPTER NINE

Mell rode up to the hotel and climbed wearily down from her horse then tethered him loosely to the hitching post. She was totally exhausted mentally and physically and the strain showed plainly on her expressive face. She climbed the stairs and entered the main lobby slowly.

The clerk looked up instantly then smiled in pleasure at the sight of her as he waved down the hallway towards his private rooms. "Afternoon Sheriff your new Deputy took a private dining room. If you will follow me I'll take you to him."

Mell nodded but didn't comment as she followed the tall very skinny clerk slowly. Mell had always joked that the man was so thin and sombre looking most of the time that he should have been an undertaker. He had a long thin face with a beak like nose that he liked to look down when talking to someone. He had black hair and eyes, which just added to the effect of an undertaker. The clerk ushered her into a room silently then bowed his way out.

Mell and Jed waited until he was gone and closed the door firmly, before Jed walked over then gathered her into his arms in sympathy. Jed released her then led her to the table and sat her down in a chair. He picked up a shot glass he had waiting and handed her a generous shot of whiskey. He watched her swallow it in one gulp and he chuckled as she sat there shuddering for a few minutes in reaction then took a deep breath before relaxing back in her chair in gratitude.

Jed knelt beside her then took her hands in support and frowned in concern. "Are you okay now?"

Mell nodded in thanks then beamed down at him as she squeezed his hands in assurance. "I'm fine when did you get here?"

Jed got up satisfied that she was all right then sat across the table from her before answering as he waved towards the saloon. "Chelsie suggested I take a private dining room just in case you needed some time alone."

There was a discreet knock on the door suddenly. Jed frowned in irritation at the interruption then he sighed resignedly as he looked towards the door and called out loudly. "Come in."

A pretty slightly plump blonde waitress came in with a tray and served them lunch then poured coffee before leaving without saying a word, or even looking directly at them. She had been told to be as discreet as possible and she took her job very seriously.

Jed continued their discussion that, the waitress interrupted, as soon as she left. "I got here about an hour ago Chelsie was a big help I would probably still be looking if it weren't for her. The five men I hired will be here in less than an hour to introduce themselves I also hired Brad and Jane Anderson to move out to the ranch."

Mell smiled in pleasure as she thought of her friend Jane. "Good you did a great job and you're right, Brad and Jane will be perfect."

Mell and Jed finished the rest of their meal in silence both thinking their own thoughts. They pushed their plates away and sat back to enjoy their coffee in contentment.

Mell stood up to leave getting impatient now to get the rest of the day over with. "Why don't we go talk to the Mayor now and I'll leave a message with the clerk for the new hands to head out to the ranch instead. I can meet the men out there later. If we don't leave soon the trip to Brian's will take forever and we probably wouldn't get back to the ranch until well after midnight then we would miss our engagement supper."

Jed nodded then smirked saucily at her as he bowed obediently. "As you wish, I serve and obey!"

Mell laughed in delight at his impertinent answer then slapped him playfully for his insolence before leaving the room. They walked into the lobby where the clerk was waiting for them expectantly. Mell stopped briefly and talked to him, he was only too happy to give her new hands the message.

They walked out of the hotel then across to her office so she could pick up the report she had filled in earlier for the mayor then they headed back across before turning right and walked a block to the town hall then entered the building together.

Mell went up to the desk to talk to the secretary first and Jed followed behind her unsure where to go. Mell smiled cheekily at the steel grey haired formidable secretary that had been with Mayor Elton since he had first taken office. Lucy was almost as tall as Mell at five foot six and a half feet, but she was brawnier not fat at all just very husky and strong from helping her father on the farm. If Lucy didn't want to let you into the mayor's office she would bar you're way physically and once planted, it was impossible to move her. "Hi Lucy is the Mayor in today? I need to speak to him it's very important."

Lucy looked up then nodded and smiled at Mell as she motioned towards the mayor's office invitingly. "As a matter of fact he is and you just caught him before he left for lunch so you can go right in Sheriff."

Mell grinned down at Lucy teasingly then gestured impatiently before planting her fists on her hips in demand. "How many times do I have to tell you to call me Mell?"

Lucy shrugged dismissively but smiled in pleasure as she teased back playfully. "Sorry Sheriff when you're on duty and I'm on duty formalities must be observed."

Mell threw up her hands dramatically in simulated anger. "I give up you'll never change Lucy."

Lucy just beamed in innocent gratification then waved them towards the mayor's office.

Jed chuckled in delight at Mell's theatrics as he looked over at her curiously then lowered his voice so the secretary wouldn't hear him. "Does it bother you that much?"

Mell shook her head negatively then smirked in amusement as she pointed behind her at Lucy. "No but it's become a routine with her and only once did I forget to ask her to call me Mell then she wouldn't speak to me for two days afterwards."

Jed snorted in understanding but didn't comment further.

Mell knocked slightly then pushed open the door to the mayor's office and entered. She walked up to his desk then waited patiently for the mayor to look up.

Mayor Elton lifted his head in annoyance at the interruption, until he saw who it was then a big smile lit up his round robust face in surprised pleasure and greeting. "Well hi Mell I haven't seen you in over two weeks where have you been, it's not like you to stay away for so long unless you're on the trail?"

Mell nodded down in greeting then her expression sobered instantly. She put her report down on the desk in front of the mayor before gesturing seriously to emphasize how important the report was. "Well I have two good things to tell you, one very bad thing to tell you, and an invitation as well."

Mayor Elton laughed knowingly then propped his elbows on the desk and put his chin in his hand in attentiveness. "Well what else is new it's always a mixture of good news, and bad news with you. So you can definitely start with the good first."

Mell nodded gravely and beckoned Jed forward then pointed to him in introduction. "Mayor Elton I would like you to meet Jed Brown my new Deputy."

The mayor sat up straight all business now. He stood up and shook hands firmly when Jed leaned across the desk and offered his hand. The two men sized each other up silently neither letting go until they were satisfied with what they saw.

Jed stared assessingly at the slightly rotund mayor with his rosy plump cheeks and his almost complete baldhead. He saw mirth, honesty, and compassion in his expressive hazelnut brown eyes. When he had stood up Jed had noticed that the mayor was only half an inch shorter then Mell. Jed also noticed that the mayor's handshake was firm but not crushingly so for such a big man.

After staring intently at each other for a few minutes both men smiled an approving smile and just like that they were friends. As Jed let go of the mayor's hand he stepped back out of Mell's way.

Mell shook her head in dumbfounded amazement at the both of them then continued without commenting on their quick friendship. "I deputized Jed in the field so you'll have to deputize him properly since he will now be my full time Deputy. I also deputized a Cheyenne Chief named Giant Bear."

The mayor nodded slightly in confusion as he wondered what had happened to Greg, but he took out his bible without hesitation knowing Mell would explain after he was done and within minutes Jed was an official deputy.

Mell frowned thoughtfully to herself as she listened to the mayor's words. Yup she had known she hadn't gotten the deputies oath right, oh well it wouldn't hurt either men to think they were responsible for the innocent as long as they lived, instead of as long as they wore a badge.

The mayor rummaged in his desk and pulled out a deputy's contract that Jed needed to fill out and sign. He handed it to him as he looked up at Jed and explained what the contract was for. "This is just a formality so that if anything happens to you we can get a hold of your family, if you have any. Mell and I decided we needed this kind of information when a Deputy of hers died in the line of duty and we couldn't find out where he was from or who to contact. So we made that up to help us in case of an emergency."

Jed nodded and took the paper over to a chair then sat down to read the contract before filling in the document.

Mayor Elton motioned inquisitively at Mell. "Do you want to take a Deputy's contract to your Chief or do you just want me to add his name to our list of part time Deputy's?"

Mell shook her head negatively. "Just add him to the list."

Mell smiled down smugly at the mayor as he sat back down then motioned casually. "I'll need you out at the ranch in a week as well to be a witness to my marriage."

Mayor Elton stared up in stunned disbelief for a moment, like Mell's father the mayor had always despaired of Mell ever finding a husband. He whooped in joy as he jumped back up before leaning across his desk hugging Mell ecstatically. "When did this happen and who are you marrying?"

Mell pointed behind her at Jed when the mayor released her and could see her gesture. "There's your culprit right there and I was officially asked last night. This also brings me to the invitation we are having an engagement party tonight. Oh I guess I should tell you that Gloria and Wade are also getting married as well as Mary and her Cheyenne husband who has come to take her and Tommy home with him. So they are going to renew their vows as well. You and your wife will be the only guests tonight then in a week's time we'll have the wedding."

The mayor dropped into his chair in incredulity at all the marriages happening at once. He held up his hands in confusion to stop Mell's excited explanation that wasn't making any sense to him anyway. "I think you better start from the beginning and take it very slowly."

Mell nodded then sat down as she told the whole story again.

* * *

It was less than an hour by the time Mell and Jed walked out of the mayor's office. Mell turned to Jed with a weary sigh. "Well I'm glad that's over with we finished everything now except for seeing Brian. All our new hands should be on their way to the ranch by now and all of the relatives of the dead have been told except for one. I have to send a letter by stagecoach for that one. Let's hurry over to Brian's and get this over with."

Jed nodded thoughtfully as they strolled back to the hotel for their horses. He couldn't help thinking as he mounted and they rode out of town that the next few hours could be the most difficult ones of the day.

Brian wasn't going to be very happy with all the things they had to say to him. Number one they had to tell him about his friend Greg's death, and Greg's betrayal of Mell. They were also going to have to tell him that his sister's husband wasn't dead. Like Brian believed all these years, and that Giant Bear was taking Mary and their son Tommy away with him. He also had to be told that Mell was going to marry Jed next week.

Jed wasn't sure which piece of news Brian was going to take the hardest. Jed had a feeling that losing Mell would hit Brian harder than the loss of his sister or even the loss of his friend.

* * *

It was a long ride from town going more northeast where as Mell's place was straight north from town. It took them three hours of hard riding to get there but there weren't a lot of trees so it was easy going, more open which made it good land for cattle as well. They rode mostly in silence neither of them looking forward to what was to come.

At Brian's ranch, they both dismounted in front of the hitching rail then draped the reins of their horses so they were hanging over the railing but not looped just in case they needed to leave in a hurry.

Jed looked around curiously. The ranch house was the only other two-story house out here besides Mell's. It was a plain house with no paint and unkempt looking. There were old harnesses, broken wagon wheels, and other junk lying around. Jed wasn't impressed even a little, especially after being at Mell's place hers was so neat compared to this.

They walked up the stairs then across the veranda slowly both still dreading the confrontation to come. Mell lifted her hand to knock, but jumped back instead when the door swung open violently, and she almost fell inside.

Brian sneered in anger as he stared at the two trespassers belligerently. "What do you want?"

Both Mell and Jed could hear the fury plain in his voice but it was Jed who smelt the liquor first before Mell and he took a small protective step towards her, he just couldn't help it. Jed eyed Brian assessing him intently and he didn't like what he saw. He was shorter then Mell by a good three inches, which would make him about five foot eight. Brian wasn't fat but fairly husky with a quick temper by the look of him. He had mousy brown hair with a thick handlebar moustache that he obviously was very proud off and squinty blue eyes. He looked older then Jed by about ten years which would make him around fifty. He had grey at his temples with a receding hairline. He'd probably be bald in another five years or so. He wasn't handsome but he wasn't too ugly either, sort of in-between the two, which made him unremarkable.

Mell smiled coaxingly at Brian and motioned calmly. "Hi Brian, can we come in? I'd like to talk to you for a few moments if you don't mind."

Brian moved back obediently and moderated his tone a little but both visitors could still hear the anger in his voice. "Come in then if you must!"

Brian led the way into the den then turned and looked at his visitors in inquiry but still with that hostile chill in his voice. "Do either of you want a drink brandy or something?"

Both Mell and Jed shook their heads negatively.

Mell scowled in disapproval at Brian's back as he turned away and picked up a glass. "No Brian you know I hardly ever drink."

Brian snorted in derision as he walked over to his chair and dropped into it disrespectfully as he looked up, but he didn't invite the two unwanted visitors to sit. "Yeah I know, so I'll ask you again, what do you want?"

Mell and Jed sat down on a divan facing the chair that Brian slumped into, even though they hadn't been invited to. Mell eyed the brandy glass that Brian put down beside his chair in surprise and wondered why Brian was drinking. She decided wisely to ignore it. She cleared her throat and gentled her tone slightly not wanting to hurt him too much. "Just over two weeks ago my ranch was invaded by a group of outlaws and almost everyone was killed. The only ones to survive were Gloria, Wade, Tommy, and my father. We unfortunately were away looking for these outlaws when they hit the ranch."

At this point Brian interrupted heatedly, as he sat forward in his chair demandingly. He waved his hand around in fury. "What has that got to do with me?"

Mell was taken aback by the resentful challenging tone of Brian's question then she motioned placatingly in reassurance. "Well nothing directly."

Mell paused in surprise again as she watched Brian relaxing back in his chair, as if in relief, then she continued as if she hadn't been disrupted. But her puzzled frown remained at Brian's strange behaviour. "I only wanted to tell you because Tommy is your Nephew. I wanted you to hear it from me because it was Greg who betrayed the ranch then ended up dead. I know how close the two of you were...."

Mell scowled deeply perplexed as she quit talking in mid sentence at the rage on Brian's face as he interrupted her angrily. Brian sat forward intently then gestured in furious denial. He shouted at Mell in an angry frenzy! "Tommy is 'NOT' my Nephew! And don't you ever call him that again!"

Mell jumped up in agitation and frustration as she started pacing back and forth just as irate now as Brian was. She couldn't believe how

146

stubborn and bull headed he was. She suddenly stopped pacing and stared down at Brian in livid incredulity then motioned imploringly. "Tommy is so your Nephew whether you want to admit it or not! The other reason we stopped here is to let you know that Tommy and his mother won't be coming back here again. Mary's husband will be taking them back to his people, contrary to what you believed the Indian you killed that long ago day wasn't Mary's husband."

Brian jumped up out of his chair in a heartbeat and was standing toe to toe with Mell. He balled his fists ready to swing forgetting for a moment who Mell was. "NEVER! I'll kill them both first."

Mell stepped back hurriedly totally taken by complete surprise she hadn't expected that reaction from Brian at all. Instinctively her hands automatically dropped to her guns in reaction ready to draw if she had too.

Jed had been watching silently up to this point but when Brian jumped out of his chair in a temper to confront Mell. Jed also jumped up off the settee and put his hand on his gun in warning.

Brian saw movement behind Mell as she stepped back and noticed Jed's movement towards his gun. He threw up his hands in surrender then fell back in his chair broodingly. He hadn't noticed Mell's quick reaction, until he looked up at her, and saw her hands on her guns as well.

Jed walked over to the mantle and turned to face Brian in forewarning then stood there quietly letting Mell handle this, but making sure Brian knew that he was there. He kept his hand close to his gun so that Brian wouldn't get any more wild ideas.

Mell sighed in relief then dropped her hands from the butt of her guns as she backed up and settled back on the divan. Mell gestured consolingly at Brian as she continued the conversation. "Brian I know this is difficult for you but your sister loves Giant Bear. I will leave you now to think about coming to grips with your hatred of Indians. I hope you can come to terms with your feelings by next week. If you do you can come to the wedding."

Brian sat forward apprehensively as he stared at Mell and demanded indignantly. "Who's wedding? According to Mary, her and that bastard of an Indian, are already married."

Mell nodded then exhaled noisily in resignation and tensed for an explosion that she knew was imminent. "Wade and Gloria are getting married next week."

At this good news Brian began to relax back into his chair in disinterest. Mell ignored his reaction not finished yet then continued to speak calmly. "Your sister and Giant Bear will also be renewing their vows and I will be getting married as well."

Brian instantly surged to his feet in surprise and rage as he motioned in disbelief. "And who the hell are you getting married to?"

Mell frowned in relief at least he had forgotten his sister for the moment. She looked up at Brian but didn't rise herself as she spoke softly in an apologetic voice, aware that Brian had wanted to marry her all these years. She pointed towards the mantle where Jed was standing. "I'm marring Jed my new Deputy."

Brian stood for a moment in a state of shock then pointed over at Jed incredulously. "You're marrying him?"

Brian sputtered in outrage for a moment unable to say anything more for a moment too shocked at first. He brought his hand back in front of him and gestured sharply in demand. "Why you don't even know him! He comes out of nowhere a drifter and you decide to make him a Deputy then marry him? He's probably after you for your ranch and your money!"

Jed took a menacing step forward in anger but paused as Mell lifted her hand towards him to stop his advancement. He backed up to the mantle once more to listen.

Mell's tone turned frosty with warning and she stood up heatedly as well. So she could watch Brian's expression closely as she demanded in a deadly soft voice. "First of all Brian Jed knows that the ranch goes with my job and he couldn't get it even if he wanted it. As to my money neither Jed nor anyone else knows about that money! Where did you get your information?"

Mell's question threw Brian for a loop. He stood there sputtering for a moment not sure what to say then apprehensively cleared his throat uneasily. "Your father told me."

Mell narrowed her eyes sceptically. She doubted very much that her father had told him anything, but she decided to let it go for now, she would check with her father later. She couldn't accuse Brian of anything until she knew for sure. Mell sighed in exasperation. "Brian Jed doesn't know about any money. Actually, I don't have any, it's my father's money not mine. As for Jed being a drifter that was because he was searching for the men who murdered his family they are all dead now, so he has avenged them and is ready to settle down. As for just meeting him well that one kind of took me by surprise, but you have heard of love at first sight haven't you?"

Brian nodded mutely in reply not sure what to say.

Mell nodded thoughtfully as she remembered their first meeting and the tingling feelings that had confused her at first. "That's right I fell in love with Jed almost the first moment I laid eyes on him, and I make no excuses for that! Now if you can overcome your feelings of hatred I'm sure your sister would love for you to come to her wedding and give her away."

Brian glared at Mell in disbelief then turned towards Jed and glowered at him with intense animosity. He spit out in anger with balled up impotent fists as he turned back to Mell and almost shouted. "NEVER!"

Mell shrugged her shoulders in resignation at Brian's stubbornness then turned to leave thankfully as she threw one more statement over her shoulder in parting. "So be it Brian. But that's a real shame and your loss! Come on Jed let's get out of here!"

It had only taken them half an hour, but to Jed at that moment it seemed more like hours, as they rode away from Brian's. Jed took a moment to ponder all that he had heard during their encounter with Brian. He had known that it was going to be difficult coming here from everything he had heard about Brian. He had also learned a few unexpected things about him and about himself.

The first thing that he had noticed about Brian was the two empty brandy decanters sitting on the mantle. It was like he had lost his best friend and was mourning him. But how could Brian have known about Greg before they had told him. Nobody else knew until today unless somebody had rode out from town to tell him while they were with the mayor. Or maybe the neighbour, that had helped Wade bury the men at the ranch. But that couldn't be it because Wade hadn't known at that time about Greg.

Also why had Brian been so jumpy when Mell had mentioned the killings and Brian's involvement in the same breath? Despite the drinking the two men couldn't have been that close of friends since Brian hadn't even mentioned or commented on Greg's death even once, after he had been told. As if he wasn't surprised by that news at all. So someone must have gotten here first and told him already that's the only thing that made sense.

Jed had also been right in surmising that Brian would be more upset about learning of Mell's upcoming wedding than he had been about the news of his sister's leaving.

He also wondered how Brian had learned about this money belonging to Mell. Like Mell he doubted very much that Brian had found out from Mell's father. Whenever Mell had mentioned Brian's name Alec would frown apprehensively and tense up, it was obvious to Jed that Alec didn't like him.

Then there was what Jed had learned about himself. Although he had promised Mell last night when he had asked her to marry him that he would let her handle things as sheriff, he had self doubts that he would be able to hold back if she was actually threatened. He now knew that he could up to a point.

Jed looked over at Mell then frowning curiously as he motioned inquisitively. "What's all this about money? What was Brian talking about if you don't mind my asking?"

Mell looked over at Jed then shook her head negatively that she didn't mind his question, then she sighed in relief, glad he had finally asked her about the money and she could get it out into the open. She didn't want anything coming between them now. "No I don't mind you asking at all. Before my dad met and married my mother he was in town and entered a high stakes poker game. He won a lot of money and a deed to a house. When he went to look at the house he was shocked to find out that he was now the owner of a fancy house and gambling den. There was no way that he was going to run such a business so he sold it right away for a substantial profit. After he married my mother he bought a half interest in the ranch that he worked as foreman at. The owner was in financial trouble at the time. Well after the accident and my mother died, dad resold his share of the ranch for a nice profit back to the original owner and came to live with me. About ten years ago dad bought into a dry gold mine that a friend of his said wasn't dry. Dad gave his friend five thousand dollars to buy the land and equipment his friend needed and wouldn't you know it his friend had been right. They struck a new vein of gold three years ago and now my father is well off. Plus the lumber business brings in quite a bit of money as well. We've tried to keep it really quiet because dad didn't want anybody to know. How Brian found out is beyond me I'm pretty sure dad didn't tell him. As far as I'm concerned the money is dad's and has nothing to do with me."

Jed nodded his head thoughtfully he was sort of in the same boat himself. He came from a wealthy family back east, but because he hadn't made the money himself he felt that he had no right to it. The estates he had back home he had left to his friend to manage for him, and the money just kept building up. Jed sighed knowingly then motioned in sympathy. "I know how you feel my family moved from England when I was a baby to Boston and they went into shipping. My father had a title in England but thankfully he left it behind when we moved. But since I never had anything to do with the business I never felt I had any right to the money or the titles. My whole family is angry with me for going to Montana then when I talked my wife into coming with me, my father almost had a fit. Especially, since I was the only one in my family to have a boy at the time. Everyone else had girls so he would have been the next heir to dad's shipping company. As it turned out my father had been right but there's nothing I can do about it now."

Mell frowned sadly as Jed mentioned his dead son and she wondered what his family would think of her as she waved unhappily at Jed. "I suppose your family won't like me because I'm a Sheriff."

Jed shook his head negatively and he laughed in delight as he imagined his father's reaction to his new wife then he gestured at Mell in reassurance. "Now there you're wrong my father especially will like you. I even know what he will say after he finishes yelling at me for taking my family into the wilds with me, and not looking after them properly. He will look you over carefully then say, 'well at least you found someone as strong as you are this time. I'll expect strong grandsons from such a strong woman, and tall ones too'."

Mell laughed at Jed's imitation of his father's voice then shook her head at him in disbelief. "You're just making that up. He wouldn't say any such thing."

Jed smiled knowingly and put his hand over his heart dramatically. "Cross my heart, I'm not lying that's exactly what he'll say."

Mell shook her head in incredulity again then grinned in amusement at Jed's theatrics. "How many brother's and sister's do you have?"

Jed sighed in resignation and artificial horror as he waved in aggravation playfully trying to be as melodramatic as possible. "Too many I have two older brothers, one older sister, and two younger sisters as well."

Mell laughed at his expression of mock horror then her face turned slightly wishful. "Was it really that bad?"

Jed nodded vigorously then scowled dramatically once more. "You have no idea! We all fought constantly and my mother would get so fed up with the lot of us she would chase us out of the house with a broom. My mother never believed in having nursemaids, she wanted to raise us herself. She told me once that when she lived in England she never got to see her parents, ever, only her nurse was around and she didn't want that for her kids. But we did have a huge black housekeeper that helped her out a lot and when that woman bellowed at you, you ran for your life."

Mell chuckled in amusement as she pictured an older feminine Jed screaming at the top of her lungs then chasing her kids outside with a broom. Once she got control of her laughter she sighed yearning again as she looked back at Jed. "I always wished for a brother or sister but after my mother died I stopped wishing."

Jed smirked in invitation. "If I could I'd give you a few of my siblings, it's not all it's cracked up to be you know."

Mell smiled over at him in fake sympathy not really feeling sorry for him at all. "Maybe but if you were an only child you would wish for a few siblings as well."

Jed laughed in agreement. "Yeah you're probably right at least we all loved each other and helped one another out when we could."

Mell heaved a sigh in anticipation as she waved eagerly. "I can't wait to meet them."

Jed laughed in forewarning then shook his head in horror at the thought of Mell with his brothers and sisters. "You might change your mind later."

Mell shook her head negatively as she answered him seriously. "No I don't think so."

Jed just smiled knowingly but didn't comment further.

Mell smirked back confidently but didn't continue the conversation either as she nudged her horse into a canter wanting to get home quickly.

Mell and Jed rode the rest of the way in silence each immersed in their own thoughts. Neither of them paid any attention to the beautiful sunset as they rode west towards Mell's ranch.

CHAPTER TEN

Mell and Jed rode into the yard thankful to be home. They both saw Tommy running towards them at the same time. So they halted immediately and dismounted where they were then waited for him.

He came rushing up to them eagerly. Mell smiled at Tommy in greeting and thanks as he took the reins from her. "Well Tommy how's everything going?"

Tommy grinned in pride at getting everything done that his aunt had wanted him to do, plus a few things extra. "Well, me and Giant Bear did the bunkhouse first and it's a good thing too we just got finished when the new hands showed up here. Then we cleaned the barn and finished that about an hour ago. Giant Bear wanted to have a bath afterwards so I took him to the creek. I offered to fill a tub for him but he wouldn't go for that. He's all dressed up and pacing back and forth. He seems upset about something. Wade came to the barn just before we went to the creek and talked to Giant Bear, it seemed to help for a while."

Mell signalled in approval then her expression became serious. "And your mother she is here?"

Tommy nodded vigorously and his chest puffed up in satisfaction as he boasted. "Yes, and I did what you asked, I wouldn't let her near the barn and I didn't tell her about Jed or Giant Bear."

Mell grinned in relief then ruffled Tommy's hair in affection. "Good boy you did a good job today. You can take the horses to the barn and ask Giant Bear to unsaddle them then go up to the house and help there

154

for the rest of the night. Since you look like you already had a bath you won't need one, but I do. So you can start heating water for me please."

Tommy beamed up in delight at being given another job to do and he nodded eagerly. "Yes ma'am, when I went to the creek with Giant Bear I decided to have a bath there too. It was very cold I wouldn't want to do that in the winter I'd freeze to death."

Tommy turned without waiting to hear Mell's reply then ran back to the barn with the three horses following him obediently.

Mell turned to Jed and pointed to her left not far from the west side of the house, but not too close. "That's where I want to put Wade and Gloria's cabin."

She then turned a little farther to her left closer to the barn but further back and waved. "And that's where I want to put Brad and Jane. The screen of trees between the two cabins will give them each a little privacy from each other."

Jed nodded as he looked in the directions she indicated then he turned back to Mell as he motioned in appreciation. "Those are good spots there are a lot of trees behind where the cabins are going to be, which will be good for privacy, as well as a good windbreak for warmth in the winter."

Mell grinned in pleasure at his praise then turned towards the bunkhouse expectantly. "Let's go meet the new ranch hands you picked out."

Mell led the way but let Jed go into the bunkhouse first to make sure everybody was dressed and ready for an inspection. When Jed beckoned to her that it was all clear she walked onto the porch and through the door. The new hands were standing in a row to be inspected already.

Mell smiled in pleasure as she recognized the youngest and went up to him first. "Hi Dusty I saw your mother today. I didn't know you wanted to work for me or I would have asked you before."

Dusty beamed shyly at Mell and fidgeted slightly in embarrassment as Mell singled him out first then he shrugged off his shyness enough to answer her truthfully. "Well I would have asked before but Pa still needed me. But now that my brother is old enough, Pa said I could go."

Mell nodded then shook his hand warmly trying to put him at ease. "Good to have you aboard."

Dusty was Lucy's son, the mayor's secretary, and one of the hardest workers she had ever seen. He was very good looking and the same height as Mell. He had midnight black hair and deep brown expressive eyes. The girls just loved him but he was so bashful he would stammer in their presence and run away before a girl could even say hi. He was only twenty years old and slightly awkward with his big feet, unless he had a job to do, then he would forget about his feet and shyness long enough to get things done efficiently. She definitely approved of Dusty being chosen.

Mell turned to Kenneth next he was the exact opposite of Dusty. His looks were only medium and he wasn't shy at all, if she remembered rightly he was very bold and outspoken. It had got him into trouble a few times but nothing serious that she could recall. He had a bit of a gambling problem but she didn't allow high stakes here anyway, so it shouldn't be a problem. He had brown hair and laughing hazel eyes he was painfully slim and wiry, but not afraid of hard work at all.

Mell shook his hand in greeting and liked the firm but not crushing grip he used. Mell also liked the fact that he looked her straight in the eye with a straightforward gaze and she nodded pensively. "Kenneth right?"

Kenneth grinned pleased that she remembered him then smirked in delight as he remembered the last time they had met. "That's right Sheriff, but you can call me Ken, you helped me out of a few scrapes the last few years."

Mell smiled recalling as well the last time he had gotten in a brawl at the saloon and she had to intervene to save his hide, but she didn't hold that against him. "Welcome aboard."

Mell turned to the next man in line and she looked at him intently as she frowned in reflection. "I don't think I know you."

The man beamed good-naturedly at her then reached out to shake Mell's hand in introduction. "No you don't I'm Darrel and I used to work in the next town but they could only keep me on until after round up. So when your man happened to come into Chelsie's Saloon and offered full time jobs I jumped at the chance. Chelsie vouched for me and so did one of the hands I used to work with."

He was better looking than Kenneth, but not as handsome as Dusty. He was the oldest man there and fairly good-looking with his steel grey hair and grey blue eyes. He was husky but not anywhere near fat and he smiled or squinted a lot by the looks of the wrinkles around his eyes and mouth. He was slightly taller than Mell at six feet. His handshake was firm and he had an honest face. She smiled at him in welcome and nodded approval. "Welcome aboard."

Mell then turned and frowned in surprise at the two men she hadn't expected to see here. "I know both of you, Mark and Tomas I believe."

They both nodded and shook her hand one at a time. Mell eyed both men closely curious to hear their explanations. "I thought both of you worked for Mr. Grey so why are you here?"

Mark shrugged with a confused expression plain on his face he seemed unsure himself what was going on then he spoke first. "They fired me this morning with no warning or reason. Just told me to collect me pay and skedaddle."

He was fairly good looking with sandy blonde hair, and a scar that ran down his right cheek that gave him a rakish look. He had green eyes and was slightly taller than her at six foot one. She remembered having only one dealing with him when he had drank too much and got rowdy other than that he seemed a pleasant enough fellow. She accepted him as well. "Welcome aboard."

She then looked more closely up at Tomas. He was a big burly man almost fat and just about as tall as Jed, but not quit, and ugly as sin. He had greasy dark brown hair and blue small squinty eyes.

The first time she saw him five years ago when he had first moved to town she had looked through her wanted posters. But there was nothing on him it wasn't because of his ugly looks that she had checked. He just seemed familiar as if she had seen him before, but she could never remember from where, and still even today she still felt she knew him from somewhere.

The hairs slightly stood up on the back of her neck in suspicion but she had never really had anything to be uneasy about, and in the last five years he had never once been in trouble with the law.

Tomas shrugged dismissively not in the least concerned. "He fired me too for no reason at all."

Mell finally nodded hesitantly in welcome, but not in approval. Now she wished she had met the new hands at the hotel she wouldn't have accepted Tomas and she wasn't sure she would have accepted Mark either, but too late now. "Welcome aboard."

Mell turned to the last man in relief at getting that interview over with then smiled in welcome. "And Brad how are you? Did you bring Jane with you?"

Brad grinned back in delight then shook his head negatively. "Nah, Jane didn't come today because your man wasn't sure what you were going to do with us. She will be coming tomorrow with Mrs. Elton though."

Mell sighed in disappointment then bobbed her head in pleasure at being able to see her friend tomorrow. "Good."

Brad was a short very plump good-natured man bald with grey green eyes. His wife fit him perfectly she was slightly shorter and even plumper then her husband. They were both jolly, almost always laughing, and both were painfully honest too much so at times.

She backed up so she could look at all six men at the same time then motioned in caution. "Jed explained the dangers of working for me I hope?"

All six men nodded in agreement.

Mell waited for all their nods before she continued. "Okay all of you please follow me and I'll give you a tour then let you know what I expect of you. I'm not sure what all your strengths are yet so over the next few days, Wade my foreman, will talk to each of you separately then we will decide where to place you and what job suits you best."

They walked out of the bunkhouse and kept close to Mell so they could all hear her, as she explained some of the rules. Mell spoke as loud as she could so all of them would hear her. "The first rule is that my name is Mell, not Sheriff while you work for me. The second rule is no drinking allowed while on duty. When you're off duty you can drink, if you want, I won't say you can't. But you all have to remember that just because you work for the Sheriff, doesn't mean there will be any special privileges if you get out of hand."

Mell smiled over her shoulder to take the sting out of that comment then turned around and continued walking and talking. "You can play poker after work but I only allow small pots. You can only go up to a dollar per game. I started that rule because one of my hands got beat up by the others because he won all their pay for two months. So now I make sure that it won't happen again."

They reached the corrals and stopped, Mell turned to face the men, and a touch of menace entered her voice in forewarning. "There is absolutely no beating, using whips, or cruel spurs on my horses."

She looked at each man in turn to get her point across. The men nodded understanding when her gaze fell on them. Mell moderated her tone once she was sure her point was made and accepted by the new men. "As you know I breed and raise horses on the side. I also have a few people who bring their horses here to be bred or broke. As you can see I have three large corrals, but one of the projects for this year is to fence off a larger pasture, because I want to pick up some more breeding stock sometime this year."

Mell turned towards the barn and the men followed dutifully as she continued. "Everybody also takes a turn on guard duty Wade will organize you guys on that job. My father takes care of the breeding, foaling, and wages. So you will all need to come to the house one at a time to meet him. Wade is the foreman of course I'll send him out to meet you later. So any specific questions you have will be directed to him or my father."

Mell opened the barn doors and they entered. She looked around but didn't see Giant Bear. She looked questioningly at Jed and he shrugged then pointed up at the hayloft in silent answer to her question. Mell nodded slightly in agreement with Jed then turned back to the men. "We have twelve stalls in here the horses that are used every day are kept here as well as both of the studs. There is a tack room over to your left with everything you will need whatever is not in here can be found in the second bunkhouse. Which, we use as a storage facility in the summer, and extra beds in the fall when we start harvesting trees. If you need a horse one will be provided. If you want to buy a horse, talk to my father and he will arrange to take small payments out of your pay each month.

Another plan for this year is expanding the barn or maybe even building a second one, we haven't decided yet which way we want to go."

Mell walked out of the barn without waiting for questions and lead them towards the area she had picked for the two cabins. "The first order of business for you gentlemen is the building of two cabins. Wade will take some of you down to the saw mill it's about two miles from here, to bring up some lumber to get started."

When they reached the spot for Brad's cabin she turned to him inquisitively. "You have three children one boy, and two girls am I correct?"

Brad nodded then smiled in delight as he thought of his rambunctious children. "Yes, the girls are seven and eight and the boy is ten."

Mell inclined her head already aware of that, but just wanting to make sure. "Okay starting tomorrow you gentlemen will start building a cabin here for Brad and his family. Brad, do you want to help me draw up a plan?"

Brad shook his head negatively. "I'd be obliged if you would do that, I'm not very good with plans."

She nodded then turned and went to the spot that she had picked for Wade and Gloria's cabin. She turned back to the men and continued. "After Brad's cabin is done I want another built here. This cabin will be for Wade and Gloria who will be getting married next week. I would also like all of you bachelors to know that if you ever decide to marry a cabin here will be offered."

She waited for the men to nod that they understood then she finished up. "Now a few other things you need to know is that my father is in a wheelchair that is why we have a wood sidewalk from the house to the barn, corrals, and bunkhouse. If you want to work with the horses or at the mill you will have to talk to him. If you need something that can't wait for payday you will have to talk to him. Any other concerns you have should be directed to Wade, Jed, or to me. Jed is my Deputy but once in a while I need extra Deputy's, if you're interested let me know later. Jed is also my fiancé and we will be getting married next week. So any orders coming from him are to be carried out. You guys can start cleaning around the spots for the cabins if there are any other duties needed tonight Wade will let you know. If you don't have any questions you're free to go. Except for Dusty and Brad. I have other tasks for you tonight."

Dusty and Brad stayed as the other men left to start cleaning the ground of dead brush and debris over at the spots Mell had indicated. She smiled at both men and waved towards the ranch house. "I'm having a small dinner party tonight so I would like you two to work at the main house. The Ladies could use a couple of strong men to haul water, and such, if you have no objections to working inside that is."

Both men inclined their heads in agreement then waited for further instructions. Mell pointed in the direction of the side door. "Go to the door and tell Gloria I sent you both to help out tonight. She will put the two of you to work."

They turned and left obediently without comment.

Mell and Jed followed but more slowly. She grinned over at Jed earnestly. "Well how did I handle myself?"

Jed smirked mischievously as he motioned teasingly. "Well I think two of the men are in love already and one is only half in love."

Mell hit him in the shoulder playfully then laughed in delight. "That's not what I meant at all and you know it."

Jed rubbed his arm in bogus pain then chuckled knowingly as he smiled over at Mell. "I know and you did a very good job, I was very impressed."

Mell beamed in delight at the praise then her expression sobered as she became serious. "I'm not sure we should have kept Mark and Tomas on though. I've never known Mr. Grey to just fire someone for no reason."

Mell thought of her father's friend he lived directly south east of here in a log cabin not far from town. Mell's father had tried to talk him into letting them build him a proper home with lumber, but he absolutely refused, gripping about getting soft that way. He was a grumpy fellow but always treated his men fairly as far as she knew.

Jed frowned in concern as he gestured cautiously. "See that's why I wanted you to meet them in town first, it's not too late I can get rid of them if you like."

Mell seriously thought about it for a moment then shook her head negatively. "No I'm just being suspicious I guess, especially with everything that's happened around here lately and now with the threats Brian made. I'm just a little jumpy that's all."

Jed nodded in understanding as he sighed in sympathy. "I don't blame you for being jumpy. Let's give it some time, I'll talk to Wade so he knows to keep an eye on the two men, then if they prove untrustworthy I'll let you know immediately."

Mell sighed in relief and they walked the rest of the way in silence. They reached the main entrance and went in as dusk was settling in.

Wade met them at the door in a panic and quickly ushered them into the drawing room then closed the door. He turned to face Mell and gestured in distress. "Mell I used two excuses to get Mary here. First I told her about the murders then I told her that Tommy needed her. After I got her here I told her about the engagement party for Gloria and me, but I didn't tell her about you, and right now she's helping Gloria in the kitchen. I also went out a while ago to see how Giant Bear was doing and it's not good. He said if you weren't back in an hour he was going to come to the house."

Mell turned to Jed in concern. "You better go out there and keep Giant Bear occupied, at least until I have a chance to talk to Mary. Give me about an hour or so then I'll send her out to the barn."

Jed nodded and took off in a hurry.

Mell then turned to Wade and waved to the door. "Good work Wade I'll take over in here now. I'd like you to go out and introduce yourself to the new men they're over at the spot I picked for Brad and Jane's cabin cleaning up. You'll need to take them down for a load of lumber. And if you ask them they'll show you where you're new cabin will be set up as well."

Wade looked at Mell in surprise and gratitude. "You're going to build a cabin for me and Gloria?"

Mell smiled and nodded that she was. "Yes this is my wedding present to the both of you. If you'll follow me I'll quickly sketch a plan for Brad's cabin and yours too if you want. Or you can do your own design."

Wade hugged Mell in thanks. "Thank you it's the best gift I ever received."

Mell returned the hug affectionately then she turned away from Wade in pleasure. She led the way to the den. When they entered Mell's father

162

was behind the desk writing. Mell walked around the desk and bent down to kiss him in greeting. "Oh just the person I wanted to see."

Alec chuckled in delight as he looked up at her then shook his head in disbelief as he teased her. "No I'm not, Jed will now fill that space."

Mell shook her head emphatically as she joke back. "Never! You will always be my number two man."

Alec laughed knowingly as he looked up at Wade and chortled mischievously. He grabbed his chest in bogus pain dramatically. "You see I'm already demoted too second place."

Mell smiled down fondly at her father then changed the subject as she pointed to the desk. "Hand me a paper so we can sketch this while I talk."

Alec looked up at his daughter then smiled inquisitively. He moved his chair out from behind the desk and wheeled himself around to the other side. "You can use the desk if you like paper, pen, and ink are on top."

Mell nodded then grabbed her chair that was at all times left in the corner for her use, and pulled it to the desk then sat down. Mell looked across at her father as Wade found a chair and pulled it closer to help if she needed it. She bent down and began drawing as she talked. "Dad since you don't know about this I'll fill you in. As you know Jed and I went to town to hire five single men, but Jed suggested I hire one family to come out and live as well. That will give us an extra man and woman to help out around here. I agreed, so he hired Brad and Jane Anderson for this purpose. I highly approve of his choice since I've always liked both the Andersons, so we need a cabin built for them. I also decided it would be a good idea to build a cabin for Wade and Gloria as a wedding present. Brad's cabin will have two bedrooms, a sitting room, and a kitchen on the main floor. I want to put a loft above this. The loft will be big enough for his two girls to sleep in. I want the cabin back far enough from the trees so that later if they want we can add on. Wade can decide on how he wants his place set up, now or later if he needs time to think about it."

Mell finished the quick sketch just as she stopped talking then handed the paper of Brad's cabin to her father and waited anxiously. Wade and Alec studied it in interest both men nodded at each other Alec looked over at his daughter in approval. "Yes I like it."

Wade grinned thoughtfully then motioned down at the sketch in admiration as well. "We can use this sketch for our cabin too. We just won't add the extra bedroom or the loft until it's needed."

Mell shook her head in disagreement. "Well I think you should add the loft at least, for later use. You can always use it for storage now until it's needed."

Wade nodded as he got up to leave. "I'll go out and meet the new men then look over the building sites you picked, before taking them down for wood. I'll surprise Gloria tonight with the good news."

Alec turned to Mell once Wade left then waved in praise towards her. "This is a very good idea you had. Since your building the cabins I'll buy them some furniture as a wedding gift."

Mell shrugged dismissively at her father. She gestured in explanation. "You'll have to thank Jed it was his idea."

Alec nodded that he would definitely thank Jed later then changed the subject as he gestured curiously. "What about the families you visited today?"

Mell sighed in sad recollection as she thought of the family's reaction to the news, most of them hadn't blamed her, but she blamed herself. "It was the hardest thing I ever had to do. I gave them all a thousand dollars like you suggested. The bank manager almost had a heart attack when I asked him for eight thousand dollars worth of bank notes, divided into eight separate notes. Although I still couldn't find out any information on the other man. I'll keep trying though and when I find his relatives I'll send them their money as well."

Alec nodded then reached across the desk for a letter of authority he had made out earlier allowing Mell to take out two thousand dollars from his account and handed it to her.

Alec smiled stubbornly at her astonished look then gestured at the banknote decisively. "That's half of the money you gave out of your account today. If you find out where the other ones relatives are I'll give you that too."

Mell sighed knowingly at her father's stubborn look then shook her head dumbfounded even though she knew he would take no for an answer she asked anyway. "But why?"

Alec shrugged dismissively knowing his daughter wouldn't want to take the money. "I wanted to contribute too since I'm part owner now."

Mell frowned solemnly. "If you insist but there's plenty of money in the ranch account so it's not necessary."

With a Mulish look Alec nodded decisively. "I know I don't have too but since I knew you were paying half out of your own account. I wanted to do the same they were my friends too."

Mell nodded in understanding not wanting to argue with him then got up and walked around the desk, after putting her chair back in its corner. She bent down then kissed the top of his head in farewell. "I have to go and talk to Mary I'll see you later."

Alec went back around his desk to finish his work once she left.

Mell hurried across the hall to the kitchen to find Mary. The meeting with her father and Wade had taken longer then she had expected and she was running out of time.

Gloria turned in relief as she heard the kitchen door open and smiled in greeting as she winked at Mell in conspiracy. "Oh Mell, I'm so glad to see you. I decided not to have supper until around nine o'clock. I knew you would need time to bathe and find something appropriate to wear for the engagement party. Mary will go upstairs with you and help you out. We put out some dresses earlier for you to try on and I also asked her to have a female talk with you, since she's been married twice now. I told her you were getting married with me but I didn't tell her who you were marrying I figured you would want to tell her yourself. Since your mother isn't here to advise you Mary can give you a few tips perhaps."

Mell beamed in thanks at Gloria for giving her an excuse to get Mary upstairs alone. "Why thank you Gloria how thoughtful of you."

Mell gave Gloria a thumbs up sign, behind Mary's back, as she ushered her out the kitchen door. Mell rushed Mary upstairs not even allowing her to talk or ask any questions, afraid that Giant Bear would show up before Mell could tell her friend.

As they entered Mell's bedroom she stopped short in surprise and delight. The sight before her was unbelievable! Her bed was covered with an assortment of gowns there was five of them, all in a variety of styles and colors, enough to dazzle anyone's eyes! But even from here Mell could tell that the styles were fairly old. Mell turned to Mary in surprise and wonder as she gestured in awe. "Where in the world did all these gowns come from?"

Mary smirked in delight as she turned to Mell then pointed up above their heads. "Your father told us that there were two trunks in the attic filled with your mother's clothing. Some have been worn but many of them are still new looking. They should fit you, your father told me you're about the same size as your mother was, except you're a little taller than her. But we can alter them if necessary."

A knock sounded at the door unexpectedly and both Mell and Mary turned in surprise. Tommy entered followed by the new ranch hands Dusty and Brad. They carried a large tub and several buckets of hot water inside as the two women moved back out of the way. It took several trips to fill the tub but finally it was full of steaming hot water.

Before they left Mell called Dusty over and she motioned in request. "Can you let Tommy eat with you tonight at the bunkhouse?"

Dusty nodded and left the room closing the door behind him.

Mary led Mell to the tub then started helping Mell undress. She stepped into the water in pleasure then sat down and she sighed blissfully as the hot water enveloped her completely, except for her knee's sticking up because she was a little too long for it.

Mary walked over to the bed and picked up one of the gowns then turned and regarded her friend as she held it up to show Mell. "While you're soaking Mell I'll show you these lovely gowns and you can choose which one you like best."

The two girls spent the next few minutes giggling and laughing over the dresses as Mary showed them off. Mell settled on a pretty turquoise gown that was perfect for her. Mary set the gown aside then walked over to the tub and began washing Mell's long hair.

Mell groaned in contentment no one had ever bathed her before and it sure felt good to be pampered. After her bath Mell wrapped a towel around herself then went to sit beside Mary on the bed so they could talk.

Mary removed all the dresses except for the one Mell had chosen to wear, after putting them away, she settled herself down beside Mell. She turned slightly so she could see her friends face better. Mary's curiosity was killing her and she waved chidingly. "You know Mell I never thought the day would come when I would see you get married. I didn't think there was a man good enough for you and that included my brother. But Gloria assures me that this man you're marrying is well brought-up. I wouldn't know since I never knew you were even seeing anyone, let alone contemplating marriage. I'm also very curious to know who this man is, she wouldn't tell me so what's all the secrecy about?"

Mell laughed at Mary's put upon expression then gestured in apology for not telling Mary about Jed. But things had happened so fast she hadn't had time to tell anyone. "I'm sorry I couldn't tell you sooner, it just happened so quickly. I'll explain everything in a moment then hopefully you'll forgive me. As for me I didn't think I'd ever get married either this kind of took me by surprise too. I just couldn't find a man strong enough for me, but Jed that's his name, is definitely man enough to handle me."

Mary nodded her head in understanding. She remembered back to that fearful time in her life when she got married, but then she had met her second husband, and everything was good for a time at least. "Yeah I remember how scared I was when I left home. At least you don't have to worry about leaving here but I didn't have a choice in the matter Brian forced me to marry this guy I didn't even know. Then the war party attacked us and everything changed for the better. I fell in love with my savage then when I found out that I was pregnant I got really scared and ran away. I think that was the worst mistake of my life. I should have stayed in the Indian village and waited for my husband to come back. You know I had actually arranged to go back to the village after the baby was born. But Brian killed my Indian guide so I couldn't go back."

Mell had listened quietly up to this point then decided that now was the time to mention Giant Bear. Mell smiled hopefully then took a deep breath to calm her nerves as she prayed that this question wasn't too late for Giant Bear and Mary's future happiness. "Mary, if your husband was here now, would you still go back with him?"

Mary nodded vigorously not even hesitating for a moment as she sighed wishfully at the thought of her husband. "Of course I would, I love him more than my life. The only thing that's kept me going all these years was my son."

Mell took a deep breath for courage then reached over and took Mary's hand in support before she continued. "Mary those three men your husband was looking for, that had killed his first wife, all those years ago were actually after me. They found me two weeks ago. You see I met up with two men who were tracking these killers and I hired them unknowingly. I found out later they were after men that wanted to kill me for something that had happened when I was fifteen and they stayed to help me catch them. One of the men I hired is my husband to be Jed and the other is an Indian Chief, named Giant Bear!"

Mary stared at Mell in shock, speechless for a moment. She whispered in total disbelief her voice was barely above a murmur by the time she finished speaking. Tears filled her eyes then spilled over but she didn't wipe them away. "Giant Bear is here? Now! Are you sure? Does he know about his son and me?"

Mell nodded unhappily as she squeezed Mary's hand in compassion. "Yes he knows Mary, but we didn't tell Tommy about him we figured you would want to do that. Giant Bear is waiting for you in the barn very impatiently I might add!"

Mary sat still for a few minutes in uncertainty as the tears continued to stream down her face. She wasn't sure what to do at first then suddenly she jumped up unexpectedly and pulled her hand away from Mell's. She reached down and gave Mell a bear hug in gratitude. "I love you Mell!"

Mary stood up quickly then with a cry of joy she raced out of the room, not even bothering to wait to hear Mell's reply that she loved her too.

Mell smiled ecstatically in relief as she watched Mary disappear, her question to Mary hadn't been too late after all, and she couldn't be happier for her friend especially now that Mell had found love too. She now understood why her friend had grieved for her husband for so long.

CHAPTER ELEVEN

Jed and Giant Bear were in the barn waiting impatiently and for about the third time Giant Bear gestured anxiously at Jed. "What is keeping her? Do you think she does not want me anymore?"

Jed exhaled noisily in annoyance he was just about to reassure Giant Bear again when a figure streaked past him and fell into his friend's arms. Jed broke into a wide grin of relief and he silently melted away.

Giant Bear stood with his feet braced as the squirming crying bundle he held began pouring loving kisses all over his face. He grinned, as she kept repeating over and over in hesitant Cheyenne. "I love you. I love you!"

Giant Bear knew that this was the only phrase she knew in his language and it warmed his heart to hear her saying it. Even that she would remember it after all these years of being apart amazed him.

He pulled away and took her hand then led her towards the ladder leading up to the hayloft. He helped her up the ladder before gently lowering her into a bed of straw with his blanket covering it, and he settled himself beside her. He gathered her close as he whispered tenderly. "Oh my Golden Dove when I found out that you were here I was both gladdened and angry. I don't understand why you left my people but right now I want you too much to question you. I will love you first."

Mary nodded in relief not wanting to talk of unpleasantness so soon. She gladly lifted her face for his kiss. Giant Bear tenderly kissed Mary's tear streaked face and ran his hand up her dress to feel her inner heat.

169

He mumbled irritably to himself as he tried to undo her dress but Mary would have none of that too impatient to wait any longer. She stood up then pulled her bloomers off before kneeling down then pushed her husband onto his back and lifted her dress as she straddled him.

Giant Bear chuckled knowingly too impatient himself and flipped aside his loincloth then sheathed himself fully within her body for the first time in nine years.

Mary groaned in ecstasy, but at the same time she gave a small gasp of pain, as Giant Bear's large manhood filled her to capacity. It was almost like it had been the first time around but not quite. She held them both still for a long moment so she could adjust to having her husband inside her again.

Giant Bear held still for a moment in relief at the tight feel of his wife surrounding him. He had heard Mary's small gasp of pain, it made him glad, because it meant that she hadn't been with another man while they were apart. Mary was so tight his manhood wanted to explode but he tried to hold back as long as possible.

Mary felt the tightness ease somewhat so she lifted up slightly then sat back down firmly as she gasped in pleasure at the feeling of his sleek manhood fully sheathed inside her.

They both gasped in unison at the gratification then Giant Bear grasped Mary by the hips impatiently and flipped her onto her back with them both still joined together. Mary could clearly hear the strain in her husband's voice as he groaned out in apology. "I am sorry love, but I cannot wait any longer!"

Mary moaned in satisfaction as Giant Bear slammed into her again and again but she didn't complain too impatient herself to wait.

Giant Bear fused their mouths together to stop some of the noise Mary was making knowing others were still around then he started to erupt deep within her. Mary felt Giant Bear's explosion and it triggered her own climax as she groaned against his lips with an intense mixture of ecstasy and pain.

Giant Bear broke their kiss then dropped his head on the blanket beside Mary's head panting in contentment and relief, as he continued to lie on top of her. It took him a few minutes to catch his breath before he rolled onto his back beside her in fulfilment. He gave a sigh of pleasure as he felt Mary cuddle up against him happily.

As his breathing came back to normal he turned on his side to face Mary then propped himself up on his elbow. He frowned in demand as he stared down at her intently. "Golden Dove it is now time to tell your story."

Mary sighed apprehensively then motioned pleadingly. "I was hoping for a little more time."

Mary paused hopefully but Giant Bear made no response just stared down at her intently waiting patiently. She knew she had no choice now as she sighed in resignation then looked into his eyes, and began reluctantly…"*Everything was going fairly well after you left Little Antelope was helping me to adjust to your way of life and, had even taught me a few words of your language. The only problem I was having was adjusting to your Medicine Man I was so afraid of him. Then when I was pretty sure that I was pregnant the Medicine Man must have suspected it also because he started coming to the tepee and chanting when I was inside. Little Antelope tried to explain that the Medicine Man was only trying to scare evil spirits away so that I would have a healthy baby, but that just terrified me more. So when I was about four months pregnant I begged Little Antelope to take me home so that my baby could be born there. He refused at first but I begged, pleaded, and cried until finally he gave in. But he said that he would only help me if I would promise to return when the baby was born. Of course I agreed because I had already planned to do that. Everything went well until we reached the ranch Brian was the first to see us and he came galloping up to us in concern, or so I thought. When he saw Little Antelope he drew his gun. I tried to get in front of him but he pushed me off of my horse and took the bullet in his chest. I crawled over to him sobbing it was entirely my fault I should have known that my brother wouldn't stop to ask question. For several days I was hysterical but finally calmed down when I realized that I would lose the baby if I didn't. Brian didn't realize that I was pregnant at first and I could only hide it for a while, I began to show at about six months. When he questioned me as to whether it was my husband's I answered yes, I couldn't tell him about you, I was too afraid of what he would do. So I let him believe what he wanted to I think he was planning on taking the ranch my child would have inherited if it had been my first husband's baby like he thought. When the baby was born it was easy to see that he was part Indian. His hair was black at first, then lightened, and his skin dusky he had my blue eyes though. Brian was so furious with me that he threatened to kill Tommy that's what I named the baby. I wouldn't let him come even one step near the little one. I kept a loaded gun under my pillow that Mell gave me for protection, after he tried to sneak into my bedroom one night. After that he more or less ignored Tommy as long as I kept him out of the way. I think the only reason he stopped trying to kill Tommy was that he thought Little Antelope was the boy's father. It wasn't until Tommy reached the age of five that more problems started, every time Brian came anywhere near Tommy he would hit him or yell at him calling him names like dirty half-breed and such. After several months of this abuse I decided that it would be best for our son if I got him away from Brian. I had befriended Mell not long after I had Tommy so I asked her to take him. I figured him living at the Sheriff's would effectively stop my brother he's been here ever since. I come to visit him every chance I get, but now Brian has decided that I should marry again. He's looking for another husband for me who lives far away from here and wouldn't know about Tommy."*

It was very quiet for a while as Giant Bear digested Mary's story solemnly then Giant Bear scowled angrily as he stared down at Mary intently. "Little Antelope is dead?"

Mary nodded in misery as she whispered brokenly. "Yes."

The fury in Giant Bear's voice was quite evident as he looked down at his wife grimly. "His family will have to be told when we get back to my people. You will have to tell them how well he died so they will know he died bravely protecting their Chief's wife and unborn child."

Mary nodded mutely in agreement.

Giant Bear glowered and his voice became deadly serious. "As for your brother I think I should pay him a visit."

Mary shook her head in horror and put her hand on Giant Bear's chest in supplication as she begged desperately. "Oh no Giant Bear please! He's my brother and I love him in spite of all he's done."

Giant Bear nodded in understanding and his voice softened slightly as he looked down at his wife's pleading look. He couldn't refuse his beautiful Golden Dove anything. "All right Golden Dove this time I will listen to you."

Giant Bear laid down beside his wife quietly neither spoke for awhile, both deep in their own thoughts. Giant Bear decided to lighten the mood as he turned his head and looked inquisitively at Mary. "Well my Golden Dove how would you like to marry me in the white man's way? This engagement party tonight is for us too."

Marry shrieked in pleasure then turned and threw herself on Giant Bear ecstatically. "Oh yes Giant Bear that would give me the greatest pleasure!"

Giant Bear rolled Mary over onto her back once more as he propped himself up over top of her then grinned down at her mischievously. "We will find our son and give him our good news later but right now I want to make love to you slowly and without any clothes between us this time. I swear you white women wear too much clothing!"

Mary sighed blissfully and encouraged her savage husband to have his way with her again.

* * *

Gloria walked into Mell's bedroom shortly after Mary left with a big grin of delight on her face. Mell smiled in humour as she looked at her. "Did you see Mary, Gloria? She went out of here like her skirts were on fire."

Gloria nodded and chuckled as she pointed towards the stairs. "I sure did we met on the stairs then she grabbed me and twirled me around. I thought we were both going to end up at the bottom of the stairs then she threw her arms around me and hugged me before rushing down the rest of them. I couldn't say anything since I was all out of breath by the time she let me go. I figured I'd better come up and help you finish getting dressed because that's the last we'll see of Mary for a while!"

Mell sighed as she motioned in confusion. "When I told her that Giant Bear was here all she could do was cry and hug me. Then she took off running. You know I've been sitting here thinking about all the tragedy that's been happening around here lately and then all three of us women find love amidst the disaster. It makes me wonder about life."

Gloria nodded thoughtfully. "That's true but life is strange, sometimes it takes a tragedy to make us realize what where missing in life. But enough of this I'm not going to let you think anymore about it right now. We have some men to dazzle and only about an hour to get everyone ready. Your dad is already waiting in the den, Jed's almost finished getting ready. I gave him instructions to go out to the barn in an hour and bring Mary and Giant Bear into the house. It's time for everyone to don his or her finery. The Mayor and his wife are due to arrive in about half an hour or so. Let's see what dress you chose and get you all prettied up then I'll go and see what I can do about myself."

Mell stood up and held the turquoise dress out to show Gloria anxiously as she frowned inquisitively. "What do you think?"

Gloria grinned as she eyed the dress in approval. "That's the one I had hoped you would pick. It'll bring out the color of your eyes. These beads I brought up will match the dress perfectly and I'll twine them in your hair. I brought my sewing kit along so while I take these stitches out you can dry your hair some. I also want to talk to you about what happens between a man and a woman when they marry. I'm sure Mary never got around to it before she left."

Mell blushed furiously as she recalled what had happened between her and Jed last night. Mell smiled in bewilderment as she eyed Gloria in surprise as she worked on her dress. "Gloria you've never been married so how would you know?"

Gloria shook her head in wonder at how innocent Mell was. Not once in the last year had Mell ever noticed Wade sneaking into Gloria's room or them slipping out to the barn together. Alec had known of course but had kept their secret.

Considering the fact that Mell had grown up among men as well as owned her own ranch, and was a sheriff to boot. It was really amazing how Mell had stayed so innocent for this long. Well this was her chance to find out. Mell could hear the curiosity plain in Gloria's voice as Gloria paused and looked away from her work long enough to gaze at Mell. She gestured inquisitively then asked her question. "I don't understand how you can still be so innocent?"

Mell sighed forlornly as she gestured in aggravation before Gloria looked back down at what she was doing. "It's not so hard really, my mother died before she got around to discussing what happened between a man and a woman. She realized early in my life that she couldn't prevent me from becoming a tomboy so she decided to protect me by forewarning the men to keep me away from all the things she didn't want me to see.

She warned them with the threat of death and if you would have known my mother you would have listened too, she was a real formidable woman. She hadn't needed to really because the men who worked at the ranch were just as protective of me as my parents were. My father always kept me occupied somewhere else when breeding or calving season was upon us. To this day I'm not allowed near the corrals at breeding or foaling time. As for being Sheriff I still haven't had much contact with that side of life. Pam always knew I was a woman and too young to be in her place anyway. Then my father talked to Pam and since then every time I've been called in on a disturbance the man that keeps the patrons in line meets me in the lobby with the wrongdoer already subdued. I've never been allowed anywhere in the house except the lobby. None of Pam's girls have been allowed to speak to me directly except to give evidence in my office."

Gloria snorted in irritation still pulling the stitches out of Mell dress as she talked. "Your father should have done something about it you're definitely at a disadvantage as a Sheriff because of it. One thing you could do before you get married is go and talk to some of Pam's Ladies, they will teach you everything you need to know and probably things you don't want to know!"

Mell laughed in delight as she nodded. "You're probably right I wouldn't want to know! As for talking to me about it you really don't need to, Jed's teaching me but I do have a few questions."

Gloria nodded and grinned in amusement. "Okay, ask away."

Mell took a large fortifying breath still not sure she should ask such a question but the inquisitiveness was killing her. So she decided to jump in with both feet and asked in a rush before she could change her mind. "I want to know about the sac that lies between a man's legs. There are two hard things inside what's it for?"

Gloria looked up startled then stared at Mell in utter amazement as she shook her head in disbelief. "I didn't think you were that innocent!"

Mell shrugged in embarrassment and waited impatiently for Gloria's reply. Gloria finished ripping out the hem of Mell's dress without speaking not sure how to tell Mell at first so wanted to give herself a moment to think. She shook the garment out before hanging it up.

Gloria sat down on the bed and patted the spot beside her invitingly bidding Mell to sit down with her. When they were both settled Gloria turned to Mell trying to explain as best she could. "Well that's what makes a man you did notice that your stud has similar balls on him did you not?"

Mell shook her head negatively. "Well no I never really noticed I guess I should look."

Gloria laughed in delight and shook her head in humour. "Well, you can look if you want but after I explain it hopefully you won't need to. Now those two hard balls inside his sac store's a white substance that makes babies. When you make love this substance goes inside you and makes you pregnant."

Mell nodded thoughtfully. "Well that makes sense last night Jed showed me what the white stuff looks like and he called it his seed."

Gloria's eyebrows rose in surprise. "You made love last night?"

Mell blushed in embarrassment and shook her head negatively. "Well not really I was too frightened so Jed is going slowly and showing me different ways of making love. He said this way I'll have time to get used to him."

Gloria smirked as she laughed knowingly remembering Mell's comment from this morning. "Oh that's what you meant earlier when you said I needed to get used to Wade."

Mell nodded then sighed in disgust. "Yes I didn't know that most prospective brides know more than I do."

Gloria chuckled in delight at having that mystery solved then waved consolingly. "Well truth be told, most women don't know much about it until their mother tells them, and you would have known earlier if your mother had still been alive. Most women don't like to talk about it so you would be amazed at how many don't know even the small amount you now do. Okay, I'll let Jed teach you what you need to know so enough of this we need to get you ready."

Mell smiled in pleasure as she went to sit at her vanity then she looked at Gloria behind her in the mirror as Gloria picked up Mell's brush to work on her hair first. "What fun to be so pampered!"

Gloria grinned back then got to work on Mell's tangled wet hair without saying a word.

* * *

Alec was still sitting behind his desk in the den, although he had went and changed earlier, when a discreet knock sounded. He looked up inquisitively. "Come in."

Jed walked in and smiled in greeting as he waved towards Alec's desk. "You shouldn't be working today."

Alec smirked at Jed then put down his pen as he motioned inquiringly. "The work never stops around here but I'm just writing letters nothing serious. What can I do for you?"

Jed sat in the chair in front of the desk then gestured down at his suit in explanation. "Well first off I want to thank you for lending me this suit. I didn't bring anything fancy with me I think I might suggest to Mell that we should go to Boston for our honeymoon. That way she can meet my family and I can arrange to bring my stuff down at the same time. I also wanted to give you this."

Jed took the package from his pocket then handed it across the desk to Alec. Alec took the box and smiled his thanks. "Thank you."

Jed grinned back then continued. "Chelsie asked me to deliver it to you."

Alec grinned mysteriously for a moment then opened it before passing the box back to Jed so he could see what was inside. "Beautiful aren't they, the necklace was Mell's mothers and her grandmother's before her. The earrings and bracelet I had Chelsie make. I had a friend searching for a long time so that the stones would match, but it was Chelsie who actually found them. A friend of hers in Ireland helped us out."

Jed nodded in admiration as he handed it back to Alec then he pulled out his little box with the wedding ring for Mell and handed it to Alec for him to inspect then waved in explanation when his hand was free. "Well Chelsie said she had finished that ring just the other day and she did mention being inspired by the design on your commission into making it. So I have to thank you for that too."

Alec smiled in pleasure at the beautiful ring then handed it back. "Chelsie is like that she seems to get inspired easily she's been talking about opening a goldsmith shop for awhile now and she wasn't just talking about jewellery either but had mentioned clocks and other things. We have a lot of discarded lumber and trees here so we could help her with wooden basses for clocks and such. It wouldn't cost much too build her a shop since I have all the lumber here it would be a good investment."

Jed nodded thoughtfully. "I was thinking along the same lines I'd be real interested if you wanted to do it a goldsmith shop would be a novelty around here. I don't recall seeing one anywhere that I've been too except Boston of course, it has almost everything."

Alec nodded then rubbed his hands in anticipation and delight. "Great she'll be here for the wedding so if you're that interested we can talk to her about it then?"

Jed beamed at Alec's enthusiasm. "That's okay with me."

Alec changed the subject. "I would like to thank you for suggesting the cabins to Mell. It's a great idea."

Jed grinned in acceptance then smirked teasingly. "You're welcome. But I'm sure one of you would have thought of it eventually, if I hadn't."

Alec smiled unconvinced then shrugged. "Maybe, maybe not!"

Alec eyed Jed shrewdly for a moment then motioned invitingly. "You have something else on your mind don't you?"

Jed chuckled in delight then winked teasingly. "Nothing gets past you now I see where your daughter gets it."

Alec just nodded and waited patiently for Jed to tell him what he wanted. He had an idea but waited to see if he was right.

Jed cleared his throat hesitantly not sure if he was on thin ice or not and he didn't want to offend his future father-in-law. "Well your daughter tells me you handle the ranch and all business aspects of it."

Alec gestured inquisitively this is what he had figured Jed wanted. "Would you like to take it over?"

Jed shook his head negatively with a slight horrified look at that thought. "No way, I'll leave that in your capable hands."

Alec laughed at Jed's dismayed look then nodded in relief. "Okay, but you do have the right when you marry my daughter to take over if you want?"

Jed shook his head vigorously again in denial. "No that's okay I'd rather be out with your daughter as a Deputy than be a rancher. But I would like to suggest something I'd like to buy more land and maybe put some cattle on it. I'd pay for the additional land and cattle of course. But since you handle the business aspects of the ranch I wanted to make sure it's feasible and that the extra work load wouldn't be too much for you."

Alec leaned forward on the desk earnestly then folded his fingers together. "You do know that now that you're marrying my daughter you won't receive a wage from the town for being a Deputy any longer?"

Jed shrugged indifferently not worried in the least. "Mell had mentioned it but she was fairly vague on the subject. I don't need the money anyway but she did say that the town supplied everything we needed?"

Alec nodded then sat back in his chair and set his elbows on the arms then steepled them together thoughtfully. "Yes the town will pay all your expenses while you're on duty of course, I'll explain to you why. When Mell first came here she passed herself off as a man. She got away with it for so long because of her height mostly and she also used our last name Ray as her first name. Since the men at the ranch where she grew up had always called her that she didn't have any problems with a name change. As long as nobody looked too closely at her she was able to continue her charade for quite some time. Longer then even I thought possible and believe me she made sure nobody came close enough. But she got careless which was bound to happen sooner or later and a young boy figured out who she was. Well the game was up and she got fired but she didn't want to leave because she had fallen in love with the area so she decided to look for a place to live for the both of us. Well it didn't take her long to find this place but instead of writing me and asking for the money to buy it, which I would have gladly given her. She decided to be stubborn and do it on her own so she kept trying to find ways to make money. When she rescued the Mayor and his wife he agreed to give her this place if she would come back, and be the Sheriff again, but he was only going to give her the yard site and a hundred acres. Well Mell wasn't happy about that of course she wanted it all. So after much arguing and dealing they finally came to an agreement. It was decided that she would get it all on the condition that she never accept wages but all her expenses would be paid for when she's on the trail. The town got a free Sheriff since this land was only theirs by default. Plus all the surrounding towns now had a Sheriff, as far as I'm concerned the town got a better deal."

Jed nodded thoughtfully. "You're right I think so too. Mell told me some of it but not all, I understand more now. She also told me you only use part of the land right now."

Alec indicated agreement as he frowned. "Yes we do. At the present time we don't use the land between here and Devil's Rock. We built a saw mill west of here and have been logging that land for some time. We make sure to replant not wanting to use up our resources. It's been very profitable because we have no expenses except for extra men when we cut in the fall and the shipping of course. There's about six hundred acres that have nice big trees there's also land beyond that we want to buy up later, the trees over there are huge. We still have three hundred acres that would hold cattle if you want. I don't think we'll need extra land the grass is lush enough around here to hold around four or five hundred head of cattle right now. If you want to get bigger then that later then we could look at more land. As for buying the cattle yourself I'll have to decline that offer for one thing this ranch has made nothing but profit since we took it over. I've been trying to talk Mell into buying cattle for a while but she was afraid it would put too much of a strain on me. Oh, she didn't put it into those terms; she just kept telling me we could do it later when she retires. But now that you're here to help I'm sure we can talk her into it."

Jed sighed plaintively as he motioned in aggravation. "Well you give a pretty convincing reason about not needing me to buy the cattle and I agree the ranch should support itself in this venture but I have nothing invested in it. So it would make me feel like I had no say, or control in the project."

Alec nodded in understanding as he gestured at Jed knowingly. "I know what you mean I felt the same way when I first came here. So I'll make you the same offer that Mell made to me. I'm not aware of your financial situation but later not tonight we'll sit down together and discuss it. Then I'll let you know how much you can invest into the ranch not just the cattle. Your investment will be made on the whole ranch."

Jed thought about it for a moment then grinned as he nodded pleased. "You're right I think investing in the whole ranch would be better than investing in just the cattle."

Jed stood up and held out his hand over the desk in invitation as Alec clasped it firmly. Jed smiled in relief that Alec understood his feelings then he grinned at Alec. "It's a deal partner!"

CHAPTER TWELVE

Alec was just pouring himself a snifter of brandy when he heard a knock on the front door. He knew that Gloria was upstairs helping Mell so he wheeled himself over and opened it, a huge smile of welcome spread over his face when he recognized the mayor and his wife. "Good evening folks. Come right in."

The mayor and Mrs. Elton returned his greeting. "Nice evening for an engagement party isn't it Alec?"

Mayor Elton patted Alec on the shoulder as he walked around the wheelchair and into the lobby, so Alec could close the door.

Alec nodded as he turned towards his two guests then he smiled enticingly as he gestured towards the drawing room on their right. "I was just pouring myself some brandy could I pour some for the both of you? We might as well get comfortable while we wait for the others."

Mayor Elton grinned immediately in acceptance as he rubbed his hands in anticipation. "Sure I would love some."

Mrs. Elton shook her head negatively and declined as she waved towards the stairs leading up to the bedrooms hopefully. "No thanks, do you think Mell would mind if I went upstairs to see if she needs some help?"

Alec beamed pleased then motioned towards the stairs in invitation. "By all means go on up I'm sure Mell would be more than happy to see you. She would probably welcome your advice as well just go to the top of the stairs and turn left it's the first door you come to."

Mrs. Elton nodded in thanks then hurried up the stairs and knocked on the door Alec had indicated. While her husband and Alec went to the den instead for a drink.

* * *

Gloria opened the door at a knock then peeked out to see who it was. She grinned in surprised delighted as she opened the door wider in invitation. "Mrs. Elton come on in Mary just got here as well so we can all make a grand entrance when we go downstairs."

Mrs. Elton went in and smiled at Mary in greeting since she was the first one she saw then she turned expectantly looking for Mell wanting to congratulate her. Mrs. Elton's mouth fell open in delighted shock as she sputtered in relish. "Just look at you you're so beautiful! A lot of men are going to be kicking themselves for not trying to win you over you do realize that nobody has ever seen you in a dress?"

Mell chuckled as she imagined all the men from town seeing her in a dress for the first time. She smirked teasingly at the mayor's wife. "You're right I'll probably give everyone a shock when they see me at the wedding. Maybe I should wear pants instead. "

Mrs. Elton nodded in perfect agreement then giggled at Mell's wit. "You're probably right a heart attack might be more like it though. I don't think your father and my husband would let you get away with pants they've both waited too long to see you married as it is."

Mell beamed at all three women in turn then impulsively gave each a hug in gratitude. She stood back so all three could see the love she felt for all of them. "I don't know if I have ever told you three this but thank you. You have all supported me all these years and even when I was exposed as a woman, when I was posing as a man, so I could remain Sheriff you still stood by me."

Mrs. Elton smirked smugly as she thought of her husband's reaction to Mell being a woman. "Well all of us here knew right from the beginning you were a woman of course and tried to help you keep your secret. But after that boy exposed you to everyone else my husband wouldn't even let me speak your name never mind talk to him about keeping you on. He wouldn't even listen to me, bull headed man anyway!"

Mell chuckled at Mrs. Elton's reference to her husband's stubbornness then waved at the three, thankful to have such good friends. "I know and I appreciate everything you all have done for me over the years."

Mrs. Elton hugged Mell again before stepping back and grinned mischievously. "Come on let's go dazzle some men."

* * *

The mayor turned to Alec and grinned as he nodded his thanks for the brandy then sat down in a chair and settled back comfortably. "I can't believe your daughter is getting married after all these years."

Alec grimaced playfully as he held onto his chest dramatically as if in complete shock. "You can't believe it what about me? I've been harassing her for the last ten years to find a husband and make me a grandfather. For a while there I thought she might pick Brian but after she found how badly he treated Tommy, and that he had killed that Indian fellow she refused to talk to him much after that. Let alone marry him thank God! I've always suspected that there's something wrong with him for the last several years I've encouraged her to keep clear of him completely."

Mayor Elton nodded in understanding then waved anxiously as he changed the subject. "I appreciate how you feel Brian has always been a strange one. But to change the subject do you think Mell will quit her job now that she's getting married?"

"No it's not an option!" Both men were startled at the voice and they jumped slightly in guilt as they turned towards the door to see Jed entering the room with Giant Bear right behind him.

Jed grinned at the two men in apology as he gestured calmly. "Sorry to make you jump but the answer to your question is definitely no! Mell and I've already talked it over she will remain as Sheriff and I'll be her Deputy. However, if or when she gets pregnant I'll take over as Sheriff for as long as necessary. Then she will resume her job and I'll return to my job as Deputy."

Mayor Elton shook his head in amazement as he eyed Jed in respect. He shook his head incredulously. "I'm glad you're the one involved in this. I could never stand for my wife being that strong willed and independent! Of course it would be unthinkable for her to take on a job like Mell's in the first place."

Jed just smirked good-naturedly as he motioned consolingly. "Well gentleman, I wasn't sure I could either at first. But that was the major attraction that drew me to Mell and when you love someone it doesn't matter what she does, you'll support her either way. That and she's the exact opposite too my dead wife may God rest her soul."

Jed then turned to Giant Bear inquisitively as he pointed at him curiously. "What about you Giant Bear. Could you let your wife be that independent?"

Giant Bear frowned in thought for a moment. He slowly gave his answer as he nodded that he could not wanting any misunderstandings. "Yes Indian men are mostly dominant but there are stories in our history where a woman became a Medicine Woman and a Shaman. According to legend our first Chief was actually a woman, that's usually a man's calling. We also have a few brave hearted women like Mell as well they not only fight beside their men but perform many brave deeds."

Heads turned in surprise as Wade walked into the room dramatically then whistled outlandishly to get their attention as he pointed behind him teasingly. "Boy you guys better come out into the hall and see what visions I saw coming down the stairs!"

Jed and Giant Bear left the room first in an excited rush followed by Wade, while the mayor pushed Alec out a little more sedately to bring up the rear.

Jed stopped at the bottom of the stairs and stood there speechless for a moment! Could that vision floating down the stairs really be Mell! She was gorgeous! As she lifted up her skirt so she wouldn't trip on her dress a little higher to come down the stairs Jed couldn't help the grin that spread across his face. She wasn't wearing any slippers but was wearing the moccasins she always wore in the house! Well he wouldn't expect his hard-nosed lady sheriff to transform herself completely now could he.

Jed looked down at Mell's father as he heard the squeak of wheels beside him. Alec winked up at Jed in conspiracy. "Just like her mother always knew how to make an entrance!"

As each woman reached the bottom of the stairs they were claimed by their equally dazed partners and escorted into the drawing room for drinks since it was bigger than the den and more formal. Gloria had put in a few extra candles to light it up a little more. Shadows flickered almost eerily on the walls from the slight wind coming through the window, constantly moving the flames around.

For a while everyone mingled and talked about the day's events as they sipped their drinks companionably.

Mell walked over to the window and turned then stood quietly by herself observing her guests and fiancé critically. Jed was having a conversation with the mayor but every once in a while he would glance around looking for her almost as if he couldn't help himself. Their gazes would meet for a moment then satisfied he would return his attention back to the mayor reassured she was still there. Mell grinned in delighted pleasure to see him so formally decked out. He looked just as handsome in formal wear as he did in buckskins.

Her gaze scanned the room looking for her friends and found Giant Bear and Mary together. They looked so good and Mary looked happier then she had seen her in a long time. Giant Bear was wearing his ceremonial clothing and looked very impressive. He didn't look uncomfortable being in a white man's house at all and he seemed very tame compared to other Indian Chief's Mell knew. She wasn't sure if that was because Mary had such a calming effect on him, or if Jed had actually tamed him on their travels. Mell had a feeling that it was Mary that kept him in check, like a sleeping lion waiting to be released. Mary was very pretty in a deep blue dress with a white lace trimmed underskirt that she had borrowed from the clothes in the attic.

Mell looked to the right of Mary, at Wade and Gloria next they looked cozy cuddled in a corner. Gloria had chosen a grey silk top with a full black skirt, and a white petticoat peeked out at the bottom. Wade was handsome in a brown western style suit and he looked ecstatic.

Next Mell's glance fell on her father conversing with the mayor's wife. He had also dressed up for the occasion he was wearing his best black suit complimented by a snow-white shirt, and silver cuff links. She was always proud of him and he seemed happier than he had been in a very long time. Mell smiled in loving pride as her father threw back his head and laughed in delight at some remark Mrs. Elton made. It was so good to hear him laugh with such unrestrained humour. It had been a long time since she had heard him laugh that way.

The two were standing by the fireplace and Mell happened to look up at her mother's smiling portrait. At that moment a puff of wind danced the candles flames and Mell saw her mother's mouth move eerily almost as if her smile widened in approve. Mell blinked and suddenly everything was back to the way it had been. Mell shivered slightly in reaction then looked away hurriedly.

Mell stared at Mrs. Elton she looked beautiful as usual with her sandy blonde hair up. Her deep blue eyes sparkled in mirth as she laughed with her father. Her spectacles kept slipping down her nose every time she looked down at him. She was slim and petite at four foot nine inches tall and her husband was huge compared to her. Mell had always giggled when she saw them together Mrs. Elton could walk under her husband's arm without even misplacing a hair on her head.

Mell had been afraid of Mrs. Elton at first when they had first met and not just because she was afraid of being discovered. But because Mell had met a lot of Ladies like Mrs. Elton and they had always looked down their noses at Mell because she preferred to be in pants then in a dress. Mrs. Elton had calmly taken her aside on their second meeting and informed Mell that as long as she didn't disgrace the town or her husband she wouldn't let on that she knew Mell was a woman, and the two had been friends ever since. Mrs. Elton was a Lady in every sense of the word but she didn't put on airs as others did and Mell was grateful to have her as her friend.

Mell's inspection was broken suddenly and she jumped slightly as Gloria touched her arm unexpectedly. "Mell your father asked the widow Donaldson to come and serve supper tonight. I forgot to tell you upstairs."

Mell smiled in appreciation then sighed in relief. "I'm glad he thought of it because I sure didn't."

Gloria grinned at the apologetic tone of Mell's voice then she shrugged in understanding. "Well you had a lot on your mind but I think he had another motive for inviting her."

Mell frowned puzzled by that remark as she gestured curiously in confusion. "What motive are you talking about Gloria?"

Gloria smiled mysteriously as she waved toward Alec in explanation. "Well in all the years I've known your father he's never once went to the kitchen except for meals. Coffee and snacks I usually bring to him unless you're around then he will sit in the kitchen with you. Since Mrs. Donaldson has been here he's been in and out of the kitchen all day with the lamest excuses."

Mell pondered that bit of information for a moment in surprise as she stared over at her father for a moment. She looked back at Gloria as she gestured slightly in disbelief. "You don't think that he has feelings for her, do you?"

Gloria frowned seriously in worried speculation. "You wouldn't mind if he's found somebody else would you?"

Mell instantly shook her head negatively in reassurance at Gloria's expression. "No, in fact it would ease my mind a lot if I knew that someone would be here to care for dad if something ever happened to me. It just comes as a bit of a shock I had no idea he liked anyone."

Gloria enthusiastically nudged Mell gently as she waved towards Alec knowingly. "Well, keep your eye on them tonight I'll bet you there's another romance brewing. Oh there's Tommy supper must be ready."

Everyone instantly paired up for supper.

Mell called Tommy over to her then motioned towards her father. "Tommy will you please push my father into the dining room for me?"

Tommy nodded as he walked over then he whispered up at Mell curiously as he gestured towards his mother in bewilderment. "Aunt Mell what's with my mother and Giant Bear?"

Mell put her arm around Tommy and gave him a hug of reassurance before pushing him gently towards her dad. "You'll have to wait until after supper Tommy then your mother is going to have a talk with you."

Tommy nodded in puzzled agreement then went over and whispered something in Alec's ear, without asking any more questions. Alec nodded in permission up at Tommy, and Tommy proudly wheeled him into the dining room.

After everyone was seated Mell called Tommy over to her again she waited until he got closer than she waved towards the bunkhouse in invitation. "Tommy I talked to Dusty earlier and you're invited to join the men tonight for supper."

Tommy's expression brightened then he sobered in seriousness as he asked Mell one more question before he left. "Okay Aunt Mell, but before I go is Giant Bear my father?"

Mell looked across the table at Mary with an eyebrow lifted in question. Mary knew what she was asking and nodded her head vigorously in permission.

Mell turned back to Tommy and inclined her head in agreement gently. "Yes Tommy Giant Bear's your father."

The young boy's face lit up in joy as he smiled smugly at figuring that one out by himself. "Good!"

Tommy turned and raced out of the room without a word to his mother or his long lost father.

Mell glanced towards Mary and watched the tears fill her eyes sympathetically then Mell grinned over in encouragement. Mary smiled back bravely then Giant Bear took her hand and whispered his own support to her so she turned away from Mell.

Mell looked at the food that was already on the table and smiled knowingly. Mrs. Donaldson had made most of Mell's father's favourite food. There was a beef pot roast with carrots, potatoes, green beans, and turnip artfully set up in the middle of the table. Over to the left of there was fresh baked bread. She had also made cabbage with a cream sauce. There were two bottles of thirty-year old red wine, out of the cellar, to go with the pot roast.

Mrs. Donaldson came in just as Mell finished examining the table. Brad following her obediently with a pot of soup probably french onion if Mrs. Donaldson stayed true to Alec's tastes.

Mell really looked at Mrs. Donaldson for the first time and liked what she saw. Her hair was a shocking red with just a hint of grey at the temples. She was a tall and willowy woman, but not too skinny. She was in her late thirties and had a very pleasant smile. Her eyes were a deep green almost emerald and they held a hint of mischief and honesty. Mell could also see determination with a hint of a temper that probably went with her red hair.

Mrs. Donaldson went to Mell's father first and dished him up some soup. Then she bent down conspiringly to whisper something to Alec, which made him laugh in delight. She also took the opportunity to touch him lightly before she went to the next person.

Mell turned and smiled at Gloria who had been watching her expression anxiously not sure whether Mell would approve or not. Gloria sighed in relief as Mell nodded her blessings.

The rest of the evening passed quickly toasts were given to everyone's continued health and happiness. The mayor and his wife departed after expressing their sentiments that the evening had been very successful but declined the offer of staying for the night even though it was late. The mayor joked that the horses new the way home and he could sleep on route if he got too tired.

* * *

As Mell and Jed were getting ready for bed she turned shy again. "Can you turn your back while I put my nightshirt on?"

Jed shook his head negatively as he waved towards Mell's nightgown in disapproval. "I'll turn around while you take your dress off, but as to the nightie sorry no nightclothes allowed in bed."

Mell blushed furiously then nodded. While Jed's back was turned she struggled to get out of her dress. After a few moments of silence except for the rustle of clothes Jed heard her use a few choice cuss words. He winced slightly at a particularly vulgar word that he had never even heard before. Trying not to laugh at the frustrated curses she was using he asked mildly with his back still turned. "Having trouble Mell?"

Mell growled in frustrated anger. "Yes I can't get out of this damn dress, could you come and help me please?"

Jed turned around slowly then couldn't help but burst out in uncontrollable mirth at the sight of Mell. She had managed to tangle herself up in her dress and petticoats. It now looked like the petticoat was the dress and it was twisted around her backwards. How she had managed that he wasn't sure.

It took him a few moments to stop laughing before he could even move towards her to help out. He courteously turned his back once she was straightened out. He waited until he heard the blankets rustling before turning around. He blew out the candle then started undressing to spare her any more embarrassment. But the moon was still large enough that Mell had light too see by.

Mell grinned in pleasure as she watched Jed undress realizing he didn't know that she could see him in the near darkness. She couldn't help asking him curiously. "Jed did you notice anything different about my father today?"

Jed shook his head negatively then remembered it was dark, so answered cautiously not sure where her question was going. "No not really except that he seemed very happy."

Mell decided to be more direct as she sighed in exasperation. "Did you notice that he paid a lot of attention to Mrs. Donaldson?"

Jed shrugged thoughtfully as he remembered the evening but continued to undress. "Well yes, but I think he was just trying to make her feel more comfortable and welcome."

Mell shook her head negatively men just didn't notice anything unless it was pointed out to them. "No that's not it I think he really likes her. Do you think that now I'm getting married he feels free to find a lady friend or maybe even a wife, since he doesn't have to stay here and worry about me anymore?"

Jed got into bed and sighed plaintively as he held up the blankets inviting Mell to move closer as he changed the subject. "I really couldn't say Mell, but forget about your father for the moment. Come on over here and give your husband-to-be a kiss I've been waiting for this all night."

Mell turned towards Jed obediently then cuddled up against him so he could have his way with her as he draped the blankets around them. He sat up slightly then propped himself up on his elbow as he turned on his side and bent his head to kiss her passionately.

He flicked his tongue out as he backed off a little and began lightly tracing her lips with his tongue before pushing it inside her mouth to deepen the kiss. Jed lifted his head up further and kissed her eyes first then her cut little nose before going down to her stubborn chin. He moved to Mell's side then flicked his tongue around her ear lobe before traveled slowly down to her neck as he gently bit her.

Jed scooted down further on the bed still propped on his arm as he nibbled his way downwards until he reached her breast. When he found her nipple he gently nipped it before he soothed the bite by flicking his tongue around it.

In response Mell moaned in delight and ecstasy arching her body in invitation wanting more, of what she wasn't sure she just wanted more.

Jed began suckling harder and deeper on the nipple at Mell's obvious enjoyment. Mell cried out in exquisite pleasure at the feelings racing through her body still wanting more.

Jed let his fingers stroll lightly teasingly down her belly once he was sure she was ready for him until he reached her thighs. Mell trustingly opened her legs to accommodate him without any hesitation this time. The trust Mell showed made Jed grin in relief against her nipple, he rewarded her by lightly stroking her bud with his fingertip. While Mell was distracted by Jed's finger he brought his head down and nibbled on her belly until she was squirming in delight.

Jed prolonged the pleasure as long as he could as he peeked up watching Mell's reaction intently as she giggled and writhed. While she was still distracted trying to get away from his teasing lips he lifted himself up then laid completely within her thighs.

Mell jumped in shock not realizing what he was up too at first as his tongue flicked out suddenly and touched her bud for the first time intimately. She shivered in hesitant surprise not sure if she liked the feeling at first, but as his tongue continued to caress her the feelings of astonishment slowly disappeared as the pleasure took over and she relaxed slightly. It wasn't until he removed his tongue then began rubbing her bud more firmly with his thumb that she was able to let go totally and enjoy the moment.

Jed removed his hand once he felt her relax completely. He began massaging her thighs as he slowly pushed her legs farther apart to give himself more room. He continued to push them up until her knees were sticking up in the air and he was satisfied. This gave Jed better access to her inner heat then without warning he parted her petals and plunged his tongue inside her to taste her juices.

Mell gasped in scandalized pleasure as she whimpered slightly in protest. So he brought his mouth up to her bud again and began lightly suckling then lapping at it before she could objection.

Jed lifted his hand and carefully pushed his finger inside her secret place. He didn't want to accidentally pierce her maidenhood in his eagerness. Mell gave a slight muffled scream of disbelief as she climaxed long and hard.

She was still seeing stars when she felt Jed lift his head then laid it on her belly to give her time to recover. Mell reached down absently and ran her hands through his hair but didn't speak totally thunderstruck and out of breath as the tremors of pleasure continued racing through her body uncontrollably.

Mell felt dazed she had never experienced anything like this before. When she got her breathing under control again tears filled her eyes unexpectedly.

Jed lifted himself of her hastily, he had been watching her closely not sure what her reaction would be as he scooted up the bed then gathered her in his arms in concern and fear. "Did I hurt you Mell?"

Mell mutely shook her head in denial.

Jed frowned in worry not convinced in the least since she was still crying as he propped himself up on his arm again, so he could study her expression intently. "Then why are you crying?"

Mell took a deep unsteady breath and wiped her tears away angrily as she shrugged confused. Since her mother had died she had hardly ever cried and now since meeting Jed that's all she seemed to do any more. She reached up tenderly and stroked Jed's face in reassurance as she tried to explain her tears. "You didn't hurt me Jed. On the contrary I've never felt such pleasure before, I'm just so happy that's why I'm crying!"

Jed sighed in relief as Mell dropped her hand and cuddled closer. Women were strange sometimes. He still wasn't sure what to do so he laid down and just held her quietly until she got herself under control.

Suddenly without any warning she sat up the tears completely gone, as if they had never existed, as she exclaimed in speculation and revelation. She turned slightly and looked down at Jed in amazement. "You weren't kidding when you said love making gets better were you!"

Jed chuckled in delight at Mell's quick mood change as she turned around further then bent down and started feathering light kisses on Jed's chest and neck as he teased in amusement. "Just wait until we're married the best is yet to come!"

Mell sighed against Jed's nipple plaintively as she whispered. "I'm not sure I'm going to live through it then!"

Jed laughed at Mell's response then he shuddered in pleasure as Mell suckled on his nipple then mischievously bit it playfully. Mell then transferred her attention to his other nipple giving it just as much attention as the other one had.

Jed groaned deep in his throat and gave a slight gasp of surprise as Mell let her lips travel down to his stomach without him having to prompt her in anyway.

Mell realized that he was ticklish as he giggled slightly and squirmed so she spent several minutes digging her fingers into his ribs as he laughed startled at Mell's playfulness then he gasped for breath in delight when Mell moved her head lower and just laid there with her head on his belly gazing at his manhood curiously.

Of course it was too dark to see details but light enough with the moon shining through the window to see the size and shape of him. Then she reached out experimentally and tentatively lifted it up to feel the texture, shape, and size of him.

Jed groaned in amusement as he watched Mell curiously trying to see in the dark then he moaned as she finally decided it was too dark to see so lifted it up and used her hand to inspect it instead.

Satisfied at the feel of him she let him go then reached down further and picked up his sac then squeezed gently feeling the hard little pebbles inside with her hand curiously wondering how that little sac could produce babies.

Jed gasped in torture as he tried patiently to wait for Mell to finish her inspection. Mell let go of his sac then picked up his manhood again and frowned intriguingly as she noticed some fluid on the tip. She hesitated for a second then finally bent her head and hesitantly touched her tongue to the tip of his manhood to taste it.

Jed groaned and arched up slightly in encouragement as she took the tip of his manhood into her mouth and suckled gently. Jed squirmed in ecstasy and sucked in his breath stunned waiting to see what she would do next. He wasn't sure if he could stand much more of this agonizing pleasure.

Mell smiled in satisfaction at Jed's gasps of delight as she lifted her head up to look up at him as her hand continued to caress him intimately. Jed couldn't hold back any longer as he exploded with a groan of disappointment. He had hoped to prolong this a little longer but Mell's inquisitive innocence wouldn't allow that.

Mell looked back down instantly and watched Jed's manhood empty itself then she bent down once more and tentatively touched the tip of his manhood with her tongue to see what it would taste like. Jed's manhood bucked once more in her hand in reaction as if trying to rise again but then it started shrinking slowly unable to rise so soon. Mell squinted and watched in fascination wondering how something that large could shrink to something that small and so quickly. Mell looked up at Jed to find him smiling broadly at her interest.

He reached down and pulled her up beside him on the bed for a deep kiss then propped himself up and stared down at her tenderly. "I can leave the candle on tomorrow night if you want?"

Mell nodded eagerly up at him. "Yes I would like that."

Jed chuckled at her earnest expression as he teased. "Well, what do you think of your second lesson in the art of pleasing your husband?"

Mell smiled up at him mischievously. "I like it I never expected lovemaking to be so enjoyable, if I had known sooner! I might have tried it long before now."

Jed growled in simulated anger then proceeded to tickle Mell unmercifully for her impertinence. Mell wriggled around trying to get away from him laughing and gasping as her eyes filled with tears of mirth. Finally she couldn't stand the tickling any more as she gasped out desperately in surrender. "I give up I was only joking!"

Jed grinned down at her devilishly as he teased her playfully. "Don't you forget that I'm the man…The only man for you!"

Mell giggled again in delight then sighed in contentment as she reached up and gently stroked Jed's face tenderly as she whispered lovingly. "I love you so much Jed!"

Jed gathered her close to him as he smiled. "I love you too."

He gently kissed her then laid back on the bed for some much needed sleep, but then decided to continue the conversation Mell had started earlier about her father. "Now we can talk about your dad are you worried that he might like Mrs. Donaldson?"

Mell shook her head negatively as she turned her head towards Jed to talk. "No not worried really I was watching them at dinner and they look good together."

Jed smiled in sympathy as he too turned his head to watch her expression remembering Mell's pain when discussing her mother. "You don't resent the fact that your father is thinking of another woman are you?"

Mell analyzed her feelings closely then shook her head decisively. "No my mother's been dead a long time now and it would relieve my mind if there was someone else out there who would love him if something ever happened to me."

Jed sat up instantly and propped himself up so he could see her face better as he vowed solemnly. "Nothing is going to happen to you I promise."

Mell frowned up at him in earnest warning. "Don't make pledges you might not be able to keep. The job we do is very dangerous and sometimes events are beyond our control."

Jed sighed in reluctant agreement then changed the subject again. "I talked to your father tonight."

Mell's eyebrows lifted inquisitively in surprise. "Oh, and what did you talk about?"

Jed smiled reassuringly and tweaked her nose playfully. "We just talked about the ranch and maybe putting cattle on here. He said I didn't need to buy more land right now because the land you have will support four or five hundred head."

Mell nodded thoughtfully. "That's true and if you're going to try cattle you shouldn't get too big at first until you decide whether you want to stick with it or not."

Jed grinned at that good advice. "You're right I'll start slowly and work up to a full herd. Your father also said that I couldn't buy any cattle because there's more than enough money in the ranch accounts to pay for the cattle I need. But he did suggest I do the same thing he did when he moved here and invest in the ranch instead of just the cattle."

Mell frowned curiously wondering where this conversation was going. "Yes that's what he did we had the ranch appraised and he gave me half the value so that we would be equal partners. But because you're going to be my husband you will already have part of my share so you don't need to worry about that."

Jed scowled irritably as he shook his head earnestly in denial. "No the ranch is yours and unless I invest in it I don't want anything to do with it."

Mell sighed puzzled by Jed's adamant refusal at sharing the ranch with her. "So you're asking me if you can invest in the ranch is that it?"

Jed nodded emphatically. "Yes, would you mind if I invested in your ranch?"

Mell shook her head in impatience. "Well why didn't you just say so I don't mind at all but you don't have too what's mine is yours."

Jed smiled down at her impatient tone then nodded decisively. "Yes I must or I wouldn't feel like I'm a part of it. I would just feel like I'm using you and we don't want that."

Mell reached up and brought his head down for a deep kiss too cut him off. When she finally let him go she smiled up at him encouragingly. "Jed whatever makes you feel more comfortable and happy here, is okay with me!"

Jed laid back and pulled her against him sleepily content now that he had that conversation out of the way. "Okay, but I still had to make sure you wouldn't mind."

Mell turned then cuddled closer as she yawned sleepily. "Good night, I love you."

Jed chuckled in delight, as Mell's yawn, almost drowned out her goodnight. "I love you too good night."

CHAPTER THIRTEEN

Tommy woke earlier than usual as he jumped out of bed eagerly and quickly got dressed in anticipation. He raced down the stairs to the kitchen forgetting his Aunt's rule about running in the house in his excitement.

Mrs. Donaldson jumped in surprise as Tommy came barrelling through the kitchen door and almost collided with her. Tommy came to an abrupt halt and gestured in apology as he looked up at the red headed new addition to the household sheepishly. "Oh I'm sorry Mrs. Donaldson I didn't think anyone would be up yet."

Mrs. Donaldson grinned as she reached over and ruffled his hair playfully. "It's all right Tommy but where are you going in such a hurry?"

Tommy's smile turned shy almost instantly as he shrugged in embarrassment. "I wanted to grab some breakfast for me and Gi...I mean my father."

Mrs. Donaldson turned away to hide the tears that suddenly sprang to her eyes at Tommy's hesitation. She walked over to the oven to give herself time then took a pan of freshly baked buns out and set them on the counter. Alec had told her Tommy's story the night before, but she didn't think Tommy would appreciate any sympathy. Once the buns were on the counter she turned back to Tommy her emotions back under control and waved towards the cupboard above the counter. "I'll put some butter on some of these buns for you if you look up there you'll find some apples."

Tommy nodded happily as he turned towards the cupboard indicated then put two of them in his pockets.

Mrs. Donaldson finished putting butter on the promised buns then placed them in a basket that she saw sitting on the back of the counter. She added a few strawberries that she had found in the cellar from last year. It was the last of them, along with a small jar of cream and two spoons. She started putting porridge into a bowl next.

Tommy walked over closer to Mrs. Donaldson then looked at her earnestly. He fidgeted for a moment undecided whether he should ask her or not then finally blurted out in a rush before he could change his mind. "Mrs. Donaldson do you think Giant Bear would mind if I called him father?"

Mrs. Donaldson caught off guard by such a personal question from the young Tommy, finished putting the porridge into the second bowl to give herself a moment. Hoping her answer wouldn't get Giant Bear into any trouble as she put them into the basket. She looked over then smiled at Tommy in encouragement as she turned with basket in hand and held it out to Tommy. "I'm sure he'd love that Tommy your mother is with your father now, so when you go wake them up tell your mother to come and see me. I could use a helping hand today."

Tommy beamed shyly in thanks as he took the basket then he grinned up at her eagerly. "Thanks Mrs. Donaldson I'll send my mother over right away."

Tommy raced out of the room with his father's breakfast carefully held out, not wanting to spill anything inside, feeling grateful to Mrs. Donaldson for providing him with an excuse to visit with his father alone without hurting his mother's feelings. Tommy reached the barn door then slipped inside carefully and walked to the bottom of the ladder. He looked up at the loft earnestly then fidgeted for a moment suddenly unsure of himself. He mustered his courage then called up hesitantly. "Mom, can I come up?"

Mary's head popped over the top of the ladder instantly as she grinned down at him in pleasant surprise. "Just wait down there Tommy we'll be right down."

Tommy turned dutifully away from the ladder then went over to a pile of straw and sat his basket down beside it before plopping down gleefully waiting patiently in anticipation. He looked towards the ladder expectantly but the minutes ticked by without either parent showing themselves. To remind his mother he was there he called out too eager to wait any longer. "Mom Mrs. Donaldson needs you in the kitchen today she said."

Tommy heard his mother mumble something but didn't catch what she said. He sighed resignedly and waited disgruntled now but tried to be tolerant. It wasn't long before Mary came down the ladder, although it seemed like forever to her son, she stood in front of him then grinned down at his displeased expression but didn't feel one bit sorry.

She laughed at his look and squatted down for a good morning hug. It wasn't until she stood back up that she noticed the basket. Mary cocked her head curiously as she looked back at her son inquisitively. "What do you have they're Tommy?"

Tommy got up eagerly before whispering in conspiracy. "I brought some breakfast for me and my…. father."

Mary hugged Tommy in encouragement with a sad sigh at his uncertainty then held him away so she could see his face as she frowned in concern. "You're not too upset at me are you Tommy, finding out about your father the way you did?"

Tommy moved back then thought about it for a moment. He shook his head negatively in reassurance as he looked at his mother. "No, I'm just glad I have a father! Do you think he would mind if I hung around him today?"

Giant Bear stepped into the light having stayed in the background listening, not wanting to intrude. He smiled in encouragement down at his son as he nodded pleased that he wanted to spend time with him. "I would be very happy to have you with me today son!"

Mary grinned up at her husband in loving praise. "You speak a lot better English now than when we first met. I can see you'll have no trouble talking to Tommy, so I'll go now, and leave the two of you alone to get acquainted."

Giant Bear kissed his wife good-bye then reached up and tweaked her nose playfully. "You can thank Jed for the English lessons. He taught me well!"

Mary nodded she would definitely thank Jed for his good teaching abilities then she turned to her son for a final good-bye. "I'll see you two later."

Mary turned and slipped out the door quickly.

Tommy and Giant Bear stood regarding each other assessingly for a moment in silence. Tommy broke the silence as he smiled hesitantly up at his father then waved down at the basket he had brought. "I have some breakfast for us. I wasn't sure what you would like but Mrs. Donaldson helped me put it together."

Tommy's voice trailed off uncomfortably, as if unsure of what to say next, unnerved by his father's silence. Giant Bear moved closer to his son then put a hand on his shoulder in reassurance. "Whatever you have there will be fine with me."

Tommy nodded in relief then squatted down to unwrap everything blissfully as his father knelt beside him.

* * *

Mary went to the back entrance of the house and slipped into the kitchen. The delicious smells wafting in the air caused her to inhale deeply in appreciation then her belly rumbled loudly in hunger, causing her to grimace in embarrassment. She turned towards Mrs. Donaldson as she heard a chuckle behind her. Mary smiled in delight as she rubbed her belly hungrily. "Something sure smells good! I'm starving!"

Mrs. Donaldson nodded knowingly, having heard Mary's belly give her away, with a big grin. She motioned in reproach as she waved away the Mrs. "First of all, please call me Jessica all my friends do. Secondly, with all the excitement going on around here someone had to make sure everyone eats properly. Sit down please I was expecting you so I have your breakfast all ready."

Mary smirked cheekily at Jessica as she sat down obediently in grateful thanks. "Thank you for giving me such a good excuse so I could leave my son and husband alone, that way they can get to know one another without my interference."

Mary looked down then inhaled deeply in appreciation as Jessica sat a bowl of hot porridge with strawberries and cream in front of her. She looked back up at Jessica then grinned gratefully in anticipation. "Oh my favourite thank you!"

Jessica beamed down in satisfaction at Mary's obvious pleasure in the breakfast she had painstakingly made. She pointed upwards at the ceiling in explanation. "I already took breakfast to Mell and Jed I'm just about to take some to Alec. Once everyone finishes eating we'll all meet here in the kitchen to discuss decorations, dresses, and what not! Oh I almost forgot will you tell Mell if she comes down before I get back that Mrs. Elton will be here soon as well. She told me last night that she would pick up the material for the dresses, that's her wedding present to you Ladies, on her way back she will also pick up Jane and Sarah to help make them."

Mary grinned up in relief at having more helping hands on such short notice then nodded in appreciation. "That's good when I finish my breakfast I'll start making some bread while I wait for everyone else to arrive."

Jessica turned away from Mary satisfied everything was in control then picked up the breakfast tray she had waiting, and hurried down the hall to Alec's room in anticipation. She knocked softly then hesitated for a moment as she heard Alec's muffled call from inside the room. "Come in!"

Jessica shook off her nerves then entered with a flourish and walked quickly over to the bed before he could protest that it wasn't proper for her to be there. She put the tray across Alec's lap before removing the cloth dramatically. Nervously she began rearranging things on the tray trying to hide her uneasiness as best she could. Finally she peeked down at Alec shyly, but with a slight hint of invitation in her face. She made sure though that it wasn't too obvious. Alec smiled in thanks up at her in appreciation for her efforts. "Thank you it looks delicious!"

Jessica smiled bashfully at Alec's approval then turned away. Sure he had gotten her subtle message and went over to open the drapes to let the sunshine in. From there she went over to the closet and pulled out the chair. Mell had told her this morning where to find it when Jessica had asked. She pushed it across the room and set it within easy reach. She then returned to the closet and called out over her shoulder inquisitively. "What would you like to wear today?"

Alec finished his breakfast quickly then sat back with a contented sigh. He sipped his coffee thoughtfully as he watched Jessica. Of course he had noticed the invitation plain in her glance, but wasn't totally sure what she meant by it. He watched her take out his chair then go back in his closet. He heard her muffled question and thought about it for a moment before answering her. "I think my black pants and blue shirt will do for today."

Jessica rummaged in the closet until she found the required garments. She brought them out along with socks and the moccasins he liked to wear inside. She walked over to the bed and deposited everything within easy reach of his hand. Jessica turned away slightly so Alec couldn't see her sly smirk as she asked with a hint of hope in her voice, that she tried hard to hide, but wasn't quite successful. "Do you need any help?"

Alec coughed slightly to clear his throat so Jessica wouldn't hear the laughter in his voice as he caught a quick glimpse of Jessica's crafty smile. He shook his head negatively. "No thank you Jessica I think I can manage now."

Alec patted the bed beside him in silent invitation between the enticement in Jessica's eyes and the sly hopeful smirk he finally figured it was time for a serious talk. "Come sit for a moment."

Jessica hesitantly sat on the edge of the bed ready to jump up if he made an improper advance and she quivered slightly in hope. She had waited a long time for this with any luck he would finally ask. Alec smiled at her shy uncertainty.

He put his coffee cup down on the tray and removed it to the bedside table out of the way. He turned back to face Jessica then reached over and took her hand in his tenderly. "Jessica, look at me."

Jessica turned until she was facing Alec fully then looked him straight in the eye boldly unafraid but nervous just the same. Alec squeezed her hand gently in encouragement as he continued more sure now of himself with what he saw in Jessica's eyes. "We have known each other for several years now and we have both been widowed for a long time. I have a proposition for you."

Jessica tensed instantly thinking the worst and her emerald eyes flashed dangerously giving away her thoughts. Alec just chuckled in delight at the spirit and fire he saw plainly in her eyes. He held up his free hand in apology before she could say anything. "I'm sorry I'm not doing this very well, but hear me out before you yell at me."

Jessica's eyes softened instantly in understanding then she nodded slightly in confusion not saying a word waiting for him to finish, still very much hoping to hear what she wanted. Alec smiled in relief as he saw Jessica's eyes soften slightly and he put his free hand on top of their locked hands. Then he tried to explain again this time in a different way. "I loved my wife very much and when she died I didn't think I could ever feel that way again. It didn't really matter to me because Mell needed me so much at the time. I sometimes wonder if I would have survived my wife's death if Mell hadn't needed me. But now Mell is getting married and I finally feel that I'm ready to try living again. I'll always have a place in my heart reserved for my dead wife of course, but I would like to try love again. Not too many people know this but I'm fairly well off and I've always wanted to travel, but I didn't want to go alone. I have liked you very much for a long time so I wanted to ask you this. After Mell is settled would you like to come with me? We could get married quietly later if you are concerned about your reputation, but we don't have to if you would rather not. Then we could live here after were done traveling and help Mell and Jed with the ranch."

Jessica smiled radiantly at Alec but ignored the, if you would rather not question in relief, then nodded emphatically in eagerness. "Yes I'll marry you and I must tell you that I have thought a lot about you for a long time too! I also loved my husband with an intense passion but like you I feel it's time to put him away. I think we can find as great a passion together as we had with our dead spouses. But I think it will be a little different too, more comfortable maybe, not as all consuming. I'm not sure if that's the right words or not I hope you know what I mean though."

Alec smiled in understanding then chuckled knowingly. "Believe it or not I think I do. Even though I'm in a wheelchair I can still make love to a woman so the passion part is no problem either!"

Jessica blushed deeply then leaned forward boldly. "I'm so glad to hear that."

Alec's response was smothered in slight surprise as Jessica took the initiative and claimed his lips for a deep kiss. Alec broke the kiss reluctantly and sighed regretfully as he pulled away. "As much as I would like to stay here and prove to you that I can still make love to a woman, everybody is probably waiting for us. I hope you don't mind but I would like to keep this quiet for a while. At least till after the young one's are married. Jed wants to take Mell to Boston on a honeymoon so maybe we could meet them there and have a quiet wedding, if that's okay with you?"

Jessica sat up slightly breathless and smiled sweetly in satisfaction, glad she had initiated the kiss it was more of a test than anything else, and she had been proven right as her body tingled then flushed slightly in passion. "I agree that we shouldn't say anything right now, I like the thought of a quiet Boston wedding. There's no one I would care to invite except my children who won't come no matter where it is. So that suits me just fine! As for living here, I like that idea as well, I've always admired your daughter even before I met you."

Alec pulled a surprised and giggling Jessica down for one more passionate kiss. He let her help him get dressed after all. There was a lot of laughter and wrestling before he was ready but both were happier then they had been in many years. It showed clearly in their sparkling eyes.

* * *

Mary finished up the promised bread then put it to the side to rise before covering it with a towel. She was just turning away to get herself a cup of coffee when Jed and Mell came in. Mell took the breakfast tray from Jed and put it the counter then turned to Mary with a grateful smile as she accepted two cups of coffee from a grinning Mary. Mary passed on Jessica's good news about the mayor's wife coming with extra help as they each found a chair at the table. They just sat down when Wade and Gloria arrived and they too found seats.

Jessica pushing Alec's wheelchair arrived last. Both were still slightly flushed from their playful bout in the bedroom. They tried hard to hide their red faces as Jessica pushed Alec to his spot at the head of the table, before sitting in the last chair.

Mary instantly jumped up and got the newcomers a cup of coffee before taking her seat once more. It took a few minutes before order was restored when it was they all sat quietly sipping coffee in contemplation, each deep in their own thoughts.

Mell shook off her thoughts of last night then looked around at all her friends and grinned in contented pleasure. Her gaze rested on Mrs. Donaldson and she beamed across the table at the red head trying to put her at ease, as she noticed a slight flush in the widow's cheeks. Mell mistook the flush for embarrassment so tried to make her feel more welcome as she leaned forward earnestly. "How's the guest room Mrs. Donaldson comfortable I hope?"

Jessica smiled at Mell, before glancing around and included everyone in her look, she turned back to answer Mell as she motioned pleadingly. "Please everyone call me Jessica no more 'Mrs.' it makes me feel old. To answer your question I slept very well thank you."

Mell was the first one to hear the carriage and instantly she got up in excitement, but before she hurried out, she turned to Gloria. "I'll go see about the Ladies, Gloria will you make some more coffee then get everyone settled in the dining room. It's much bigger and we won't be so crowded in there."

Mell rushed out of the kitchen, after Gloria nodded in agreement, then down the hallway. She opened the front door and was instantly enveloped in a big hug. Mell laughed in delight and pushed away from an ecstatic Jane. "Well hello there I'm so glad you came today."

Jane smiled broadly as she let her friend go reluctantly. "Wouldn't miss it for the world, besides I need to see where I'll be living from now on don't I!"

Mell laughed in delight at Jane's boldness. "To the point as usual, well if you'll follow me I'll show you where you and your family will be living."

Mell turned to Mrs. Elton then gestured in invitation. "You and Sarah can come too if you want?"

Mrs. Elton smiled regretfully then shook her head negatively. "No I think we'll go and visit with everybody else if you don't mind. I want to introduce Sarah anyway."

Mell nodded then stepped out of the doorway and waved down the hallway to the right. "They're all in the dining room waiting for you tell them we'll be back in a few minutes."

Mell grabbed Jane by the hand in excitement not even bothering to change out of her moccasins. She ran down the porch to the stairs pulling Jane along insistently. Jane pulled back from Mell and laughed heartily, slightly out of breath. "Mell slow down just because you wear pants don't mean the rest of us do!"

Mell blushed slightly in embarrassment as she let go of Jane's hand reluctantly. She turned to her and gestured in apology. "Oh sorry Jane I forgot myself."

Jane grinned good-naturedly then reached over and grabbed Mell's hand then pulled her into a hearty embrace. "It's okay I forgive you."

Jane let Mell go and they walked the rest of the way more slowly chatted excitedly as they walked. They both quieted suddenly as they heard the banging of hammers before they got there and they quickened their steps slightly. Mell smiled over at Jane and motioned proudly at the frame of the building already stared. "This will be your cabin when it's ready."

Jane beamed radiantly over at Mell then she turned and gazed around in approval. "Wow this is a gorgeous spot I like it already."

Mell turned away from Jane at a loud shout coming from the direction of the new building. Brad raced over and swept Jane up then twirled her around playfully. He gave his wife a passionate kiss and hug before he set her back on her feet and stepping back. "I missed you last night."

Jane gazed adoringly at her husband then she reached up and stroked his cheek tenderly. "I missed you too."

Mell cleared her throat to get their attention and chuckled slightly as both her friends gave a guilty start at forgetting her presence. They turned to her with identical embarrassed expressions. She smirked then motioned at Brad in invitation. "Brad, show your wife the sketch of her new home?"

Brad nodded quickly trying to hide his discomfited face and pulled it out of his pocket. He showed it proudly to his wife in excitement. "See there's two bedrooms downstairs, a sitting room, and a kitchen. Then there's a loft upstairs that will be large enough for the girls to sleep in."

Jane smiled down in delight as she gazed at her new home. "Oh it's gorgeous thank you Mell with all my heart."

Jane turned and pulled Mell into another hug to show her gratitude. Mell squeezed Jane gently then grinned to herself. If Jane were going to be staying here she would have to get use to all this hugging. She was just one of those type of people that loved to show affection. Mell pushed her away tenderly. "Come on and I'll take you back to the house to meet everyone."

Jane nodded as she stepped back. She turned to her husband for one last kiss and hug. Both women turned away from Brad and hurried back to the house. They went straight to the dining room where everyone was impatiently waiting and talking. Mell made introductions then they all sat around drinking coffee and chatting eagerly waiting for Mell to tell them what was expected of them next.

Everyone quieted as Mell handed out assignments. She looked at each group as she called out their names to see if there were any objections to anything she had to say. "Okay everyone I would like Mrs. Elton, Sarah, Jane, and Jessica to make the dresses because they will take the longest. Gloria and Mary can do the cooking. Dad can do the invitations with my help and I'll deliver them when I go to work. I'll also gather supplies and decorations for the house while I'm in town. Wade I would like you to take Giant Bear and Tommy then gather poles and some of the planks the men are using to make me a platform and an archway for outside. I'll give you a sketch of what I want. The hands can keep building the cabins. Wade you and Giant Bear can help them after you're done making the archway and platform for me. Jed can also help Wade until I go to town then he can come help me with supplies and decorations. Anybody who finishes their tasks first can help wherever they think they can do the most good, would anybody like to add anything?"

Mrs. Elton spoke up instantly as she pointed in request at Mell. "Before you do anything we need measurements."

Mell grimaced not looking forward to standing in one place but she finally nodded as she got up. "Okay I'll meet you upstairs after I make the sketch of the archway and platform for Jed and Wade."

Mrs. Elton nodded satisfied then everyone got up and followed Mell out of the dining room to start their assignments. She moved out of the way so everyone could pass by her. Mell waited until her father came out before walking behind his chair then pushed him towards the den, while Jed and Wade followed behind. They entered and Mell pushed her father to the front of the desk then left him there, before going behind it.

Mell pulled her chair over then sat down as she took out paper, ink, and pen. Both Wade and Jed gathered close to Mell's father to watch what she was doing. Mell gave verbal instructions while she drew the design so they wouldn't miss anything. "Okay I want a raised platform putting the planks side by side but only tacking them together lightly so that they can be reused later when we are done with them. The platform is for the minister to stand on only so that the guests can see him clearly. You might want to add a lower platform in front so we can stand on it, that way everyone can see us too. I also want two poles about the size of your forearm, and tall enough so that the minister isn't blocked. I want another pole to nail across the top of the other two. This one doesn't have to be as wide, but it should be quite long. The archway should be placed about a foot in front of the platform so that we have to go through it first. It needs to be wide and tall enough so it isn't blocking the view. If you can try to peel the bark off the poles then tack the archway together. But don't put it up right away because we need to decorate it first."

Mell looked at her father inquisitively. "Dad, would you start making a list of names to send invitations too. Only make ones for people around here and in town there isn't enough time to invite people from too far away. I'll hand deliver them since most can't read, but they'd be upset if they didn't get one. I can always read it to them while I'm there. I'll take Jed and Wade out and show them where I want the platform set up while you do that."

Alec nodded when Mell looked in his direction then wheeled himself around the desk to start his list. Mell put her chair back in its corner then led Wade and Jed out of the den.

* * *

Mrs. Elton led her three helpers upstairs into the spare room. They pushed all the furniture into a corner to give themselves more space then started bringing in the supplies they needed from the wagon. Mary walked in just as they finished. She looked around until she spotted the mayor's wife then walked over to her and gestured apologetically. Knowing Mrs Elton had already gotten the material but she hoped that she could return it. "Mrs. Elton you only need to make two wedding dresses because I don't need one. I hope you can return the extra."

Mrs. Elton smiled slightly in relief that would give them more time to work on the other two, she wasn't worried about the extra material she would find a use for it sooner or later. She frowned in puzzlement. "Well it will definitely make it easier, but are you sure you don't need one?"

Mary bobbed her head emphatically as she waved towards her home. "I have my Indian bridal dress hidden at home and I think Giant Bear would like me to wear that, if nobody objects that is."

Mrs. Elton shrugged that it was okay by her. She motioned slightly in anxiety. "Well that makes sense, but I heard about the threats your brother made. Will you be able to get it before the wedding?"

Mary nodded vigorously as she pointed towards town. "Yes Brian goes to town every day at three o'clock. I was going to ask you if I could borrow your wagon for a bit to go gather some of my things while he's gone."

Mrs. Elton frowned apprehensively at the thought of Mary going to her brothers alone. She put her hand on Mary's arm in caution. "Sure you can use my wagon but I don't think you should go alone!"

Jane stepped forward immediately not liking the thought of Mary going by herself either. "I'll get my husband and we'll take her."

Mary smiled in thanks then grimaced slightly not wanting anyone else to get hurt if her brother showed up unexpectedly. She turned to Jane as Mrs. Elton's hand dropped from her arm. "That's very kind of you but are you sure? It could cause you and your husband trouble."

Jane beamed reassuringly then reached out and patted Mary's arm in support. "Nonsense! We'll be happy to help you."

The two women turned to leave but stopped short suddenly almost in guilty surprise, as they noticed Mell standing by the door. Mell scowled at the two conspirators chidingly. "I'll go with you as well, just in case Brian comes home unexpectedly. That way there's nothing he can do to stop you since the Sheriff is with you."

Mary's smile was a little strained as she nodded. "Okay, but you have time to have your measurements taken before we leave. I'll meet both of you downstairs when you're done here."

Mary left quickly and closed the door softly. Mell watched her leave in surprise then frowned pensively at the closed door in suspicion. "Well that was easier than I thought it would be. I was sure she would insist on going alone."

Jane laughed knowingly as Mell turned to her. "I think I'd better go down and keep an eye on her. I think you're right it was much too easy!"

Mell turned back into the room as Jane left, relieved now that she didn't have to worry about Mary slipping away by herself.

* * *

Twenty minutes later Mell was striding purposely towards the den to let her father know where she was going just in case there was any trouble. Mell knocked softly then walked in at her father's muffled response to enter. She walked to the desk then smiled down at her father in apology, when he looked up at her inquisitively. "Sorry but I'm going to have to run out on you, dad."

Alec grinned up at his daughter knowingly then laughed as he motioned teasingly. "That's okay I'm sure I can manage on my own. I just had this feeling that you'd find a way to get out of such a boring job as writing invitations."

Mell chuckled at her father's expression and walked around the desk then bent down to give her father a kiss. "Good I'm definitely not disappointing you then! Unfortunately I'm not looking forward to this either. I have to take Mary over to Brian's to collect her belongings. Writing invitations might be boring but it's probably safer."

Alec frowned slightly in apprehension but new better then to protest. He accepted her good-bye kiss then motioned in forewarning as she stood back up. "Okay but if you're not back by dark I'll send out the cavalry."

Mell chuckled as she walked towards the door she turned back as she opened it. Her expression now serious, she agreed with his statement that she might need cavalry. "Okay! See you later."

Mell closed the door behind her and was on her way to the front door when Jane met her in the hallway. Jane smiled then gestured chidingly. "There you are we're waiting for you! We saddled Lightning Mary didn't think you would want to ride in the wagon with us."

Mell smiled then nodded curtly. "She's right! One of us should have a horse for a quick getaway just in case."

Jane laughed in delight and disbelief all too aware of Mell's aversions to wagons. She stopped at the door as she waited for Mell to strap on her gun belt and change out of her moccasins. "That's the lamest excuse I've ever heard of for getting out of riding in a bouncing wagon."

Mell chuckled at being caught red handed by Jane as they headed out the door. She sobered in seriousness as she looked over at Jane. "It might be a lame excuse but a true one just the same."

Before they got within hearing distance of Mary and the others Jane leaned closer to Mell then whispered cautiously in warning. "It's a good thing I went to keep an eye on Mary. She was headed for the door when I went down the stairs. I pretended I didn't know what she was up to but I stayed close to her after that."

Mary scowled down angrily at Mell from the seat of the wagon when they reached her and she snapped irritably. "You sent Jane to watch me didn't you?"

Mell frowned up at her irritated friend and nodded decisively not sorry in the least that Mary was angry with her. "Yes I did! I know you don't want anyone else involved but think of it this way. If Brian came home unexpectedly he would lock you up and throw away the key. That would mean that Giant Bear, Jed, and I would have to come to your rescue. Do you really want your husband and brother to be fighting over you? One or both could end up dead!"

Mary sighed forlornly then nodded pacified she hadn't really wanted to go alone anyway. But hadn't wanted to ask Mary was just glad that her friend had found out in time. "You're right of course as usual. I'm sorry for snapping at you."

Mell reached up and took Mary's hand then squeezed it gently in support. "It's okay I forgive you!"

Mell let go of Mary then turned away to mount Lightning. She turned to Brad and nodded. "Okay let's get this over with!"

Brad nodded then clucked to the horses.

* * *

It took them several hours to reach Brian's ranch because of the wagon and Mell frowned in concern. It had taken longer than any of them had anticipated. Mary jumped down instantly without any assistance too impatient and afraid that too much time had passed. She hurried to the barn to make sure that Brian's horse was still gone. She came back in a rush a few minutes later and grinned in relief up at Mell. "His horse isn't here we only have a couple of hours at the most, if where lucky, before he gets back so let's hurry!"

Mell nodded as she dismounted then handed the reins to Brad after he helped his wife down. "You stay here and keep watch I'll call you when we need you."

Brad took Mell's reins then tied Lightning loosely to the back of the wagon. Mary led the way and ushered them into the house quickly. She called out questioningly as she looking around expectantly. "Mrs. Jenkins! Where are you?"

An older woman around sixty came out of the kitchen and hurried over to Mary in obvious relief. Mary was taken by surprise when the older lady rushed up to her then gave her a warm hug in greeting. "I've been so worried about you Mary! Brian's been storming around the house ever since the Sheriff came and told him you weren't coming back. He's been muttering nasty things under his breath ever since that he figures nobody could hear."

Mary smiled reassuringly as she gently pushed away from the elderly housekeeper. "I'm okay Mrs. Jenkins. I just come for my things."

Mrs. Jenkins frowned then wrung her hands in agitation as she eyed Mary pleadingly. "I'm sorry Mary but I have orders not to let you have anything."

Mell stepped away from the door with her badge pinned firmly on her shirtfront so the older lady could see it plainly. "It's okay Mrs. Jenkins I'm here to see that she gets her belongings without any problems."

The housekeeper smiled in relief then nodded. "Oh that's different, with you here Sheriff I can let her have them, but I can't help or I'll get fired."

Mary sighed in relief then reached out and patted her hand in sympathy. "That's okay Mrs. Jenkins, Mell and Jane is here to help me."

Mrs. Jenkins hurried back to the kitchen without another word. Mary beckoned Mell and Jane to follow her upstairs to her room. She pulled two large trunks out of her closet and started throwing things inside. "Just throw in everything you can find and I'll sort it out later."

Mell and Jane nodded then quickly followed her example. None of them bothered to fold anything or even looked at what they were packing. They just threw everything in the trunk that they could lift. When they finished Mary took a last look around then crawled under her bed to retrieve the two large parcels she had hidden there so very long ago. Not once in all these years did she dare take them out. She stuffed them in one of the trunks and they lashed the lid down securely. The three girls pushed and groaned as they dragged one then the other trunk to the top of the stairs. It had taken them nearly an hour to clean out Mary's room.

Mary sighed painfully as they got the trunks close to the stairs and she stood up in relief. "That's everything except for one more trunk downstairs in the storage room. It's my hope chest and already packed."

Jane nodded and started downstairs immediately as she called over her shoulder. "I'll get Brad to help with the trunks."

With that Jane hurried as fast as her chubby legs could go downstairs then outside. She returned a moment later with Brad. He grinned teasingly as he looked at Mary questioningly. "Just two trunks?"

Mary shook her head negatively then pointed downstairs. "No there is one more in the storage room but we can get that last."

Brad nodded then heaved one trunk up onto his broad shoulder and carried it downstairs by himself. The three women managed to carry the second one down on their own. By the time they reached the bottom of the stairs, Brad was back, and hefted it up then carried it out to the wagon. He returned quickly to join the others at the storage room where they were trying to push the hope chest out into the hallway. Brad tried to lift it by himself but it was too heavy, so they all joined forces, and got it outside then loaded it into the bed of the wagon with the others.

Just as they finished they heard the sound of horses approaching the ranch. Deadly silence fell as everyone froze instantly. Mell turned towards Brad and spoke urgently. "Untie Lightning and drop the reins then get the Ladies into the wagon as quickly as you can!"

Brad did as he was told and had just finished climbing into the wagon himself when the two horsemen entered the yard. Mell turned to face Brian immediately then waited for him to ride up and speak. Brian stopped in front of her then smiled triumphantly as he gestured insolently first at Mary then at Mell. "Well if it isn't my wayward sister and the Lady Sheriff! What the hell are you doing here sneaking around my house stealing things?"

Mell relaxed her stance and dropped her arms in readiness, just in case Brian got any foolish ideas, so that her hands were in easy reach of her guns. "We didn't take anything that was yours and since I am the Sheriff everything was done legally."

Brian dismounted and handed the reins of his horse to his hired man. He turned to face Mell and copied her stance. "My sister is to marry someone from South Dakota, the rest of you can leave but she stays!"

Mell smirked complacently as she shook her head negatively. "Let me bring you up to date Brian! Your sister is over twenty-five and a widow, so she can go where she wants and can marry whomever she chooses. She doesn't have to marry if she doesn't wish to."

Mell called back over her shoulder. "What about it Mary do you want to stay here and marry the man your brother has chosen?"

Mary shook her head emphatically then answered verbally not wanting to distract Mell by making her turn to see her answer. "No, I do not want to stay here and I refuse to marry anyone my brother has chosen for me!"

Mell nodded decisively she hadn't turned to ask Mary her question but had kept her gaze locked on Brian's not giving an inch. "You have your answer Brian. I suggest that you go into your house and let us leave now before it's too late."

Brian weighed Mell's stance and her willingness to use her guns. He lifted his hands away from his own reluctantly and backed away knowing he was no match for Mell. "Have it your way this time Sheriff but you haven't heard the last of me!"

With that parting shot Brian turned then stormed to the house and slammed the door angrily behind him. Mell let out the breath she had been holding and quickly mounted her horse. "Let's get out of here before he tries something stupid!"

Brad didn't need to be told twice he clucked to the horses before turning them around and they headed back towards Mell's.

* * *

Jed and Giant Bear were just walking towards the barn when the sound of horses and a wagon reached them. They looked at each other in relief then waited for Mell and her party to come into view. Jed studied Mell intently for any signs of injury and Giant Bear did the same with Mary. When they were both satisfied that neither was hurt both men visibly relaxed.

Mell reached them first and wearily dismounted. She turned as she eyed both men distrustfully as they just stood there saying nothing. Dusty rushed up from the barn and took Mell's horse away. Mell scowled at the two men angrily and asked suspiciously. "Going somewhere you two?"

Jed shook his head negatively then shrugged dismissively. "Not anymore, why didn't you tell us you were going to Brian's? We were both very worried when we found out."

Mell shrugged her shoulders stiffly then scowled irritably. "I told my father where we were going. I didn't know that I had to report to either of you when I go somewhere?"

Jed held up his hands in surrender then dropped them as he motioned placatingly. "I'm sorry I didn't say it right. I just meant that as your Deputy I should have been with you."

Mell sighed in apology then shrugged as her anger drained away instantly. "No I'm sorry I'm just not used to having a Deputy with me all the time."

Jed pulled Mell into his arms in relief now that her annoyance had dissipated. "Well please try to remember in the future and I'll try not to question you when you go without me."

Mell kissed Jed in apology.

Giant Bear left the two of them alone then walked over to the wagon and scolded Mary for not telling him her plans.

Jed stepped back inquisitively then waved curiously. "Did you have any problems?"

Mell shook her head negatively in relief. "Not really Brian wasn't there when we arrived but he showed up just as we were leaving."

Mell went on to tell Jed everything that had happened then turned to Giant Bear when she finished. "Would you take the big trunk to the barn since Mary doesn't need that one Jed would you and Brad haul the other two trunks up to Mary's room please? We can wait until tomorrow to go to town for supplies since it's already too late it's almost dark."

Jed nodded then started to lift one end of a trunk but stopped at Giant Bear's remark. Giant Bear stepped forward insistently as he pointed towards the barn. "All of Mary's trunks can go to the barn she will be staying there with me now."

Mary smiled widely up at Giant Bear in pleasure then nodded eagerly. "As you wish!"

CHAPTER FOURTEEN

Mell woke up the next morning and groaned in dismay at the sound of rain drumming on her window drat just what she needed a wet soggy ride first thing in the morning. She turned to cuddle back up to Jed and found him gone she frowned in annoyance. It was the first time since they started sleeping together that he wasn't there when she woke up and she was slightly disappointed.

She turned onto her back then stretched and yawned sleepily wondering where he had gotten to so early in the morning. A soft hesitant knock caught Mell's attention and she cocked her head inquisitively it couldn't be Jed knocking of course. She called out sleepily after checking to make sure she was decently covered. "Come in."

Mell smiled in delight as Jessica entered with a breakfast tray and she sat up instantly now wide-awake. "Good morning you don't need to bring me breakfast every morning Jessica."

Jessica beamed amicably and whispered in conspiracy even though no one else was around to hear. "I know that but I enjoy doing it. But don't tell anyone!"

Mell chuckled at her dramatics then nodded in pleasure not really having any objections. "Okay, if you insist I won't complain too much. Do you know where Jed is by any chance?"

Jessica grinned as she nodded then put the tray across Mell's lap before looking at her. "Yes he told me to let you sleep and to tell you when you woke that he went hunting with Giant Bear this morning."

Mell nodded her thanks then dug into her porridge hungrily while Jessica tidied up her room. Mell finished her meal then sipped contentedly on her coffee as she watched Jessica cleaning. She smirked at Jessica when she looked over to see if Mell was finished yet. Mell motioned teasingly. "You're going to spoil me bringing me breakfast and cleaning up after me all the time!"

Jessica sighed wishfully as she thought of her family. "I enjoy doing things for people it's been kind of lonely since my husband died and my kids left to start their own families."

Mell inclined her head in sympathetic understanding then gestured curiously. "How many kids do you have if you don't mind me asking?"

Jessica beamed proudly as she shook her head negatively. "No I don't mind you asking. I have two boys who left before my husband died and one girl who left last year to get married my husband's been dead three years now."

Mell frowned wishfully hoping someday to have her own kids. She changed the subject as Jessica walked over to the bed. "Is everyone else up yet?"

Jessica nodded then gestured across the hall to the spare room. "Mrs. Elton and Sara arrived ten minutes ago and I'm on my way to help them now that you're done. Jane is finishing her breakfast then she will be up to help us later. Mary and Gloria are already in the kitchen baking up a storm. Your father is in the den finishing up the invitations."

Mell sighed in satisfaction and approval. "Okay can you find out from the Ladies if they need anything from town, if they do make a list and I'll pick everything up after work."

Jessica took the tray from Mell's lap and left.

Mell got up and rummaged in her closet for clean pants, shirt, long johns, and socks then quickly got dressed. She left her room and went across the hall into the sewing room. She grinned at everyone gathered cheerfully. "Good morning Ladies."

Everyone returned the greeting almost simultaneously as they looked up quickly then they all looked back down and continued their sewing as if they hadn't stopped even for a second. Mell chuckled slightly at the busy ladies then turned to Mrs. Elton inquisitively. "Was there any trouble in town yesterday without me there?"

Mrs. Elton shook her head negatively as she smiled up in reassurance. "No John told me to tell you that everything was quiet he figured you'd be asking."

Mell nodded in relief she had been slightly worried with no sheriff or deputy around for the last two weeks anything could have happened. She had been in town the day before of course, but not long enough Mell gestured inquisitively. "I'll be going in to work today but before I go is there anything you need me to do?"

Mrs. Elton shrugged negatively. "No not today but tomorrow we need to do a proper fitting before the hem can be adjusted so you're free to go."

Mell grimaced in relief not looking forward to all those layers of silk and lace she was required to wear. She left the ladies without another word then went to see her father next.

Mell knocked on the door of the den before entering then walked over to the desk. Alec smiled up playfully at Mell as he motioned teasingly. "Well sleepy head how are you this morning?"

Mell walked around the desk then bent to give her father a good morning kiss. "I'm fine how are you feeling this fine morning?"

Alec smirked smugly in triumph as Mell stood back up. He waved down at his desk proudly. "Just great! I have two more invitations to make out then I'm done for the day."

Mell laughed in delight at her father's self-righteous attitude as she patted his shoulder in congratulations. "Well I guess I'll just have to find something else for you to do."

Alec held up his hands in surrender as he shook his head. He grimaced as if horrified by that threat. "No that's okay I already have a lot of things I need to do without you adding more!"

Mell chuckled at her father's appalled look. "Okay I'll leave you to finish and I'll pick them up before I leave I'll also need a list of provisions for the week, and anything else you think we might be needing for the wedding, that you can think of before I go."

Alec nodded as he motioned down at his desk. "Okay I'll have everything ready for you in about an hour is Jed going with you?"

Mell shrugged slightly in irritation. "I don't know he went hunting with Giant Bear. If he's not back before I leave he'll have to meet me at my office!"

Alec smiled knowingly up at his miffed daughter. "I'll give him the message when he gets back."

Mell shook off her exasperation then motioned in inducement. "I'm going to the kitchen to have a coffee so why don't you finish up here and come have a cup with me before I go? Hopefully the rain will let up by the time we're finished!"

Alec grinned pleased. "Okay sounds like a good idea to me."

Mell nodded good-bye then turned and left the den. She went to the kitchen next and as she entered she sniffed loudly in appreciation. "Something sure smells good in here!"

Mary turned in surprise not having heard the door then she smiled at Mell as she waved towards the kitchen table invitingly. "Sit down Mell I'll bring you some coffee and a fresh bun with lots of butter on it."

Mell sat down instantly without having to be told twice then rubbed her hands in anticipation as she beamed over at Mary in delight. "Sounds too tempting to resist!"

Mary chuckled perceptively then humming softly to herself she finished up the promised bun. She brought the bun, coffee, and a jar of raspberry jam to the table then set them in front of Mell dramatically before stepping back and returning to her baking.

Mell just finished putting a generous heap of raspberry jam on her bun when Jessica entered with a list of the things the ladies wanted. Jessica smiled down at Mell in apology for interrupting her meal. Mell groaned in disappointment then put it down as she took the paper Jessica handed her. Jessica pointed down at the items on the page. "Here's the list you requested there's not much just a few odds and ends Mrs. Elton forgot to bring with her when she came."

Mell scanned it before nodding as she looked up at Jessica. "Okay I'll pick these up today."

Jessica saluted in farewell before she turned then left to go back and help the ladies upstairs with their task.

Mell picked up her bun then took a big bite in pleasure, out of the mouth-watering morsel, as it continued emitting heavenly smell. Mell groaned in anticipation as she closed her eyes in delight. She savoured the sensation of the hot buttered bun in ecstasy. Mell sighed in gratification as the raspberries hit her taste buds then she groaned in bliss. It was better than lovemaking she chuckled to herself, as she thought of the last few days, well maybe not!

Mary giggled at Mell as she turned around at the groan of contentment. She watched Mell take her second bit in exactly the same manner then she turned away satisfied that she was enjoying her treat.

Mell was halfway through her bun when Jed walked in dripping water everywhere. Mell looked up at his bedraggled appearance then smirked in amusement it served him right for leaving without her this morning.

Jed quickly bent down and gave Mell a wet kiss making sure to drip on her just because she had such a smug look on her face. Mell pushed him away in simulated anger but couldn't help grinning in delight. "Oh you're soaked get away from me!"

Jed smiled down at her and opened his arms invitingly as a mischievous light entered his eyes. "Come give me a hug darling!"

Mell laughed then shook her head emphatically as she shook a scolding finger up at him. "Not on your life buster go and change into dry clothing before you catch a cold!"

Jed saluted smartly in false servitude. "Aye, aye Sheriff!"

Mell chuckled as she watched him leave with his head hanging low, as if his feelings were hurt. She finished her bun quickly before any more interruptions could wreck her enjoyment then she sat back to drink her coffee while she waited for her father and Jed to come.

Mary came over with the coffee pot and poured Mell another cup she smiled her thanks then finished her second cup of coffee. Mell heard the door open behind her and she turned expectantly. She smiled up in approval as Jed walked in with dry clothes and his hair all slicked back. "Well you certainly look better not like something the cat dragged in!"

Jed winked down at her teasingly. "I feel better too."

He walked around the table and sat across from Mell. Jed looked up then grinned in pleasure as Mary placed a cup of hot coffee in front of him, as well as a steaming fresh from the oven buttered bun. "Thank you Mary the bun looks delicious and the coffee is appreciated."

Mary smiled gratified by his appreciation and turned back to her baking in satisfaction.

Jed turned back to Mell inquisitively as he waved towards town. "Are we going to the office today?"

Mell nodded decisively as she watched Jed enjoy his bun almost exactly the way she had. "Yep! Dad is finishing the invitations so I want to deliver them today and I need to order supplies at the store as well. Dad's coming to have coffee as soon as he's finished then we can go."

Jed mumbled his mouth full. "Sounds good to me the rain's letting up some and I saw some clearing to the north. Hopefully the rain will stop before we leave."

Mell sighed in relief glad the rain was letting up already. "That's good I definitely wasn't looking forward to riding in it. Speaking of riding where did you go hunting this morning?"

Jed pointed to the north before putting jam on his last piece of bun as he looked back at Mell. "Giant Bear wanted to teach Tommy how to track so we took him out to the open field between here and Devil's Rock. Deer love high grass and they like to bed down in it just as much as they like eating it. We'll be having deer steaks tonight for supper. Right now Tommy is learning how to skin and clean a deer."

Mell rubbed her hands together then grinned in anticipation. "Good! I haven't had a deer steak in a long time."

Mell heard the door opening behind her so she turned and smiled hello as her father entered. Alec beamed back in greeting then turned to Jed. "Did I hear someone say something about deer steaks?"

Jed laughed in delight then shook his head in amazement. "Nothing gets by you, yes we got a two year old buck this morning thanks to Giant Bear."

Alec pushed himself up to the table then rubbed his hands together in delight almost exactly the way his daughter had. "Oh good I love deer meat."

Mary brought Alec coffee and a bun then smirked saucily as she set them down in front of him. "Finally decided to join us did you?"

Alec grinned devilishly up at her then smacked her behind as she turned around. "That's for being impertinent to your elders!"

Mary chuckled benevolently over her shoulder at Alec then looked directly at Mell and winked good-naturedly. "Some men have no respect!"

Mell smiled indulgently at the two of them then reached over and lightly slapped her father's arm in rebuke playing along. "Behave yourself!"

Alec put on a hurt expression and sighed forlornly as he turned to Jed. He gestured hopefully looking for sympathy. "See what I've had to put up with Jed all these years? All these women in my household taking advantage of a poor old man in a wheelchair!"

Jed laughed incredulously in disbelief as he shook his head not in the least sorry for Alec. "And you love every minute of it!"

Alec grinned in delight at having his bluff called and nodded decisively. "You got that right!"

Mell smiled affectionately at her father then changed the subject. "Did you bring me everything I need?"

Alec nodded then pulled out a pile of papers that he had tucked under his leg and set them before her. "The list of kitchen supplies is on the top then there's the ranch supplies, all the invitations are there as well and a list the hands made up of some things they would like."

Mell looked through the lists as she continued speaking. "Have you met all the new hands yet dad?"

Alec inclined his head slightly when Mell looked back over at him inquisitively. "Yes I met them yesterday and added their names to the payroll."

Satisfied Mell finished her coffee quickly in silence before standing up with the papers in her hand. "Good I'll see you tonight then."

Mell bent and gave her father a good-bye kiss then left the kitchen and went to the front door. She took her gun belt down then buckled it on before grabbing her badge off the little shelf and pinning it on. She coiled her long thick blonde hair into a bun on top of her head then put her hat over top firmly, to keep her hair in place, and exchanged her moccasins for her riding boots.

Jed had followed Mell silently after patting Alec's shoulder in farewell. He also buckled on his gun belt before pinning on his badge. He grabbed his hat on the way out as the two of them walked to the barn to saddle their horses.

Mell entered the barn first then walked over to where Tommy and Giant Bear were bent over the deer carcass in deep discussion on how best to skin a deer.

Tommy looked up at Mell in surprise then smiled in delight. "I'm learning how to hunt and skin a deer Auntie Mell!"

Mell smiled down in approval then patted Tommy on his shoulder in congratulations. "That's very good with you two big hunters around we'll have lots of meat for winter."

Tommy nodded eagerly and gestured to his father ecstatically. "My father is taking me hunting again tomorrow then he's going to teach me how to shoot a rifle and how to fight with a knife."

Mell's smile was slightly strained this time as she motioned at Tommy. "Go wash your hands then help Jed saddle the horses for me please Tommy."

Tommy jumped up instantly then rushed outside to wash at the water pump. Mell frowned down anxiously at Giant Bear as she pointed behind her at the retreating Tommy. "Is this really necessary Giant Bear? I know he's going to be living in an Indian village but maybe you're going a little too fast. I'm not sure he needs to learn knife fighting yet he's a little young after all."

Tommy came rushing back in and Jed left the two of them to talk privately. He distracted Tommy so he wouldn't hear what Mell and Giant Bear were discussing.

Giant Bear sighed in aggravation but tried to be patient realizing that Mell was only looking out for his sons interest, as he was. "Mell I know that you practically raised Tommy but you have to realize that Indian children his age already know how to do the things I'm teaching him. If he's going to fit in with the other boys his age I need to teach him everything before we get to the village. If I don't he will find it very hard and the other boys will make it even harder on him to adjust, especially since he's a Chief's son they will expect him to lead them. I have already had this fight with Mary I'm trying not to go too fast for him but he seems to learn everything very quickly and asks for more!"

Mell frowned in thought as she remembered one time before the Cheyenne had moved out of Northern Dakota into South Dakota and Montana that she had visited one of the villages and saw some of the tests of bravery that the boys endured to reach manhood. She nodded her head slightly now worried as she realized that Giant Bear was right. Her adopted son would be no match for those boys. "All right I'll do what I can to help him along as well."

Giant Bear smiled in relief at having Mell's support then motioned imploringly. "I was hoping you'd teach him your technique of fighting."

Mell sighed then inclined her head she had already decided she would show Tommy what he needed to know. "I will but you know Mary won't like it."

Giant Bear gestured meaningfully having already clashed with Mary today then he shrugged dismissively. "I know but he has to learn!"

Mell changed the subject and pointed curiously at the deer hide. "What are you going to do with the skin?"

Giant Bear smile softened as he thought of his wife and son. "I'm going to cure it and Mary is going to make Tommy some buckskin's."

Mell nodded in disappointment, she had hoped to have it. She turned to smile at Tommy as he handed the reins to her. "Would you like something from town Tommy?"

Tommy beamed shyly then shook his head negatively. "No Auntie Mell I don't need anything."

Mell waved good-bye to father and son and along with Jed left the barn to mount their horses. Jed mounted then motioned inquisitively behind them at the barn when Mell turned to him before they rode off. "Did Giant Bear ease your mind a bit Mell?"

Jed pulled the lead rope for the packhorse tighter so the horse wasn't too far behind then tied him to the back of his saddle as he waited for Mell's answer.

Mell sighed irritably as she turned her horse towards town. "He explained why it was necessary to rush Tommy a little and I agree with him but I still don't have to like it!"

Jed leaned over then reached out and took her hand as they rode along. "He'll be all right Giant Bear would never do anything to hurt him."

Mell frowned forlornly as she thought about it sadly. "I know he wouldn't. It's just that Tommy has been my son as well as Mary's for so long that I can't help resenting Giant Bear a little for taking him away from me."

Jed sat back as he let go of Mell's hand after giving it a comforting squeeze then nodded knowingly. "I know Mell but Giant Bear is right. If Tommy is going to survive in an Indian village we have to prepare him before he gets there otherwise the other kids will make it miserable for him."

Mell scowled apprehensively then gave in as she gestured in surrender. "Then I guess I'll have to help him as much as I possibly can. Giant Bear asked me to teach Tommy some of my fighting techniques and I even have a few tricks you haven't seen yet."

Jed grinned in relief but deep down he had known she would. He chuckled as he thought about Mell's last statement. "Well I'm definitely going to have to watch so I don't learn the hard way what tricks I haven't seen yet!"

Mell just smiled secretly without comment then nudged her horse into a faster pace. They reached the edge of town before the rain finally quit completely and the sun came out. Mell sighed in aggravation it just figured. She turned to Jed then waved towards town. "I need to hire another Deputy today."

Jed raised his eyebrows in surprise then frowned in simulated hurt. "Oh, and are you firing me already?"

Mell laughed at Jed's expression then shook her head negatively. "No but since neither of us lives in town and I'm sure you don't want to stay here to do night duty. I need someone to patrol at night while were away."

Jed grinned in relief and nodded emphatically that he definitely wouldn't stay in town at night by himself. "In that case I'll help you find one and you're right, I wouldn't like night duty. I plan to spend all my nights with you!"

Mell blushed at Jed's suggestive tone and smiled back shyly as they rode up main street. Mell turned away to hide her blush then waved towards their right. "I want to go to the store first and drop these lists off. One of Charlie's young boys will deliver the supplies if I catch him before he goes."

Jed nodded and followed Mell obediently. They dismounted at the store and went in together. Mell went up the isle and spoke to the man behind the counter, while Jed stayed behind to browse through some of the clothes on display. Mell grinned in greeting at the rotund storeowner. "Hi Charlie how are you and that pretty wife of yours?"

Charlie shook Mell's hand firmly in friendly greeting. "Morning Sheriff we're both doing just fine. What can I do for you this fine morning?"

Mell gestured hopefully as Charlie let go of her hand. "Has Graham left to do the deliveries yet?"

Charlie shook his head negatively. "Not yet why?"

Mell sighed in relief then held out the lists. "Good I have some supplies I need and I figured he could deliver them for me."

Charlie nodded agreeable then took the lists. "Sure thing Sheriff let me have a look at what you need."

Mell waited patiently while he looked them over. She took the opportunity to study him a little closer. Charlie had been here way before she moved to this area. He was almost completely bald with just a little bit of grey hair on the sides of his head. He was huge and fat weighing close to three hundred pounds with a double chin and green blue piercing eyes. He was taller then her at six feet one with a laugh that was heartfelt and deep.

The old sheriff that had hired her had shown her a wanted poster on him but after buying Charlie's Mercantile he had hung up his guns and the old sheriff had left him alone as long as his guns stayed hidden. Besides how could she arrest someone who smelt like cinnamon all the time, every time she got anywhere near him she couldn't help taking a big sniff he just smelt so delicious.

Charlie nodded as he went down the list then he looked up with a smile of satisfaction. "Yep I've got everything you need but that's a mighty lot of supplies you're getting this time around you having a party or something?"

Mell grinned mischievously as she dug into her inside pocket where she had put the invitation. She had made sure to put Charlie's on top since she knew this would be her first stop. "Yep you could say that this is for you as well."

Mell handed him the invitation dramatically. Charlie took the envelope in surprise and opened it then looked up from the invitation with a smile of pleasure plain on his face. "Well I heard you were getting married congratulations!"

Charlie shook Mell's hand warmly and looked over at Jed. "And you must be the new Deputy, who's marrying our Lady Sheriff, congratulations to you too!"

Jed walked over immediately then shook Charlie's large beefy hand warmly in gratitude. "Thanks."

Mell waved down at the invitation hopefully. "Can you and your wife come Charlie?"

Charlie nodded emphatically. "Sure thing Sheriff I'll even close the store down that day. I wouldn't miss seeing you married for all the tea in China."

Mell smirked in delight at Charlie's solemn vow since he was always lamenting the fact that he couldn't get any tea on a regular basis. Mell turned to leave then looked back inquisitively as she motioned hopefully. "Oh have you seen Gary around today?"

Charlie shook his head negatively. "No not since Millie let him get away from her last week."

Mell sighed in disappointment. "Well if he happens to come in today tell him to come see me at the office please."

Charlie nodded in agreement. "Sure thing Sheriff."

Mell waved good-bye then turned and left with Jed following close behind. They mounted their horses once more then rode over to Mell's office to dry out. They weren't quite soaked but unpleasantly damp, still it was very uncomfortable and Mell needed to show Jed a few things anyway.

Mell walked ahead of Jed into the office and went over to a wood cook stove then lit a fire first to make a pot of coffee. She sat at her desk and pulled out some old reports her other deputies had made and handed them to Jed so he could study them. "Every night before I leave I write a report similar to these. My Deputies also have to write one even if they are along with me at the time. That way the Mayor, who is also the judge, and town leaders know what we're doing. I won't look at yours except the first couple to make sure you're doing it right and you won't be allowed to see mine. That way it's all legitimately told without either of us being able to lie about anything."

Jed nodded in surprise and curiously began reading the reports.

Mell got up and poured them both a coffee that was finished then sat at her desk again after she gave Jed his. They both sipped the hot coffee appreciatively as Jed continued his study of the reports. Mell smiled over her coffee cup at Jed's intense expression. "These reports have to be handed in to the Mayor every night, Lucy the Mayor's secretary, makes up a copy of the originals then once the Mayor and town leaders see the reports I get the copy's back but not the originals."

Jed finished reading then he handed the reports back to Mell. She rummaged through her desk again then pulled out some more papers. Mell looked over sympathetically and smiled at Jed's groan of protest at the thought of more papers to be filled out. She still handed them to him regardless of his protest. "This is an arrest sheet every time you arrest someone even if it's just a drunk you have to fill out one of these. I made up these forms because my Deputies kept arresting people for no good reason so after they had to fill in these they quit arresting people so often. The report we send to the Mayor is for the towns benefit because I had a few cases thrown out for lack of evidence with a lot of your word against mine so to speak. So that's why we both have to fill in one every day without seeing what the other has written. That way the town has more of a case against the outlaws."

Jed took the papers and scanned them but they were pretty straight forward so he handed them back to Mell with a nod but without comment.

Mell took the papers and put them back in her drawer so Jed could use them as a reference later when he did his first one. She looked up as her voice became deadly serious at the end of her statement. "You can follow me around for the next few days until you become familiar with my routine. I also want you to read my law book at the house. It won't tell you everything but it gives some good pointers and things to watch for. If you're not sure about something ask me don't bull ahead trying to figure it out for yourself. I have lost a few Deputies because they didn't ask and either got fired for doing wrong, or ended up dead. You'll also have to go through my 'wanted' papers and memorize the faces. I don't kill anyone unless I absolutely have to even if a poster says kill on sight. Only when I have no choice or someone's life is in jeopardy. Any Deputy that is caught doing so is dismissed immediately then charged as a criminal. Any questions so far?"

Jed shook his head negatively just as serious. "No but I might have some later though."

Mell nodded pleased then stood up. "Okay let's go."

Mell walked outside with Jed following. She immediately went to her horse and loosened the saddle girth, since she wouldn't need him for a while. She grabbed her whip that was always hooked to the back of her saddle.

Jed followed her example then he untied the packhorse and tied him to the hitching post, before loosening his girth strap as well.

Mell waited for him patiently then turned towards the stagecoach office first when Jed joined her. He walked beside her, listening attentively as she talked explaining why she did what she does. "I make this round every morning when I get to town, then every evening before I leave, and always on foot. I spend enough time in the saddle during the week I really don't want to ride around town too unless I have too. I always check the stagecoach first since all my Deputies from the surrounding towns send in their reports by stage. Unless it's an emergency then they either come themselves to report or send a pony express rider."

Mell walked into the building once they reached the entrance and went straight to the counter as she nodded cordially to the skinny short bald man behind it. She grinned slightly in humour to herself because every time she saw him she wanted to laugh. He reminded her of a little weasel with his sharp beak like nose and thin almost nonexistent lips. His thick glasses made his brown eyes look huge and ferret like. He was

232

scrawny and awkward looking and only stood at five foot one. "Morning James, have anything for me today?"

James nodded that he had as he smiled across the counter in pleasure. He knuckled his forehead in greeting before reaching under the counter. He pulled out some papers then laid them on the counter in front of her. "Morning Sheriff your reports are in and there are two new wanted posters."

Mell inclined her head in thanks as she reached in her vest and pulled out an invitation then placed it on the counter beside her papers. "I have a letter for you as well."

James grinned and picked up his pen to write all the information down so he could send it on the next coach. "Where would you like me to send it to?"

Mell chuckled and shook her head at the misunderstanding. "No not where it's for you and your mother."

James beamed in pleasure at getting a letter and nodded in delight. "Oh thank you!"

James took the letter off the counter then opened it. He looked up sadly after reading it and shook his head in regret. "I would love to come but I can't. I have to look after the stagecoach."

Mell sighed in disappointment then gestured hopefully. "What about your mother?"

James shook his head negatively then shrugged in apology. "Sorry she has no way to get to your place without me."

Mell frowned thoughtfully then she motioned imploringly. "What if I could get her a ride there and back?"

James grinned then nodded. "That's different if you could get her a ride I'm sure she would love to go."

Mell smiled in delight as she waved teasingly. "Good I'll even make sure she gets an extra piece of wedding cake to bring home for you."

James chuckled in anticipation. "Thank you Mell I'll look forward to the cake."

Mell then turned to Jed and made introduction. "James this is my fiancé Jed he's also my Deputy."

Jed inclined his head slightly in greeting then reached across the counter to shake hands. "Nice to meet you."

James nodded and beamed then winced slightly at Jed's firm handshake, but didn't pull away until Jed did. Jed realizing he had gripped a little to firmly let go immediately so he wouldn't hurt the little man any more.

Mell picked up her papers then turned after waving good-bye. She looked down at the wanted posters as she walked then passed them to Jed one at a time as she finished with them. Jed looked them over carefully then passed them all back when they were both done. Mell folded them in half and put them away in her belt so they wouldn't occupy her hands as she walked.

They went across the street and turned right then continued walking until they came to the two-story house at the very edge of town that Jed noticed on their first trip. It was still fairly quiet and dark being so early in the morning. This must be the place Dan had referred to as 'Pam's Place' and sure enough just above the door was her name, but not what kind of place it was. They entered and the huge burley man at the entrance nodded pleasantly at Mell then left without comment to let Pam know the Sheriff was here to see her.

Jed raised his eyebrows in surprise then grinned devilishly but didn't say anything. He looked around at the plush overly lush furniture with paintings on the wall of half naked women lying suggestively on couches.

Mell just smiled innocently over at him when he looked at her and sat on a chair by the door without speaking waiting patiently.

CHAPTER FIFTEEN

It wasn't long before a slightly plump middle-aged woman with midnight black hair ample hips and huge breasts that were almost totally out of her bodice came in. She had crystal clear green eyes with huge black irises that almost took over the green. The hair was obviously coloured and was probably mostly grey since she looked to be in her late forties.

Mell liked her despite her profession because she was direct and always honest without a conceited bone in her body. Plus she loved to laugh it was always hearty and honest, especially at herself. She smiled in delight when she walked in and saw Mell. "Well hello Sheriff I was wondering when you would be back to see us. Running a little late aren't you?"

Mell grinned then stood up respectfully. "Good morning Pam how are you and the other Ladies this fine day?"

Pam laughed boisterously in humour shaking her head in disbelief as she planted her hands on her ample hips in incredibility. "You know Sheriff you're a gem. You are the only woman who dares to walk in here never mind calling us Ladies!"

Mell smiled slightly in scepticism that she was the only one to call them all ladies but didn't comment. Instead she took out an invitation and handed it to Pam.

Pam took the envelope tentatively fearing the worst then opened it and raised her pencil thin eyebrows in surprise as she looked up at Mell in incredulity. "You want me and all my girls to come to your wedding. Are you serious?"

Mell nodded innocently then frowned slightly mystified by the look of mistrust on Pam's face as she gestured anxiously. "Yes, if you want to come that is."

Pam suddenly reached out and hugged her spontaneously to hide the tears in her eyes. She pushed Mell away slightly so she could look at her. "Darling I wouldn't miss it for the world but I can't speak for everyone else. I'll ask them for you though."

Pam stepped away from Mell wiping the tears away then turned to Jed. She eyed him up and down appreciatively then turned to Mell and smirked mischievously. "I suppose this gorgeous hunk of a man is the one marrying you?"

Mell grinned at Pam's direct teasing question then motioned in introduction. "Pam this is Jed my fiancé and he's also my new Deputy."

Jed smiling devilishly had watched his fiancée in disbelief at first then in humour as she innocently asked a lady of ill repute to attend her wedding, as if it wasn't always done by other women, nothing would surprise him about Mell now. He took Pam's hand then bowed over it before kissing it gently in greeting. "Charmed!"

Pam giggled in delight as she turned her head back towards Mell then winked outlandishly. "Well Mell I have to give you credit you can sure pick them!"

Mell beamed indulgently but without a shred of jealousy at the two of them as Jed and Pam flirted back and forth for a few minutes. Mell broke in with business on her mind. "Pam did you have any problems since I've been away?"

Pam turned away from Jed instantly all business now herself. "No it's been really quiet lately."

Mell nodded in relief then waved in farewell. "Good! We'll see you tonight then on my final rounds."

Pam escorted the pair to the door then opened it for them as she gestured in pleasure. "Thanks for inviting us Mell I'll always love you for that."

Mell smiled good-bye still slightly mystified by all the fuss as Pam closed the door behind them.

Jed looked at Mell sideways in speculation. "You really amaze me sometimes Mell."

Mell turned slightly towards Jed then smirked pleasantly as she motioned calmly. "Maybe I'm just more liberal than most women."

Jed chuckled in agreement as he turned back towards the sidewalk ahead of him. "I guess you are at that!"

They passed several houses the town office and the hotel without stopping since Chelsie's Saloon was always third on the list to visit. Mell pushed the batwing doors open then stepped inside. She stopped to wait for her eyes to adjust before looking around then walked over to the bar and smiled at Chelsie in greetings. "Good morning Chelsie how's business?"

She grinned in delight at Mell before turning around to pour them the coffee that she had waiting. She turned back and set the cups on the counter before looking at Mell with a sly smirk. "Just fine how is the bride-to-be?"

Mell beamed warmly in reply. "Just Great!"

Mell rummaged inside her pocket and found Chelsie's invitation then handed it to her dramatically. Chelsie opened it excitedly already guessing what was inside then she looked up and grinned in delight as she nodded in acceptance. "Well thank you! I'll definitely come, but I'll have to ask the girls before I can say whether they will come or not."

Mell sighed in relief glad her friend was coming at least. She became all business as she changed the subject. "Okay how did things go lately any problems?"

Chelsie shook her head negatively. "No problems at all Sheriff."

Mell nodded glad to hear that then turned around to see who was all there while she sipped her coffee. Mell put her cup down then took out her invitation and rummaged through them before pulling out the ones she wanted. She put the others away then turned to Jed. "Wait here I'll be right back."

Jed inclined his head in agreement as his eyes followed Mell curiously as she walked away. He turned to Chelsie and accepted more coffee. He smiled his thanks before pointing over his shoulder towards Mell in humour. "I think Mell is inviting the whole town to our wedding."

Chelsie nodded decisively as she motioned matter of factually. "Of course if she didn't invite everyone they would think she was mad at them for some reason. We all love Mell and appreciate the things she's done for us. This town was pretty wild before she came here as a Deputy the Sheriff then was pretty old and couldn't do much about it. Then this tall skinny boy with a pretty face came out of nowhere and helped clean up the town. Some of us knew that she was a woman of course but after she proved herself we all turned a blind eye and pretended we didn't know. After she got fired the town turned completely lawless again we had two Sheriffs die one after another. Lucky for us she saved the Mayor and his wife so the Mayor gave in and asked her to take her job back. We have all lived a better life since. More women came out here and settled as soon as word spread that the town was safe once more. Now we have a town that's growing and prospering all because she makes sure that the law is enforced. Not just for this town mind you but for several other towns as well."

Jed sighed in understanding. "I can see that everyone loves her and I must admit it doesn't take long to fall under her spell. I loved her from the first day I met her, although I didn't want to at the time."

Chelsie smiled knowingly but didn't comment as she refilled his coffee cup and Mell's also as she saw her turn towards them. Mell grinned in thanks at Chelsie then looked at the two of them speculatively wondering what they had talked about that seemed so serious. She sipped her coffee as she shrugged in unconcern and turned around curiously as she heard someone enter the saloon.

It was Gary and Mell smiled in greeting as he sauntered towards her. She studied him speculatively as he got closer he was six feet, gangly, and awkward looking with his long, long legs and big feet. He had sandy brown hair and deep honest brown eyes. He had a thick brown handle bar moustache that he kept neatly trimmed and he was always playing with it proudly. He wasn't a fast gun but he didn't panic in bad situations. She knew that because she had watched him a few times.

Gary smiled back hesitantly unsure why the sheriff would be looking for him. "Charlie told me you were looking for me Sheriff."

Mell nodded relieved she wouldn't have to go looking for him. "Yes I was Gary do you remember asking me for a job a few months ago?"

Gary frowned slightly in puzzlement as he motioned curiously. "Yes you told me you didn't need anyone."

Mell shrugged nonchalantly. "That's right at the time I didn't, but now I need another Deputy. If you're still interested that is, you'll be working from five at night until five in the morning."

Gary gestured ecstatically. "Yes of course I'm still interested and I'll gladly take the job."

Mell inclined her head in relief then waved up the street. "Go see the Mayor right away and he'll swear you in. Meet us at the hotel for lunch afterwards and I'll explain your duties."

Gary turned immediately then headed for the door with a noticeable spring in his step.

Mell waved good-bye to Chelsie as she and Jed left the saloon. She turned down the street and crossed over to the store then entered with Jed following curiously.

Mell walked up to the counter and yelled into the back so Charlie would hear her. "Charlie!"

Charlie came hustling out in surprise and went behind the counter with a troubled frown. "Did you forget something Sheriff?"

Mell shook her head negatively then motioned placatingly. "No but I have a favour to ask you. When you come out to the ranch for my wedding would you pick up James's mom since you live next to her then bring her along with you. James can't leave the stagecoach office and his mother has no other way to get out to my place?"

Charlie smiled in relief. "Sure I will just tell James that I'll pick her up in the morning."

Mell nodded gratefully before waving good-bye. "Thanks Charlie I'll see you later on my evening rounds."

Mell and Jed walked out of the store then down the street a ways before crossing to the hotel for lunch. As soon as they entered the hotel

Mell walked up to the desk. The reed thin clerk looked up and smiled in greeting. "Hello Sheriff how's your day going so far?"

Mell beamed back then she rummaged inside her shirt. "Fine Dan how's business?"

Dan shrugged his bony shoulders nonchalantly. "The same as usual nothing exciting ever happens around here."

Mell grinned sympathetically then handed him an invitation. "Maybe this will help."

Dan opened the envelope and read it then looked at Mell with a wide smile. "Wouldn't miss it for the world your new Deputy the lucky man?"

Mell nodded as she made introductions since the two of them hadn't been introduced last time they were here. "Yes this is Jed. Jed this is Dan."

The two men shook hands cordially. Dan chuckled as he winked at Jed in conspiracy. "So you're the lucky man who managed to steal Mell's heart. Well, there will be a lot of disappointed men on your wedding day. I think half the men in town are in love with Mell, even the married ones."

Jed smirked confidently. "I'm sure I can handle the competition."

Mell grinned in delight and shook her head in horror at the two of them then beckoned Jed to follow her into the restaurant without comment. Mell picked a table in the back corner that was positioned so that both their backs were to the wall and the whole room was open to their view.

The waitress came over immediately and poured coffee for the two of them. "Morning Sheriff. How ya doin today?"

Mell smiled up at her in greeting as she studied Gary's wife. She had strawberry blonde hair and steel grey eyes. She was tall for a woman at five foot five, pretty but not beautiful. She was as slim and awkward looking as her husband. She had a heavy accent and she controlled her husband with an iron fist. "Fine Millie and how are you this fine day?"

Millie shrugged nonchalantly. "Doin jus fine tank ya."

Mell nodded glad to hear that and rummaged through her invitations then looked up inquisitively. "I hired your husband today as a Deputy. I hope you don't mind."

240

Millie shook her head negatively. "Nah! He wants ta be Deputy for longest time. I jus hope he doesn mess it up likes he does all da udder jobs."

Mell found the invitation and handed it to Millie. Millie turned it over anxiously not being able to read she had to ask in embarrassment. "What dis for?"

Mell smiled sheepishly then explained having forgotten that Millie couldn't read. "It's an invitation for my wedding next week. I hope you can come."

Millie smiled down grateful that she didn't have to pretend to read it and nodded hesitantly not sure if she could go or not. "Well, I can no promise I try!"

Mell nodded in understanding. "Okay. I hope you can come though. Can we have a couple of your specials Millie and order one for your husband too. He'll be joining us shortly."

Millie nodded as she tucked the invitation in her apron pocket then turned towards the kitchen. "Sure Sheriff."

Mell waved around the room before getting up. "I'm going to hand out invitations. I'll be right back."

Jed watched her circulate around the room talking and laughing with everybody as she handed them out. She was just returning to their table when Gary came strutting in. Proud as a peacock with his new deputy's badge pinned on for everybody to see. They both sat down together and Mell smiled over at Gary inquisitively. "Well the first thing I need to know is can you read and write?"

Gary shrugged slightly in embarrassment. "I can some but not very well."

Mell sighed not surprised and motioned placatingly. "That's all right Gary. We'll just have to improvise."

She then proceeded to tell him the rules. They were almost exactly the same rules she had given Jed except for the last. "Now, you remember if you have any problems that you can't handle come to me I'll handle them. Absolutely no heroics do you understand me?"

Gary nodded anxiously. "Sure Sheriff if a gang comes to town and it looks like trouble. I'm to come and get you not handle it myself right?"

Mell smiled in relief. "That's right and every morning after work I want you to go over to the Mayor's office and give Lucy a verbal report she will write it up for you."

Gary gestured eagerly. "Okay. I can handle that. What about when you're gone on the trail who do I report to then?"

Mell inclined her head in approval at the question. "When I'm not here you'll report any problems directly to the Judge the same as you would to me."

Gary grinned proudly up at his wife as she set a bowl of soup in front of him. "Millie look I'm finally a Deputy!"

Millie glanced at his badge briefly then beamed proudly. She gave him a quick pat on the shoulder in appreciation then left too busy to stay any longer.

The rest of their meal was eaten in silence.

* * *

Mell sighed in relief as they headed out of town. It was six o'clock and later than she usually stayed. But she had accomplished everything she had set out to do today. Gary had settled into his new job very well. All the invitations but two were given out and everyone had accepted tentatively if not outright except James. Jed had been introduced to quite a few people and so far had no problems with anybody. Or with the rules of being her deputy, so far that is.

Jed gazed around curiously as they headed northeast they hadn't been this way before. They couldn't be headed to Brian's it was further east of here. He turned to Mell then motioned inquisitively. "Where are we going this will take us longer, won't it?"

Mell turned to Jed and grimaced slightly in discomfort not really looking forward to the next few hours as she explained why they were taking a different route home. "We're going to take the long way I have to drop my last two invitations off. We'll go to Mr. Grey's ranch first he's a friend of my father's then go to Brian's on our way home."

Jed sighed in aggravation then motioned in annoyance. "I'm definitely not looking forward to seeing Brian again!"

Mell frowned then shrugged consolingly. "Neither am I. But I have to give him at least one more chance before I give up on him! I really don't know what's come over him lately he's never been this bad before?"

Jed made a face in reluctant agreement he supposed they had to give Brian one more chance. As for what's gotten into him Jed really couldn't say since he didn't know anything about Brian at all. "I guess so."

They rode in silence for a few minutes then Jed turned to Mell curiously with a questioning look. He just had to ask the question it had been on his tongue all day. "Mell, why do you carry a whip around town?"

Mell grinned slightly at Jed's curious question then answered truthfully as she shrugged self-consciously. "Well, you know the ban on killing. I don't like to kill unless I'm given no choice. So I use the whip to control situations that might get out of hand. I've always been better with a whip then a gun anyway. I modified it just slightly. It's not quit as long as it was but then I added three extensions on the end, similar to a cat of nine tails, with fairly sturdy hooks. They almost look like fishhooks but barbed on both sides."

Mell shook her head irritably at herself as she tried to explain, fishhooks was not the right description. She snapped her fingers as she got an idea. "Not fishhook but like an anchor for a boat. I used antlers from a deer since they are tougher then wood. I carved them myself it was pretty difficult to get them thin enough so the ends wouldn't be too heavy when released. It will catch on someone's clothes or flesh and hold tight no matter which direction you're aiming. It can do a lot of damage if you're not careful. Even kill! For instance if someone gets drunk and starts smashing things or shooting his gun off. I'll wrap the whip around him to hold him tight while I disarm him. It's very effective and has saved me from killing more times than I can count, but it's not effective all the time. If for some reason I figure the whip is no good in a situation or won't help me, and I have to use my gun, I always try to aim for the gun hand or arm."

Jed nodded in understanding and they rode on in silence for a few more minutes before Jed turned to Mell again questioningly. He had been thinking of that report she had received this morning but this was the first opportunity he had to ask her about it. "What do you think about the report your Deputy Ted sent you?"

Mell shrugged undecided it had puzzled her too but she wasn't sure what to do about it yet. "I'm not sure what to think. He has no idea why a hired gun showed up yesterday out of the blue but according to Ted he hasn't caused any trouble so far. I'm not sure if I should wait until or if he does! Or whether I should go and check it out myself before the wedding."

Jed nodded thoughtfully as he asked curiously. "How far is the town from here?"

Mell sighed in aggravation then shrugged annoyingly. "You could be there in two days from the ranch if you rode hard. Three and a half to four days if you take your time. With our wedding only six days away I'm not anxious to go and possibly have to postpone the wedding."

Jed nodded not liking the thought of having to postpone it either but another scenario kept running through his head and he motioned in worry. "I see your point but what happens if we don't go now and put a stop to whatever he has planned then he makes his move the day before our wedding. We would have to postpone the wedding anyway if that happens. If we go now we should be back in plenty of time I hope."

Mell nodded thoughtfully. "I know and that's what I'm wrestling with right now. Should I or shouldn't I, but I'll make a decision tonight and let you know what I'm going to do as soon as I decide."

Jed sighed in relief then left it at that as they rode into Mr. Grey's ranch yard. Mell rode over to a man who was walking towards the house and they stopped beside him as she tipped her hat cordially in greeting. Mell studied him then grinned in humour the short bow legged old cowboy always wore a hug floppy hat that covered his slightly receding steal grey hair. You could just barely see his watery blue eyes and craggy aging face under the hat. He was close to sixty-five and showing his age more and more as his beard and thick handlebar moustache finally turned as steal grey as his hair on his head. "Evening Mr. Grey, do you have a few moments to talk?"

Mr. Grey eyed Mell sourly but nodded curtly. "What do you want Sheriff?"

Mell raised an eyebrow in surprise and hurt at his bitter tone of voice and curt nod. The use of her professional name instead of her real name surprised her as well. She ignored his tone of voice then reached into her pocket and pulled out his invitation before handed it down to him expectantly. He reached up and took it reluctantly then opened it tentatively. He squinted at it in the fading light but was still able to read it clearly. He then tried to hand it back angrily as he shook his head negatively. "I'm not coming and neither are my men or I'll fire the lot of them!"

Mell sat back in her saddle in shocked surprise not having expected that at all she didn't take the invitation back but left it with him. Mr. Grey had been her father's friend since they had moved to the ranch and he had never turned down an invitation to come and visit him. Mell shook her head in confusion as she gestured anxiously still ignoring the invitation he was holding up to her. "Why not even if you don't care to come and see me married I figured you would want to come and see my father at least!"

Mr. Grey growled in rage as he motioned in fury. "Me and your father were friends until you killed Greg!"

Mell's mouth fell open in shocked surprise not having expected that explanation for his actions at all. She snapped her mouth shut angrily and growled back just as irate in explanation even though she didn't think he deserved one at this moment. "I wouldn't have killed Greg if he hadn't taken my father hostage and tried to kill us both. Plus, he murdered all of my men at the ranch except Wade!"

Mr. Grey scowled up suspiciously and dropped the invitation she refused to take on the ground before he turned away without any further argument then stormed to his house without another word.

Mell ignored the invitation still on the ground then turned to Jed and gestured in livid confusion. "This is unbelievable! I just don't understand. He's been my father's friend since we moved to the ranch."

Jed shrugged bewildered but not knowing Mr. Grey he couldn't really say anything to help her. "I guess he figures Greg was a better friend than your father."

They turned their horses and headed out of the yard as Mell brooded in troubled silence totally perplexed by all that had happened. She turned to Jed with an unconvinced expression as she shook her head in disagreement. "That can't be the reason. Greg and Mr. Grey hardly ever spoke to each other never mind spent time together. I don't even think they liked each other much."

Jed frowned then gestured placatingly. "Talk to your father and see what he thinks. Maybe he has the answers."

Mell nodded still upset and they turned and continued to ride towards Brian's in silence now going more east then north. They were about a quarter of the way to Brian's ranch when they spotted a rider coming fast. Mell squinted in the fading light then turned to Jed as she gestured for him to stop. "I think its Brian but I can't be sure yet in this light we'll wait here just in case."

Jed frowned in suspicion also sure it was Brian and he loosened the flap that held his gun in the holster when riding just in case of trouble.

Brian savagely pulled his horse to a stop when he was close enough to be heard but not too close. His horse squealed in pain at his master's rough handling but Brian ignored him as he snarled angrily at the two he hated as he leaned forward in rage. "I hope you weren't on your way to my ranch. You're no longer welcome there Sheriff!"

Mell sighed in aggravation even though she hadn't expected a warm welcome then pulled out his invitation and held it out to him. "I just came to give you this."

She held it out to him and waited but he didn't take it. Brian sneered as he sat back in his saddle and refused to come any closer. "What is it?"

Mell frowned angrily when he refused to take the envelope and snapped impatiently. "It's an invitation to my wedding and your sister's renewal vows."

Brian glanced at the envelope in disdain then at Mell with the same look of contempt plain on his face. With a last look of rage at the envelope he cruelly put spurs to his horse and galloped away without looking back or even touching the envelope.

Mell scowled in frustration but had expected he wouldn't accept it and tucked the envelope back into her pocket. She turned to Jed in impotent anger. "I guess the answer is no!"

Jed and Mell turned their horses west away from Brian's and headed home silently without any more talking. Both were glad Brian had shown up so they didn't have such a long ride back to the ranch.

* * *

It was late by the time Mell and Jed reached the ranch. Dusty and Tommy ran out of the barn and took their horses reins immediately. Dusty unhooked the packhorse's lead rope and they led all three horses to the barn to be unsaddled then bedded down for the night.

Mell and Jed entered the house still barely talking and both sighed in relief as they took off their gun belts, badges, boots, and hats. They just finished undressing when Alec entered the hallway and he smiled in exasperation. He looked both of them up and down in reproach. "Well, look who finally dragged themselves home! Where have you two been? We've been waiting for you two for hours."

Mell smiled apologetically and went over then bent down to give her father a fond kiss. She stood up still smiling this time more in apology down at him. "I'm sorry we're so late but it took longer than I thought to deliver the invitations. I also hired Gary as the night Deputy and I had to show him what to do."

Alec nodded placated by the apology and he grinned up at Mell in forgiveness. "Apology accepted. We saved supper for you two so come to the kitchen and eat while you fill me in on the day's events."

Mell pushed her father while Jed followed silently. Jessica turned and smiled in greeting at Mell and Jed as they entered. "I heard your voices so I put your supper on to heat up."

Mell beamed gratefully then motioned hopefully. "You wouldn't happen to have fresh coffee on as well? It's cool tonight."

Jessica smirked smugly then nodded agreeably. "Of course I do! Sit down and I'll get you both some."

Mell and Jed sat at the table then thankfully sipped the hot coffee Jessica put in front of them both finally able to relax and enjoy the rest of the evening.

Alec watched the two of them unwind and drank his own coffee in silence. Not wanting to interrupt their time of respite with questions right away. He decided to tell them of the goings on at the ranch instead of asking them about their day. Questions could wait until after they ate.

Alec smiled over at the two of them then cradled his cup in two hands as he continued to watch them relax. "Your supplies came in just after lunch. The hands continued building the cabin after the rain quit and it dried up a little. Wade, Tommy, and Giant Bear helped them after your platform was built. I was out looking at the cabin just before dark and it's coming along very nicely. It's amazing how fast a cabin can be built when ten people do it together. At this rate they should be done in a few days then they can start on Gloria and Wade's cabin. Mrs. Elton and Sara left just after supper they said to tell you that if you didn't get home too late that Jessica could help you try the dress on and pin up the hem for them."

Mell and Jed continued to listen to Alec while they ate, but made no comments, only nodding at the appropriate times. Alec finished his description of the day's happenings at the ranch then lapsed into silence.

Mell and Jed finished eating then pushed their plates away and sat back contentedly sipping their second cups of coffee. Mell smiled at her father grateful that he had rumbled on to give them time to finish eating. "I'm glad they're doing well on the first cabin."

Alec nodded then waved impatiently. "Now let's hear about your day."

Mell smiled in humour at her father's impatience and obliged him. She left nothing out and if she forgot something Jed reminded her. It took a good half hour to tell him everything and when they finished Alec sat there with a pensive frown more worried about the hired gun then his friend's strange behaviour. Alec looked at Mell in concern. "This hired gun showing up just before your wedding worries me. Is he going to stay where he is or is he going to show up here on your wedding day?"

Mell frowned thoughtfully then gestured hopefully. "That's what I've been wondering. It could be just a coincidence or maybe not. We could slip down there and be back before the wedding."

Alec motioned with a worried frown. "If for some reason you're going to be late send a rider with a note and I'll let everyone know that the wedding is postponed until you get back."

Mell smiled at both men in surrender. "Okay, I give up! We'll go tomorrow morning as soon as we're up. One of the men will have to go to town in the morning for me and let the Mayor know where we went at least. The Mayor can deputize him and he can look after the day shift until I get back. I would suggest Dusty he's a little shy but he's not a hothead so he should be okay for a few days."

Alec pointed at himself. "I'll look after that for you."

Mell nodded in relief then motioned inquisitively. "What about your friend Mr. Grey. Any thoughts about why he's acting so strange all of a sudden?"

Alec thought it over for a few moments then shook his head negatively. "I have no idea why he's acting as he is but I'll definitely have to find out."

Mell sighed in disappointment she had hoped her father could shed some light on his friends strange behaviour. "Well if you think of anything, let me know."

Alec inclined his head then he gestured curiously. "Okay. What time are you leaving in the morning?"

Mell shrugged undecided. "I'm not exactly sure but as early as I possibly can."

Jessica walked over to get their attention she had been listening but had remained quiet until now. "I have a suggestion."

Mell smiled up at the pretty red head then she nodded in permission. "Okay, I'll listen to any proposal that gets me back here before my wedding day!"

Jessica grinned in sympathy at Mell's pleading tone. "Well, if you will come up and try on your dress. I'll work on it while you sleep and wake you up at three o'clock that way you will be out of here by four. I'll have breakfast made for you so that way you can eat before you go. The Ladies can finish your dress while I sleep in the morning."

Mell looked at Jed in question and he nodded in agreement. Mell turned back to Jessica and motioned at her gratefully. "Okay as long as you're sure you don't mind."

Jessica shrugged then smirked teasingly. "I don't mind at all, especially if it will help you get back in time for your wedding."

Mell frowned at the image of all the guests showing up and their disappointed faces when she didn't. "Yes, I would certainly hate to miss it!"

Mell turned to Jed inquisitively. "Well, are you going to bed now or are you going to talk to Dad until I'm done with my dress fitting?"

Jed waved towards Mell's father. "I'll talk to your dad until you're done then I'll join you after."

Mell nodded and got up then left with Jessica. Jed and Alec talked about the ranch for half an hour then Jed went to bed as Jessica came in for coffee.

* * *

Jed entered the bedroom and smiled teasingly over at Mell. "Well, how did the fitting go?"

Mell grimaced in pain and aggravation. "Now I know why I don't wear dresses! They're difficult to get into and even more difficult to get out of."

Jed laughed in delighted at Mell's face then blew out the candle before getting undressed then got into bed. "Go to sleep Mell. We only have a few hours so no lessons tonight then a long ride tomorrow."

Mell sighed in disappointed agreement then gave Jed a goodnight kiss before cuddling closer and both were asleep in moments.

CHAPTER SIXTEEN

Mell woke to the sound of someone banging on her door insistently. She checked to make sure they were both covered up before mumbling sleepily. "Yes!"

Jessica popped her head in the door then grinned in apology. "Sorry but it's three o'clock!"

Mell groaned tiredly. "We'll be right down Jessica thanks."

Jessica smiled in sympathy then closed the door as Mell nudged Jed impatiently. "You awake?"

Jed sighed plaintively then yawned before mumbling. "Yes I'm awake!"

Mell got up and dressed quickly then threw some of her clothes into one side of her saddlebag that she pulled out of her closet. Then she grabbed an extra buckskin shirt and pants for Jed as well as the new pair of dress pants and a shirt that he had bought before they left town yesterday. She put them in the other side of her saddlebag. She turned as she slung it over her shoulder to see if Jed was up and dressed yet.

Mell smiled compassionately as she caught him sitting on the bed fully dressed smothering another sleepy yawn. "You can carry the other saddlebag with the food and other necessities that we'll pick up in the kitchen."

Jed nodded then got up to hold the door open for her. They went downstairs and entered the kitchen together. Mell's eyebrows rose in surprise to see her father sitting in his chair at the table, calmly eating breakfast waiting for them. Mell put her saddlebag on the floor then leaned down and kissed her father good morning before walking over to the counter then helping herself to porridge and coffee without comment. Jed followed her lead as they sat down to eat in silence before sitting back and sipping their coffee reflectively.

Jessica came over and gave Jed a saddlebag bulging with food on one side. On the other side were flint, medicines, toilet articles, a coffee pot, and a small axe that stuck out a little ways.

Jed smiled up in appreciation at Jessica's thoughtfulness before taking the saddlebag and setting it on the floor beside his chair. "Thanks Jessica!"

Jessica smiled in acknowledgment then turned back to the sink as she busied herself washing breakfast dishes.

Alec waved to the door inquisitively. "Are you two ready?"

Mell and Jed immediately got up then grabbed their saddlebags before following Alec out to the entryway. Alec watched as the two put on gun belts, jackets, badges, and their hats before grabbing the rifles propped in the corner for them. When they were ready Mell turned to her father inquisitively. "My rain slicker isn't here?"

Alec motioned towards the barn in explanation. "I sent Jessica up to wake Tommy and sent him out to the barn to saddle your horses. He took your rain slickers to tie on to the back of your saddles. He also took out two bedrolls inside you'll find a skillet, extra bullets, as well as a hunting knife each."

Mell smiled gratefully then bent down and gave her father a hug then a kiss good-bye. "I'll see you in a few days. Please ask the Ladies to finish the dresses and ask them if they can decorate the house, the platform, and the archway for me since I won't be able to myself like I'd planned."

Alec chuckled in sympathy then gestured consolingly. "I'll ask them for you and don't worry so much between the lot of us we'll get everything done by the time you get back I promise."

Jed walked over and shook Alec's hand in farewell. "I'll take good care of her I promise!"

Alec shook Jed's hand firmly then smirked up at him teasingly as he chuckled knowingly. "I wouldn't be too sure of that if I was you! She just might end up taking care of you!"

Jed laughed in delight as he winked at Mell playfully. "Yeah, you're probably right!"

Mell rolled her eyes at the two of them then waved good-bye to her father as they left the house and walked down to the barn. They entered just as Tommy and Giant Bear were leading the horses out of their stalls fully saddled and ready to go.

Mell walked over to Tommy and put her saddlebag on Lightning. Then she turned and ruffled his hair affectionately in farewell. "You behave while I'm away and I promise that when I get back I'll teach you the proper way to handle a knife."

Tommy grinned up at Mell in excitement as he nodded emphatically in delight then he pointed behind him towards the packhorses stall. "I'll be so good nobody will even know I'm around I promise. We didn't know if you wanted your packhorse this time but I didn't think you would since you want to get there and back in a hurry?"

Mell shook her head negatively. "No you're right we don't need him this time."

Mell turned and hugged Tommy good-bye then led her horse out of the barn while Jed and Giant Bear talked. She had just mounted when Jed led his horse out then mounted beside her. They turned and waved to Tommy and Giant Bear as the two came out of the barn to say good-bye before they urging their horses into a trot to warm them up then into a gallop.

Mell led Jed in a southwest direction that would skirt the town and take them directly to Miller's Creek. They maintained their speed for an hour before finally slowing to a trot for another hour then to a walk for an additional hour. Once the hour was up they started all over again.

Mell and Jed did this twice more than camped for a quick lunch and coffee. They rested their horses for about an hour then mounted and repeated their earlier routine. Camp was set up again around six o'clock that night. But this time they unsaddled the horses and rubbed them down to give them both a much-needed rest.

Mell smiled over at Jed tiredly. "We'll have supper here, and give the horses an hour and a half, or better yet two hours to rest up for the last leg of the journey. It's another four hours of hard riding before we get to where I want to camp for the night it'll be around midnight when we get there and I'm definitely not going to feel like cooking."

Jed nodded then walked around collecting deadfall to start a fire with while Mell took out their food then placed it where she wanted the fire to be so it would be in easy reach.

While Jed was starting the fire Mell went over to her saddlebags and rummaged in the extra one that Giant Bear had thoughtfully hooked behind her horse then took out some oats to feed the horses with. In the other side was hay but she decided to leave the hay for when they stopped for the night. She had to wait for the fire anyway and feeding the horses kept her occupied while she waited.

The fire was ready when she came back so she threw potatoes, carrots, and deer meat into the skillet her father had provided with some water from her canteen and a little flour for gravy. Within half an hour they were enjoying their stew.

Jed dug in greedily and even had seconds before Mell could finish her first bowl. Mell smiled teasingly at Jed across the fire as she watched his enjoyment in gratification glad he was take pleasure in the food she had cooked. "I have enough meat and vegetables left over for another stew tomorrow if you like."

Jed grinned in delight as he looked at Mell across the fire. "Best news I've heard all day!"

Mell laughed in satisfaction as Jed rubbed his belly appreciatively and finished her stew then let Jed have what was left in the pot since she was full anyway.

Mell smirked saucily over at Jed as she gestured at all the dirty dishes. "I cooked so you can do the dishes!"

Jed groaned in mock dismay then nodded in reluctance before gathering up the dishes and heading for a small creek in the distance. When he got back Mell was sitting propped against her saddle cleaning and oiling both her guns. Normally this was Tommy's job but he had been busy with his father the last few days and Mell needed something to do for another half hour anyway.

Jed went over to his saddle then picked it up and carried it over to Mell then he sat back against his saddle as well. He rolled two cigarettes one he handed to Mell after he lit them with a stick out of the fire the other one he stuck in his mouth before taking out his own kit then cleaned and oiled his guns as well.

Mell finished first and reloaded then put them back in her holster before she threw what was left of her cigarette into the fire. The two hours were up so she started breaking camp while Jed finished cleaning his gun.

Jed finished loading and put it back in his holster before getting up to help Mell finish breaking camp. He looked over at Mell curiously as he motioned inquisitively. "What are we doing first when we get to town?"

Mell sighed plaintively as she hefted her saddle onto Lightning's back. "The first thing I'm doing is heading for the hotel to take a hot bath."

Jed grinned teasingly over his horses back at Mell as he did up the girth on his saddled. "Feeling saddle sore Sheriff?"

Mell smiled over her shoulder at Jed's teasing tone. "Not really I just don't usually like to push my horses this hard and since I need to stable Lightning for awhile anyway to give him a rest, I might as well relax myself!"

Jed smirked in disbelief not convinced by her explanation at all. "Well, I certainly like your way of thinking. I'll even admit to feeling a little saddle sore even if you won't!"

Mell laughed playfully and gave in as she gestured plaintively before mounting her horse. "Okay, I admit to feeling a little saddle sore! You'd think with all the riding I do I wouldn't have this problem!"

Jed mounted and chuckled at Mell's grimace of pain. "I don't think it really matters how much you ride. The only time I can recall not being saddle sore is when I rode Indian style with a blanket for a saddle!"

Mell smiled and nodded thoughtfully as she recalled that at one time that was the only way she would ride. Now that she thought about it at that time she never knew what a saddle sore was. She shrugged dismissively then nudged her horse. "Let's go!"

They rode hard for the next four hours luckily they had a three quarter moon so could see quite well and only slowed once to give the horses time to rest. They reached their campsite around midnight after unsaddling both horses and feeding them some hay the two put their sleeping bags together then dropped into them in exhaustion. They slept for a few hours then continued their gruelling pace the next day with one exception they didn't stop at midnight this time but kept going hoping to get to the hotel before dawn.

Mell and Jed exceeded their expectations as they arrived at the hotel just after three in the morning. Mell was relieved they had made it in two days not an easy feat by any means since normally it took almost three days to get here under ordinary riding conditions. They were both exhausted and Mell patted her sweat encrusted exhausted horse in sympathy.

Immediately she roused the stableman to look after their horses she flipped a fifty-cent piece at him for his troubles. "Please take special care of them we've ridden them pretty hard the last two days and they're both exhausted."

Mell and Jed gathered their rifles and saddlebags except for the one Giant Bear had given them for the horses then they limped painfully into the hotel, once they were satisfied that the stableman was taking good care of their horses.

Mell decided not to take her whip so left it tied to her saddle. She figured it wouldn't do her any good in this situation anyway. Mell walked up to the desk while Jed hung back a little and waited for her.

The man at the desk looked up and stared in surprise for a moment not expecting to see the sheriff so soon. She had only left a few weeks ago. "Well Sheriff Ray what are you doing here? We weren't expecting you for another three weeks at the least."

Mell smiled at the desk clerk then grinned he was the complete opposite of the hotel clerk in Smyth's Crossing. He had blonde hair, was short, and chubby with a friendly twinkle in his hazel brown eyes. The two hotel clerks were so different in looks and manner that it always made Mell chuckle when she thought of the two of them at the same time.

Mell tiredly put a finger to her lips in a silencing motion. "Well John I need to speak to Deputy Ted but I don't want anyone else to know I'm here yet. So can you keep quiet about it please?"

John nodded perplexed then grinned reassuringly. "Sure I won't tell anybody that you're here."

Mell sighed in relief then nodded her thanks as she pointed behind her at Jed. "We need a room and a bath if it's possible this time of morning."

John beamed accommodatingly then waved in agreement. "Both are possible for you Sheriff. Rooms ten and eleven are available if you like."

Mell leaned over the counter then whispered in conspiracy. "Just one room John that man over there is Deputy Brown and my fiancée so he can share my room."

John moved over slightly so he could see Jed better for a moment in surprise then turned back to Mell with a big grin a mile long as he reached out and shook Mell's hand in best wishes. "Well congratulations Sheriff! It's about time you decided to get married!"

Mell nodded as she let go of John's hand then stepped back from the counter with a conspiring grin. "Just don't tell anyone for now okay."

John frowned then motioned knowingly. "But you do know there's going to be a few disappointed men around here, especially Deputy Ted. He's been in love with you for years, although I do know a Lady who will be very happy to hear about this. Claire has been in love with Deputy Ted for just about as long as he's been in love with you."

Mell smiled pleased that her marriage would help Claire with Ted. "Well it should work out for the two of them now that I'm out of the picture."

John nodded happily in relief maybe now Claire would quit mopping around here. "Do you want me to send for Ted right away?"

Mell shook her head negatively. "No. Send a boy around nine o'clock to bring him here. I would also be much obliged if you could send breakfast up to our room around eight."

John inclined his head in assent then took a key from the shelf and handed it to Mell. She smiled in thanks then waved in approval. "Oh, when you make out the bill for the town make sure you add a half dollar tip for yourself."

John beamed in pleasure. "Well thank you Sheriff!"

Mell gathered the things that she had put up against the counter while they talked and waved good-bye then she headed for the stairs and their room.

Jed smiled over at the desk clerk then touched the brim of his hat in goodnight without saying anything as he followed Mell upstairs. He stood back waiting as she unlocked the door. They entered and hung up their saddlebags on the hooks put there for that purpose.

Jed fell on the bed in exhaustion and watched as Mell took their clothes out of her saddlebags then hung them up in the closet. Before she too sprawled on the bed beside him just close enough that they were touching slightly.

Jed groaned in reluctance as he rolled off the bed to answer a knock on the door. He peered out cautiously then opened the door wide to let in the boys carrying a large tub. Behind them a girl with brown hair and grey eyes followed carrying a tray holding a steaming pot of coffee along with ham sandwiches and cake. The girl was willowy and pretty but only medium height at five foot three.

Jed grinned in delight as his belly rumbled slightly in hunger at the sight of the food. "We didn't order that but I must say it's more than welcome!"

The woman set the tray down carefully on the nightstand beside the bed then turned to Jed with a smile as she waved down the hallway. "The clerk told me to tell you that there are tubs down the hallway for men. If you'll come with me I'll show you where they are. You can return there in half an hour and one of the tubs will be filled for you."

Jed followed her to the bathing room before heading back for a quick bite to eat before his bath. Three boys passed him in the hallway carrying buckets of hot water to fill his tub.

Mell sat up reluctantly, but the coffee smelt so inviting that she just couldn't refuse the invitation then poured herself a cup. She was eating one of the sandwiches when Jed came back. Mell smiled in greeting then pointed at the door. "Leave the door open the boys will be back with the bath water in a few minutes."

Jed left the door ajar as bidden then walked over and poured himself a cup of coffee before he began munching on a sandwich hungrily as he waited. He just got settled on the bed as they both sat there compatibly sipping their coffee when four boys came in with two buckets of water each and filled the bathtub.

Jed dug into his pocket and pulled out four pennies one for each boy then before they left he flipped them high. The boys caught their pennies and grinned in thanks.

Mell smiled at them sympathetically as they smothered yawns. "You can go back to bed after you fill the tub down the hallway. I'm sure the clerk won't mind if you wait until later to empty the tubs."

The boys nodded gratefully and left closing the door behind them gently. They went to give their brothers the good news.

Mell and Jed ate everything on the tray and had another cup of coffee before Jed had to get up and answer another knock on the door. It was the same girl that had showed him where to bath but this time she was carrying a supply of towels and soap along with a pail of warm water to wash Mell's hair.

Jed smiled in greeting, grabbed clean clothes, then turned and waved good-bye to Mell as he headed for his own bath.

Mell grinned gratefully at Claire then removed her shirt and walked over to the tub so that Claire could wash her hair. Mell bent over and made sure that all her hair was floating in the bathwater so they wouldn't make too much of a mess.

Claire sighed wishfully. "You have such beautiful hair Sheriff."

Mell beamed even though she knew Claire couldn't see it. "Well thank you Claire. I think your hair is beautiful too."

Claire nodded gratefully at the praise then tipped the bucket of warm water a little too wet Mell's hair as she asked curiously never having seen the sheriff with a deputy before. "Who's the man with you Sheriff if you don't mind me asking?"

Mell groaned in pleasure as Claire massaged soap into her scalp vigorously. "That's my new Deputy he's also my fiancée."

Claire paused for a moment in surprise then continued washing Mell's hair. Mell didn't need to see Claire's ecstatic grin she could hear it in her voice. "Congratulations Sheriff. I am so glad to hear that!"

Mell chuckled knowingly. "I'm sure you are! It wouldn't happen to be because of another Deputy we both know would it?"

Claire giggled in delight. "I think everyone knows that I'm in love with him except the man himself. He just vexes me so at times. He can't see what's staring him in the face!"

Mell laughed and stood up a little so that Claire could rinse her hair. "All men can be obtuse when they want to be."

Claire handed Mell a towel to wrap her hair in then she went over and picked up the tray. She turned and smiled gratefully at Mell when she saw the two bits lying on the tray. "Thank you!"

Mell inclined her head in farewell. "I'll see you tomorrow Claire. Oh can you please keep our engagement a secret for the moment we don't want anyone to know yet."

Claire quickly agreed then closed the door behind her.

Mell undressing after Claire left then she crawled into the tub with a thankful sigh. She looked at the closed door with a smirk as she thought of Claire. Of course she would run to see Ted as soon as she could get away that's why Mell had told her. She laid back to enjoy the hot water and was fast asleep in moments.

* * *

Jed finished his bath and dressed quickly then hurried back to the room. He looked at the bed when he entered expecting Mell to be in it already but she wasn't there. He looked around perplexed then spotted Mell sound asleep in the tub.

Jed chuckled in delight before throwing his dirty clothes into the corner then grabbed a towel that was beside the tub and placed it on the bed. He quickly got undressed not wanting to get his clean clothes wet then he went over to the tub. He scooped Mell up into his arms gently not wanting to wake her. Leaving a trail of water he carried her over to the bed then laid her on the towel carefully.

Mell murmured in her sleep but didn't wake up.

Jed dried her off as best he could and rubbed her hair to dry it a little before he put her under the covers. He grinned down at his fierce little sheriff and chuckled normally he wouldn't have been able to get away with coming into the room without her being instantly aware of him. The fact that she never even woke up when he lifted her out of the tub made him glad she was getting use to having him around. That she trusted him enough to be able to relax completely and let her guard down meant the world to him.

He chuckled in disbelief at himself as he looked down and found himself in a state of arousal from just drying Mell's body but he ignored it as he snuffed out the light. He crawled into bed beside her then gathered her close as he sighed in contentment and was fast asleep within minutes.

CHAPTER SEVENTEEN

Mell woke to the feel of Jed stroking her breast tenderly. She stretched and yawned contentedly then turned to Jed inquisitively. "Good morning. How did I get to bed? The last thing I remember is lying back in the tub."

Jed chuckled in delight as he remembered finding Mell in the tub. "I came back from my bath and you were sound asleep in the tub so I carried you to the bed then dried you off as best I could before tucking you in."

Mell stifled another yawn still more asleep then awake. "What time is it?"

Jed tweaked her nose playfully. "Our breakfast should be here soon."

Mell kissed him lightly then rolled off the bed. "Well we better get dressed then. I really don't want Ted to see me like this. I just might give him a heart attack."

Jed chuckled then got up and got dressed as well. They just sat back down on the bed when a discreet knock was heard. Jed got up to answer it, while Mell tried to comb the knots out of her hair.

Jed peeked out then opened the door wide to let a girl of about seventeen in. She wasn't the same girl from last night this one had short black curly hair and she was taller. The young girl set a loaded breakfast tray beside the bed then left with a smile of thanks after Jed put a penny in her hand. He lifted the cloth away from the tray and smiled hungrily in delight at the bacon, eggs, and two buns with jam spread on top. He sighed loudly in pleasure.

Jed looked over at Mell then grinned sympathetically at the look of pure torment on her face as she tried to untangle a stubborn knot in her hair. Taking pity at her plight he gestured enticingly. "Mell come over here and have breakfast. Then I'll get the knots out of your hair for you later once we finish eating."

Mell groaned in relief as she dropped her brush on the bed thankfully and obediently scooted over to sit beside him then started eating hungrily.

Jed finished first and picked up the brush then knelt behind her on the bed and gently but methodically attacked the stubborn knots. Mell finished her breakfast and put her head back in delight then sighed in pleasure as Jed finally got all the knots out but kept brushing her hair anyway in contentment. He had never brushed a woman's hair before nor realized how much he would enjoy doing it or even how aroused he would become just from such a little chore. Jed chuckled at himself as he lovingly continued to brush Mell's hair even though there was no need to now. "I love your hair I hope you never cut it."

Mell smiled knowingly at the way Jed phrased his request for her not to cut her hair. He didn't say she couldn't, only that he hoped she wouldn't, very diplomatic of him she couldn't help thinking. Jed wasn't the only one feeling frisky all of a sudden as she grinned savouring the sensation. She would have to get him to brush her hair more often now that she knew how it made her feel.

She groaned in disappointment when a knock on the door caused Jed to lay the brush aside and get up to answer it. Jed chuckled knowingly at the groan and the look of disappointment on Mell's face as he strode over to open it just as reluctant as Mell was.

The man on the other side of the door looked at Jed in confusion as the door opened. He gestured in apology. "I'm sorry I must have the wrong room!"

Jed smiled in greeting as he saw the badge pinned to the man's vest. Jed shook his head negatively in reassurance. "No you don't not if you're looking for the Sheriff that is."

Jed opened the door wider so that Ted could see Mell then beckoned him to come into the room. Jed shut the door softly and turned to evaluate Ted. He was tall at six foot two but not as tall he was. He had sandy blonde hair with deep, deep brown eyes almost black and a fairly handsome rugged face. He was slim almost painfully so it gave him a lanky look. His gun hung low on his hip and was well cared for.

Ted was studying Jed just as intently. Mell got up and made the introductions when both men continued to stare at each other without either looking away. The two men shook hands once introductions were finished then they nodded cordially at each other in greeting.

Ted turned to Mell inquisitively. Now that he saw the two of them together he realized Claire was right even though he had refused to believe her when she had told him. "I heard you were getting married but I didn't want to believe it. Congratulations to both of you, although I should dislike the man for stealing you away. I have always known that you were never really interested in me."

Mell smiled in apology she had known Ted was in love with her for a long time now, that's why she had told Claire last night. Mell motioned consolingly. She grinned teasingly. "But I know a Lady who works here who's very interested in you."

Ted blushed slightly in embarrassment then sighed knowingly. "You're talking about Claire of course. I've known for awhile how she felt but I wasn't ready yet."

Mell nodded in understanding then waved towards the door. "Let's go down for coffee and talk there."

Mell turned to Jed then shook her head negatively as he reached towards the table beside the bed where he had put his badge. "Jed, don't put your badge on right now. We don't want anyone to know about you just yet."

Jed frowned in puzzlement but nodded as he buckled on his gun belt and put his hat on but left his badge on the table obediently. He watched as Mell buckled on her gun belt but instead of putting her hat on she just tied her hair back with a ribbon and she left her badge on the table as well. Jed raised his eyebrows in surprise but she just shrugged then gestured self-consciously. "I'm not on duty. I'm just another woman going to have coffee in the dining room."

Jed looked Mell up and down suggestively then chuckled in disbelief. "No one would ever take you for just another woman!"

Ted smiled at the two of them as they bantered back and forth, he grinned in delight when Mell blushed a fiery red. He had never seen her blush before not even when they had to go into the whorehouse.

He opened the door then led them down to the dining room. They took a corner table that gave them a view of the whole room. Ted watched as Jed and Mell both set their chairs against the wall and sat down. He sighed shrewdly and took a chair across from them but made sure he wasn't in the way of their view. Ted smiled over at Mell in apology. "Well, I didn't expect you to rush down here until there was actual trouble. I just wanted you to be aware that there might be, but so far he's keeping to himself."

The waitress came over and poured them coffee. Mell waited until she left before shrugged dismissively. "We're getting married in four days. We figured that we better find out what's going on now. I would hate to miss my own wedding!"

Ted sighed sadly as Mell referred to her wedding once more then shrugged of his feelings. He became deadly serious as he waved in warning. "Well, it's a good thing you did come anyway. We had another hired gun show up last night."

Mell raised her eyebrows in surprise as she motioned in irritation. "Another one what are they up to? Do you know who they are?"

Ted inclined his head knowingly. "The one that came first and has been here for a few days is called Diago, he's Mexican. The one that showed up last night is the same one you chased out of town a couple of years ago, Samson I believe his name is."

Jed frowned pensively at the names and Ted seeing the look on Jed's face gestured curiously. "Do you know either of these men?"

Jed frowned troubled as he remembered back to that horrible day and he shuddered in revulsion as he remembered what Diago had done to that poor girl. "Diago, I had a run in with him a few years ago. He was only about twenty at the time and already a mean son-of-a-bitch I thought I had killed him! I can't see him being any better now than he was then."

Mell sighed in aggravation as she turned to Jed. "Well, this sure clinches it. Two hired guns both with a grudge against one of us here at the same time. I don't like the sound of this at all."

Ted looked from one to the other in concern then turned and directed his question to Mell in confusion. "You think they're after the two of you but whatever for?"

Mell frowned thoughtfully as she explained everything that had happened at her ranch since she had returned from her rounds of the surrounding towns. Ted waited until she finished then he shook his head in disbelief. "That's unbelievable and I can see why you'd be concerned! But who would you suspect of hiring the two gunmen if all the outlaws are dead? Unless they had been hired before the others died?"

Mell shrugged puzzled herself. "I don't know. I suppose it could be just a coincidence."

Jed nodded as he thought about it then he shook his head in denial. "It could be but I wouldn't want to bet on the odds. Do you know where they're staying Ted?"

Ted shrugged in apology. "No I don't know where Samson is staying. But Diago is staying at the Saloon. When Samson arrived last night they both stayed completely away from each other and totally ignore everyone else."

The waitress came over and refilled their coffee cups then motioned enquiringly at Mell. "Would you like some lunch Sheriff?"

Mell glanced at the two men questioningly they both nodded. She looked back up at the waitress as she smiled in thanks. "Yes, you can bring the men whatever is on special and put it on my tab but I'm still full from breakfast."

The waitress left and Mell turned back to Ted as she gestured curiously. "Are there any wanted posters on these two men?"

Ted nodded affirmative. "Yes, for both of them dead or alive pretty hefty rewards too. Samson's is for five hundred alive and two hundred dead. Diago's is one thousand, dead or alive, preferably dead it says."

Mell sighed resignedly. "Well, it looks like Diago is one step away from a 'shoot on sight' poster."

Ted frowned pensively. "I had the same thought myself but I figured I'd better wait for you first. I was sending you another message this morning, good thing Claire came to see me early."

Mell inclined her head in relief glad Ted had more sense than to take on a situation he wouldn't be able to handle himself. "You did the right thing. Those men are far too dangerous for you to handle on your own."

Ted waved resignedly. "Tell me about it! I know my own limitations very well."

The waitress arrived with two bowls of thick beef stew and hot buttered biscuits on the side. The three fell silent as they ate. When they were finished the waitress came back with a piece of apple pie each along with more coffee. She served the desert first and even gave one to Mell before she finished clearing the table. She grinned over at her. "I figured you wouldn't say no to the cook's homemade pie!"

Mell chuckled in agreement. "You know me too well Linda."

Linda smirked knowingly then left without comment. Ted waited for her to leave before he motioned curiously at Mell. "Do you have a plan or an idea as to what you're going to do now?"

Mell nodded she had came up with the idea while the two men were eating. She waved at the two men enticingly. "I have a plan but first I would like to hear if either of you have thought of anything, or if you have something to add now would be a good time before I tell you."

Ted shrugged in bewilderment. "The only thing I can think of is an ambush. Catch them one at a time then throw them in jail and find out what they're up to."

Jed shook his head negatively as he motioned decisively. "No! Diago is as slippery as a newborn foal. He's been caught and put in jail several times already but he always escapes then ends up killing anyone who has had anything to do with his capture. That's why he's still loose. Nobody wants to be his next victim."

Jed turned to Mell anxiously as he gestured in forewarning. "I know you don't like to kill Mell but I think you're going to have to bend your rules this once. If these men are after us they will stop at nothing to kill us. That includes going after our loved ones and killing every one of them until we show ourselves. That's Diago's favourite method of flushing his prey out."

Mell frowned pensively then finally nodded reluctantly. "I think you're right! But how do you suggest we go about it? Should we let it be known that we're here and let them come to us, or do we go looking for them forcing their hand?"

Jed shrugged undecided. "A little of both I think Ted can go to the saloon first and let it be known that we're coming for a drink in celebration of our wedding. We'll leave fifteen minutes after he does and walk up the street slowly. If they're after us they will probably meet us out on the street. If not they'll either leave town immediately or stay in their room until we leave the saloon."

Mell thought about it for a few moments then nodded before gesturing hopefully. "I'm of two minds in a way I'm hoping they'll meet us and we can put a stop to their reign of terror. On the other hand I'm hoping they won't, which would reassure me that no one has hired them to come after us. But either way I'll still have to deal with them now or later. As Sheriff it's my duty to stop them no matter what!"

Jed nodded calmly even though inside he wasn't calm. "I'm also hoping that nobody hired them. But if there is still someone out there who wants us dead that badly we'll have to find out who it is then put a stop to them. Before anyone else gets hurt."

Ted looked at Mell thoughtfully still not convinced by their idea that someone had hired the gunmen. "I think you might still want to keep in mind that maybe they weren't hired but will still meet you on the street, because they hate your guts. For instance Samson wants to get back at Mell because he's dealt with her before and knows that he can't handle her by himself. So he gets a hold of Diago to help him kill her then the two of them can take over the town. Or Diago finds out Jed is here and wants revenge. So he wires Samson because he heard Samson hates the Sheriff out here so they make a deal."

Mell and Jed looked at each other in surprise then they both looked at Ted in admiration. But it was Mell who spoke for the both of them. "Well Ted. Now I know why I hired you! Even if you're not a fast gun you always out think your opponent and manage to get the better of them. I think you're right. All this worrying about who hired them and you give us the reason without even trying."

Ted blushed in pleasure at the praise then smiled at Mell in thanks glad he had contributed. "Well, like you said that's why you hired me. Now what time do you want me to go to the saloon?"

Mell grinned at Ted's blush of pleasure and sighed thoughtfully. "Two o'clock I think is the perfect time. The sun will just be starting to go down and should be behind us by the time we meet the gunmen so we'll have that advantage at least."

Linda came back to the table to pick up their dirty plates. Jed looked up at her inquisitively. "Do you have the time?"

Linda nodded. "It's close to twelve thirty."

Jed inclined his head in thanks then turned back to Ted. He pointed over his shoulder towards the front entrance. "Ted you better go out and start spreading the rumours about Mell coming. Don't mention my name at all or that I'll be coming with her. If anyone asks you don't know who I am or whether I'll be with her."

Ted got up then left. Mell turned to Jed with a troubled frown. "You think they're after me and don't know that you're here!"

Jed shrugged dismissively. "I don't know for sure but the only way for them to know about me is through someone in your town, if Ted is right that is. If someone from your town had told them about me they would have told them that I could be found there not here. But everyone knows that you travel to all the small towns around your own. So it would make sense for them to wait quietly until you showed up here then catch you when your guard is down. They could not only take over this town but all the others as well. There would be no one to stop them!"

Mell sighed thoughtfully. "You're probably right. I just hope they won't guess what we're up to and hightail it out of town."

Mell and Jed quickly finished their coffee and went upstairs to get ready for the fight of their lives.

* * *

Mell and Jed walked out of their room to go to their meeting with the outlaws. Mell impulsively touched Jed's arm to get his attention before they even reached the stairs. Jed turned immediately already guessing what she wanted and needed then quickly enfolded Mell in his arms and kissed her deeply with all the passion he felt for her. Mell broke the kiss reluctantly then smiled up at him lovingly before whispering passionately. "I love you!"

Jed kissed the tip of her nose in reassurance. "I love you too and remember I won't be far behind you!"

Mell felt calm and content now that Jed had reassured her of his love, that's all she had really wanted. They went down to the lobby together Mell turned with a final wave as she gave Jed a bolstering smile then left without him.

They had decided that Mell would walk out alone to give the outlaws a sense of victory with Jed following a little way behind her. When the outlaws came out to meet Mell she would go out into the middle of the street and Jed would catch up to her there then they would meet the outlaws together. They had also decided that Mell would take on Samson since she had dealt with him successfully before and Jed would take on Diego again.

Mell turned and looked up at the sun just behind her then nodded her head in satisfaction. Her estimate had been correct the position of the sun would be a definite asset to them today. She turned back towards the east end of town and she walked to the edge of the sidewalk so she would be as close to the road as possible. She sauntered slowly and confidently towards Jake's Saloon, as if she didn't have a care in the world, but inside she was very worried about Jed. She had never seen Jed use his gun so had no clue what the outcome of today would be.

Mell was just about at the Saloon when two men walked out purposely into the middle of the street arrogantly. Both with a confident swagger then they turned and stared at her intently. Mell smiled in relief as the outlaws came out to meet her and she walked off the sidewalk then ambled slowly towards the middle of the street. Before slowing her pace even more so that Jed would have time to catch up to her. She walked slowly and purposely towards the men taking her time. She was just about to the spot she had picked out to stop when Jed walked up beside her and slowed his step to match hers.

Jed didn't say a word to her and neither of them took their eyes off the outlaws. He did reached over for a quick moment and squeezed her hand before letting go quickly, so that both their hands would be free. Mell was observing the two men closely and saw them look at each other in confusion. Mell smiled to herself in relief well it looked like Ted was right. The outlaws hadn't known about Jed. She reached the spot she had picked out and stopped confidently. Mell smirked nastily at Samson. "I thought I told you to stay out of my towns or I would kill you next time."

Mell relaxed her stance and dropped her hands beside her guns to be ready to draw at a moment's notice as she saw Samson readying himself.

Jed frowned angrily at Diego as he too readied himself. "Well we meet again Diego! Do you remember me?"

Diego shook his head negatively in confusion then snapped his fingers as he remembered suddenly. "Yes, it wasn't far from the Montana border. I'd been hired to kill a man squatting on someone's property when you and the biggest Indian fellow I've ever seen shot my employer instead. You also took a shot at me but luckily I moved a little and the bullet just missed my heart. It took me six months to recover so I owe you one. Where is that Indian fellow by the way?"

Jed smiled grimly as he remembered Giant Bear's rage. "Lucky for you he's not around at the moment. If I remember correctly he would like to talk to you about the Indian woman you cut up after you finished raping her."

Diago shrugged nonchalantly. "What does it matter she was just a whore anyway!"

Samson broke in glaring in hatred at first Jed then Mell as he turned to her fully. "Who the hell is this man? This is none of his business!"

Mell smirked in delight as she taunted. "This is my Deputy Jed and also my fiancée. So you see it is his business!"

Samson scowled furiously then hissed in warning. "Enough talking I'll give you one chance to get out of North Dakota or I'll kill you!"

Mell glared insolently then taunted Samson knowing that when he was angry his reflexes slowed considerably. "Sorry to disappoint you Samson but I'm not going anywhere. Besides the minute I turned my back to you, you would shoot me. I'm just a little surprised that you had the guts to face me. Usually, you lurk around corners and shoot people in the back."

Samson growled in rage and went for his gun just as Mell had anticipated. He stared in shock as he saw Mell's smoking pistol pointed at him. His gun had hardly moved from the holster before her bullet struck his heart and he fell over backwards. He was dead before he hit the ground.

Jed waited patiently while he listened to Mell taunting Samson but he didn't take his eyes off Diago. The Mexican drew his gun at the same time that Samson did and Jed was ready as he drew his own. But he wasn't as fast as Mell was or even Diago but the Mexican made a fatal mistake as he turned his gun on Mell first.

Mell caught Diago shifting his aim out of the corner of her eye and since she had drawn both her guns in preparation of helping Jed it only took a slight movement of her wrist to shift her aim. Mell's bullet hit first then Jed's entered Diago's body a half a second later. The Mexican was dead before he even knew what hit him.

Mell and Jed turned as one to stare at each other anxiously they both eyed each other from head to toe to make sure that they were unharmed. Mell put her guns away and took a hesitant step towards Jed. Jed took the final step and swept Mell into his arms for a long passionate kiss of relief at their close call.

It wasn't until a tremendous cheer arose around them that they realized the whole town had surrounded them. Since Mell took over as sheriff gunfights were outlawed and it was rare that the town got to see one. Every person in town had heard about the gunfight and they were now cheering and clapping their approval. Not only because of the demise of the two outlaws. But also for the passionate kiss they had just witnessed. Mell pushed away from Jed in embarrassment and blushed a fiery red at being caught kissing with such wild abandon.

Jed put an arm around her in relief as he bent down and whispered lovingly. "I love you Mell!"

Mell smiled up at him adoringly. "I love you too!"

Ted pushed his way through the crowd and shook Jed's hand first then Mell's. "That was the best shooting I've seen in a long time. But

I'm sorry Jed. If I had to put money on one of you it would have to be Mell!"

Jed chuckled as he nodded calmly without a shred of jealously. "I don't blame you. If Diago hadn't messed up and turned his gun on Mell first. I'd probably be dead now instead of him. He was definitely way better than he used to be."

Mell shuddered in reaction in his arms and he squeezed her reassuringly before letting her go. Jed looked around at the crowd and shouted loud enough so everybody could hear him. "First drinks on me!"

All the men cheered in thanks then rushed for the saloon. Jed turned to Ted and waved down at the bodies. "Will you see to them while I buy my bride-to-be a shot of whiskey to calm her nerves?"

Ted nodded then flipped a coin at a boy to go and get the undertaker for him. Jed put his arm around Mell again then steered her over to the saloon. She was still shivering slightly in reaction at Jed's close call. When they entered everyone cheered and a space was made for them so that they could reach the bar. Jed smiled in greeting at the man behind the bar and put out his hand for a shake. "You must be Jake. I'm Jed Brown Mell's new Deputy. Can I get two shot of whiskey one for me and one for the Lady please?"

Jake was tall but not as tall as Jed and hefty but not fat. He was just very muscular and he reminded Jed of a miner turned saloonkeeper. He had black hair and light brown eyes. He shook Jed's hand it was firm but not crushingly so. "Sure thing Deputy!"

Jake poured them each a shot and handed them across the counter. "Are ya really getting married to our Sheriff or was that just a ruse to get the gunmen out?"

Jed grinned in conspiracy as he leaned closer to the bar to be heard above the noise. "That was no ruse Jake. We're really getting married in four days."

Jake roared in glee then banged loudly on the bar to get everyone's attention as he hollered above the noise. "Next drink is on the house. Mell is really getting married!"

Jed heard a few groans of disappointment in the crowed but everyone cheered and came over to shake Jed and Mell's hand in congratulations.

Mell smiled in gratitude at everyone in the crowded bar then hollered out. "Next drink is on me!"

The men cheered again and a toast was given to their very own one of a kind lady sheriff. Mell drank to the toast then turned to Jake. "Make out the bill and send it to the Mayor make sure to add a tip for yourself. I think its time for us to head home!"

Jake nodded in thanks and handed Mell a paper to sign before starting to write down the drinks and amounts. Jed waited until he finished then paid for his round in cash before flipping a silver dollar Jake's way. Jake expertly caught it then saluted in thanks.

Mell touched Jed's arm pleadingly. "Let's go home Jed."

Jed nodded in full agreement then steered Mell through the crowd but it took them quite a while to get through the doors since everyone kept stopping them along the way for handshakes and more congratulations.

Mell took a deep breath of fresh air when they reached the sidewalk just outside the saloon and looked towards the spot where the two outlaws had died. The bodies had been removed already thankfully. Mell looked up at Jed as she waved down the street. "I need to talk to Ted then I'd like to stop at the store before we go."

Jed followed Mell to the sheriff's office. They entered the building and found Ted already writing up his report. Mell walked up to the desk and cleared her throat slightly to get his attention. Ted looked up in surprise then smiled in greeting when he saw who it was. "Well neither one of you look that bad for the ordeal you just went through."

Mell laughed in delight then motioned agreeably. "It's amazing what a few shots of whiskey can do for a person."

Ted chuckled knowingly then gestured curiously. "What can I do for you Sheriff?"

Mell pointed down at the report Ted was making out. "We want to leave right away so I'd like to know if you would send a note in your report to the Mayor let him know where not going to Smyth's Crossing just yet but straight to the ranch so tell him know we'll be at home when he gets this."

Ted sighed in disappointment then waved enticingly. "I can if you like but why don't you stay over until tomorrow morning, it's getting pretty late?"

Mell shook her head negatively. "I made a promise to a boy and I must keep it. Plus I need to finish getting ready for my wedding."

Ted nodded in understanding then got up and walked around the desk for a congratulations hug from Mell before he turned to shake Jed's hand. "I'll see you when Mell comes back this way."

Jed inclined his head in farewell. "I'll look forward to it."

Mell and Jed saluted in good-bye and left the building. Mell walked slowly towards the store trying to find a way to get rid of Jed then she looked sideways at him slyly. "Do you need anything from the store?"

Jed shook his head negatively. "No nothing that can't wait until we get home."

Mell smiled in relief as she pointed towards the hotel hopefully. "Well why don't you go to the hotel and have our horses saddled while I grab a couple of things?"

Jed nodded not suspecting a thing and took off across the street. Mell rushed into the store and walked up to the counter. The storeowner turned in surprise at the sight of the sheriff. "Well hello Sheriff what can I do for you? I didn't even know you were back in town?"

Mell grinned knowingly at Luke he was completely opposite of Charlie. He was short and slim almost mousy appearing with thick glasses that always fell down his nose. He had blonde thin hair and dark green eyes. She knew he wouldn't be aware that she was in town because he almost never left his beloved store, unless his wife made him go for something. Mell smiled hopefully. "I'm looking for a pocket watch for my fiancée."

Luke nodded pleased that he had one then reached under the counter. "I have just the watch for you."

He opened an engraved box and pushed it towards Mell. She bent down to inspect the watch and gasped in surprise. It was a beautiful gold watch with a rearing black horse engraved on the front. Mell picked it up and opened it then smiled in delight when it played a tune. She set the watch down then nodded eagerly. "I'll take it."

Luke smiled knowingly then wrapped it while Mell walked around the store waiting for him to finish. She noticed a new rifle in a display case and went over and took it out in interest. Luke walked over after he finished wrapping her watch as he noticed her interest sensing another sale. "That's a repeater rifle. It will shoot fifteen bullets before you need to reload. Here let me show you."

Mell handed it to him in interest then watched closely. Luke took ten bullets out of the box on a stand and started shoving in bullets one at a time. Mell watched in amazement as he loaded all ten bullets into the chamber, as she shook her head in disbelief. Luke then beckoned to Mell to follow him and he led her out the back door where he had a target set up ready for anyone wishing to try out the new rifles. He explained how the gun worked first. "After you put the bullets in and push the lever over then down it's ready to fire the first shot."

He fired the gun then lowered it to show Mell how to get rid of the empty bullet. "Then to expel the shell you just pull up the hammer and pull it back to where you had it when you loaded it."

Mell watched in amazement as the empty shell popped out. Luke smiled in delight at her surprised expression. "Now to fire the next bullet all you do is push the hammer over again and down."

Luke lifted the rifle then fired again and the gun responded. Mell watched closely as he expelled the bullet again and reset it for the next shot. Luke handed the rifle over to Mell for her to try. "You try it."

Mell took the gun then hefted it. It was light as a feather she put it to her shoulder then fired a shot and waited for the recoil but it was so light she hardly even felt it. Smiling in delight she had the rest of the bullets expelled within moments. She looked at Luke then smiled widely. "How many of these do you have?"

Luke shrugged in apology. "Not many yet only four but they should be in the store at Smyth's Crossing by now. If not all Charlie has to do is get a hold of 'Winchester Repeating Rifles' in Boston. Make sure he tells them that the model number is 1866 and they'll send him some."

Mell sighed slightly in disappointment at not being able to get more then she grinned good-naturedly. "Okay I'll take all four and as much ammunition as you have for them."

Luke led the way back into the store. Mell walked to the counter then waved down at the rifles in explanation. "Just wrap up the rifles in an oil cloth and the bullets as well."

Luke smiled enticingly. "Is that everything Sheriff?"

Mell laughed then held up her hand in surrender. "It'll have to be. I don't have any more room left for anything else. You can put two of the rifles and most of the bullets except for two boxes on the town's tab. For the rest I'll sign a bank note."

Luke frowned in disappointment that she didn't want anything else then tallied up the town's bill first so Mell could sign it. He then filled out a bank note on the two rifles, two boxes of shells for each gun, and the watch. Mell signed it then tucked the watch away in her shirt pocket under her vest and gathered the four rifles, which had two boxes of shells in each wrapping. Mell left in a rush and carried her burden to the hotel.

Mell smiled at her horse as she passed the hitching post but didn't stop. She rushed into the lobby and she grinned over at the clerk but didn't stop there either, as she ran up the stairs and kicked at the door to be let in. Jed opened the door and jumped back out of the way as he stared at Mell in surprise. She almost barrelled into him on her way in and set the bundles on the bed. Jed's eyebrows rose in indignation as he turned to her then laughed. "Well, what do you have there?"

Mell smiled up at him in delight then told him about the new guns. Jed walked over speculatively and uncovered one of the rifles then examined it. He put it back reluctantly and smiled at Mell in approval. "Well I can't try one here so let's get going. I can try one when we stop for the night."

Mell nodded excitedly. "The horses are out at the hitching post so all we have to do is pack up. We can stick the rifles in our bed rolls for now."

Jed motioned around the room then grinned teasingly. "I've already packed everything and as you can see it's already on the horses."

Mell looked around in surprise and noticed that there was nothing left in the room. She smiled at Jed in approval. "Okay let's go. I have to stop in the lobby and sign my bill on the way out. Oh did you get our provisions out of the cold room?"

Jed nodded his head in pride. "Both are already done Sheriff! All we have to do is get on our horses and ride off into the sunset."

Mell laughed and handed him two of the rifles to carry. "Well let's go then."

Mell and Jed raced down the stairs together then walked across the lobby and waved good-bye to the clerk as they left the hotel. But they didn't stop too eager to get home. They put the rifles inside the bedrolls then mounted and rode out of town. Mell smiled over at Jed. "I want to reach the campsite we used last night so we'll have to ride hard if we're to reach it by midnight."

Jed nudged his horses into a gallop immediately without argument eager to get there as well. They arrived just before midnight as Mell had hoped and they unsaddled the horses and rubbed them down good in apology for pushing them so hard.

Mell made beans with hardtack too tired for anything else. Jed got stuck doing dishes again and when he got back Mell took out one of the rifles then showed him how to use it. After they practiced for awhile in the dark not even sure if they hit anything but both were now more proficient in loading and firing rapidly. They sat by the fire and had one last coffee before bed. Jed smiled at Mell hopefully. "Who are you giving the rifles to?"

Mell grinned at Jed's optimistic tone of voice. "Well there's one for you and me of course. Then I figured I would give one to Tommy and one to Giant Bear as parting gifts. I'll go to Charlie's and order more for the men later."

Jed rubbed his hands together in anticipation. "Thank you I'd love to have one."

Mell chuckled knowingly at Jed's eager voice and pulled out his other gift then handed it to him dramatically. "I never had a chance to get you a wedding gift before but I found something in town that I think you'll like."

Jed took the gift in surprise then opened it. He smirked in surprised delight as he realized that she had gotten him a watch just because he had asked the waitress for the time. He held it closer to the fire so that he could see the decoration on the front then opened it and smiled in pleasure when he heard music coming from it. Jed leaned over and gathered Mell into his arms then kissed her passionately. He smiled down at her gratefully as he let her go. "It's beautiful and I'll think of you every time I look at it, come to bed now we have a long trip ahead of us tomorrow."

Mell kicked the fire out then followed Jed to the bed he had made for them earlier while she was cooking. They kissed goodnight then cuddled close together both were asleep in moments too exhausted for anything else.

CHAPTER EIGHTEEN

Mell and Jed woke just before sunup and had a quick coffee then finished off the beans from the night before. Mell got up from the fire then retrieved one of the rifles and two boxes of shells then threw them to Jed one at a time so he could catch them. She then grabbed her own rifle and two boxes of shells for herself. They both spent twenty minutes practicing before they went to saddle up their horses. Mell took her old nickel one shot rifle out of its sheath. It had been made in Paris by a man named B. Houllier and put it in the oilskin to be retired. She put her new lighter repeater rifle in the sheath on her saddle in glee with a satisfied thunk it settled perfectly inside. Jed did the same and Mell smiled over at him in delight. "This new rifle is ten pounds lighter. I like it already."

Jed grinned in agreement then mounted. He took out his new watch and looked at the time speculatively as he looked over at Mell. "It's five thirty I'd like to get back to the ranch in time for supper tomorrow night. Do you think the horses would stand such a hard ride?"

Mell smiled saucily over at him. "I'll race you!"

With that she dug in her heels and raced away. Jed smiled indulgently after her as he tucked his new watch into his pocket securely then kicked his own horse into a gallop as he raced to catch up to her.

* * *

Mell and Jed rode into the ranch yard at five o'clock the next day and grinned at each other in delight they had made it for supper as they had hoped. They had only stopped once today to give the horses a much

280

needed rest and for a quick bite to eat just after lunch. Both horses were foam slicked and blowing hard but not dangerously so.

Dusty and Tommy came running out of the barn at the sound of running horses they both stopped short in surprise at the sight of Mell and Jed nobody had expected the two back until at least tomorrow. The two boys looked at each other in concern at the conditions of the horses then turned back and walked over as Mell and Jed dismounted. They grabbed their saddlebags, new rifles, and bedrolls. Mell smiled in greeting at Dusty and Tommy then her tone became serious. "The horses are pretty exhausted take special care of them for me boys."

Tommy nodded solemnly already aware of what to do. This wasn't the first time he had seen Lightning like this, but not very often did it happen. Both boys turned away and trotted the horses slowly towards the barn in concern.

Mell and Jed raced each other to the house where Alec was waiting in the entryway having heard the commotion as well. Plus Wade had run in as soon as he saw them coming to tell Alec. He grinned in satisfaction they were earlier then he had thought they would be and that was a good sign that everything had gone well.

Mell set her stuff down then rushed over in relief for a big hug and kiss from her father not even bothering to remove her outer cloths first. Alec smiled up at Mell curiously as she stood back up. "Well that certainly didn't take long. I wasn't expecting you guys back until midnight tonight or tomorrow morning."

Mell smiled grimly as she remembered the ordeal of the last few days. "I'll explain everything when we're all together. Are Wade and Giant Bear having supper with us tonight I want them both here as well?"

Alec nodded that they were then he explained the progress at the ranch so far. "Yes but Mrs. Elton, Jane, and Sara left a little while ago. Mrs. Elton said to tell you that your dress is done except for a final fitting to make sure everything is right. The archway and platform are decorated except for a few flowers that we figured you'd want to put on. Hopefully, it won't rain until after the wedding. Brad and Jane's cabin is almost finished and the floor on Gloria and Wade's cabin has been started.

Everyone is waiting for you in the kitchen right now including Giant Bear and Wade."

Mell and Jed hadn't been idle while Alec talked. They both took off their parkas, gun belts, boots, and hats then put their badges away on the shelf. Before changing into moccasins then reaching down and grabbing their new rifles and bedrolls. Mell smiled down teasingly at her father. "I have a surprise for everyone after supper."

Mell turned to Jed then gestured down the hallway to their left. "We can put these in the den until after we've eaten."

Jed headed there obediently with Mell following him. Alec followed the two of them trying to pry out more information. "What do you have they're Mell? Those are definitely not the rifles I gave you when you left here."

Mell deposited her bundle on the divan and walked over then patted her father on the shoulder teasingly before going behind his chair and pushing him towards the kitchen. Mell grinned devilishly at Jed behind Alec's back so he couldn't see. "Sorry Dad. You're just going to have to wait until after supper like everyone else."

Alec sighed in disappointment as they reached the kitchen. Mell pushed her father inside then up to the table. Mell smiled in greeting at everyone as she and Jed sat down in the two empty chairs that were together. Tommy came in just as Jessica put the roast on the table and smiled over at Mell hopefully. "Dusty called Brad in to help him so I could come and eat is that okay Aunt Mell?"

Mell smiled and nodded permission then waved at the empty seat for Tommy to sit. She waited for Jessica to have a seat as well before giving a quick blessing on the food then everyone dug in. They all ate in silence until the meal was finished. Mell sat back in her chair to enjoy her coffee as she watched Jessica, Gloria, and Mary cleared the table then they brought more coffee before sitting down as well. Once everyone was seated again Mell told them everything that had happened except for the rifles of course, she wanted that to be a surprise. Alec waited until she finished then he gave a relieve sigh before gesturing thankfully. "So our fears were groundless. Nobody hired them to disrupt the wedding."

Mell smiled grimly as she nodded in aggravation. "That's right all they wanted was to get rid of me so they could take over the towns I look after."

Alec sighed angrily. "Well that's bad enough I suppose. Although now the story will spread and hopefully it will make anyone else with the same ideas think twice before attempt it."

Jed shrugged not convinced by that reasoning. "Maybe and maybe not, someone else could still try it but with a lot more men now that they know that two didn't succeed."

Mell scowled irritably as she nodded. "That's the trouble about being a Sheriff in such a large area. Outlaws are constantly trying to take over and they keep trying to get rid of you. This isn't the first time this has happened of course and it probably won't be the last."

Alec nodded thoughtfully but didn't say anything very much aware that his daughter was in constant danger.

Mell turned to Tommy in anticipation. "Go out to the bunkhouse and tell all the men to meet us at the target practice area I us behind the ranch house. We want to show everyone something."

Tommy grinned in anticipation of a surprise then ran out. Mell turned to Jed then waved towards the den. "Will you go to the den and grab our surprise then meet us outside beside that old oak tree behind the house?"

Jed nodded with a grin of delighted anticipation then left. Mell pushed Alec down the hallway and outdoors to the porch where he changed into his other wheelchair. It was specially made for running on the dirt and grass in the yard and had slimmer tires for better traction on rough or wet terrain. Everyone else followed closely behind chattering excitedly wondering what all the fuss was about. Mell smiled over at Wade as she stepped away from the wheelchair. "Will you push dad the rest of the way? I need to go and talk to Jed before everyone arrives."

Wade nodded with a puzzled frown but Mell ignored him and sprinted around the house to join Jed. He was waiting patiently for her and when she arrived he handed her the rifle that was hers along with the half empty box of shells that they had used the last two days to practice with. Mell smiled at him in delight. "Should we fire one at a time or would you rather that we shot together for effect?"

Jed grinned back eagerly then waved dramatically. "Let's shoot together and give them a real show!"

Mell smiled mischievously then gestured ahead of her at the old oak tree she used for practice and smiled innocently up at Jed. "As you can see I've got two targets against the oak for practice. Now that we're a little more proficient in loading and firing let's make a little bet. We'll each fire two full rounds and the one to hit the target the most has complete control tonight in bed and the loser has to do whatever they're told."

Jed smirked wickedly as he nodded. "You're on!"

Just then the others from the house were arriving so Mell handed Jed her rifle then took four steps back so that everyone would stop where she was at and not get too close. She waited for them to get to her in anticipation. Right behind Alec came Tommy, followed by the men from the bunkhouse. Mell waited until everyone was gathered then listened to all the excited curious questions for a moment before she held up her hand for silence and everyone hushed expectantly. "I'm not going to answer any questions right now. All I want you to do is stand here quietly then watch and listen until I come back here. Then I'll answer all your questions."

Alec grinned up at her knowingly as he motioned towards the targets. "Going to put on a show are you?"

Mell smiled teasingly down at her father without answering him then winked in conspiracy at him before turning and joining Jed. Jed handed her rifle to her and they each grabbed fifteen extra bullets. Normally Mell didn't allow a loaded rifle in the house but since she hadn't wanted anyone seeing her load the rifle for the first time she had made an exception this time. Jed grinned down at her cheekily. "Let the best man or woman win!"

Mell grinned up at him in complete confidence but didn't comment. Both lifted their rifles at the same time then set themselves ready to fire. Mell waited a few moments dramatically to extend the silent anticipation behind them before finally shouting loudly so everyone could hear her. "Get set! Go!"

Both rifles fired as one then continued firing for an unbelievable fifteen times. It took them approximately one minute to expel all fifteen bullets before both were reloading as quickly as they could. Jed was slightly ahead but not by much. Two minutes later both rifles were firing again. When the last bullets were fired they were both neck and neck. They lowered their rifles then turned and grinned at each other in delight. It was a tie!

Wade pushed an excited Alec over to them and he beamed up at his daughter in amazement as he motioned incredulously. "That was amazing! I counted every shot and timed you as well. You both shot thirty bullets in fewer than four minutes. I've never heard of such a thing happening before. Let me see that rifle."

Mell smiled cheekily down at her father then handed him her rifle and Jed handed his to Wade so he could check it out as well. While the rifles were being examined and passed around in excitement Mell and Jed turned as one to go and inspect the targets in anticipation to see who had won the bet.

They inspected Mell's target first and she grinned saucily over at Jed when they counted thirty bullet holes. Only two of them were dead center but she hadn't missed once! Then they went over and inspected Jed's target but they only counted twenty-nine holes. Mell was just starting to smile in triumph when Jed noticed that one of the holes in the center was slightly bigger than the rest. He pointed to it and Jed grinned in triumph at her disappointment. "Looks like neither of us win. We both hit the target thirty times."

Mell sighed in regret then grinned good-naturedly as she pointed at Jed's target in approval, twenty out of thirty bullets had hit the center. "It's a good thing we never bet on who could hit the bull's eye the most or I'd have lost for sure. You definitely have way better aim than I do."

Jed smirked devilishly. "I'll have to remember that in the future and bet on it next time."

Mell laughed in delight at Jed's gloating look as they both turned then went back to join the crowd as they answered excited questions. Mell and Jed spent the next hour showing everyone how to load and reload the rifles. Finally it was full dark and nobody could see any more. Mell smiled at everyone even though they couldn't see her smile in the dark. "Tomorrow when I get back from town I'll demonstrate and everyone can take a turn. Even the women if they want they're is not much of a kick to these rifles, so they should learn how to shoot them as well. But right now I need a coffee!"

Mell turned to Tommy as the men from the bunkhouse turned away talking excitedly as they left and went back to their card game. "I want you to come to the library with us as well."

Tommy frowned perplexed usually he wasn't allowed in with the adults and was always banished to the bunkhouse. "I'm not in trouble am I Aunt Mell?"

Mell smiled tenderly as she ruffled his hair affectionately then she draped her arm around his shoulders as she led him back to the ranch house. "No you're not in trouble I promise."

Jessica walked up to Mell then gestured enticingly as they entered the house. "I'll bring coffee and apple pie to the den for everyone if you like."

Mell smiled gratefully over at Jessica then she led the rest to the den as Jessica scurried ahead of them heading to the kitchen. Mell turned to Jed just as they reached the door then handed him her rifle. "Would you please put this in the gun rack for me and grab a couple of extra chairs while you're at it?"

Jed nodded and Wade followed him to help with the chairs while Mell went to the divan and transferred both bedrolls to the floor. She sat down and beckoned Tommy to come over and stand in front of her. She waited until he reached her then she took both of his hands in hers as she looked up at him earnestly. "Tommy since the day you were born and your mother put you in my arms I've loved you with all my heart. When your mother brought you here for me to look after, at the age of six I have thought of you as a son. Always in the back of my mind I've pictured you staying with me and taking over my ranch some day. But now your father is taking you away to live with him, so as your adopted mother, I have two gifts to give you. One I would have taught you later when you were older. But tonight and tomorrow then every day until you leave here I'll teach you my techniques of fighting so that you can always protect yourself from harm. Since I won't be there myself to protect you any longer the other gift I have for you is also for your protection I'll give you instructions in its use as well. But your father will have to help you on your journey so you can get really good with it."

Mell let go of Tommy's hands then bent down and unwrapped one of the new rifles and two boxes of bullets then handed them to Tommy. There wasn't a dry eye to be seen as everyone felt Mell's pain at being parted from her adopted son. Tommy reached out then took the gifts from her reverently and examined them before setting them on the floor out of his way so that his hands would be free. Then he dropped onto his knees and reached out for Mell as he cried unhappily on her shoulder for a long moment.

Mell held him tenderly crying as well until he stopped then she let him go reluctantly. As he sat back he smiled shakily at Mell as he wiped his face with his sleeve. Mell too was wiping her face clean of tears. As Mell looked around she saw all the others in the room drying their tears as well no one there could help but feel the pain of Tommy and Mell's parting.

Tommy paused while he waited for Mell to look at him again then he motioned down at the rifle. "Aunt Mell, thank you for the wonderful gifts. I'd also like to say that I've always thought of you as my second mother and I also thought I would live here forever. But I hope you understand why I have to go with my father now even though I love you so much and will always be grateful for the love you have given me."

Mell smiled in understanding as she wiped more tears away. "Yes Tommy I understand why you must go. But always remember if you ever need me I'll come to you no matter what. Now take your new rifle upstairs and come back in an hour. But remember no loaded guns in the house ever!"

Tommy grinned, as he stood back up then saluted smartly in humour. "Yes Ma'am!"

Tommy scooped up his rifle and bullets then ran out of the room still crying slightly. Mell bent down then unrolled the second rifle and took it along with the two boxes of bullets to Giant Bear. She sighed sadly as she handed the rifle over to him. "Since you are taking two of the most important people in my life away with you I give you this gift so that you can always protect them."

Giant Bear waved to his wife and she scurried from the room aware of what he wanted. Once his wife was gone he turned back to Mell and accepted the gift graciously. He pointed behind him in the direction his wife had taken. "I thank you for your generous gift. I also have something for you Mary will bring it in a moment. The gifts I have for you are prized by the Cheyenne and are rarely given away. I have carried it with me since I started this journey unsure of why I brought it. But the Great Spirit told me to bring it and that I would know what it was for when the time came. I give it to you because without your help my son would not have survived and grown so strong in spirit."

Mary came into the room just then and there were gasps of admiration and disbelief at what she carried. Giant Bear passed his new rifle to Jed to hold for him as he took the white buffalo robe from Mary and placed it around Mell's shoulders in formal ritual. Then he took a white medicine bag made from the same buffalo and put it over Mell's head so it nestled between her breasts. Then he took out his hunting knife and took Mell's hand in preparation. "From this day forth you shall be known to the Cheyenne as 'White Buffalo'."

He cut into Mell's palm and then his own before he joined their hands to mix their blood. Still he continued talking as if they were in an Indian ceremony. "The White Buffalo has very strong medicine and will protect you as long as you wear your medicine bag. His spirit can find you anywhere but beware, never take it off or the White Buffalo will lose you. You are now a blood sister and friend to all the Cheyenne especially the Bear tribe."

Giant Bear bent and kissed Mell on each cheek before releasing Mell's hand. Mary passed Mell and Giant Bear each a clean cloth to wrap around their hands before he could enfold Mell in an embrace. Then he stepped back and gestured deadly serious. "If for any reason you ever need me for anything in the future go to any tribe of the Cheyenne and let them know your need. I will come to you or die trying!"

Mell smiled tremulously, flabbergasted so choked up in emotion that she had to clear her throat several times before she was able to speak coherently. "This was totally unexpected I'm not sure what to say! But I do want you to also promise me the same thing. If you ever have need of me as a Sheriff or as your friend just get a message to me through any Sheriff's office and I'll come."

Giant Bear nodded solemnly and once again they embraced this time in promise to seal their pact. Mary stepped forward as soon as Mell moved back from Giant Bear and she too embraced Mell barely able to contain her glee. "Hello White Buffalo adopted sister of the Cheyenne and blood sister of Chief Giant Bear! I am Golden Dove married to Chief Giant Bear of the Cheyenne!"

Jed came over next and hugged Mell tenderly then spoke in Cheyenne gravely as he stepped back to see her face. "White Buffalo adopted sister of the Cheyenne and blood sister of Chief Giant Bear. I am Grey Wolf blood brother to Chief Giant Bear and adopted brother to the Cheyenne."

Alec wheeled himself over to Mell once Jed moved away to let the others have their turn with her. Mell bent down and kissed his cheek. Alec also spoke in Cheyenne very much aware of what the white buffalo hide represented to the Cheyenne. "White Buffalo adopted sister to the Cheyenne and blood sister to Chief Giant Bear. I am 'Stands Tall' friend to all Cheyenne and also your loving father."

Mell smiled down at her father and tears filled her eyes in joy as she too spoke in Cheyenne. "It's been a long time since you spoke of your Indian name so openly not since mothers accident have I heard you speak it."

Giant Bear and Jed looked at each other in shocked surprise they had both heard the tales of Stands Tall. When Giant Bear was a youngster he had even been taught a little knife trick by Alec which he had used to save a young boys life. But because of the wheelchair Giant Bear hadn't realizing who Mell's father was plus the Cheyenne had figured he had died a long time ago. Giant Bear stepped forward then nodded eagerly. "Yes I did not see it before because of the chair but now that you have spoken your name I truly see you! Now I know why I thought I knew you even though I couldn't remember from where and why your daughter's fighting skills seemed so familiar as well."

Alec smiled up at Giant Bear as he too remembered. "I recognized you too, it took me some time to remember, but it finally came to me a few days after you arrived. Although at the time you were only a little older than Tommy and were not yet named Giant Bear."

Giant Bear stroked the hide he was wearing thoughtfully as he remembered. "It was actually because of you and that trick you taught me with the knife that I became Giant Bear. Without your teaching I probably would have died instead of the bear!"

Alec shook his head negatively in denial. "You were fated to become Giant Bear. If the Great Spirit hadn't used me to help you he would have found another way."

Giant Bear grinned unconvinced then shrugged unknowingly. "Yes you could be right."

Mell was glancing from one to the other speculatively then smiling in delight as she remembered the stories. "Dad this is the boy you used to tell me stories about!"

Alec smiled in agreement then nodded. "Yes he is but his tribe moved to Montana before you were born so I never did see them again."

Mell spotted Tommy coming in so she looked down at her father in farewell as she touched his shoulder. "I'll be in the library if you need me."

Alec smirked up at Mell then gestured teasingly in warning, before patting her hand that was on his shoulder. "Okay just don't wreck the place please!"

Mell grinned down saucily then winked mischievously before she turned and left without speaking. Mell took Tommy into the library and they moved the furniture over against the wall to give themselves more room. Mell had picked the library because it had the most available space since there were only a few chairs and the divan to move. She put the two chairs one in front of the other but made sure that they were facing each other as she sat down then motioned for Tommy to sit in the other one so they could talk. Mell gestured at Tommy inquisitively. "Did you bring a knife?"

Tommy nodded eagerly and took it out of its sheath then handed her the knife his father had given him. Mell took it and examined the blade critically then checked it for balance by using her first finger on her right hand. She laid the knife blade down on top of her index finger close to the hilt and it balance there once she removed her hand then she nodded in approval. Mell noticed movement by the door but didn't say anything to Tommy as Jed and Giant Bear settled back in the shadows to watch. Mell turned her attention back to Tommy. "This is a very good knife Tommy. See how it balances when I hold it in the center?"

Tommy grinned enthusiastically. "Dad gave it to me when we went hunting. He said all hunters need a good knife."

Mell frowned as her tone became cautious in forewarning. "Your father is wise and you should always listen to his advice. But I have always taught you that no matter who advises you all decisions in your life are yours to make, not somebody else's. I've also taught you to listen to your instincts. Gut reaction can save your life just as often as good advice, especially in a knife fight. You have to learn when to use your instincts and when to use your head. Nobody can teach you that it's something you learn as you gain experience. Now when you're in a knife fight, never hold your knife straight out like most people do. Always hold it hilt backwards with the flat of the blade against your arm. This gives you better control because it's actually your wrist that controls how deep and at what angle you're going to drive the knife home. If your arm is held stiff and your knife is pointed straight ahead, chances are your wrist is also locked. So all you can do is stab straight ahead and hope that your opponent doesn't have a longer reach than you do. Because I was smaller and weaker then the boys my age I had to adapt to a different fighting style. Wrestling was especially difficult for me at first, so when one of the older hands at the ranch I grew up at saw the difficulty I was having. He taught me how to box which gave me the footwork I needed to keep away from my bigger opponents. To get away from the stiff-armed jabs I'm going to give you some exercises to do. Now watch closely and I'll explain as I demonstrate. Hold the knife lightly not in a death grip. Only when you're actually going to stab someone do you need to tighten your grip. Only the first two fingers and your thumb should be holding the hilt the rest of your fingers need to be loose so that they are only there to keep the knife in position. Now bring your knife up to the left side of your arm but don't twist your hand. Only you should be able to see the knife at this point, your opponent should only be able to see the tip of the blade just sticking up past your arm slightly. Now move the knife to the right side of your arm and the knife should now be completely visible to your opponent, which means that all you should be able to see is the tip of the blade against the side of your arm sticking up. Okay now you can tighten your four fingers but loosen your thumb so that you can move your thumb to the very end of the hilt then pull the hilt down slightly so that the knife is sticking straight out of your fist. It should now be completely straight but in a horizontal position then tighten your grip fully. You should now be ready to use the knife."

Mell handed Tommy the knife hilt first. "Now you try it but try not to cut yourself."

Tommy copied her but slowly and hesitantly. Mell smiled in approval then took the knife away. "Okay. Now I want you to turn your wrists counter clockwise in a fist without a knife then with your hand open now reverse direction. Good now lift your hand up and down, like you're nodding with your hand but strain it. Go back as far as you can go and as far down as you can go with a fist then open handed. Do these exercises twice a day with both wrists. I think at first you should find a stick as heavy as your knife but the same length and use that to practice with until you think you're ready to do the exercises using your knife. This is how it should look when you finally become proficient with it."

Tommy watched closely as his aunt passed the knife from one hand to the other. Not once did the knife stop moving or her wrists but she never once moved her arms or shoulders. Tommy sighed dejectedly as he watched her. "It's going to take me years to be able to do that!"

Mell smiled consolingly over at Tommy as she finished then flipped the knife in midair and caught it blade first as she handed Tommy back his knife hilt first before putting her hands in her lap. "Actually, you'll be surprised at how fast you can learn to do this if you practice twice every day. You can put the knife away now we won't need it anymore tonight."

Mell watched in satisfaction as Tommy immediately put his knife in its sheath then laid it on the divan beside him before turning back to Mell expectantly. Mell waited until he was facing her once more and she had his full attention then continued her lessons. She made sure to gesture as she talked to make sure her point was getting across as strongly as possible. "Now most people who fight with a knife circle each other with the knife held straight out in front of them then they jump in and stab straight ahead. If they manage to hit something they're darn lucky. That is a crude method but don't get me wrong it can be very effective at times to throw your opponent off balance. But you should think of it as a dance instead one movement should flow into the next freely. Like in any dance you must train yourself to move effortlessly. At first balance, speed, and knowing what you can or cannot do will come only with time. You always need to remember that every part of your body can be used as a weapon, knees, elbows, head, hands, and feet can all be lethal if used properly. This method of fighting can be used for knives, tomahawks, and especially hand to hand fighting. When I learned to wrestle then box I had to teach myself how to stay away from a bigger opponent it was just natural for me to use my flexibility to my advantage so I came up with a routine that I do before bed. I call it a dance but it isn't really. I'm just calling it that so you can understand it's more of a method of stretching to the limits of my ability."

Mell got up then turned to Tommy as she stepped away from the chairs to give herself more room as she pointed to herself. "I'll show you my dance first which will be different than yours. There are some things that I can do that you cannot and it has nothing to do with being a man, or a woman. It has to do with being flexible and how you're put together. I can kick straight up and touch my nose with my leg. But I saw a woman once in a circus that could wrap both legs around the back of her neck. I tried for a long time to do that but I just couldn't do it. Now watch me closely Tommy and try to feel the dance as well as seeing it."

Mell moved further back closer to the center of the room then knelt down on her knees. She knelt there for a moment with eyes closed listening to something inside her that only she could hear. Suddenly she began to move slowly and was no longer on her knees as every move she made was turned into a different move effortlessly. Her dance was well practiced and had taken her years to perfect but that didn't mean that she never tried to add other moves that she could think up. Always she was changing never wanting to become predictable.

Tommy watched his Aunt Mell in fascination he had never seen her so intense before or so beautiful. She kicked, twisted, and rolled, sometimes all at the same time. Every move she made flowed into the next move with no breaks or stops. Finally she stopped in the exact same spot and position she had started in.

Tommy clapped loudly in approval and the awe was clear in his voice as he motioned eagerly as his Aunt looked over at him expectantly. "Wow! That was amazing. Do you really think I can learn to do all that too?"

Mell smiled indulgently then nodded emphatically over at Tommy before gesturing in caution. "Some of it you will learn easily and some of it you will have to train yourself to do. Now one thing I will tell you, that I probably shouldn't because your mother will shoot me, is that I taught her this dance. The only reason I'm telling you is because you will need someone to train with and she can help you."

Tommy stared at Mell in surprise then grinned in delight as he clapped his hands in glee. "She can? I never knew that!"

Mell grinned as she waved for Tommy to come over to her. "Yes she can. Now come over here and I'll show you some exercises that you can do every day. Once you can do these exercises without thought or effort you will know that you are ready to put together your own dance. Once you learn your dance it will be time to add your knife. From that time forward you can practice with a knife, tomahawk, and of course with nothing in your hands at all."

Tommy nodded eagerly then got up to begin his lessons.

* * *

Jed and Giant Bear listened then watched quietly without a word spoken between them not wanting to intrude or distract the pair from their intense concentration. When Tommy was doing his exercises and they were both sure they wouldn't be heard Jed turned to Giant Bear with a grin of satisfaction. "I've seen a similar technique used by the Chinese in Boston, but its way different too. Mell only scratches the surface of what they do hers are just basic kicks, turns, and spins that she put into a dance like rhythm."

Giant Bear shrugged dismissively having no clue as to who the Chinese were or even what they were. "I don't know who they are but if my Golden Dove knows how to fight like White Buffalo I better be careful! White Buffalo must have taught her after she came back here because she didn't know it when we first met. I do remember though that Stands Tall had a similar way of fighting but different. He held his knife like White Buffalo and did some kicking but not like she does."

Jed nodded thoughtfully as he waved towards Mell in complete amazement. "It looks like White Buffalo trained herself to do most of the things she does. She said it wasn't really a dance but it looks like one to me she makes it look so easy. She's managed to completely amaze me now and I won't be surprised by anything she does anymore. I've never met a woman like her in all my travels. She's definitely unique!"

Giant Bear sighed knowingly. "That is why the White Buffalo spirit claimed her as one of his own in our history only two others have been named White Buffalo, it's been over a hundred years since one has been named, but they were both men and both had strong medicine. This is the first time in our history that a woman has been named. The fact that she is also white with no Indian blood in her will cause many of my people to question me on my decision to name her as such. She will come to me when my people are in the gravest need but my dream did not tell me when or why this would happen or even who would be named. There was only a sense of needing to take the hide and the medicine bag with me on my journey. With a quick glimpse of a female buffalo walking towards me as my people cried out in the distance. Of course the Cheyenne believe that the white buffalo represents a female spirit."

The two men lapsed into silence suddenly both wondering what was to come as they turned back to watch Tommy and Mell.

* * *

Mell grinned down at Tommy then she clapped in approval. "Very good I think that's it for tonight. Remember though that your kicks should get higher until you reach your limit. Practice tomorrow while I'm at work and then I'll show you more. If for some reason I'm unable to finish teaching you your mother can do so."

Tommy nodded as he got up then walked over to Mell for a goodnight hug before grabbing his knife off the divan and turning to leave. He spotted Jed and his father sitting in the corner so went over to say goodnight to them first. Mell smiled lovingly up at Jed as he walked towards her after Tommy left. "Well did you learn anything tonight?"

Jed laughed in delight as he tweaked her nose playfully. "Yes. Never pick a fight with you!"

Mell chuckled in disbelief not believing for a moment that they wouldn't fight then turned away without comment as she started moving the furniture back with Jed and Giant Bear helping her silently. Mell picked up her buffalo robe that she had set aside earlier then turned and smiled at the two men enticingly. "Since I missed my coffee and pie in all the excitement I think I'll go to the kitchen for some. Either of you want to join me?"

Giant Bear shook his head negatively. "I think it is time for me to go back to the barn. Mary will be waiting for me."

Mell nodded in disappointment then watched him leave before she turned to Jed inquisitively. "Well how about you?"

Jed smiled eagerly then rubbed his hands together in anticipation. "I'd love some!"

They walked to the kitchen together in silence then entered. Alec was already they're enjoying another piece of pie and coffee. He grinned up at Mell inquisitively. "Well White Buffalo how does it feel to be blood sister to Giant Bear?"

Mell sighed tiredly as she sat down in the chair beside her father. "I'm not sure yet. Everything happened so fast I don't think I really feel any different except maybe more whole like I'd been missing something all this time!"

Alec nodded knowingly remembering back to his younger days. "I had the same feelings when I received my Cheyenne name. How did the lessons with Tommy go?"

Mell smiled in pride and approval as she thought of Tommy. "Very well he'll make a fine warrior one day."

Mell grinned up at Jessica in thanks as she set pie and coffee before her. "Thank you!"

Alec looked curiously at Mell when she turned back to him after Jessica turned away. "Are you going to town tomorrow you two?"

Jed and Mell both nodded but it was Mell who answered. "Yes I need to make a report tomorrow on what happened and I want to check on Gary to make sure he's doing all right."

Alec nodded he had known they would be going but asked to make sure. "Good I want to go to town as well so why don't the two of you meet me at the hotel for lunch?"

Mell motioned curiously as she cocked her right eyebrow inquisitively. "Sure we can meet you. Is there a specific reason you're going to town or is it just to get out for the day?"

Alec nodded that there was. "I have an appointment with my lawyer and I'll probably visit the Mayor as well. Brad is coming with me so he can pick up Jane and the kids they need to get some furniture for their cabin anyway so they can move into it tomorrow. It'll be nice to have young ones running around again."

Mell face lit up eagerly as she rubbed her hands together in anticipation. "It'll certainly be different we've only ever had one kid around and he was always so serious and quiet most of the time you didn't even know he was there. Having three small children running around will take some getting used to!"

Jed grinned over at Mell teasingly as he winked suggestively. "Well, you better get used to it pretty fast if we're going to have one or two kids of are own. Although having your own kids is different than looking after someone else's."

Mell blushed slightly at the reference to her having children. "I suppose it is different but until we have one or two of our own I won't know for sure!"

Jed smiled devilishly then couldn't help teasing her some more. "Well in two days we can try as often as you like."

Mell's blush deepened and she quickly changed the subject. "Well I don't know about you two but I'm exhausted. If you'll excuse me I'm going up to bed."

Alec's laugh of delight followed Mell out the door at the deepening blush staining his daughter's cheeks as she raced out to escape Jed's teasing. He hadn't seen her blush in a long time and it gladdened his heart to see it. Alec chuckled once more then turned to Jed. "Well it's certainly going to be nice having another man around the house."

Jed grinned hopefully as he gestured anxiously. "I hope I live up to all your expectations for a son-in-law."

Alec smiled indulgently as he winked reassuringly. "All you have to do is make my daughter happy. That's all I ask."

Jed nodded eagerly. "That's easy to do because that's what I want as well. Have you come up with some figures for me so I can buy a share of the ranch?"

Alec shook his head negatively. "No, but that's one of the reasons I'm going into town tomorrow. There's an assessment we had done last year on this place at the lawyer's office. I'll pick it up then we can discuss it tomorrow."

Jed finished his coffee then got up to leave. "I'll wish you a goodnight then sir. I'll see you in the morning or for lunch if you're not up when we leave."

Jed took the stairs two at a time and quietly entered the bedroom. He quickly got undressed then slipped under the blankets beside Mell. She turned in her sleep and cuddled close but didn't awaken. Jed smiled down at her lovingly then laid back and drifted off to sleep.

* * *

Alec smiled up at Jessica hopefully as she walked over and pulled him away from the table to take him to bed. "Going to tuck me in Jessica?"

Jessica grinned down wickedly then bent down close to his ear and whispered suggestively. "If that is all you want Alec?"

Alec nodded solemnly pretending not to hear the suggestive note in her voice then looked up with an innocent grin. "That's all I can think of at the moment."

Jessica chuckled in disbelief and continued pushing him into his bedroom then over to the bed so he could lift himself out of the chair. Once he was out of his chair she pushed it over to the closet and stored it inside. Alec sat on the edge of his bed waiting for Jessica in anticipation not moving a muscle. She walked over to the bed then stood in front of him thoughtfully staring into his eyes unsure at first if she should continue. She only hesitated for a moment as she saw the passion flare up in Alec's eyes suddenly. She smiled teasingly then reached over and started undoing the buttons on his shirt slowly without asking permission.

Alec sat very still and waited eagerly not wanting to push her into something she didn't want to do. His breath caught in hope as he waited to see what she would do next. Jessica pulled out his shirt and finished undoing it. She unhooked his cuff links then put them on the nightstand before turning back and removing his shirt completely.

Alec hadn't worn his long johns today because it was just too hot out for them so Jessica had an unobstructed view of his chest. She ran her hands over his muscles then smiled in admiration. Because Alec had to lift himself in and out of his chair constantly his chest and arm muscles had hardened over the years even more then when he had the use of his legs. Jessica smiled mischievously as she looked up teasingly. "For an old man you certainly have a nice physique."

Alec laughed devilishly as he wrapped his arms around her so she couldn't get away. "I'm not that old woman. Come here and I'll prove it."

Jessica grinned saucily as she slipped out of his reach mischievously. She paused playfully for effect then started to undo the buttons on the front of her dress. Alec watched breathlessly then groaned in torture as she finally dropped her dress to the floor and stood in front of him completely naked. She wasn't wearing any petticoats or a corset having planned this moment earlier. She had ran to her room while everyone else was occupied then stripped out of them in preparation for this moment so she stood there completely naked.

Alec caught his breath in delighted surprise then looked her over. Her breasts weren't large but they were high and firm just under a hand full. If he hadn't known better he would have thought she hadn't had any children because her stomach was slim and firm. You had to look very closely to see any stretch marks. Her hips were just slightly rounded and the hair at the junction of her thighs was just as red as the hair on her head. Her legs were long and firm with slim ankles and small feet.

Jessica waited for a moment so he could get a good view before walking towards him slowly teasingly. She got close enough so that she could push him backwards onto the bed but not close enough for him to grab her. He was now lying on his back and she removed his slippers and socks then she unfastened his pants before pulling them off. Jessica stood over him a few moments once he was completely naked and admired his body before she climbed on top of him for a passionate kiss.

Alec groaned against her lips in pleasure as their bodies came into partial contact. He touched both her breasts tenderly then lightly squeezed her nipples before he ran one hand down the side of her body. He reached her hip then brought his hand across her stomach then down and gently cupped her secret place. Alec shuddered in pleasure as he felt her heat and the moisture that said she was ready for him, which was a good thing it had been so long that he didn't think he could wait much longer. Alec put his hands around her waist and lifted her a little without breaking their kiss so that he could enter her fully. When she was ready but he didn't rush her letting her control the penetration not wanting to hurt her.

Jessica gasped in pain and pleasure as she slowly lowered herself onto his engorged manhood it had been such a long time for her too. As he entered her slowly she shivered in ecstasy then pushed down more fully. Jessica finally broke the kiss reluctantly once the pain had receded and sat up to get a deeper penetration.

Alec grasped her hips in demand and pushed her down harder. Jessica lifted herself up on her own this time before coming down hard again. Alec couldn't hold back any longer and he pulled Jessica down for a deep kiss as he grasped her hips then pushed her up and down faster so they could both erupt together. Jessica collapsed on top of Alec in exhaustion then after a few minutes she chuckled deep in her throat as she panted softly. "Well you certainly proved to me that you're not too old!"

Alec caught his breath then gasped still slightly breathless. "I'm not too sure about that I definitely feel old now!"

Jessica laughed in delight then rolled off Alec so he could pull himself up to the headboard. They cuddled for a bit then Jessica got up and went to the washbowl. She brought it back with her along with a cloth then she proceeded to give Alec a sponge bath. Alec's manhood quivered a few times as if trying to rise again and Jessica chuckled in satisfaction. She sponged herself off next then put the washbowl away before getting dressed. Alec smiled at her sleepily with a slight wistful plea plain in his voice. "You don't have to go to your room. I think my daughter is old enough not to mind if you sleep here with me."

Jessica reached down then tenderly stroked his cheek before shaking her head in denial. "I know she wouldn't but until we're married we should at least keep up appearances."

Alec nodded in disappointment he had known she wouldn't stay. "Whatever makes you happy."

Jessica bent down and kissed him goodnight then slipped out the door silently without comment. Alec yawned sleepily as he stared at the door for a few moments hoping she would change her mind. Then fell asleep still hoping.

CHAPTER NINETEEN

Jed woke instantly at the sound of an insistent knock then reached down and pulled the blankets up before summoning softly. "Come in."

He gently nudged Mell awake she grumbled in annoyance but obediently opened her eyes. Gloria came in with a breakfast tray and smiled at the two of them cheerfully. "Good morning, it's time to get up I figured you two would want breakfast before you leave."

She walked over then deposited the tray in Jed's lap ignoring Mell's discontented mumble as Gloria stepped back and folded her hands in front of her. "Brad is up and seeing to your horses they'll be ready to go whenever you are. Everyone else is still sleeping. Do you need anything else before I go?"

Mell waved Gloria out in dismissal as she sat up then poured a coffee for her and Jed. "No you may go."

Gloria turned to the door and closed it softly behind her. Mell grinned over at Jed in sleepy delight. "I could get used to this pampering in no time if I'm not careful."

Jed laughed in humour. "Well I think you better get used to it because between Jane, Gloria, and Jessica you'll be waited on every day!"

Mell smiled in contentment but didn't comment as they ate their breakfast in silence then they finished up the coffee before getting dressed. Mell finished first then picked up the tray before gesturing over at Jed. "I'll take this to the kitchen while you grab our new rifles from the gun rack then I'll meet you at the front door."

Jed nodded then finished quickly and left first. Mell followed more slowly as she took the tray to the kitchen and set it on the counter. Gloria came bustling over then shook a chiding finger at Mell in gentle rebuke. "You don't have to bring the tray down I can pick it up when I go up to clean your room."

Mell shrugged negligently a slight note of warning in her voice. "That's okay I don't think it will strain me too much to bring the breakfast tray down."

Gloria nodded as she held up her hands in surrender then smiled consolingly. "If you wish!"

Mell grinned good-naturedly at Gloria's diplomatic answer then waved good-bye. "See you after work!"

Mell left the kitchen without another word and hurried to the front door to put on her gear. Jed was already there dressed and waiting for her patiently. Mell finished and Jed handed her one of the rifles as well as their last box of shells. They went outside together loaded both rifles then flipped on the safety before going to the barn. Their horses and the packhorse were tied up at the corral waiting for them as promised.

Brad came out of the barn then touched the tip of his hat in respect and greeting at Mell. He waved towards the house hopefully. "If you don't mind after you're done with the archway I'd like to break it down and make a hitching rail for the front of the house. It would save you time to have your horses tied up there instead of having to walk all the way here to get them."

Mell inclined her head in approval. "Sure you can make one if you like."

Brad nodded his thanks before turning to go to the bunkhouse for breakfast his job done. Mell and Jed mounted after he tied the packhorse to the back of his saddle and they headed for town. Jed looked at Mell inquisitively as he pointed behind him at the packhorse. "Why don't you just keep a packhorse in town instead of taking one from here all the time?"

Mell shrugged dismissively. "I don't know I really hadn't thought about it I've just always brought my own besides sometimes I don't get to town before I have to go so this is easier."

Jed nodded in understanding and they rode the rest of the way in silence. When they entered town Mell stopped at the store first. Before dismounting she turned to Jed and motioned towards the office. "You go on ahead and make coffee then start your report. I'll see if Charlie has any of these repeating rifles yet and some bullets before joining you."

Jed turned his horse away from the hitching post. Mell dismounted and entered the store she looked around expectantly then spotted Charlie. "Morning Charlie, how are you today?"

Charlie smiled in greetings then walked over to Mell as he grinned curiously. "I'm doing just fine Sheriff. I heard you had to run to Miller's Creek nothing serious I hope!"

Mell shrugged solemnly. "Nothing we couldn't handle but while I was there I came across some new rifles, called Winchester Repeating Rifles model number 1866. Have you got them here yet?"

Charlie pointed towards the back of the store then grinned in humour. "Just came in last night I haven't even had time to put them out yet."

Mell smiled in delight. "Good! I'll take eight if you have that many?"

Charlie frowned in thought then nodded. "I think there's a dozen but I'm not sure. How much ammunition would you like?"

Mell deliberated for a moment then held up her fingers in explanation. "If you have enough I'd like two boxes of ammunition for each rifle. You can put seven rifles on my tab as well as the ammunition. One rifle with two boxes of ammunition and six extra boxes of bullets can be put on the town's tab."

Charlie was writing her instructions as they talked and he looked up inquisitively. "Do you want me to have the rifles delivered?"

Mell shook her head negatively. "No dad's coming into town later he'll be stopping here so you can send them with him except for the one rifle and two boxes of shells. I'll take them with me now. Oh, I'll also take the extra boxes of ammunition with me now as well please."

Charlie inclined his head amiably as he waved behind his counter in invitation. He continued the conversation as Mell followed him. "No problem Sheriff, you getting excited about your wedding tomorrow?"

Mell sighed irritably then shrugged resignedly. "Unfortunately I haven't had time to get excited yet."

Charlie looked over his shoulder in concern as he motioned curiously then turned away and continued walking. "Being the Sheriff is a big job are you going to continue on being Sheriff now that you're getting married?"

Mell harrumphed decisively. "Of course that was agreed upon even before I told Jed I would marry him."

Charlie chuckled knowingly as he stopped at the crates then turned with a grin as he gestured in relief. "I figure it was but a lot of people are asking that question. Now I can relieve everyone's mind."

Mell watched silently as Charlie grabbed a bar then forced the lid of the crates open. It only took a few moments before Charlie handing Mell her rifle and the ammunition she had requested. Mell smiled her thanks then turned and headed back to the front of the store as she called back over her shoulder. "Write it up for me Charlie I'll see you later."

Mell left the store then mounted her horse awkwardly not wanting to put the rifle and ammunition away, since she only had a short distance to go then rode to her office. She dismounted just as precariously then walked inside and propped the rifle beside the coat rack. Gary smiled over in greeting, as Mell went over to her desk then deposited the ammunition before walking over to the stove to pour herself a coffee. She took the pot over and filled the men's cups as well before sitting down at her own desk then sipped her coffee in appreciation. Mell grinned at Gary as she smiled inquisitively. "Did you have any problems while I was gone?"

Gary shook his head negatively. "No nothing unusual."

Mell sighed thankfully then motioned towards the door. "You can go home to bed once you're done at the Mayor's office. Oh by the way one of my men will come in tomorrow instead of me so as soon as he comes go to the Mayor's office and give your report. So the Mayor and Lucy can leave as soon as you're done."

Gary nodded agreeably then grinned as he thought of his wife's nagging the last few days. "We'll be out for the wedding tomorrow too. Millie is very excited about it so I couldn't say no well I guess you could say that I didn't get a chance to say no!"

Mell smiled enthusiastically. "Good I was hoping you would come."

Gary finished his coffee then got up to leave. "Guess I should mossy on over to the Mayor's office then home for a sleep before my next shift."

Mell pointed towards the rifle she had brought in. "Oh, I almost forgot the rifle I brought in is for you and you can take two boxes of shell's off my desk as well."

Mell got up then went over picked up the rifle then handed it to Gary to inspect. He looked it over eagerly then smiled in thanks. "Well thank you kindly it's beautiful."

Mell put her hand out for the rifle then motioned towards the bullets. "Bring me a box of bullets and I'll show you how to load it before you go."

Gary did as he was told then watched avidly as Mell showed him how to insert the bullets then she handed it to him. "When you get home you can practice loading and firing it."

Gary nodded eagerly as he took the rifle from her then he waved in farewell as he turned to leave. "I sure will and thank you again. See you tonight."

Mell waited for him to leave then walked back to her desk and took out paper, pen, and ink to write her report. There was absolute quiet except for the scratching of two pens as they both wrote furiously. Only once did Mell look up and that was to smile in thanks when Jed got up to pour them the last of the coffee. Mell sighed and threw her pen down thankfully.

Jed still wasn't finished so she rifled through the wanted posters and took out Samson's and Diago's then she wrote across the front of both posters in big letters...'Deceased'.

Jed dropped his pen on the report then sat back with a sigh of resignation as he looked over at Mell plaintively. "I'm definitely not going to like this part of the job."

Mell laughed knowingly then gathered her report and the two wanted posters before getting up and walking over to Jed's desk. She put Jed's on top of hers to read critically then grinned distractedly, as she looked at Jed for a moment, then back down at the report. "You get used to it after awhile!"

She scanned his then nodded in approval as she looked down at him. "You did a good job for your first real report now that I'm satisfied that it has everything in it that a report should have I won't ready any more of them. It'll now be up to Lucy to help you if you do something wrong."

Jed smiled up at Mell gratefully. "Thanks!"

Mell inclined her head in acknowledgment then gestured towards the door. "Let's do our rounds so we can meet Dad for lunch."

Jed watched Mell walk over to her desk then split up the boxes of bullets and handed half of them to Jed. They left the office and both stopped to loosen the girths on their horses then put their bullets away. Mell grabbed her whip before heading for the stagecoach office. Mell went in first and smiled cheerfully at James in greeting. "Good morning. How are you and your mother doing today?"

James grinned thankfully at seeing Mell and Jed back so soon. "Great! Mother's really looking forward to your wedding tomorrow. I heard you had some problems at Miller's Creek. The Deputy who took over your shift wasn't sure if you'd be back in time for the wedding though."

Mell smirked teasingly across the counter. "You think I'd be late for my own wedding?"

James laughed negatively in relief. "We were all hoping you wouldn't be. We've all been waiting too long for you to get married as it is."

Mell chuckled in delight. "Well I don't plan on disappointing anyone at this late date!"

Mell handed James the two wanted posters. James looked them over and whistled as he looked up in disbelief. "Both of them at the same time, I've never heard of them working together before!"

Mell exhaled noisily in satisfaction. "You won't hear of it again either. Will you send a message to all the Sheriffs for me? You'll also have to send one to the Governor and one to the Pinkerton Agency as well."

James grinned in pleasure. "Gladly Sheriff!"

Mell nodded in thanks then motioned inquisitively. "Anything for me today?"

James shook his head negatively but handed her a couple of letters for her father. "Nothing for you just for your father."

Mell sighed relieved that was good news then she stuck the envelopes in her pocket before waving good-bye as they headed out. She turned to

Jed and gestured down the street. "I want to go to the Mayor's office first today."

Jed followed her without comment across the street then turned left. They went in and Mell smiled cheekily at Lucy. "Is the Mayor free Lucy?"

Lucy grinned in greeting as she nodded that he was. "Yes he is Sheriff. Go right in."

Mell groaned in anger then bantered with Lucy for a few minutes as Jed looked on in humour. He grinned at the two women as they repeated the performance of the other day. Mell just smiled back at Jed cheekily as they left Lucy's desk and walked to the mayor's office. Mayor Elton looked up from a report then motioned in relief at the two of them as he held up the paper he was studying. "Well, I see that you're finally back. I got this report from Deputy Ted late last night, but I want to hear what happened from you two?"

Mell and Jed both sat down as Mell related everything that had happened. She then handed him their reports so that he could read them later, usually she gave them to Lucy, but Mell had known the mayor would want them right away this time.

The mayor sighed in aggravation as he took the reports then layed them on the desk to read later. "I read Ted's report last night if it's not one thing it's another! At least they didn't have anything to do with your wedding! I think we should talk about hiring a Marshal again South Dakota has one and it might be time for us to have one as well. I've talked to the Governor about it a few times but you've always done such a good job that we decided to let it be for now."

Mell broke in frowning angrily then leaned forward intently as she gestured sharply in exasperation. "We don't need a Marshall! I can still handle things and now that Jed is with me all the time I'll have back up if I need it."

The mayor frowned in displeasure as he put his hands up in surrender. "Okay, don't get mad about it. I agree that now that Jed is with you it will take some of the load off. If you think the two of you can handle it I'll leave it at that for now! But sooner or later we're going too have to talk about it seriously. We have more and more people coming to settle here and more towns are springing up every year. You're not going to be able to keep up pretty soon!"

Mell sighed in aggravation as she sat back then waved resignedly. "I know that but we don't need one yet."

Jed cleared his throat to get their attention. "What's the difference between a Marshal and a Sheriff?"

Mayor Elton shrugged negligently as he explained to the confused Jed. "Well a Sheriff looks after one town and the surrounding area. A Marshal doesn't look after any town but he tours the whole countryside and helps any Sheriff that needs backing up. Plus he looks after people in out of way places that don't have a Sheriff close to them. The Marshal also goes from town to town picking up men who are wanted in other areas, once their caught. He takes them to the place where the criminal will be tried and if needed executed or jailed."

Jed nodded thoughtfully but didn't say anything more wanting to think about that for a bit. Mayor Elton turned back to Mell inquisitively as he changed the sensitive subject. "Well are you ready for the big day tomorrow?"

Mell shrugged then motioned impotently. "I'm not sure you'll have to ask my father. I haven't had time to do anything never mind think about it! Which reminds me Dad is coming to town and he said something about visiting you. We're supposed to meet him for lunch later."

Mayor Elton smiled in pleasure and anticipation. "When you leave let Lucy know your father is coming and tell her to let him right in."

Mell nodded as she got up and headed for the door. Jed followed after waving good-bye to the mayor. Mell stopped at the front desk for a moment to give Lucy the mayor's instructions then they left. Once outside they turned left and headed for Pam's place. They went in and waited in the lobby while Pam's hired man went to tell her to come out to see them. They didn't have long to wait as Pam came bustling in with a wide smile of pleasure. "Well Sheriff it's about time you got back thought for sure that we were going to have the wedding without its star attraction."

Mell laughed in horror at that thought as she shook a finger in warning at Pam. "No chance of that! I've waited too long to miss it now. Besides do you know the first thing I'm going to do after I get back from my honeymoon?"

Pam smiled puzzled then shook her head negatively. Mell smiled mischievously as she waved inside Pam's house dramatically. "I'm going to come in here and walk through your house!"

Pam and Jed both laughed uproarsly at that statement. Pam was the first one to gain control as she sighed in delight before wiping the tears of mirth away. "Well once you're married you can come in anytime you like. And if you ask I'm sure the girls can give you some good advice as well."

Mell smirked in satisfaction at the choking noises behind her from Jed. Mell's expression became serious as she turned all business. "Well how did things go while I was gone?"

Pam's expression sobered as well as she thought about last night. "One of my girls was beaten up again. I would have handed him over to you but I didn't know until after he left."

Mell motioned knowingly then scowled fiercely. "George again?"

Pam nodded grimly. "Yes, he gagged her this time so she couldn't call out for help. We didn't find her until closing time. He did a real number on her too. He's been real good since you had him in jail last time so I didn't even hesitate in letting him in. Besides, all he usually does is slap the girls around a bit but doesn't hurt them all that much. But this time he almost killed her! The doctor's been with her all morning and just told me a few minutes ago that she'll make it."

Mell frowned grimly then sighed in aggravation. "I'll go and pick him up then I'll talk to Mayor Elton about a public flogging this time and a jail term of at least six months. I'll also ban him from all of my towns that way all the Ladies will be safe from him."

Pam nodded in relief then watched Mell stalk from the room in a rage she had never seen Mell this angry before and for a moment she felt sorry for George. Until she thought about Mary Jane that is, her face-hardened and she didn't feel sorry for him any more only furious.

* * *

Jed rushed to catch up with Mell he had never seen this side of her before she hadn't even waited for him. He matched his stride to hers and wisely didn't say anything knowing she wasn't in the mood for conversation. They reached Chelsie's saloon and Mell uncoiled her whip as she barrelled through the doors in fury.

Complete silence fell instantly as a man in the corner jumped up and reached for his gun. But he wasn't fast enough as Mell rushed up quickly and with a swift flick of her wrist the whip coiled around him and held him fast. Mell jerked hard on the whip in anger and the man fell forward. It happened so fast he couldn't save himself from the fall and he landed hard face first on the floor with a loud grunt of surprise and pain.

Instead of loosening the whip Mell handed it to Jed to hold then she walked over and disarmed the man at the same time she searched him for hidden weapons. When she was satisfied that she had them all she hauled him to his feet bodily and pushed him towards Jed in anger. "Take him and lock him up then fill out an arrest warrant and put my recommendations on the bottom of it then take it to the Mayor for his decision, tell him I'll fill out a report later."

Jed nodded and didn't dare refute her in her present mood besides he actually agreed with her. Keeping the whip wrapped around the man Jed pushed him outdoors and into the street. Mell turned to the bar her mood improving now that George had been so easy to find and catch. She had known this would be were he would be waiting. George was always predictable and even waited at the same table after beating up one of Pam's girls. Mell walked over to Chelsie then motioned casually as she leaned against the bar. As if a few minutes ago she hadn't been in a furious rage. "Morning Chelsie how's business?"

Chelsie grinned good-naturedly as she waved teasingly. "Well Sheriff that's the most excitement we've had in weeks. And to answer your question business is just fine. I knew something was up with George he came in here and started drinking as soon as I opened at ten. He sat in his usual corner and just watched the doors for you without moving. Did he beat up one of Pam's girls again?"

Mell scowled angrily. "Worse than usual this time the doctor wasn't sure if the girl was going to live but Pam said the worst was over now and she should make it."

Chelsie whistled grimly. "No wonder you were so mad!"

Mell nodded then accepted the coffee Chelsie offered her gratefully and waited for Jed so they could finish their rounds.

* * *

Jed pushed George in front of him down the main street exactly in the center of the road so people could stare and wonder at the strange sight of the helpless George walking dejectedly with head hanging. He hoped the riders veering out of their way and the town's people got a good lesson once the word spread of what George had done. Jed didn't loosen the whip until he got George inside the sheriff's office then into a cell. When the whip was loosened the three pronged, snake like coils dropped harmlessly to the floor now useless without its mistress to wield it. He eyed George as he looked for the marks from the prongs that Mell had made out of deer antlers. And sure enough he saw three gouges in George's vest one was even bleeding slightly.

He left the cell then closed and locked the door behind him before coiling the whip back up into an inconspicuous circle. He studied one of the three coils and frowned thoughtfully. It was as long as his arm and made of two braided rawhide strips that ended in the antler hook. Mell had been right they looked more like an anchor then a fishhook. He frowned it kind of reminded Jed of a bolas that some of the natives used. A bolas was two or three strips of rawhide with rocks tied to the ends when thrown they wrapped around the legs of an animal and would hold them fast. This did the same thing but because it was used on humans that could unwrap a bolas she had used hooks that would tangle in someone's clothes or flesh.

Jed stood for a moment longer outside the jail cell in contemplation as he looked down at the now innocent looking whip. He had seen men use whips on livestock lots of times but this was the first time he had seen it done on a person. It could also be used as a punishment tool, cat of nine tails it was called; it did a lot of damage to a man's back. The power and precision needed to wrap the long snake like coil around a body without injuring or killing him took a lot of talent and years of practice.

Now he could see why Mell carried her whip all the time as far as he was concerned she was better with a whip then with a gun and that was saying a lot. He shook off his thoughts as he left the cells then went to

312

his desk took out an arrest warrant and filled it out quickly. At the bottom he wrote Mell's recommendations then got up and headed out the door. George hadn't said a word since his capture and Jed barely glanced at him as he left.

Jed walked over to the mayor's office and saw Brad and Jane. They were just turning the wagon around after dropping Alec off and were headed for the store. Jed grinned up at them as Brad stopped the horses but he waved them on wanting to see Alec right away. "See you at lunch!"

Brad nodded as he inclined his head then clucked to the horses to continue on without speaking as Jed turned away and entered the mayor's office. Jed approached the receptionist's desk and smiled down hopefully at Lucy. "I need to speak with the Mayor and Alec. Is it okay if I go in?"

Lucy nodded permission as she waved in invitation. "Go ahead Deputy. I'm sure they won't mind."

Jed tipped his hat politely in thanks then turned away and walked down the hallway before stopping in front of the door then knocked politely. He entered at the mayor's impatient call. "Come in!"

Jed smiled in apology as he closed the door behind him then he nodded in greeting at the two men before walking over to the desk as he held up the paper he had in explanation. "Sorry to interrupt gentleman! But I have an arrest warrant that Mell wanted me to bring over right away."

Jed handed the document to the mayor as Alec grinned up at him questioningly. "Who's Mell arresting now?"

Jed shrugged not really knowing the guy then he motioned angrily as he explained to Mell's father the circumstances of the guy's arrest. "A man called George seems he likes to beat up on Pam's Ladies. But this time he went too far and almost killed the girl. Mell is recommending a public flogging, six months in jail, and a ban from all towns she presides over as Sheriff."

The mayor nodded angrily as he looked up after reading the report. "I agree except he'll get a year in jail instead of six months."

Alec nodded then changed the subject as he gestured inquisitively at the mayor. "Any thoughts about hiring a Marshal we've talked about this before and now that Mell's getting married it would be better to have a Marshal so she doesn't have to travel all the time."

The mayor shook his head plaintively as he thought of Mell's reaction earlier when he had suggested it. He frowned in annoyance. "I tried to broach the subject with her earlier this morning but she almost bit my head off again!"

Jed interrupted as he sat down in the chair beside Alec's wheelchair then he smiled eagerly this is what he had wanted to discuss with both men and he was glad that they had brought it up. "I might have a suggestion if you would like to hear it."

Alec turned towards Jed then smiled hopefully over at him as he motioned in invitation. "Sure we'd like to hear it."

Jed grinned at the two men enticingly as he waved casually. "Well, the Mayor described the difference between a Sheriff and a Marshal to me earlier but Mell doesn't want to give up her towns where as you two want to lighten her load a little. So why don't you make her the Marshal and me a Deputy Marshal. That way every town has it's own Sheriff so she doesn't have to run back and forth constantly to keep the peace. It will lighten the load for her in the sense that she won't have to worry about being in two places at once. Or that desperado's and hired guns would be forever trying to take over her towns. She'll still have to travel from town to town, which is what she really loves to do. That way everybody is happy!"

The mayor and Alec looked at each other in amazement at how easily Jed had solved their problem then they grinned in complete agreement at each other. The mayor turned to Jed with a smile of thanks. "Well young man I think you have the perfect solution to our little problem."

Alec nodded proudly then smirked. "Yes he's definitely going to be an asset to the family!"

The mayor chuckled at the boastful Alec then looked from one man to the other in contemplation. "Okay now that we have reached a solution how do we approach Mell with it?"

Jed laughed devilishly at the two men as he got up to leave. "I'll leave that up to you two to figure out. If I don't get back to the Saloon soon Mell's going to come looking for me!"

Alec smiled teasingly up at Jed as he motioned resignedly. "He knows when to make an exit too. That's just fine leave us poor men to figure out how were going to approach Mell on this sensitive issue I'll meet you in about an hour for lunch."

Jed chuckled in delight at Alec's teasing then inclined his head in farewell to the two men without comment. He didn't stop at the desk this time but he made sure to wave at Lucy as he passed her on his way out then he hurried to Chelsie's hoping Mell wasn't angry with him for taking so long.

* * *

Mell smiled across the bar at Chelsie glad she had gotten rid of Jed so easily. "Do you happen to have wedding bands for men?"

Chelsie grinned then nodded that she did and waved one of her girls over to tend bar for her. Chelsie turned back to Mell then beckoned her to follow. "Just come this way and I'll show you what I have."

Mell followed Chelsie into her back room obediently then watched as Chelsie opened her safe and brought out a small box. She turned and smiled at Mell as she brought the box over to her desk. "I only have a few at the moment because most men won't wear rings."

Mell nodded just thankful to have a few to choose from and opened the box. There were a dozen rings in all and each one had a different design. She examined them carefully then picked up one that featured three stars and each star held a small diamond. She ran her fingers over the surface to make sure it was smooth and wouldn't catch on anything. She looked back over at Chelsie then held out the ring. "I'll take this one it looks like it might fit him."

Chelsie grinned as she motioned in reassurance. "If it doesn't bring it back and I'll make it fit."

Mell nodded towards the ring. "How much do you want for it?"

Chelsie looked the ring over critically then looked up at Mell. "Well there's three tiny diamonds in it and it has a unique design which took me a long time. It's also the last one I made in Ireland. I made it for one of the Ladies of the court, a Duchess to be I think, but she didn't come for it before I left so I took it with me. I'll take one hundred for it. If that's too much there are cheaper ones in there that is also very nice."

Mell shook her head negatively. "No I'll take that one. Hand me a paper and pen I'll make out a bank note."

Chelsie handed her the items requested as she wrapped the ring while Mell wrote out the note. Chelsie sighed hopefully as she looked up at Mell and handed her the wrapped ring. "I heard the railway was coming this way. If it does I might be able to sell my jewellery cheaper. Most people cannot afford any of these specialty ones that I showed you but I do have a separate case full of ones that are under fifty dollars, but they're not as good as this case is unfortunately."

Mell waved irritably with a disgruntled sigh she had heard the same rumours. "Well you're probably right going to Boston will be quicker and cheaper by train. But speaking as a Sheriff I'm definitely not looking forward to it because if it passes too close to any of my towns, it's likely to cause me nothing but grief. I'd definitely have to give in to the Mayor then about hiring a Marshal."

Chelsie smiled placatingly well aware of Mell's opinions of marshal's then she motioned teasingly. "Well, you wouldn't want that now would you?"

Mell sighed in aggravation ignoring Chelsie's teasing tone as she shook her head in denial. "No, I love all my towns and would hate to have to stay in just one while someone takes over the others and wrecks all the work I've done so far."

Chelsie nodded as her expression became serious knowing that Mell wouldn't appreciate her teasing then she took the box of rings and the banknote then put them away in her safe before both women left then went back into the saloon. Chelsie shooed her girl away then went back behind the bar and poured Mell another coffee. Mell took a sip then looked at the clock behind the bar that Chelsie had made in aggravation. "I wonder what's taking Jed so long. If he's not back by the time I finish my coffee I'll have to go look for him."

Chelsie laughed knowingly. "Well, now that you're getting married you'll have to get used to waiting you know what men are like when they start gossiping. But usually they wait until after the wedding before they make you wait."

Mell was still chuckling in delight when Jed came in and gestured in apology. "Sorry it took me so long but your father was at the Mayor's office."

Jed looked at both women perplexed as they looked at each other and laughed in conspiracy. He shrugged off their laughter not sure what it was all about, but he was pretty sure he didn't want to know, then continued as if he hadn't been interrupted. "Your father said he would meet us in half an hour for lunch."

Mell nodded as she turned back to him and took back her whip as Jed held it out to her then she waved to Chelsie before they left. Mell sighed in anger as she thought about George then looked over at Jed and motioned curiously as they walked. "What did the Mayor have to say?"

Jed grinned reassuringly over at Mell. "I wrote down everything you recommended and he agreed to everything except the jail term. He extended the six month to one year."

Mell sighed relieved. "Good!"

They walked down the sidewalk slowly looking into buildings, but not entering any until they reached the hotel. They went inside and Mell smiled over at the clerk. "Any problems the last few days or strangers in town?"

The clerk shook his head negatively as he waved in reassurance. "No everything's been quiet here."

Mell nodded in relief then they went into the dining room to wait for her father. They walked across to a corner table and once again they put their chairs against the wall so that they could both see the whole room. Millie walked over with the coffee pot and two cups then smiled at both of them cheerfully. "Coffee Sheriff?"

Mell nodded as she grinned up at Millie inquisitively. "Please Millie. My father and the Anderson's will be joining us so we'll wait for them before we order. How's home life since Gary started working for me?"

Millie smiled in pleasure as she poured them each a coffee. "Jus great he loves it and causes me no grief anymore."

Mell winked up in approval. "Well that's good news. I promise to keep him so busy he'll hardly have any time to cause you grief!"

Millie laughed in delight. "Suits me jus fine Sheriff."

Mell sipped her coffee reflectively as she looked over her cup at Jed then she sighed contemplatively. "Well tomorrow's the big day. Are you ready Jed?"

Jed smiled teasingly then chuckled knowingly. "I've been married before so I do know some of the things to expect. But then again marriage to you will be way different you're always so full of unexpected adventure. You're very unpredictable unlike my first wife."

Jed was rescued from explaining his remarks, as Mell frowned inquisitively, by the arrival of first Jane followed by Brad pushing Alec's chair. Jane arrived first and sat down in excitement as she gestured in delight then grabbed Mell's hand eagerly. "Oh Mell you should see all the furniture your father bought us he said it came with the house and he wouldn't let us pay for anything he even bought us new dishes and pots with a huge wood cook stove that will keep the whole cabin heated with lots of room for cooking we're going to pick the kids up from my mother's place on the way out of town and we're going to move into the cabin as soon as we get back."

Mell smiled in pleasure at Jane's excitement and squeezed her hand but knew better than to try to say anything until Jane was finished. When Jane paused for breath Mell interrupted hurriedly. "Well he's right. We promised you a place to live and it should come with everything. I'm glad you're happy with the arrangements and it will be nice to have your kids running around. As for the wood stove you need a big one, because you'll be cooking for the men in the bunkhouse as well as helping out at the ranch house."

Millie came over with coffee and everyone ordered the special. Alec waited until Millie left then looked over at Mell sadly. "I heard what happened at Pam's last night. Any problems capturing George?"

Mell shook her head negatively with an angry scowl. "No he knew I was coming for him and waited at Chelsie's. Chelsie said he was there as soon as she opened and he just sat in his usual corner drinking watching the doors for me."

Alec shook his head pensively. "Something must have set him off. He's been so good since you had that talk with him."

Mell gave an angry shrugged as she waved in aggravation. "Doesn't matter sooner or later it was bound to happen once a women beater, always a women beater it won't ever change!"

Alec nodded regretfully then changed the sensitive subject quickly seeing Mell getting angrier as they talked about it. "I suppose so! John was telling me that the railroad is making good progress. If they keep on the way they're going they should be here in the next two years or so. It looks like it'll be going straight through our town. He also heard that the telegraph will be coming soon too, as the Mayor he gets information before the people hear it, and he's pretty sure that the telegraph will make it sometime later this year or early next year."

Mell sighed in frustration. "The telegraph will definitely be welcome since it takes too long by coach to get messages. But I had hoped that the train wouldn't come this way!"

Jed looked at Mell in surprise as he motioned curiously. "Why would that upset you? With the railroad going through here the towns will grow and prosper."

Mell tried to explain her fears as she turned to Jed. "I know it's a good thing that the town will grow and prosper but think of it this way the more people in town the more crime, which means I'll have to give in to the Mayor and let him hire a Marshal."

Alec and Jed looked at each other then smiled secretively before turning their attention back to Mell. Jed couldn't help asking even though he was sure he knew what the problem was already. "So what's the problem with that what's wrong with being a Sheriff in just one town?"

Mell sighed disconsolately as she waved plaintively. "They're all my towns and some strange man will come in and wreck everything I've accomplished."

The food arrived and the conversation was cut short as they all ate quietly each deep in their own thoughts. When they were finished eating Jane and Brad got up to leave. Jane smiled down at Alec. "We'll grab the kids and the rest of our things then come back and pick you up."

Alec inclined his head in acknowledgment. "Okay I'll be here when you finish."

Jane waved good-bye and they left. Millie came over and refilled their coffee cups before cleaning the table off. Alec waited until she finished then turned to Jed as he pulled out a paper from inside his pocket then handed the paper over for Jed's inspection. "Here's a copy of the estimation done on the ranch. This figure is what you would have to pay to each of us to become a full partner. Now, if you don't have enough money I have another suggestion. Since it's Mell's ranch you could just pay me my half and we could each own one quarter with Mell having controlling interest."

Jed shook his head negatively. "No, I have plenty of money to pay both of you. But Mell has the final say if she wants controlling interest then I'll just pay you. If she doesn't mind a three way partnership I'd prefer that."

Mell looked from one to the other then nodded at the two men agreeably. "I don't mind a three way partnership but it's totally up to you two. I don't mind either way."

Jed sighed in relief. "I'll head over to the bank right away. Do you want the money put in your own accounts or in the ranch account?"

Alec looked at Mell inquisitively then turned back to Jed when she shrugged not caring one way or the other. "Well since we're selling a piece to you it should go in our private accounts."

Jed nodded then got up to go. "Okay I'll be back in a couple of minutes."

Alec watched Jed walk away in surprise then turned to Mell thoughtfully. "I'm not sure if that man has more money than brains or if he's just worried not wanting people to think that he's using you for your money. He didn't even blink an eye at the amount!"

Mell motioned over at her father teasingly. "Well if I remember rightly I had this problem once before with another man who refused to have anything to do with the ranch unless he could pay his own way."

Alec sighed reproachfully at his daughter but pretended he hadn't heard her last comment. "Well, since I was in his place once I guess I can understand his determination to pay his own way."

Mell chuckled in delight as her father ignored her teasing then changing the subject as she gestured hopefully. "Is everything ready for the wedding tomorrow?"

Alec grinned in reassurance. "Except you need to try your dress on one more time when you get home tonight you also had two wedding gifts show up very early this morning, a two-year-old steer, and a three-year-old sow both are butchered already for the wedding. The sow is probably already in the underground oven we hastily dug this morning. The steer will be cooked tomorrow."

Mell's eyebrows lifted in surprise as she waved inquisitively. "Oh, and who would send them over as a wedding gift?"

Alec chuckled at Mell's surprised expression. "Daniel Grey, you must have made him feel guilty, but he still isn't coming to the wedding I'm told."

Mell sighed irritably as she shook her head angrily. "I didn't think he would. Once that old goat makes up his mind about something you have to practically hit him on the head with proof before he'll budge."

Alec laughed at Mell's accurate assessment of his friend but he didn't say anything as Millie refilled their coffee cups.

Jed walked in a few minutes later and smiled in satisfaction. "Okay all done the bank manager said the money should be in your accounts by next week once he gets conformation from my bank in Boston!"

Alec grinned in relief glad to have that all settled then took out another paper from his pocket and handed it to Jed when he sat down. "We all need to sign this. You can read it first and give it to me later. All it says is that you have bought into the ranch on a three-way partnership and that your share of the profits will automatically be transferred to your account each year. It also says that if anything should happen to either of us their share automatically goes to Mell since it is her ranch. If something happens to Mell then her share is divided between us or goes to her children if she has any."

Jed nodded then put the contract in his pocket so he could read it later. They had more coffee and a piece of pie, while they waited for Jane and Brad. Finally the two showed up and Mell pushed Alec out to the wagon then gave him a kiss. Brad and Jed helped Alec get in then put Alec's chair in the bed of the wagon for the trip back to the ranch. Mell and Jed waved good-bye before returning to their duties.

CHAPTER TWENTY

The day of the wedding turned out to be beautiful. The sun was shining gloriously and the temperature was mild not to hot. There was just enough wind to keep the bugs away but not enough to cause any problems with the outside decorations.

Mell woke in surprise at the sound of the birds cheerily singing and the sun shinning brightly in her bedroom window. She had never slept this late before. She rolled over to cuddle up to Jed but he was already gone. Mell stretched contentedly and laid her head back on the pillow in excitement remembering that today she wasn't going into work, but getting married instead.

The last week had gone well she supposed, while she had been showing Jed the ropes and taking care of the hired guns in Miller's Creek. Gloria, Jessica, and Mrs. Elton along with Mary, Jane, and Sarah had spent the week sewing two wedding gowns and preparing food for the wedding reception.

Everyone in town and the surrounding area had been invited and the only ones to refuse their invitations had been Brian, James, Mr. Grey, and their men.

Pastor Dan was going to perform the ceremonies. He had balked a little about joining a white woman and an Indian in matrimony. But he had come around when told that they were already married and a sizable donation to his church had made him happy to renew their vows.

Mell heard a knock on the door but before she could answer Gloria walked in carrying a tray laden with food. Mell had just enough time to grab her blankets and cover herself decently. Gloria grinned teasingly as she saw Mell comfortably sprawled on the bed. "Well lazy bones I brought you some breakfast. You're not allowed to do anything today. You're to eat all of it and in about an hour's time the boys will bring up your bath water. Your dress is ready and everything is going smoothly so far. The guests should be arriving around two o'clock or so. When the boys bring your bath up Mrs. Elton will come up as well and help you get ready. You're not even allowed to leave your room until your father comes to escort you."

Mell nodded then scowled chidingly as she shook her finger reproachfully at Gloria. "What about you? It's your wedding day too and here you are running around waiting on me."

Gloria laughed good-naturedly as she deposited the tray on Mell's lap unceremoniously. "We gave instructions to Wade to disappear until we're finished the morning chores then I'll also be banished to my room. Mary will take over for me then since she's already married it doesn't matter if he sees her. She'll have time to get ready later."

Mell grinned satisfied with that explanation and sipped her coffee contentedly. "Can you hand me my dressing robe please?"

Gloria turned away to look for the robe. "Sure."

Mell sighed apprehensively as she all of a sudden felt a shiver of forewarning course down her spine. "Has anyone heard from Brian yet?"

Gloria shook her head negatively as she put the dressing gown on the bed where Mell could reach it easily then looked down at Mell fretfully. "No, and it's making Jed nervous. He's posted some men on guard duty just in case there are any signs of trouble. Mary's still upset about her brother turning down her invitation but she knew he would. Tommy has adjusted very well to Giant Bear. Ever since the engagement party he's had a grin on his face a mile long. He follows Giant Bear around everywhere and tells everyone that he's his father. He never stops asking about his Indian heritage and the village where he will be living. He's also been practicing with that rifle every chance he gets and every time we look around he's practicing his kicks and rolls, or twirls that stick around in imitation of a knife."

Mell grinned in delight as she thought of Tommy then her expression sobered restlessly as she thought of Brian again. "I'm glad Jed posted some guards. I have a feeling that we haven't seen the last of Brian."

Gloria frowned irritably at the thought of him. She turned to leave not wanting to continue discussing Brian, she had never liked him, and like Mell's father she had feared Mell would marry him. Mell waited until Gloria reached the door before calling out curiously. "By the way how's the romance going between my dad and Jessica?"

Gloria turned the doorknob but didn't leave right away as she turned back towards Mell and grinned in delight. "Fine I think Mrs. Donaldson is beginning to enjoy being chased."

With that comment Gloria left the room and softly closed the door behind her. Mell slowly ate her breakfast but her mind wasn't on what she was doing as she thought about Brian and his threats. The more she thought about him the more nervous she became. Surely he wouldn't be crazy enough to attack Mary and Giant Bear here with all these people around! Would he? She shook her head negatively as she decided that he wouldn't be that stupid.

She shook off her nervous feelings decisively then turned her thoughts to Jed instead and the perfect week they had spent together making love without consummating their relationship when they weren't too exhausted to do so that is. But tonight they would go all the way and make love fully. She definitely wasn't afraid of the experience any longer. She had lost her fear and shyness when it came to Jed's body after the first night but hadn't let on enjoying their nights together as they were. Jed had explained to her last night that there would be some pain in the beginning when he entered her body for the first time. But it would be brief and then she would never feel pain again.

Mell grinned it wasn't the pain she had been afraid of she had known a lot of pain in the years she had been a deputy and sheriff. Especially once everyone found out that she was a woman and they had to test her out. More then once she had been stabbed, shot, and she had even supported a few black eyes with a fat lip or two. That was before she had made a reputation of never backing down and that she always got her man or woman no matter where or how.

So pain had never entered her mind when she first looked at Jed fear of loosing herself was more terrifying then pain. If she was totally truthful with herself it was the fear of her own femininity that had scared her the most. Jed made her feel vulnerable, tiny, and for the first time in her life like a woman. That's what really scared her so bad no other man in her life had ever made her feel this way. It had terrified her to feel so vulnerable and it made her feel like she was losing control of herself.

Mell heard another knock on the door so hastily shook off thoughts of Jed. She set aside the tray before hastily getting up then putting her robe on. She sat back down on the bed and called out expectantly already knowing it was Mrs. Elton and her bath water. "Come in!"

A beaming Mrs. Elton entered followed by the boys carrying a large tub and pails of water. She walked over to the bed demandingly as she put her hands on her hips in sternness. "Come on Mell it's time to get ready."

Mell grinned up at Mrs. Elton but waited for the boys to leave before stepping out of her robe obediently then crawled into the deep warm water in pleasure. She sighed in delight as Mrs. Elton scrubbed her long hair. Then Mell immersed her head for a quick rinse before kneeling in the tub as Mrs. Elton poured a pail of warm water over her head to rinse her hair of any excess soap left behind. Mrs. Elton wrapped a towel around her head then gently pulled on the towel in demand. "Lie back now so that your hair is draped over the tub that way I can dry your hair while you finish bathing."

Mell got out of the tub and dried off as Mrs. Elton held her hair out so that it wouldn't get wet again. When Mell was dried of to her satisfaction she let go of her hair then went to the wardrobe and came over with Mell's camisole, undergarments, and new corset. She put the camisole and undergarments on her first then Mrs. Elton helped her put the corset on then laced it up as tightly as she could. Mell was groaning in painful torture by the time Mrs. Elton felt it was tight enough to suit her. Mell moaned then finally managed to take enough of a breath to gasp out plaintively. "Why do women torture themselves with these contraptions?"

Mrs. Elton grinned sympathetically. "Well it all started with a woman who was too fat to get into her favourite dress. So she had someone make a corset so that she could fit into the dress instead of being smart and altering the dress. Well when other women saw the woman who used to be fat they asked her how she got so slim so fast. Now you can imagine that it wasn't long before every woman was wearing it and now we're stuck with them."

Mell sighed forlornly at that explanation then waved at the door pleadingly with a smile of innocence. "Mrs. Elton could you ask Gloria for the turquoise combs that hold up my vale I forgot them."

She nodded not suspecting a thing then went over to the bed and picked up the breakfast tray. "Would you like more coffee as well?"

Mell grinned eagerly it would keep her busy hopefully long enough to do what she needed to do. "Sounds good to me I'll be stuck here for awhile so more coffee sounds great."

Mrs. Elton inclined her head in sympathy then left. As soon as she left Mell rushed over to the bed and quickly pulled on her stockings. She groaned in pain as she bent over in the tight corset but she didn't let that stop her. Once her stockings were on she strapped onto her right leg what looked like a garter. But was actually a small pouch with a pistol that she always carried even when she wore pants.

Mell then hurried to the closet and pulled out her petticoat then quickly put it on. She was gasping for breath as the tight corset tried to cut off her air supply as she hurry not wanting Mrs. Elton to catch her in the act of arming herself even on her wedding day. She then grabbed a knife and her Indian Medicine pouch that she had hidden under her pillow then stuck them into a deep pocket in her petticoat.

Gloria of course had guessed what the pocket was for when Mell had requested it but she had kept her secret. Mell just finished putting her wedding gown over her head and was pulling it down when Mrs. Elton came back into the room. She stopped short in surprise when she saw that Mell was already dressed. Mell smiled guilelessly over at her as she smoothed her dress down. "Oh just in time to help me do up these buttons and to help me on with the blue garter."

Mrs. Elton sat her tray down on the vanity then turned and smirked at Mell teasingly. "It took you a long time to decide to get married and now you're in such a hurry you can't even wait for me to help you get dressed!"

She laughed in delight at Mell's fiery blush then motioned playfully "Just teasing Mell now how about sitting down at your vanity and while you enjoy your coffee I'll fix your hair before we do up the buttons on your dress?"

Mell smiled in relief that Mrs. Elton didn't suspect a thing as she did as she was told and sat down at her vanity.

* * *

Jed and Giant Bear walked out of the house followed by a faithful Tommy. Once on the veranda they paused a moment to look around. Giant Bear turned to Jed inquisitively as he waved demandingly. He had spent too many years with Jed to be fooled by Jed's calm expression. He switched to Cheyenne so Tommy wouldn't understand. "What is wrong Grey Wolf? You have been uptight all morning."

Jed sighed in confusion as he turned and looked at his friend then shrugged uneasily as he too switched languages. "I don't know Giant Bear. I've just had this gut feeling all morning that something isn't right. I keep thinking about the threat's Brian made when told about your remarriage to Mary. I just have this feeling that he's up to something it's just been too quiet since he made all those threats."

Giant Bear nodded in understanding with a shiver of foreboding as he frowned in surprise. "I have to admit that I have the same expectation of danger but the guests will be here in about an hour. What can we do we can not call off the weddings now on just a hunch so what can we do to protect everyone?"

Giant Bear frowned thoughtfully as he turned to Tommy suddenly more worried then he cared to admit as he gestured demandingly and switched to English so Tommy could understand. "Do you have that knife I gave you handy?"

Tommy nodded solemnly in confusion he hadn't understood what they were saying but he could feel the tension in the air and it bothered him. "Yes it's in my room."

Giant Bear smiled reassuringly trying not to scare him. Jed had told him the threats Brian had made in regards to his son and wife. "Do you remember where to stab a man should one attack you?"

Tommy pointed down at himself as he remembered his father telling him that stabbing a man in his groin area if held from behind would make the man let go of him instantly. Giant Bear grinned proudly then nodded towards the house in demand. "Good I want you to go get it and stick it under your shirt where you can reach it easily. Then I want you to stay close to your mother and guard her for me, okay!"

Tommy frowned in surprise at his father then turned towards the house without questioning why. His chest puffed up slightly in pride at being given such a serious job as protecting his mother then he ran into the house. Jed chuckled at the pleased Tommy then he turned towards Giant Bear and his expression sobered in anxiety as he waved after the young boy. "Tommy sure is proud of being your son isn't he? But do you think he's ready to stand up to a man in a fight? I know you and Mell have been teaching him as fast as you can and that he's learned quite a few tricks already but I don't think he's ready yet for such a fight."

Giant Bear smiled proudly at the progress his son was making then he frowned troubled as he shook his head fretfully. "He is learning the art of knife fighting well. You are right though he is not ready yet but I sent him up to his mother for two reasons. One to keep him away from me in case Brian attempts to kill me, the second reason is so that I will know where he is at all times. This way I can keep track of him and Mary at the same time."

Jed nodded in approval then he sighed in resignation as he pointed up towards Mell's room. "Good thinking friend. As for Mell I already know that if it comes to a fight she'll be right in the middle of it. I think we'll have to warn our guests to be on the watch at all times and to keep their guns handy. I'm going to check on the men I have stationed around the ranch to make sure that everyone's ready just in case of trouble."

Giant Bear solemnly gestured towards the barn. "Okay I will go to the barn and check on the horses and Mark then I will get dressed in my ceremonial clothes while I am there."

329

Jed walked with Giant Bear towards the barn neither speaking now both apprehensive wondering if they had thought of everything. Giant Bear turned to go inside and Jed walked over to the corral to get his horse.

Jed wasn't even half way to his first lookout when he saw a rider approach so he brought his horse to a halt to check on who it was. The guests shouldn't be arriving yet. As the man got closer he recognized Mark and Jed frowned in surprise. Mark stopped in front of Jed then he smiled reassuringly as he pointed behind him. "I took a look around and there's not a soul in sight."

Jed nodded without comment and waved Mark on his way then Jed turned his horse suspiciously to watch him as he rode back to the ranch slowly in no apparent hurry. Jed's eyes narrowed dangerously he hadn't asked Mark to do any scouting his job had been to remain at the barn. Jed changed his mind about checking on the lookouts for now and rode over to the bunkhouse. He would get Tomas to keep an eye on Mark just in case. After speaking to Tomas, Jed went in search of Giant Bear.

As Jed came around the side of the barn he saw Giant Bear walking toward the veranda so he changed directions and quickly caught up to Giant Bear then motioned inquisitively behind him at the barn. "Did you talk to Mark Giant Bear?"

Giant Bear nodded that he had in unconcern. "He was just coming in as I was leaving. He did not say much except that he was out scouting on your orders."

Jed shook his head angrily in suspicion. "He implied the same thing to me but I gave him no such orders. I talked to Tomas and he promised to keep an eye on Mark for me."

Giant Bear inclined his head in agreement then waved at the cloud of dust coming up the road. "I think it is time for you to get ready. I can hear carriages coming. I will greet the guests and warn the men for you so you can go and change."

Jed smiled in thanks then totally forgetting about Mark in his excitement he turned and hurried up the steps before slipped in the door.

* * *

Mell stood at the window watching the guests arrive anxiously, not sure if she could go out there in front of her friends and the towns people.

Her gown was beautiful it was all white with turquoise glass beadwork artfully sewn on the bodice. The neck was cut very low and showed off her large breasts to perfection. The waist was snug but the skirt flared out and swept the floor. White shoes adorned her surprisingly small feet and peeked out below her skirts.

At first she had balked at the shoes but gave in when Mrs. Elton threatened to burn her moccasins if she dared ware them under her beautiful wedding dress. She had placed a blue garter above Mell's left knee for Jed to remove and throw to all the bachelors when it was time. Mrs. Elton had swept her hair up and held it in place with turquoise combs, which the long net veil was attached too.

Mell wasn't sure how she would manage walking in the dress without disaster. She grinned at the picture of herself getting all tangled up in the dress and the long veil then tumbling down the stairs head first in front of all her guests.

Mell turned in surprise as she heard the door opening and saw her father enter the room then he stop short at the sight of her. In his lap were two cases a long black velvet case and a smaller blue one. Mell glided over to push her flabbergasted father further into the room as he sat there staring in shocked surprise. She closed the door before walking back around the wheelchair then turned to face him. Alec smiled mistily up at her as he wiped a tear away. "Forgive me for staring so but every time I see you in a dress you remind me so much of your mother that it hurts."

Mell knelt down then leaned forward against his legs and kissed him tenderly not daring to bend over again in the fear of passing out from lack of breath. "I know dad. I did wear a dress once at the other ranch and I've always remembered the look of sorrow and pain that was on your face. So until the engagement party the other night I've never worn another dress. Perhaps it's a good thing can you imagine me trying to be a Sheriff in a dress?"

Alec laughed in humour at the mental picture of Mell chasing an outlaw with skirts hiked up so she wouldn't trip on them. He shook off his thoughts and picked up the long black case before opening it. He turned it around and showed Mell what was inside. "Mell I have two things for you. One is very old and once belonged to your great grandmother, and one is new. The necklace was passed down to your mother so now it rightfully belongs to you."

Alec took the necklace out of the box then held it up for Mell to see. Mell's breath caught in awed wonder. It was gorgeous the necklace was made with diamonds. Two perfectly matching small teardrop ones on each side of a large center one all three were flawless. The chain holding the diamonds together was made out of pure gold and was so tiny Mell was afraid to touch it in fear of breaking it. When the diamonds caught the light in a certain way a bluish green light would sparkle. Mell smiled at her father in surprise. "It's beautiful!"

Alec chuckled at Mell's reverent look then handed her the smaller velvet case. Mell opened it and gasped at the diamond earrings and bracelet both in a teardrop design to match the necklace. Mell was overwhelmed as tears sprang to her eyes. She motioned incredulously as she looked up at her father. "Oh dad they're so gorgeous! I've never dreamed of owning anything so beautiful."

Alec smiled indulgently then pointed at the necklace. "The necklace has always been yours. There has just never been an occasion to present it to you before now. The bracelet and earrings are new they are a gift from me."

Mell still kneeling turned so that her father could fasten the necklace. Then she turned back around and clipped the earrings on before holding out her arm so her father could put the bracelet on her wrist.

Mell reached out and hugged her father in loving thanks for the beautiful gifts as he leaned forward. "I love you dad."

Alec smiled fondly and wiped the tears from his eyes so they wouldn't fall on his daughter's beautiful dress as he hugged her back fiercely. "I love you too Mell."

Alec pushed her away from him and stared at her sadly for a moment. "You're so exquisite and you look just like your mother did on our wedding day. I still miss her unbearably at times."

Mell nodded her head too chocked up to speak as she wiped the tears away then she grinned mischievously as she took her fathers hand in hers. "I do too but I think Mrs. Donaldson is a very nice lady."

Alec eyed her warily for a moment then smiled in relief at Mell's pleased look. "You don't miss much do you? I'm glad you don't mind I think it's time that I stopped mourning for your mother now that you'll have a husband to take care of you I'd like to do some traveling. I think that Jessica might be a perfect companion."

Mell was very happy that her father was moving on with his life, he had been mourning her mother far too long as it is. "Dad I know you'll be very happy with Jessica. This is the best news I've had in a long time all I've ever wanted is your happiness!"

Mell hugged her father again then stood up as she got a naughty look on her face at Alec's reference to Jessica being the perfect traveling companion. She couldn't help teasing him a little more. "Jessica might or might not be a perfect traveling companion but it doesn't hurt that she's gorgeous as well."

Alec grinned wickedly but changed the subject without comment. "I think it's time. Let's go!"

Mell laughed at her father's refusal to remark but she had caught his sinful smirk and decided to let him off the hook. She walked around the chair then opened the door before pushing her father into the hallway, where Brad and Darrel waited patiently to carry him downstairs.

* * *

Outside in the yard all the guests were assembled in excitement to witness the ceremony. They were seated in rows facing an archway decorated with all types of wild flowers and a buzz of excitement could definitely be heard as they talked with friends and neighbours.

Standing in front of the archway up on a dais was the minister. Just below him on a smaller platform on the minister's left hand side was Jed, on the right hand side stood Wade. Giant Bear stood in between the two on solid ground since he was only renewing his vows. This way Jed and Wade would be the focus of everyone's attention.

Suddenly the guests hushed expectantly as Alec was seen approaching. He stopped his wheelchair dramatically for a moment at the edge of the guest's seats then Tommy and the mayor joined him instantly.

This way the men waiting on the other side of the archway had an unobstructed view of their brides to be. The guests all rose to their feet respectfully when the mayor's wife stood up and started singing the wedding song, accompanied by the piano that the men had taken out of the drawing room this morning.

The three brides approached their escorts slowly as Jane and Brad's daughters threw flower pedals in front of them and the boy held Mell's wedding train. The mayor's youngest grandson held Gloria's. Mary didn't have a wedding train since she was wearing her Indian bridal dress.

Mell came first she was slightly ahead of Gloria with Mary following behind the two. There were exclamations of shocked surprise and admiration as the town's people caught their first and only glimpse of Mell in a dress.

The three women halted beside their escorts and each woman put their hand on their arms proudly as they slowly proceeded to the front of the archway in anticipation. They halted a little distance from the waiting men so that they were directly under the archway, as the minister called out loudly so that all the guests could hear him. "Who giveth these women to these men in holy matrimony?"

Alec looked up at his daughter in pride and his voice drowned out the excited whispers of the guests as he looked away from his daughter and towards Jed with tears in his eyes. "I Alec Ray give my daughter Melissa Ray to Jed Brown in holy matrimony."

Mell bent down for her father's kiss of blessing then she whispered quickly. "I love you dad."

Alec smiled lovingly up at his daughter then whispered as he lifted Mell's veil for the traditional kiss. "I love you too and may God bless you and keep you happy forever!"

Mell waited for her father to lower her veil then she stood up straight in excitement and walked over then up onto the platform to stand by Jed. Gloria took Mell's place with her escort and the minister repeated his question. Mayor Elton did the honours for Gloria since her father had passed on several years ago.

The question was repeated a third time reluctantly and even the now quiet guests could hear the reluctance in the minister's voice. Tommy forgot his line in his excitement since he was his mother's escort and yelled out in confusion. "I do."

Tommy kissed his mother as the guest's laughed. Mary smiled at her son's flustered answer and embarrassed red face then turned away and walked over to stand beside Giant Bear. The three couples then turned to face the minister solemnly holding hands. As the guest's hushed expectantly so they could all hear.

* * *

Tomas watching from the barn wiped tears from his eyes as he grinned evilly. Weddings always made him cry he turned away from the barn window and walked over to the dead man lying on the floor. He looked down at Mark and placed his foot on him disdainfully as he nudged him playfully. "Well Mark I sure fooled Jed when I sent you out on his orders. Jed thought it was going to be you causing trouble!"

Tomas threw back his head and gave an evil sinister laugh then he went to the corner picked up a can of coal oil and he proceeded to pour it over the straw on the floor at the back of the barn. He then turned and looked at the horses in admiration. "That should give the men time to get all the horses out in time especially you Lightning. He promised me that I could have you as soon as he gets control."

Tomas went back to the window to watch the rest of the ceremony satisfied that he was ready and everything was going according to plan.

* * *

Six people said. "I do!" simultaneously.

Then the grooms were lifting the veils for the traditional kiss. The preacher waited until the kiss was finished then waved them all over to a small table for their signatures. The mayor had put it there earlier for this purpose.

Once all six signed their names the papers were taken to Alec and the mayor to witness the signatures. A cheer of joy went up from the crowd as the six stood on the platform surveying their guests proudly. Their lady sheriff was married at last!

Mell stiffened suddenly in alarm as she heard her horse scream in terror. She looked towards the barn in dread and saw puffs of smoke poring from the windows. Mell pointed and screamed above the noise of the cheers...."THE BARN'S ON FIRE!"

Everyone turned as one and raced for the barn to save the horses. Just before Jed and Mell reached the door two shots rang out.

Mell screamed Jed's name in panic and fear as he collapsed with blood pouring from his chest. At the same time she heard Mary's scream of grief and turned slightly to see Giant Bear collapse with blood streaming down his face. Then everything turned black suddenly as something hit her on the head.

* * *

Everyone was running around in a panic screaming. Gloria keeping her head ran over to Mrs. Elton in demand as she gestured anxiously. "Help me herd all the women and children into the house. Hurry please!"

Mrs. Elton had turned white in shock but she shook herself and between the two of them they managed to get everyone inside safely. Gloria frantically searched among the women in the house for Mell and Mary but couldn't find either of them. She ran over to Jessica in a panic as she waved in urgency. "I can't find Mell or Mary so I'm going back outside to take another look. In the mean time try and keep everyone calm."

Jessica watched Gloria leave in concern then she herded all the children into the hallway then up the stairs to her room with Mrs. Elton's help.

* * *

Gloria ran out of the ranch house in a panic looking for Mell and Mary. She tried shouting above the noise first as she cupped her hands around her mouth. "Mell, Mary! Where are you?"

Gloria gave that up nobody could hear her in all this noise and she stumbled over to Mell's father in fear. "Alec I can't find Mell or Mary but I've gotten all the other women and children inside the house safely away from any stray bullets."

Alec frowned in fear then pointed to his left towards where the mayor was standing surrounded by arguing men. "Good job Gloria! Now we've got to get everyone calmed down. The Mayor is over there please ask him to come here there's just too many people running around for me to get to him."

Gloria did as she was bid.

Alec looked up at the mayor in relief as the two managed to get to him then he motioned to all the guests still running around not sure in which direction to go. "We need to get everyone calmed down. I've tried but haven't had much success any suggestions?"

Mayor Elton sighed in exasperation, as he looked around at all the foolish people running around for no reason. "Let's try this first!"

The mayor put two fingers in his mouth and gave a loud sharp whistle but nothing happened. When that didn't work he shrugged resignedly then took out his gun and fired a shot into the air expectantly.

Everyone turned to look in surprise and when they saw the mayor holding a smoking pistol, quiet descended instantly. The mayor's voice boomed out in demand. "Can I have everyone's attention please?"

Everyone gathered around glad to finally have someone take control. Alec smiled up in appreciation at the mayor. "Thank you."

He then turned to speak to all his guests. He pointed to a group standing off to his right. "I want you men to get the horses out of the barn and put the fire out."

About ten men rushed towards the barn instantly without question. Alec then turned to the rest unrelentingly. "Mell and Mary are missing. So are Jed and Giant Bear."

Gary stepped forward instantly and waved towards the barn. "Jed and Giant Bear are both dead. One's lying over by the barn doors on the right, and the other one is lying on the left side of the barn."

Alec gasped in shocked denial as he started shaking in reaction. "No they can't be!"

* * *

Mell came too instantly as she heard the sound of someone groaning. At first she thought that she had made the sound but as she lifted her head to investigate she saw someone slinging a bound and gagged Mary over a horse. Mell quickly dropped her head against the saddle as she realized that nobody had noticed that she was awake.

Mell moved slightly in experiment but realized in disappointment that she was already tied belly down on a horse and gagged as well that's why her mouth hurt so much. She moved again this time squirming slightly so she could check on her hidden weapons and was relieved that no one had checked her when she felt the small pistol still strapped to her thigh and the knife hidden under her dress.

Mell heard footsteps suddenly coming closer so she deliberately went limp hoping she could fool them into thinking she was still unconscious. Somebody grabbed her by the hair and started to lift her head up to check on her but paused half way as he called out to someone instead. "Is she awake yet?"

Another deep voice answered him but Mell couldn't tell who either man was by their voice. "I just checked her and she's still out cold."

The man holding her head by the hair grunted in disgust without checking to make sure himself then let go suddenly without warning. "Okay let's go!"

Mell ground her teeth in pain trying not to make any noise as she let her head hit the saddle with a hard thwack, much harder then she intended as the lights went out once more.

CHAPTER TWENTY-ONE

Mayor Elton pushed Alec over to Giant Bear first he was closer not having reached the barn in the panic of finding his son and wife. The mayor left Alec then bent down to examine the wound on Giant Bear's head then checked for a pulse. He turned to Alec thankfully as he motioned in relief. "He's not dead thank God. Whoever shot him wasn't very good. The bullet just creased him he'll be fine in a bit except for a bad headache."

Alec sighed in elation as he pointed to the men on his left. "You four take him to the house so Gloria can see to him."

Alec looked up at Gloria pleadingly. "Gloria go with them and patch him up please."

Gloria nodded reluctantly wanting to stay to help find Mell and Mary but obediently directed the men to the house, while Mayor Elton pushed Alec over to Jed who was lying face down.

The mayor left Alec again then knelt down as he gently pushed Jed over in dread fearing the worst by the amount of blood on the ground and examined the wound carefully before checking for a pulse. He turned to Alec with a gratified sigh as he waved pleased. "Jed's alive too but he's losing a lot of blood. The bullet went clean through just below his left shoulder. Just missing his heart by the looks of it he's very lucky! A little further down and he would have died instantly."

Alec turned ecstatically to four more men standing by waiting as Mayor Elton got up and walked back over to Alec. "Please take him up to the house to Gloria quickly so she can stop him from bleeding to death."

Alec then looked up at the mayor pleadingly once he saw his new son-in-law on his way for treatment as he waved in panic. "What about Mell and Mary?"

Mayor Elton turned to the remaining men questioningly but they all shook their heads at his unspoken enquiry. The mayor turned back to Alec and put his hand on his shoulder consolingly. "I'm sorry no one seems to know what happened to them. They just seemed to have disappeared."

Alec gave the mayor an anguished look that he tried to hide from the others. Then they all look towards the barn at a shout as they saw some of the men returning carrying a body. They put the body down gently and Dusty came over then motioned sadly. "Mark is dead his throat was slit. The fire is out and we put all the horses over in the far corral. Whoever set the fire didn't want to kill the horses so cleared the area around it, so that the fire wouldn't spread."

Alec exhaled noisily pleased that none of the horses had been harmed. Looking around at all the men gathered he motioned pleadingly. "Pick four men who are good trackers and send them out to see if they can find out what happened to Mell and Mary, someone must have taken them they just couldn't have disappeared without a trace. Then gather all the guests in one group and the new hands in another group then see who's missing."

Alec turned to one of his hands then waved towards the ranch house. "Kenneth will you help me over to the house so I can check on Jed and Giant Bear's progress, Darrel please saddle up their horses, as well as Lightning and Mary's horse. I know Jed and Giant Bear will waste no time in going after the women when their finally able to ride."

Alec kept his expression under careful control as Kenneth pushed him towards the house and up the ramp to the front door. Once they entered the house Alec looked up at Kenneth in gratitude. "Thank you I can manage now."

Kenneth inclined his head in farewell then left. Alec waited until he was gone then let the emotions he had been hiding blaze to the surface for a moment as he shuddered in fear and terror at the loss of his daughter. He dropped his head in his hands in despair. He stayed like that for a while fighting for control then he took a deep fortifying breath and when he looked back up his face was expressionless once more. He was in complete control again then he went towards the den where he knew he would find Gloria working on the two men.

Gloria was just coming out and put her finger to her mouth to indicate that he should remain quiet. She had quickly changed out of her wedding dress and put on an apron. Her apron was full of blood as she wiped her hands on it to clean them. Then she went behind his chair and pushed him into the kitchen where they could talk without disturbing her patience. Once inside she pulled off her apron in distaste then threw it in the fire pit to be burned as she pulled a clean one out then put it on thankfully. She washed her hands then poured them both a coffee still without speaking and brought a plate of sandwiches over to the table. She then sat down across from him.

Alec sipped his coffee reflectively then put the cup down and dropped his head into his hands as he ran his fingers through his hair in frustration. He sighed dispiritedly as he dropped his hands then looked across the table at Gloria pleadingly. "I'm getting too old for this Gloria I don't know how much more I can stand. If something happens to Mell I don't think I could survive it!"

Gloria took his hand sympathetically and held it for a moment already aware that Alec wouldn't survive if his daughter got killed. He squeezed her hand a little in gratitude then frowned in surprise as he looked around and wondered why it was so quiet. There should have been women and children running around. He looked back at Gloria inquisitively. "Gloria, where did you put all the women and children?"

Gloria smiled mysteriously as she took her hand away from Alec's then picked up a half a sandwich and set it before him. "You better eat this or I won't tell you!"

Alec held his two hands up in surrender at Gloria's stubborn look. He grinned, as he obliged her. "Okay, okay I give up. I'll eat if you'll answer my question."

Gloria waited patiently without comment then smiled in satisfaction when he picked up the sandwich and bit into it. She smirked as she pointed up. "Jessica and Mrs. Elton are upstairs keeping the women and children busy."

Gloria then waved her hand towards the den and continued as Alec obediently took another bite of his sandwich. "Jed is lying on the couch in the den. I had a hard time with his wound I had to heat a blade up then push the tip inside the wound to cauterize it. Just to stop the bleeding then packed it full of herbs. I also put a couple of stitches front and back before bandaging it as tight as I could in order to stop the blood loss. The bullet must have hit a vein that's why there was so much blood on the ground. He came too briefly but I gave him some willow bark tea and a drop of laudanum for the pain. He should sleep for another half an hour or so. Giant Bear is in the library I had to physically hold him down and tell him that he had to sleep for at least an hour before I would let him up. He didn't settle down until I told him that several men were out tracking and that I would wake him the minute they found out where the women were taken."

Mayor Elton walked in the kitchen just then and sat down heavily in a chair in exhaustion. Gloria got up and poured the mayor some coffee. At the same time she refilled Alec's cup along with her own. He looked at Alec and frowned dejectedly as he held up three fingers in aggravation. "We have three people missing. One is your new man Tomas and the others are two guests Gerald and Philip. The men I sent out to track the kidnappers aren't back yet but it shouldn't be too much longer I hope."

Alec nodded sadly then banged the arm of his chair sharply in confusion with a closed fist. "I still can't figure out why this is all happening. Who would want to kidnap my daughter and Mary? It just doesn't make any sense."

Mayor Elton shrugged in sympathy then reached over and patted his friend's hand consolingly. "I'm sorry Alec but your daughter has a lot of enemies out there. It could be someone she has arrested at one time or it could be a family member of someone she has had to kill and they want revenge."

Alec shook his head negatively in disagreement not believing that. "No I don't think so if it was for that reason why did they take Mary too?"

Giant Bear and Jed walked into the room suddenly both a little unsteady so they sat down right away not wanting to fall down. Gloria jumped up instantly in concern as she chided both men for their stubbornness. "You weren't supposed to get up for at least another half an hour!"

Mayor Elton got up and poured the two men coffee then refilled everyone else's, while Gloria checked both men's wounds. Gloria went to Giant Bear first and removed the bandage. It was an ugly red and purple color but the bleeding had thankfully stopped. She put a finger in front of his eyes and moved it back and forth. "Let your eyes follow my finger if you feel dizzy let me know."

Gloria nodded when she was satisfied that Giant Bear would have no lasting problems she decided to leave the bandage off since the cut had quit bleeding on it's own. She turned her attention to Jed more concerned about him since his wound was more serious then Giant Bear's. She removed the bandage carefully and was happy to see that the bleeding had stopped and the stitches seemed to be holding. She nodded in gratification as she bent down and looked into his eyes but found them clear. "Do you feel at all dizzy or light headed as if you're going to pass out?"

Jed shook his head negatively then answered truthfully. "I felt a little dizzy when I first got up but right now I feel fine."

Gloria sighed thankfully as she replaced the bandages so he wouldn't reopen the wound again then she sat down. Alec turned to her anxiously. "Can you pack some provisions and anything else you think Jed and Giant Bear will need to go after Mell and Mary?"

Gloria quickly left the room without argument.

Alec turned to Jed and Giant Bear as he motioned apprehensively. "Do you two have any idea who would want to kidnap Mell and Mary?"

Jed and Giant Bear exchanged significant glance of perfect understanding. Jed turned to Alec and answered for both of them. "Yes we're both pretty sure it is either Brian or Daniel Grey. Maybe even both of them who did it."

Alec looked shocked for a moment then spread his hands out in stunned disbelief. "But why I've never really trusted Brian but I never would have thought he would stoop to kidnapping, as for Daniel he's been my friend for years."

Jed sighed sadly at having to accuse Alec's friend, but he couldn't rule out the possibility, he was pretty sure Brian had been heading to Daniel's place the night they had tried to give him an invitation. "We're not absolutely sure but the other day when we went over to tell Brian about what had happened here and about Mary's reunion with Giant Bear he was very angry and upset already, which seemed strange to both of us. Then when we told him that Mell was going to marry me he got real mean! Brian made a lot of nasty threats and he accused me of wanting to marry Mell for your money, which I didn't know anything about. When Mell asked him how he knew about it he said that you had told him."

Alec interrupted angrily as he shook his head emphatically in denial. "I never told him any such thing! So you think he's doing it for the money Mell will inherit after I die?"

Jed nodded then motioned in explanation. "Yes, but we're not sure why he took Mary as well, unless it was just to prevent her from remarrying Giant Bear since he did threaten to kill her if she did. As for Daniel Grey he blamed Mell for killing Greg and was pretty nasty about it. The two men we hired Tomas and Mark were both his before they came to us. Mell had thought it was strange that Mr. Grey would just fire two of his men without a reason. But then again we have no idea why he would take Mary so were not too sure about him. Or it could be that Brian and Mr. Grey are working together. When we left Mr. Grey's ranch after he refused the wedding invitation, we bumped into Brian halfway between the two ranches. He could have been headed for Mr. Grey's place, which would make your friend Daniel a suspect."

Brad walked in unexpectedly then gestured in apology for interrupting. He frowned in confusion. "We found the place where they had horses waiting right away but we couldn't figure out where they went from there."

Jed and Giant Bear got up instantly ready to go immediately. "Just show us the place and we'll take it from there!"

Jed turned then looked down at Alec reassuringly as he put his hand on Alec's shoulder in promise as he vowed solemnly. "We'll find them I swear. We will bring the Ladies home or die trying I guarantee it!"

Alec nodded in relief satisfied by Jed's vow and knew he meant every word. "God speed and safe journey!"

Jed and Giant Bear left without saying another word determination written all over their faces. Half an hour later Jed came back to get the provisions Gloria had put together for him. Alec met Jed at the front door for news but there wasn't really anything to report so he went back to the kitchen in disappointment.

He entered warily frowning in worry at the mayor as he pushed himself up to the table. "John, I've waited years to see my little girl get married I had almost given up on it when Jed showed up out of nowhere! Mell is such a strong woman and her ideas scare most men away. Now she's finally found someone who is willing to accept her the way she is and we might lose her before she finds out what she's been missing for so long."

Mayor Elton reached over in sympathy and patted Alec's hand consolingly. He smiled in reassurance. "You won't lose her Jed will bring her back. He promised!"

Alec sighed dispiritedly and shrugged in annoyance at himself as he tried to lighten his tone. "I pray it will turn out all right but I just can't help but feel frantic."

Mayor Elton frowned knowingly he was just as apprehensive but was trying not to show it so he could be strong for his friend. He smiled up at Gloria gratefully as she poured him and Alec some fresh coffee. John turned his attention back to Alec as he shrugged off his anxiety and looked at the mayor pensively. "Well I think I'll send a few men over to Daniels to make sure he's not involved. I'll go as well, it'll keep me busy for a while so I'm not sitting here brooding. Besides I need to make sure my friend isn't involved it will help put my mind at ease. Can you stay here and let the guests know that they can go home if they wish or they can stay in the hopes that someone will show up tonight. But my guess would be that it will be several days before we see anyone, maybe we should send them all home and call them back later?"

Mayor Elton got up instantly, wanting to help any way he could, then put a hand on Alec's shoulder in support. "Don't worry about the guests I will look after them. I'll have the men saddle your mare for you just sit tight and have something to eat before you go."

Alec nodded in thanks and watched him leave.

Jessica came in shortly after the mayor left and sat across from Alec then took his hand in encouragement concerned about him. "How're you holding up?"

Alec smiled over at her in reassurance as he squeezed her hand gratefully. "Well I was feeling sorry for myself just a few minutes ago, but John straightened me out. I'm taking a few men and going over to Daniel's to make sure he isn't involved in Mell's disappearance. The Mayor is going to stay here and take care of any of the guests who wish to stay. I suggested to him that he should probably send them all home and we can call them back later if they want. Will you help him please? If any of the guests want to stay, you'll have to find places for them to sleep. There's an old bunkhouse we don't use very often have our men clean it up and the guests can stay in there if they wish."

Jessica smiled comfortingly then nodded pleased that he trusted her to look after his guests. "Of course I'll help him now do not fret so much we'll look after them."

Alec nodded gratefully and smiled. "Thank you!"

Jessica got up to leave then leaned over unexpectedly and kissed Alec quickly before she turned and left. Alec saw Gloria watching him with a gloating expression. He was saved from any comment as the mayor entered. "Your horse is ready to go Brad, Darrel, and Deputy Gary will be going with you just in case."

Alec looked up at his friend gratefully and smiled in thanks before pointing across the hallway. "Good, can you go into the den and bring me one of the new repeater rifles?"

Mayor Elton turned immediately to leave then threw over his shoulder before going out the door. "Sure I'll meet you at the door."

Alec pushed himself out of the kitchen then down the hallway to the entryway. He got his coat off a hook and put it on then reached over and took his boots off the rack. It took him a few minutes but he wrestled them on before he grabbed his hat off a hook. The hooks were put there especially for him and were wheelchair height so he didn't have to bother anyone else to help him dress.

The mayor came striding down the hallway with the rifle and thirty bullets. He handed them to Alec and watched as he put fifteen bullets into the gun then flipped the safety on, before pocketing the rest of them. The mayor motioned at the new rifles in approval. "Those are sure better rifles by far than the single shot rifle. But they might cause more problems later, as more and more people get ahold of them."

Alec was aware that the new rifles would be trouble later but was too preoccupied to worry about it now as he wheeled himself outside. The mayor walked behind Alec's chair then grabbed the handles and assisted Alec down the ramp. Not bothering with his outside chair since they didn't have far to go to get to where Brad and the others were waiting.

Brad grinned down at Alec in pride as he waved over to where the new cabins were being built. "I hope you don't mind but the men were milling around with nothing to do. So I asked them if they wanted to help finish Gloria and Wade's cabin while we're gone and they all agreed. Wade is directing them so he told me to tell you that he can't come with us."

Alec inclined his head in approval. "No I don't mind at all actually it's a very good idea."

Brad smiled gratefully at the praise and helped the mayor lift Alec onto his horse before strapping in one of his legs, while the mayor strapped down the other one. The mayor handed Alec his rifle then shook his finger up in caution. "You be careful! We don't know what Daniel will do if he's really involved. I don't want to tell Mell when she gets back that I let her father get himself killed while she was away!"

Alec reached down and shook his friends hand in reassurance. "Don't worry so much John. We'll be back before nightfall hopefully."

The mayor waved good-bye as he watched them ride away.

Brad rode on the left side of Alec and Deputy Gary rode on the right side with Darrel bringing up the rear. Alec pushed the horses as hard as he dared. Just before they got there Alec slowed his horse then turned to the deputy on his right to give him instructions. "Gary, when we get there will you go up to the door and get Daniel to come out to see me?"

Gary nodded his head in agreement. "Okay."

Alec spoke up so all the men could hear him. "I'll talk to him first and see if it's safe to go in. If it is Brad and Gary can carry me in that way I can keep both of you with me just in case. Darrel you can stay with the horses. So that we have someone to watch our backs and no one can sneak in without us knowing."

Alec turned in his saddle and looked at Darrel questioningly then smiled in acknowledgment when Darrel inclined his head. Alec looked at the other two expectantly and received their nods as well, just as they entered the yard. Alec halted a few paces away from the hitching rail that was in front of the house then nodded to Gary to go. Gary dismounted and handed his reins to Darrel then walked up to the door and knocked loudly. He smiled calmly at the man who opened the door. Gary pointed behind him in explanation. "Afternoon Mr. Grey Alec would like to talk to you if you have a moment."

Daniel looked at the deputy's badge pinned to Gary's shirt and frowned puzzled wondering why Alec would send a deputy to get him to come out. He looked over the deputy's shoulder at Alec then turned back and frowned at Gary in confusion. "Just give me a moment while I get my boots on."

Gary inclined his head then turned and walked back to Alec. Alec smiled down at Gary in praise. "Thank you. At least we know he's here and doesn't have an armed guard around the place which would make me a little nervous."

Gary shrugged not worried in the least. "He didn't seem upset to see me or you either only a little surprised by my Deputy's badge."

Alec sighed relieved then looked towards the front door of the house as it opened. Alec put the rifle across his saddle casually then leaned on it as he bent down slightly so he could hear him better. Daniel walked down the veranda then up to Alec's horse. He smiled hesitantly up at him as he motioned inquisitively. "Afternoon Alec what can I do for you?"

Alec inclined his head in greeting down at his friend as nonchalantly as possible. "Well I just wanted to thank you personally for the wedding present you sent over for Mell."

Daniel grinned in relief then smiled cordially. "I'm glad you liked it. I have never been to a wedding so I wasn't sure whether it was an acceptable gift or not."

Alec's face sobered suddenly in disappointment as he waved with his free hand curiously. "I also came to ask why you didn't come to the wedding."

Daniel's smile disappeared suddenly as he shifted slightly in embarrassment then he shrugged in apology. "Well, I kind of felt bad at the way I talked to Mell the other day."

Alec exhaled noisily reassured at the slightly guilty look on his friends face. "Well since I'm here how about a glass of brandy to toast the newlyweds?"

Daniel grinned thankfully at the forgiveness on Alec's face then pointed behind himself at the house. "Sure have your men bring you in. I'll go tell the housekeeper and she'll bring us a tray."

Daniel turned hurriedly and trotted off quickly before Alec could change his mind.

Brad got off his horse and helped Gary unstrapped Alec's legs. They lifted him off carefully while Darrel held the reins of all the horses. Alec handed his rifle to Darrel once Brad and Gary had a good hold on him and wouldn't drop him if he moved around. "You keep this handy. We won't be long."

Darrel nodded and tethered the horses to the hitching rail to free up his hands then he casually leaned up against it himself and cradled the rifle as he kept watch.

Gary and Brad carried Alec up to the door, which Daniel had left open for them, then inside to the hallway where they met Daniel waiting impatiently for them. He closed the door and led them into the sitting room. Alec's men put him on the couch carefully and sat one on either side of him then waited and watched expressionlessly.

Daniel eyed the three of them in surprise usually Alec's men left after putting him on the couch, but not this time, he didn't say anything obviously something wasn't quit right. He sat in a chair across from them then smiled nervously at Alec unsure of himself now. "The housekeeper will bring a tray in a few minutes."

Alec nodded distractedly not really interested in refreshments then leaned forward slightly before pointing earnestly in demand. "What happened between you and Mell the other day?"

Daniel looked embarrassed as he fidgeted slightly. "Well I had some false information and instead of asking her about Greg's death. I just accused her of murdering him without giving her a chance to explain."

The housekeeper came in just then and brought a tray of sandwiches, cakes, and a decanter of brandy. She set them all on the small table between them. Daniel poured the brandy then handed everyone a drink before sitting back with his own. Alec continued the conversation as he frowned thoughtfully then motioned enquiringly at his friend. "It wouldn't happen to be Brian who talked to you would it?"

Daniel looked at Alec in surprise then nodded ashamed as he looked down into his glass. He took a generous gulp of the fiery liquid to boost his confidence then looked back at Alec with a pleading look of understanding. "Well yes it was. Brian came here and said Mell was caught doing something wrong so she killed Greg to keep him quiet. He said she did it to keep her ranch and we all know how much she loves that ranch."

Alec sat back in relief glad that his friend wasn't directly involved in the disappearance of Mell and Mary. "Well that's not what happened at all."

Alec spent the next half hour telling Daniel the whole story. When Alec was done he shook his head incredulously. "That's unbelievable! Mell mentioned Greg trying to kill you both but I didn't want to believe her. So I just stormed away without letting her explain further. But when I thought about it afterwards I finally decided Brian must have lied to me. So I sent over the wedding gift but was too embarrassed to come myself."

Alec frowned troubled as he leaned forward anxiously. "Daniel you're my best friend all you had to do was come and talk to me at anytime, I would have explained it to you."

Daniel shrugged self-consciously and gestured in apology. "I'm sorry Alec but Brian was so very convincing. I suppose in a way I've always been sceptical about having a woman Sheriff. It didn't take much to convince me I'm sorry to say!"

Alec inclined his head accepting the apology relieved to have this out in the open. "Apology accepted! I do have one more question to ask though regarding Mark and Tomas, why did you fire them?"

Daniel looked at Alec in shocked surprise then waved sharply in denial. "I didn't fire them Brian asked me if he could use them for a couple of days and I agreed. I haven't seen them since."

Alec sighed then explained what had happened at the wedding this morning thankful at having an explanation for the two men. Daniel shook his head flabbergasted he had figured the two men had decided to stay with Brian and hadn't checked to see where they had disappeared too. He put a fist up too his heart then stared at Alec intently as he swore vehemently "I had nothing to do with it! I swear!"

Alec nodded his head consolingly. "I believe you. I think Brian was setting you up in case things went wrong for him."

Daniel sighed dejectedly as he hung his head in shame. "I can't believe I fell for it. I should have known better."

Alec frowned as he inclined his head sadly when Daniel looked back at him. "Yes you should have! But I can't blame you completely we were all taken in by Brian."

Alec finished his drink then put the glass back on the table before motioning at Gary and Brad to finish up as well. "I must get back and see if Jed is back with Mell yet. You can come if you like."

Daniel nodded eagerly getting quickly to his feet. "Yes I'd like to come. I want to apologize to Mell personally."

Alec was pleased with Daniel's decision to come along. "Okay you're always welcome you know."

Daniel smiled relieved that he hadn't lost his best friend over his stupidity and went to get ready while Alec's men took him back to his horse.

* * *

Alec arrived back at the ranch three hours later than he had planned it was way after dark. His stomach growled angrily at him reminding him that he hadn't had supper yet. The mayor met him on the porch with his wheelchair and smiled in relief as he shook a finger chidingly at the late Alec. "I was just about ready to send a posse out to look for you."

Alec grinned over at Mayor Elton and laughed goodnaturedly as he pointed over his shoulder. "No need for that as you can see I've brought Daniel with me. Thankfully he had nothing to do with it."

The mayor inclined his head towards Daniel in greeting. "Well that's definitely good news and you're just in time for supper."

Daniel smirked devilishly as he dismounted then laughed in delight. "I always time it perfectly!"

Alec chuckled at Daniel's smug face as Darrel and Brad lifted him off his horse then carried him up the stairs to put him into his chair. Alec waited until Darrel and Brad stepped back before turning to Daniel as he motioned teasingly "Don't I know it we're going to have to find you a wife one of these days."

Daniel laughed playfully as he joshed Alec back. "Well I've been giving the widow Donaldson the eye but I don't think she's interested in me!"

Alec grinned up at Daniel mischievously. "Well normally I'd encourage you and even help you out if need be. But this time I'm going to have say find your own woman, Jessica's my fiancée!"

John and Daniel both whooped ecstatically then shook Alec's hand in best wishes. Daniel smirked good-naturedly and chuckled in delight. "Well you old coot! You snatched her right out from under my nose! But I'm happy for you. Congratulations!"

Mayor Elton nodded agreeing with Daniel. "That goes for me too. It's about time you stopped grieving does Mell know yet?"

Alec looked over his shoulder at Brad, Darrel, and Gary as the mayor walked behind his chair to push him to the house. "Put the horses away then come up to the house for supper since it's late and you three probably missed supper at the bunkhouse."

The mayor pointed in apology over at Gary before he could turn away completely knowing that he probably wanted to stay. "Gary I need you to go to town after supper and help Kenneth keep an eye on things. I have a feeling it will be at least several days until Mell gets back and I'd prefer to have more then one person on duty especially with the townspeople wanting to stay at least one night."

Gary nodded dejectedly but agreed not really wanting to go. The three men nodded farewell and left leading the horses to the barn obediently.

Alec looked up at the mayor to continue the conversation. "In a way she does. She knows I've been chasing her for the past few days but she doesn't know I caught her yet. Mell likes Jessica and she approves fully. If it wouldn't be too much trouble could you two keep this too yourselves for now Jessica doesn't want anyone to know yet."

Daniel and the mayor looked at each other then winked in perfect understanding, before both nodded innocently as they looked down at Alec.

The mayor pushed Alec towards the house. "Oh, by the way almost all the guests stayed tonight especially after I told them there would be a big announcement when Mell and Jed returned. So I sent Kenneth to town to keep an eye on the businesses. The only one who couldn't stay was Charlie he had to take James's mother home but he said he might return if he could manage it. I told him not to bother coming until I sent someone for him since I'm sure we are going to have a long wait. I told the rest the same thing but they want to stay one night at least. If nobody shows up in the morning they will go back to town. The townspeople took up a collection while you were gone they want to divide it between Jed and Giant Bear for saving the Sheriff they love and respect so much."

Alec looked up at John in surprise just before they entered the house. "Well that was very nice of them!"

Alec decided he would add to the pot as well as the three got to the kitchen for supper. After supper they sat out on the porch waiting as long as possible for the rescue party to show up before finally giving up.

Alec's prediction proved correct with no sign of his daughter or the others. So he sent Daniel out to the bunkhouse to bed down and he put the mayor and his wife upstairs in the spare bedroom, before going to bed himself even though he was sure he wouldn't sleep.

But even Alec couldn't foresee the length of time it would actually take before anyone was to show up.

CHAPTER TWENTY-TWO

In the next four days Mell came to for short periods of time but never for long. The concussion she had given herself when her head hit the saddle so hard the first day had been a bad one. It wasn't until the morning of the fourth day when she felt rough hands untying her from the saddle that she was lucid enough to realize what was going on.

She managed to remain limp so they wouldn't guess she was awake, as they carried her into a building. But she almost gave it away as she automatically tensed when she felt herself falling. She landed on something soft thankfully nobody noticed she was awake. Then she felt Mary bounce beside her in relief her friend was still alive at least. She noticed that she wasn't gagged anymore and was grateful at least she could talk now.

A worried voice to her right that seemed vaguely familiar grumbled anxiously. "Are you sure they won't think to look here?"

Mell peeked slightly hoping nobody would see her to find out who was talking and wasn't too shocked to find out it was Tomas. One of the new hands she had been suspicious of. She sighed to herself mentally in disgust, see she knew she shouldn't have kept him on! Then she stiffened involuntarily when she heard Brian's voice. "Nobody would think to look at Devil's Rock since she killed Greg here."

Mary moaned in discomfort and tried to sit up.

Brian grimaced angrily at Tomas as he pointed towards Mell. "Mary's awake again! Go check on Mell see if she's awake yet she's been out a long time. Are you sure your friend didn't hit her too hard. It won't do me any good if she dies from a head wound."

Mell decided to pretend that she was just waking up too. As footsteps neared the bed she shifted and moaned as if in pain.

* * *

The two guards Gerald and Philip stationed up on the cliffs died without a sound and two shadows drifted towards the miner's shack where the two women were imprisoned.

* * *

Mell pushed herself up painfully stiff from lying over a horse so long as she eyed Brian balefully. "I should've known you would pick my wedding day to ambush us!"

Brian chuckled nastily as he motioned in rage. "Well you bitch! If you hadn't ruined everything and been so stubborn we would've been married by now!"

Mell's voice became deadly as she remembered her father saying he thought there had been another person at his kidnapping, and things started to make sense to her in a way. But she was still slightly confused by why. "It was you, and not Greg who staged my father's kidnapping, wasn't it? But I don't understand why Tomas is involved. Or how the three outlaws I had a run in with when I was a kid, got tangled up in all this."

Brian smirked arrogantly as he waved towards Tomas in explanation. "Well my dear it's simple Tomas here is Greg's brother."

Mell looked Tomas up and down disdainfully as she looked for similarities. She had never seen the two men together at anytime so had never connected the two as siblings. But now that she looked closer she could see some resemblance. That's why he always seemed so familiar but she could never figure out why.

Brian looked straight at Mary so he could watch her expression in pleasure knowing it would make him feel good to see every ounce of shock on her unguarded face as he dropped a bombshell.

But he still directed his speech at Mell as he continued without any hint of remorse. "Tomas and Greg are my cousins and the other five you killed were my brothers. After you killed two of my brothers when you were a kid you disappeared. So Sam contacted me to find you. Little did I know you were here all that time right in front of me! It wasn't till you messed up and got discovered that I put two and two together. I dug into your background a little and accidentally found out about your father's money. Then it took me some time to find my other three brothers they were running from the law because of you! I found them in Montana. It was me who came up with the idea of kidnapping Alec to get you up here. Then I was going to come on the scene and pretend to kill the bad guys. Unfortunately, Alec was going to be killed before I could get to him. Then I was going to use your grief to get you to marry me. After that my brothers would stage an accident for you and I would end up with everything. But unfortunately those bastards you married came out of nowhere and ruined everything."

Although speaking to Mell, Brian had kept his eyes on Mary throughout his confession enjoying her changing expressions. First one of shock to find out she had other brothers and that they were outlaws. Then disgust and outrage as Brian told of his plans for Mell and Alec. Finally she gasped out in total disbelief and anger unable to keep quiet any longer. "What are you saying Brian? I never knew of any other brothers or that Tomas and Greg were our cousins!"

Brian laughed uproarsly for a moment enjoying Mary's confusion. When he gained control of himself he smirked at Mary in obvious pleasure. "My dear half sister there's a lot you don't know. You see our father was married to an older widow first who had three sons already. After they married they had three more children all boys too. I was the last one and she died giving birth to me. When I was ten years old my father kicked my five older brothers out and married your mother Irene. When I was twelve years old and you were a year old my brothers staged an accident and Irene was killed. Our father figured out who was responsible so he packed us up immediately and moved us out here. Father forbade me to mention my mother or my five brothers again. Everybody including you was told that Irene was my mother as well as yours."

Mell hadn't been idle while Brian and Tomas had their attention totally on Mary. She had managed to rip a hole in her dress and was trying to retrieve her knife. It was very hard to rip fabric quietly but she managed it. She almost had the knife when Tomas happened to look at her. She held herself perfectly still trying to look innocent then sighed softly in relief when he turned back to the conversation.

Mell loosened the knife enough to pull it out. She then slowly severed her bond hands but kept a tight hold on the ropes so they wouldn't fall and give her away. Luckily they had tied her hands in front of her instead of behind her. She slipped the knife under her thigh so it was out of sight then she started working on getting the little gun she had tried so hard to conceal from Mrs. Elton on her wedding day.

Keeping a close eye on the men to make sure they weren't watching her, she curled her legs up a bit, and started crinkling her skirt to get at the hidden gun that was strapped to her thigh. She inched her skirt up high enough to reach it then quickly pulled the pistol out then placed it under her leg in easy reach. Lady luck was with her as she pushed her skirt down then put her hands back in her lap just as Brian turned back to her.

Brian grinned nastily at Mell then looked her up and down insolently. "Now that your husbands are dead I can proceed with my plan. First of all since Tomas and Mary aren't related they can get married that will keep her quiet. As for you my dear Mell we'll also be getting married as soon as we get back to my ranch I've already got an out of town preacher waiting."

Mary looked at Tomas in horror as he grinned evilly down at her in anticipation. She shuddered in revulsion figuring she wouldn't live long under his cruel and barbaric treatment.

* * *

The two men listening outside the window had heard enough and they nodded to each other before bursting into the cabin together.

Brian and Tomas pivoted in shocked surprise then grabbed for their weapons, but they were both too late! Two shots were fired one after another. One shot came from the doorway and one surprisingly came from inside the room. Both men were dead before they hit the ground.

Jed and Giant Bear looked at each other knowingly then turned to see Mell standing awkwardly on bound feet with her little smoking pistol in her hand. Jed grinned at her devilishly in relief to see her unhurt. Then put his hand on his hip in demand as he waved his gun irritably. "Don't you think you could let me rescue you just once at least?"

Mell laughed in delight to see her husband still alive then shook her head negatively. "Not on your life! Now get over here and untie my ankles they're killing me!"

Both men obediently rushed forward to untie their wives.

Mary grabbed Giant Bear's face as best she could with bound hands and began kissing him thankfully as tears streamed down her face. She pushed him away as she eyed him in concern. "I thought you were dead when I saw all that blood on your face!"

She looked for traces of his wound and saw a deep scratch across his right temple that had turned a pretty blue and purple in colour. Giant Bear sighed thankful that Tomas wasn't a good marksman. "Two inches to the left and I would be dead. Jed got a bullet in his shoulder just above his heart. Good thing Tomas was not a very good shot! Mary I think it is time to go home before anything else happens. Do you want to say good-bye to your dead brother?"

Mary shivered in reaction as she thought of her evil half brother and shook her head negatively. "No! But I must say good-bye to Mell."

Giant Bear cut her bound hands and feet before helping her to stand. She wobbled slightly as the circulation rushed into her aching feet and she groaned painfully. Giant Bear took hold of her arm and helped her over to Jed and Mell who were in each other's arms engrossed in a deep kiss.

Mary cleared her throat loudly to get their attention.

Mell and Jed broke apart guiltily and Mell blushed a fiery red at being caught kissing with such a lack of restraint. Jed got up immediately and Mary sat down beside Mell.

She reached over and took Mell's hand remorsefully as she pleaded desperately with tears streaming down her face. "I'm so sorry Mell please forgive me. I think I was part of the reason my half brother knew so much about you and the ranch. He was always asking me questions about you after you were discovered. It was me who told him you were from South Dakota and the name of the ranch you were raised on. It was also me who told him where your father's room was and where to find his chair. I'm also the one who told him which horses your father and Wade used. I never realized how much I was telling him because he never asked me more than one question at a time. He would wait a day or two before asking another question by then I had forgotten the questions he had asked before. He had changed for the worst after I came back from Montana pregnant but after me and you became friends he seemed to calm down again, and became his old self once more. So I thought he was falling in love with you that's why I never refused to answer his questions."

Mell took her hand away from her friends then wiped the tears from Mary's face gently before hugging her fiercely trying to reassure her friend the best she could. "Don't cry Mary, we were both fooled by him for a long time. He manipulated my feelings until I respected and admired him. I might eventually have married him but thank God you told me about the Indian fellow he killed. Plus the cruel way he treated Tommy kept me from saying yes. There is no reason for you to ask for forgiveness. It wasn't your fault that he was so evil!"

Mary sat back wiping more tears away then sighed dispiritedly. "Well you might not think I need forgiveness but maybe this will atone for my actions a little."

Mary sat forward again intensely. "I have a favour to ask of you. Now that my brother is dead Giant Bear and I will be leaving for our Cheyenne village as soon as we pick up Tommy. I need to ask if you and Jed will look after the ranch. I know that Tommy doesn't want it but maybe if I have another boy some day, he might want it. Any profit you make from the ranch is yours and you can keep control until someone comes to claim it. I'll leave a letter of attorney so that you can do anything you want to with it, except sell it."

Mell looked at Jed questioningly and he nodded his assent. So Mell turned back to Mary as she agreed knowing there was no one else Mary could rely on. "Okay Mary we'll do as you ask but only as a favour to you! Not because you think you owe me anything!"

Mell put her arms around Mary and hugged her fiercely as she whispered sadly in her ear in farewell. "I'll miss you very much Mary but I know you will be happier with Giant Bear than you were with your brother. I also have a favour to ask of you, will you help Tommy continue learning my fighting techniques with a knife?"

Mary smiled at Mell when she let her go then shrugged unsure if she would remember much. "Well I never kept up with it after I took Tommy to you and he was safe, that's the only reason I wanted you to teach me. But I'm sure it will come back to me!"

Mell turned to Giant Bear next then stood up to give him a big farewell hug. "Take good care of Mary and Tommy for me Giant Bear and be happy!"

Giant Bear returned the hug awkwardly not use to showing affection. "Good-bye White Buffalo, I will always remember our bond and will come if you ever have need of me."

Mell smiled as she stepped back as she thought of their pact hating to say good-bye to her friends trying to prolong it a little. "I'll remember also and come if ever you have need of me."

Jed and Giant Bear clasped forearms in farewell somewhat embarrassed with showing their emotion. Giant Bear inclined his head in farewell. "Good-bye Blood Brother. It has been a long nine years but it is finally over. I would not trade knowing you for anything. Now because you have taught me the white man's language and customs I have a better understanding of what the Indians will face if we do not find a way to live together. I will never forget your teaching and I will pass it down to my children in the hope that we can find a way to live in peace. Even if the other tribes will not listen I will find a way myself. I hope that when we have a band meeting close to the Dakota border you will come and bring your wife for a visit."

Jed grinned as he thought about all the good times he had shared with Giant Bear. He agreed even though he knew it would be a very long time before he was to see his blood brother again. "I wouldn't miss it for the world and I thank you for sticking by me through thick and thin. Even though I almost gave up you kept me going and I will eternally be grateful for it!"

The two quickly embraced then both men turned and helped their women walk out of the cabin both were still a little wobbly. They stood there for a moment waiting for the ladies to find their balance. Jed turned to Giant Bear once more as he waved towards the ranch. "Will you tell Alec we're going to camp out here for tonight so we'll be a day behind you?"

Giant Bear nodded as he agreed. "I can do that for you Jed."

Mary and Mell hugged once more in parting both crying slightly.

Giant Bear and Mary turned away and they were gone.

Mell turned to Jed inquisitively. "We're not going home now?"

Jed shook his head negatively. "No we're going down Devil's Rock to your old campsite. Our horses are tethered there waiting already we'll spend one night before the long ride home."

Mell nodded in puzzlement but didn't question him as they set off. Neither of them looked back. They made it to camp just as the sun was sinking. It had been a long walk both were exhausted physically and mentally. Jed's shoulder was bothering him quit a bit from the hard ride, so soon after the injury, but he hid that from Mell not wanting to worry her.

Lightning saw his mistress coming and nickered in greeting. Mell hurried over to him and buried her face in his long mane then silently sobbed out her anger and grief. Jed sighed in relief as he stood there helplessly and watched Mell shaking silently as she cried. This was why he had decided to stay the night here. He had hoped Mell would cry now and not bottle it up to fester until too late. Hate was a powerful emotion and he knew that all to well.

He walked over then grabbed the two bedrolls he had removed earlier and made a bed for them so Mell could have some privacy. He then picked up some wood that was piled beside the fire pit and preceded to make a fire so that he could prepare something to eat. He just finished putting the beans and coffee on when Mell came over then dropped down beside him in exhaustion.

Mell sighed forlornly as she gestured sorrowfully. "I'm sorry Jed. I ripped my wedding dress and made a mess out of our wedding!"

Mell's breath caught on a sob suddenly and Jed pulled her into his arms tenderly and held her as she wept bitter tears into his shirt. All he could really do was hold her and let her cry it out. Jed stroked her back soothingly as he whispered consolingly. "Hush Mell it's all over now.

Those men can never hurt you again I promise. It wasn't your fault that your dress got wrecked and I'm sure it can easily be fixed."

Mell's crying ceased as she listened to him talk soothingly to her but she remained quiet and kept holding Jed closely afraid to let him go. The fact that he was alive was a miracle and she needed a few minutes to just hold him thankfully.

Jed dropped a kiss on the top of her head then smiled devilishly down at her as he teased. "As for ruining our wedding, just think of it this way. Everyone's been waiting so long for the Lady Sheriff to get married that they would have been disappointed without some action. Now you will not only go down in history as the first Lady Sheriff but they will also be talking about this wedding for the next twenty years."

Mell laughed a little in relief as Jed lightened the mood. She let him go then leaned back in his arms to taunt him back. "I don't think they will be talking about me at all. I think they will put you in the history books as the only man able to tame this Lady Sheriff and the only one who has ever had to rescue her not once, but twice."

Jed hugged her fiercely at her banter and knew the worst was over. "It was my pleasure! Now grab a dish and scoop up some beans before they burn. While I dig out the pants, boots, and shirt I brought along for you."

Mell smiled in gratitude at his consideration especially since having to ride in this corset didn't appeal to her at all and did as she was told. As she filled her dish she couldn't help commenting in pleasure at his thoughtfulness in bringing her a change of clothing. "It was very nice of you to bring me my clothes."

Mell leaned against a tree and started eating her food but she kept her eyes on Jed as he moved around afraid he would disappear suddenly and that this was all a dream. He had changed back into his buckskins and left his wedding suit at the ranch before coming to look for her. She was glad because he definitely looked better in them than he did in his finery.

Jed chuckled in delight as he turned around suddenly and caught her staring at him. He tried to be as dramatic as possible to make her smile as he fibbed just a little. "Well, I would really like to take credit for bringing them to you but it was actually Gloria who gave me the saddlebag with the clothes and food in it. She thrust it at me just as I was going out the door. I was in such a hurry! We probably would have starved before I could get you home."

Mell smiled in pleasure at Jed's first usage of the word, 'home'. She filled a dish of beans for him as he came over to sit beside her. He handed her the clothing in exchange for the food. Mell got up and began changing.

Jed chuckled in amusement and sympathy as Mell groaned in frustration as she tried to get out of her dress. He had to leave his food to get up and helped her remove them because she got tangled up again. Once he finished helping her out of her clothes he stood for a moment eyeing her corset in disapproval. "Whatever possessed you to put that thing on?"

Mell groaned forlornly as her voice took on a torturous tone of desperation. "It definitely wasn't my idea Gloria and Mrs. Elton insisted. But please quit staring at me and help me out of this darn thing!"

As he moved to provide assistance Jed couldn't help but grin at the note of misery in her voice. Then he took out his hunting knife and cut the strings dramatically but was careful not to cut the camisole under the corset.

Mell gasped in indignation she didn't like the contraption but she hadn't expected him to wreck it. "What did you to do that for?"

Jed chuckled at Mell's outrage as she stripped out of her cotton underwear it was too hot for them anyway. He frowned slightly in anger as he eyed the deep red marks all over Mell's tender skin once she removed the camisole, from the corset digging into her from being slung over a horse for so long. "I did it because I never want to see you in one of these things again!"

Mell took a deep breath for the first time in four days. She sighed relieved as she waved in agreement. "Good! Because you definitely will not catch me wearing one of these things again, they're pure torture!"

Jed sat back down in satisfaction then finished his supper as he watched Mell bend over to put on her socks, pants, and boots. She grabbed the white binding that she always used to bind her breasts. She stood up then started wrapping it around her chest as snug as she could get it.

Jed frowned angrily as he watched her for a moment silently then he motioned firmly in protest. "I don't want you binding your breasts either Mell!"

Mell looked over at Jed in surprise for a moment. She shook her head in irritation then retorted angrily in disagreement. "Well that's just too darn bad isn't it I have no choice in the matter can you see me going at a full gallop chasing some man with my breasts flopping all over the place. I'm libel to give myself a black eye? This binding controls them. Besides if I try galloping my horse without the binding it hurts like hell!"

Jed thought about it for a moment then burst out laughing at the mental image of Mell's breasts bouncing so hard, they almost hit her in the face. He held up his hands in surrender still chuckling. "Okay I concede to that but at least loosen it a little. I don't like seeing welts all over your tender skin."

Mell inclined her head slightly in agreement. She turned to him with one eyebrow cocked in amusement as she let him have this victory. "Very well but I won't loosen it by much. I'd rather have welts then sore breasts!"

Mell loosened it slightly as promised then finished dressing. She grabbed a cup of coffee from the fire for herself and one for Jed then walked over and sat down beside him. As the two of them sat sipping their coffee Mell snuggled up to Jed contentedly then her expression sobered as she thought of all her wedding guests. "Tell me what happened after I was knocked out."

Jed drew her a little closer then kissed the top of her head glad he had decided to stay here one night before the long ride home. "Well, as you can imagine there was complete kayos."

It took a good half hour to explain it all.

Mell tilted her head back inquisitively as he finished. "You're right the money was the real reason. Did you just barge in when you came to the cabin or did you listen first?"

Jed smirked down smugly at Mell as he kissed her lightly then lifted away from her so he could answer her. "No we didn't just barge in but we were tempted at first afraid for the two of you. We got there just as Brian started talking so we waited. We wanted to make sure that this time there were no other people involved. We didn't want to be looking over our shoulders waiting for some other lunatic to come after us."

Mell sighed and tucked her head back into Jed's shoulder as she waved in relief finally able to be at peace. "I'm just glad it's over we can start our life together with no more worries!"

Jed nodded then reached over with a stick and banked the fire for the night before reluctantly pulling away from Mell as he yawned. "We'll stay here tonight then go home in the morning. We won't consummate our marriage, or go on our honeymoon until then. Your father will want to see you first before we go and I want our first time together to be in our home on a nice soft bed."

Mell chuckled in full agreement and got up after putting her coffee cup down then walked over to they're joined bedrolls and crawled inside clothes and all!

Jed crawled in after her and kissed her goodnight tenderly. "Go to sleep Mell I just want to hold you tonight."

Mell sighed contentedly then cuddled close and within moments she was fast asleep exhausted from her ordeal. Jed lay gazing up at the stars for a long time before he too was finally able to sleep.

CHAPTER TWENTY-THREE.

Alec and the mayor were going back into the house after spending another useless day on the porch watching for Mell and Jed. They had spent eight long days staring out across the ranch yard towards the road leading to Devil's Rock hoping but in vain. The two were just going through the door for supper and another sleepless night when they heard the unmistakable sound of horses racing towards the ranch.

Both stopped short and the mayor pulled Alec back out of the doorway as they turned hopefully. John pushed Alec back towards the chair he had only just vacated a few minutes ago. They both stared intently down the road and saw Giant Bear and Mary riding into the yard.

Alec kept his eyes glued intently on the road behind Mary and Giant Bear expectantly, but it remained empty. There was no sign of Jed or Mell and Alec tensed in fear. The mayor put his hand on Alec's shoulder already guessing Alec's thoughts trying to calm him down but the fear was clear in his voice too. "Don't jump to conclusions yet they may have decided to camp out an extra day or so for some reason."

Alec nodded then sighed in relief as Mary hurried towards them after dismounting not even bothering to tie her horse up. She smiled down reassuringly as soon as she got close to Alec and quickly gave him Jed's message not wanting him to worry unnecessarily. "Jed said to let you know that they're going to camp out one night. We came back right away because Giant Bear wants to go home immediately, so we came to collect our things and Tommy. I'm also giving Mell power of attorney and control of my ranch until someone comes to claim it."

Giant Bear walked over to them and gestured solemnly down at Alec. "Stands Tall, I want to take my family home tonight. Will you help me with some provisions?"

Alec nodded decisively. "Of course, you have some wages coming anyway so I'll give you enough provisions to see you home instead of money. We're just going in for supper so come and join us and while we're eating I'll have Jessica and Gloria get everything ready for you. Mary you can tell me the details of what happened as we eat. After we finish eating I'll take you to my study I'm sure the Mayor will come along and help you make out your power of attorney."

Mary and Giant Bear nodded in reluctance they both wanted to leave immediately but they knew it would be awhile yet before they could go. Mary looked up at Giant Bear and shrugged in silent apology. Giant Bear grunted in agreement at Mary's look then both turned and walked into the house with Alec leading the way.

* * *

Supper just finished when Jessica came in then walked up to Alec. "Everything is ready for Mary and Giant Bear I also helped Tommy get his things ready to go."

Alec smiled up at her in thanks. "Good! Can you send Tommy to me and ask Darrel to put Tommy's saddle on Princess as well."

Jessica inclined her head. "Sure I'll be back in a bit."

Alec looked around for the mayor after she left and beckoned him to come over. Alec grinned up at his friend in anticipation. "You can present Giant Bear with the money now if you want."

The mayor went behind Alec and pushed him over to Giant Bear and his wife. Giant Bear saw them coming so stood up respectfully. The mayor walked around Alec's chair and clasped Giant Bear's hand in farewell.

The townspeople that were left, only a few of them had been able to stay unfortunately, hushed expectantly wanting to be witnesses for the others when they got called back. Alec had sent a man to town already to let the ones who had left know Mell would be arriving tomorrow so they could all come back if they wished. They strained to hear what was being said having waited patiently for this moment with silent excitement.

The mayor reached in his pocket dramatically and pulled out an envelope then handed it to Giant Bear expectantly. "Giant Bear the townspeople wanted to show their appreciation for all your help by taking up a fund for you and Mary. They all hope this money will help you on your way home."

Giant Bear looked around at all the eager faces then motioned in apology as he refused to take the envelope. "Jed has told me of this custom but I am sorry I must decline. Where we are going we will not need it. Alec has provided us with provisions for our journey so please give the money to him in payment."

Alec frowned in disappointment, but he wasn't surprised, he had known Giant Bear wouldn't accept the money. Suddenly an idea came to him and he grinned up at Giant Bear hopefully. "Giant Bear would you accept horses instead of the money?"

Giant Bear thought about it for a moment. He really didn't want to offend anyone so he finally nodded as he looked down at Alec in thanks. "Yes if you wish I will accept horses instead of money."

Alec winked up at Giant Bear glad to have found the solution so easily. "Good! Mayor Elton will take Mary into the den so she can make out the power of attorney and I'll find you some horses."

Alec reached up and took the envelope from the mayor then counted the money as the mayor left with Mary following. Alec looked around the room expectantly and spotting Herman Johnson he pushed himself over to him. He smiled up hopefully as he looked up at the grey haired old wrinkled rancher that lived on the other side of Daniel Grey's. Herman's huge handle bar moustache took up almost his whole craggy lower face and sometimes it was hard to know whether the man was smiling or scowling. Herman had always joked that it gave him an edge at the poker table. "Herman, do you still have that stud you wanted to sell?"

Herman nodded that he did. "Yes sir I do. Why?"

Alec grinned up enthusiastically then motioned inquisitively. "How much do you want for him?"

Herman told him and Alec counted out the money then handed it to him. Alec pointed towards one of his hired hands. "Go tell Brad over there which horse it is and where to find him, he'll go and get him for me."

Alec counted out the rest of the money it was a little short for the two horses he wanted to sell but he shrugged dismissively, it was for a good cause. He beckoned to Giant Bear. "Come out to the corral and I'll show you which horses are yours."

Giant Bear went behind Alec's chair to push him out to the corrals. The townspeople followed closely behind them not wanting to miss a thing. They hadn't quite reached the front door when Tommy came running up to Alec in excitement. "You wanted to see me Grandpa?"

Alec beamed up at Tommy tenderly in pleasure at the endearment. He crooked his index finger at Tommy so he would follow them. "Yes come with us out to the corrals I have something for you."

Tommy was puzzled but didn't ask any questions as he waited for his father to pass him pushing the wheelchair. He followed them obediently while the townspeople followed behind Tommy. They left the house once everyone scrambled into their outer footwear and they kept going. Once they were in front of the barn Alec beckoned to Darrel who was standing in front of the barn having a smoke. "Bring the mare that's saddled out first then put a halter and rope on Two Socks and Brandy then bring them here as well."

Darrel put out his smoke immediately before going into the barn. He came back out a few minutes later leading a dainty mare with a small saddle on her.

Alec smiled sadly up at Tommy as he took his hand then pointed at the mare with his free hand in explanation. "I wanted to give you a going away present. So I figured Princess would do you the most good where you're going. She is also bred to Mell's stud so you will have a foal next spring as well. You will always be welcome to return here anytime. We all love you and we'll miss you dreadfully."

Tommy let go of Alec's hand then bent down and hugged him fiercely in farewell as the tears streamed down his face in sorrow. "I love you too Grandpa, and if I ever come back this way, I'll come to see you I promise. Thank you very much for the horse I'll treasure her always!"

Alec smiled mistily up at Tommy as he stood back up. "May God be with you Tommy and never forget we're here if you ever need us."

Tommy nodded solemnly down at Alec in understanding then he ran over to his horse in sad excitement.

Alec wiped tears from his eyes as Darrel went back into the barn and led out a gelding and a mare then walked towards them. Alec got his emotions back under control and looked up at Giant Bear as he motioned towards the horses Darrel brought out. "Both those horses are yours from the townspeople. One is a gelding and the other one is a bred mare. Brad is on his way over to the Johnson's to pick up a stallion for you. There are also two horses in the barn that are packed with provisions for you as well. They are a parting gift from Mell and me. While we wait for Brad the men will help pack both the mare and gelding I just gave you with your belongings if you'll show them what you're taking with you."

Giant Bear looked gravely down at Alec then around in surprise at all the grinning townspeople. Never had he ever been treated with such love and respect by the whites before. It gave him hope for the future of the Indian tribes that they could all live in peace someday. He smiled at everyone in thanks as he gestured in appreciation. "I want to thank all of you for the gifts. I will cherish them always. When we have a band meeting close to the border you are all welcome to come and join us."

The townspeople cheered then they came over one at a time and introduced themselves. Giant Bear managed to slip away to help pack the rest of his horses.

After Giant Bear left, the townspeople gathered around Alec expectantly. Chelsie stepped forward since she was the official spokeswoman for the group. She had sent all her girls back to the saloon to look after things for her until she could make sure Mell was alright, Pam had done the same. Both women were very worried about their friend and they knew there would be no rest until they saw her again. "Alec we would like to know what we should do with Jed's money. Will he accept it or do we have to find him a gift as well?"

Alec thought about it for a few moments then grinned up at Chelsie in gratitude. "Well I think he might accept it, but I also know he wants to start a cattle herd. So if you want there should be enough money for a bull and maybe a couple of cows here."

Tom Carlson stepped forward eagerly then fidgeted shyly. He was painfully slim and usually too shy to speak out in a group. He was of medium height and build; with mousy brown hair the only thing that set him apart from his homely appearance was his crystal clear green eyes. "I have a Texas bull for sale."

Herman stepped forward eagerly as well. "I have two heifers for sale."

Alec eyed the two men in appreciation. "Okay how much?"

They told him what they wanted and he counted out the amount. Then Alec looked around at all the expectant townspeople as he handed both men the money they wanted. "Well there's still twenty dollars left my suggestion would be to deposit it in the bank for their children."

Everyone cheered in approval.

It took another two hours to get everything sorted out but finally Alec sat in his wheelchair on the porch with a few townspeople gathered around waving good-bye to Giant Bear, Mary, and Tommy. There wasn't a dry eye to be seen anywhere Mary and Tommy had always been a favourite among the townspeople and they would sorely be missed.

Giant Bear stopped his horses at the end of the ranch yard and the three turned then waved one last time in farewell at there friends before turning away and they never looked back again.

Alec sighed sadly then looked around in approval at all the familiar faces looking down at him expectantly. These people amazed him sometimes never in all his travels had he came across a town so willing to befriend everybody no matter what race or colour they were. He looked at Chelsie and Pam standing slightly in the background. Most towns he had been in would have shunned the two women completely since they were both women you couldn't tell your wife about. Instead they were standing here and the mayor's wife was standing with them talking, all were friends of Mell's of course which was what had brought them together in the first place.

There were two half-breed Indians, a Mexican and his wife, a Chinamen with his family, and a black man with his wife talking to the mayor. It just amazed him that they could all live in one small town without any prejudiced feelings at all.

Alec frowned in worry as he thought of the future he knew one day that it would end of course, as soon as the railroad went through their town it would all change. More people would come and like Mell in a way he was dreading it. With more people would come more crime and prejudice! They would wreck everything they had all accomplished. He just hoped the people standing here today would keep their morals and not allow others to influence them.

Alec looked up at the mayor and grinned enticingly as he waved towards the front door of the ranch house. "Okay I'm sure the Ladies have desert waiting in the kitchen for anyone who wishes to have some before bed and there is brandy in the library for the men who wish to have a night cap?"

Mayor Elton looked around with a grin at all the eager nods of pleasure from the townspeople. He looked back down at Alec and inclined his head agreeably before walking behind Alec's chair to push him into the house. "I think we would all like that very much."

The townspeople followed behind Alec and the mayor. Talking excitedly about the day and what was to come tomorrow when Mell finally arrived back with her new husband.

* * *

Jessica sat down beside Alec's chair and sighed in relief as the last guest left for their bed. It had been a long emotional day and she was exhausted. She looked over at Alec and opened her mouth to tease him but paused in surprise as she saw him staring at her so intently.

Alec reached over suddenly without a word and stroked Jessica's cheek tenderly with the back of his hand. He lifted his hand up further and twined a wayward red curl around his finger teasingly. All the while he continued to stare at Jessica intently she had done so much for him the last two weeks. He hardly even had to open his mouth and she was there to help him. But with all the people around it was hard to have a private moment with her to tell her how much he appreciated what she was doing for him.

Alec let go of the curl he was holding and went back to stroking her cheek tenderly. "I haven't had much time lately to tell you how much I appreciate everything you've done around here. I just want you to know that I do appreciate it!"

Jessica smiled over at him lovingly then closed her eyes and rubbed her cheek against his hand in pleasure then she looked back at him just as keenly. Alec caught his breath in surprise at the look of passion suddenly blossoming in Jessica's eyes and he grinned in excitement as Jessica's passion fuelled his own. He leaned over for a kiss but stopped short of her lips as he whispered lovingly. "I'm so lucky. You're so very beautiful and you're all mine!"

Without letting her say another word he caught her lips in a demanding kiss and refused to release her as he nibbled and lightly bit her bottom lip playfully before capturing her lips in another searing kiss. While she was busy kissing him back passionately Alec reached up and pulled out the comb she had holding her hair up into a bun on the back of her head. He groaned in pleasure as her hair cascaded down her back in a riot of curly red locks as he buried his hand in the thick mass of hair in pleasure.

He reluctantly pushed himself away from her then turned his chair so that he was facing her and pulled her chair around so she was facing him completely. He grabbed her by the waist and hauled her into his lap before turning his chair towards the kitchen door.

Jessica giggled in delight as she curled up in his lap not fighting even a little bit as he wheeled them towards his bedroom. Once inside she waited until he pushed them around the bed then she turned so her back was facing him as if she was going to get out of the chair. But then she paused suddenly as she felt his erection even through her dress. Instinctively she wiggled slightly and heard his surprised intake of breath, as he grew harder against her.

She grinned devilishly as she stood up and heard the disappointing groan behind her, but she ignored it as she reached under her dress and removed her bloomers but left her dress on. Then she turned suddenly and knelt down on the floor between Alec's legs then undid his buttons on his pants. She looked up at Alec teasingly as she shook her head chidingly. "Not wearing any long johns are we?"

Alec grinned down saucily at her as he winked wickedly. "Wouldn't want to disappoint anyone now would we."

Jessica laughed huskily as she reached inside his open pants then pulled out his engorged manhood. Her breath caught in surprise at his obvious pleasure as she lowered her head slowly then her tongue flicked out experimentally. Alec gasped in shocked delight that she would do that and he groaned in disappointment as she stood up suddenly and turned her back to him. Alec reached out for her to pull her back then he paused in relief as she lifted her dress up. She was just getting undressed.

Jessica lifted her dress then looked behind her teasingly as she winked playfully and suddenly sat down back into his lap with her dress hiked up around them then she wiggled enticingly.

Alec frowned unsure what she was up to for a moment then he grinned wickedly it didn't take him long to catch onto what Jessica wanted and groaning in pleasure at the idea. He lifted Jessica up while she held onto the arms of his chair for support then he placed her over his manhood and sheathed himself fully inside wet inner heat.

Jessica cried out in pleasant surprise she hadn't been sure it would work very well when she first thought of it, but now that he was inside her the pleasure was so intense, she had never felt so fulfilled before. Alec lifted her up and at the same time she pushed on the arms of the chair then locked her arms to hold herself up. Alec tried to pull her down once she was up far enough but Jessica's arms were braced so that he couldn't pull her down. Only the tip of his manhood was still inside her and she groaned as she wiggled slightly still holding herself up then suddenly she relaxed her arms and dropped back into Alec's lap unexpectedly.

Alec cried out in shocked denial as he erupted deep inside Jessica so soon, he had wanted to prolong this but the pleasure was so intense he couldn't help himself. He wrapped his arms around Jessica and refused to let her go as he layed his head on her back still shuddering in ecstasy.

Jessica groaned in disappointment she too had wanted to prolong this but her pleasure was just as intense as his as she cried out in rapture as her body erupted around Alec's pulsating manhood. She slumped slightly against Alec in exhaustion as her body continued to shudder for a long time afterwards.

Finally the two calmed down and Jessica lifted off of Alec slowly then as she had done the first time she went over to the washbowl and wet the cloth waiting there for her. She walked back over and knelt down between Alec's legs then gently washed him clean before getting up and lifting her dress then washed herself as well.

Alec watched her with his eyes half closed still slightly breathing hard then he grinned up at her drowsily as she threw the cloth into a corner then proceeded to undress him for bed. Once he was fully undressed Alec reached over and pulled a laughing Jessica into his lap once more. He pulled her head down for a deep demanding kiss. At first she struggled playfully but then suddenly she groaned in pleasure and melted against him in surrender.

Jessica stayed there for a few minutes enjoying his teasing kisses then pushed away from him and stood back up with hands on her hips as she laughed down at him light-heartedly. "Oh no you don't, come on now it's time for bed up you go."

Alec groaned in disappointment but obediently lifted himself up onto his bed then pulled himself up onto his pillow so Jessica could pull the blankets over him. He waited until she got closer then he grabbed her around the waist and pulled her on top of him cloths and all as his lips found hers in another searing kiss.

Jessica groaned in pleasure but managed to escape his arms as she rolled off the bed laughing teasingly then she turned to face him as she shook a warning finger at him. "No more tonight go to sleep."

Alec sighed in frustration then he wiggled his eyebrows suggestively. "How about a goodnight kiss then?"

Jessica laughed and shook her head emphatically. "No way that's just an excuse for you to pull me back into bed. I'm not falling for that one mister!"

Alec smirked in disappointment then stuck out his lower lip in a pout hoping it would entice her to lean closer for a kiss, but it didn't work as she giggled down at him. She put her hand up and blew him a kiss before turning for the door. Jessica opened the door then turned back once more and grinned over at Alec tenderly. "Goodnight love!"

Alec smiled back sleepily as he waved then blew her a kiss. "Goodnight I love you!"

Jessica nodded then left for her own bed.

Alec frowned dejectedly but he had known she wouldn't stay any longer. He grinned devilishly as he thought of his chair he would have never thought of putting it to such good use, but now he couldn't wait to try it again. Next time he wouldn't be taken by surprise and he would make darn sure he would last a lot longer then he had tonight. He sighed dreamily then drifted off to sleep.

The first good night sleep he was to have since Mell's disappearance almost two weeks ago and his dreams were of Jessica and a future full of love and happiness.

* * *

Jed stopped his horse suddenly then waited patiently for Mell to notice and turn back to see what he was doing as he stared up in awe at the bright full moon shining above. It didn't take long for Mell to notice and she rode back to Jed curiously. "What are you doing we could be home early in the morning if we ride all night!"

Jed looked at Mell sitting on her horse totally unaware that the moonlight was doing spectacular things to her face and hair. She had left it down this morning not wanting to take the time to put it up. Jed pointed up at the moon playfully. "Isn't it beautiful?"

Mell looked up in surprise at the moon she hadn't really paid it any attention to busy concentrating on the ground in front of her horse not wanting him to step in a hole and possibly injuring his leg. Her expression softened as she looked up then suddenly she gasped in surprise as Jed grabbed her around the waist and pulled her onto his horse demandingly as he captured her lips in a kiss.

Mell pulled away laughing huskily as Jed's passion fuelled her own. "What are you up too now?"

Jed grinned mischievously as a wild idea made him dismount in a hurry. He pulled a protesting Mell from his horse then turned and took the saddle off but left the blanket on him. He turned suddenly and started pulling Mell's clothes off first her shirt dropped to the ground then the binding around her breasts followed the shirt. He reached for the buttons on her trousers but she pulled away teasingly.

Mell giggled at Jed's haste then turned suddenly and ran away. She kept her arms across her breasts so they wouldn't bounce. She was laughing so hard it only took Jed a few minutes to catch her. Jed grinned lovingly then grabbed a fistful of her hair and pulled gently until she was looking up at him. "I love you so much woman!"

Without giving her a chance to respond he ground his lips against hers in demand. His hands were busy undoing her pants and suddenly she was naked then he stepped back and stripped out of his own shirt then his pants and finally his long johns followed until he too was naked.

Mell couldn't look away as Jed stared at her so intently then she jumped in surprise when Jed whistled for his horse unexpectedly. Jed smiled devilishly then jumped up on his horse and put his hand down enticingly so that he could help Mell mount in front of him. Mell frowned slightly in puzzlement as he lifted her up to sit in front of him. She gasped in shocked surprise as Jed turned her so she was facing him and her breasts were pressed against his naked chest.

Jed grinned at her teasingly then grabbed her by the waist and gently pulled her closer so that her womanhood was pressed tightly against his manhood. She lifted her legs instinctively then draped them over his to accommodate him. Jed groaned in pleasure then he reached down between her legs and opened her lower lips so that her bud rubbed against his manhood. He pulled her in tighter. Mell instinctively wrapped her arms around him to keep from falling as he lowered his head to kiss her passionately. But before his lips touched hers he whispered tenderly. "Trust me love!"

Mell instantly relaxed as Jed's lips claimed hers she hadn't even realized she had tensed up. Jed groaned in approval then he nudged his horse into a walk and this time he growled in ecstasy as every step the horse took rubbed Mell's bud against his manhood harder and faster.

Mell gasped in surprised pleasure as Jed nudged his horse into a trot. She couldn't believe they were doing this on a horse never in her wildest imagination would she have dreamed such a thing would be even possible never mind pleasurable. All of a sudden Jed nudged his horse into a canter and all thoughts flew from her mind as her body took over control.

The motion of the horse not only caused a pleasurable friction between their legs but it also caused her breasts to bounce slightly against Jed's curly hair on his chest so she was getting pleasure from both places.

Jed gasped in delight as he felt Mell loose control first and she screamed out in pleasure as she climaxed long and hard. Jed too couldn't wait as his horse drove him hard against Mell and his control snapped as he too yelled out his passion. Then he ground his lips against Mell in demand as he climaxed so hard he almost fell off the horse but righted himself just in time. He slowed his horse down then turned him back towards Mell's clothes, but at a more sedate walk as Mell leaned against him in exhaustion.

Mell groaned against Jed's shoulder as they rode back he was still slightly enlarged and the horse was still causing a lot of friction between them then too her surprise she climaxed again. Jed chuckled knowingly as he felt Mell's uncontrollable shivers then he sighed in disappointment as he finally shrunk too much for more pleasurable climaxes from Mell.

Mell sighed disgruntled as her clothes and her horse came in sight then she gasped in surprise as Jed lifted her up then gently let her down off the horse. But her legs were so wobbly they refused to hold her up and she sat down on the ground right where she was.

Jed laughed in delight then he got down himself and grabbed his blanket off the horse. He laid it on the ground before walking over picked Mell up unceremoniously and deposited her on the blanket until he could get his bedroll out so they could catch a few hours of sleep before continuing on in the morning.

Mell watched him walk around naked making them a bed and she grinned, the man had no sense of decency what so ever, and she was definitely glad that he didn't since she loved to watch him walk around naked. As she watched Jed also grabbed his canteen of water then splashed some on his belly to clean himself off. Mell grinned then looked down at herself she too was full of Jed's pleasure and hadn't even noticed.

Jed walked over then washed her off gently and dried them both off with the saddle blanket before lifting her up again. Mell protested laughingly that she could walk but Jed shook his head without a word then brought her over to the bed he had made for them. He climbed in with her as soon as he put her down and they cuddled up close together. Jed sat up for a moment then grinned down at Mell enticingly. "Someday we'll do that with me inside you but not yet. Goodnight I love you!"

Mell smiled up in anticipation sleepily then reached up with her hand and tenderly stroked his face lovingly. "I can't wait to try that someday but are you sure it won't hurt you it's kind of an awkward position for you to be in."

Jed chuckled as he laid back then pulled her close. "No love it won't hurt I promise!"

Mell curled up close then yawned. "Goodnight I love you."

It didn't take either of them long to fall asleep and the full moon that had caused all the excitement in the first place, caressed the lovers as they slept peacefully beneath it's warm loving light.

CHAPTER TWENTY-FOUR

Mell and Jed rode in about noon the day after Mary and Giant Bear. They would have been at the ranch sooner if they hadn't stopped to play in the moonlight last night. As they entered the yard they were both surprised at the sight that greeted them. Mell's father was the first one they noticed behind him stood the mayor, his wife, and their daughter. Actually it was the crowd of people in the background that surprised them even more. They had figured after all this time the townspeople would have gone home.

Everyone gave a tremendous cheer of greeting at the sight of them and Mell was overwhelmed by the love and acceptance she received from these people. Even though she was a woman they had continued to accept her as a sheriff and friend.

Mell jumped off her horse in excitement, wiping the tears from her eyes, she rushed over to her father then gave him a fierce hug of greeting. The tears were more from relief that she was home and everyone important to her was safe. The two were quickly swallowed up by the townspeople as everyone converged on them in excitement.

Jed sat on his horse watching a little longer amazed by it all never had he ever saw the like before. He had visited or lived in many towns between Boston and here, and even into Canada, but never had he seen a sheriff accepted or greeted as Mell was. In most towns the sheriff was only barley tolerated. He smiled as he heard Mell's laughter ring out joyously, as she returned everyone's hugs, and at the same time answered their questions as fast as she could.

Jed shook his head still slightly baffled by it all and jumped down off his horse then started loosening the saddles. Kenneth walked over instantly when he saw what Jed was doing. He warmly clasped Jed's hand in greeting before pointing over his shoulder at the crowd behind him. "You better go over and join Mell. I'll take care of the horses."

Jed inclined his head in thanks and went over to join the throng. As he made his way through the crowd Jed was surprised at how enthusiastically he was received. Everyone clasped his hand firmly in friendship and thanked him for rescuing Mell. He nodded cordially but didn't say anything still awed by it all. Jed reached Mell's father and he shook his hand affectionately in greeting. The crowd instantly hushed so they could all hear what was being said not wanting to miss a thing.

Alec tightened his hold on Jed's hand so he couldn't get away then he dramatically waited for complete silence, before he started his speech. He gestured around them with his free hand then made sure to speak loud enough for everyone to hear him. "My son, thank you for saving my daughter's life. As you can see we are all so very grateful and to show our appreciation the Mayor has a surprise for you. If you will follow us over to the far corral we will present it to you."

Alec looked up at the mayor as he let go of Jed's hand then nodded that he was ready and John dutifully pushed Alec's chair in the direction of the corrals. The townspeople followed just as excited to see Jed's reaction as Alec was. Mell walked over and took Jed's hand then entwined her fingers with his as they followed her father obediently.

As they drew closer to the far corral Mell caught her father's glance and smiled gratefully over at him as she saw what was inside. Jed could hardly contain his glee when he saw the cattle in the corral waiting for him. They stopped in front and the mayor walked around Alec's chair so that they would be the focus of everyone's attention as he shook Jed's hand amiably. An expectant hush fell over the crowd as they waited to hear what John had to say.

The mayor cleared his throat dramatically to make sure everyone was listening, as he looked at Jed expectantly. "We are all eternally in your debt not only for saving our Sheriff but also for saving our dear friend. The whole town wanted to show their appreciation. So after you left to save Mell everyone chipped in and two of your hands went over to the Carlson ranch and picked up a Texas bull that was for sale. On their way back they stopped at the Johnson's ranch and picked up two heifers. This is our thank you gift to you. We hope that in the coming years as Deputy and sometimes Sheriff when Mell is with child...."

The mayor paused and chuckled himself as everyone laughed at the blush on Mell's face at the reference to her having children. When quiet descended again John continued. "You will come to know us and serve us as well as Mell does. We also hope to buy cheap beef."

Everyone hooted again at the rotund mayor's hopeful expression at the mention of food then they cheered their approval at his speech.

Jed turned to the crowd and waited for them to be quiet, not sure what he was going to say at first then he took a fortifying breath to calm his nerves as silence prevailed. He waved around at all the people surrounding him in awe. "I am so overwhelmed by all of this I don't know what to say exactly. I suppose first off I'd like to thank each and every one of you for the wonderful gifts. I also appreciate the fact that all of you come back to finish our wedding celebration with us. I'm sure I speak for Mell to when I say thank you. I would also like everyone here to know that I would have done the same for any one of you if your woman faced the same situation as Mell did. I'd also like to say that I appreciate the faith you are all putting in me to be your Deputy and also your Sheriff, three or four times I hope."

Mell blushed furiously again and slapped Jed playfully for that last comment. The crowd clapped and whistled their approval at Jed's speech. Then each man came over to Jed one at a time and introduced himself and his family if he had any. After the last family had been introduced Alec pushed himself over to Jed's side and raised his hands for quiet dramatically. "Can I please have everyone's attention? Gloria and her helpers have set out the wedding feast they've been cooking non-stop since sunup this morning. Better late then never I always say. Everyone feel free to go into the house and eat. I would also like to extend my hospitality to all of you who would like to stay tonight."

As the guests started to leave to go up to the ranch house to eat Mell leaned closer to Jed and whispered in his ear playfully. "See I told you they would be talking about you and not me."

Jed hugged her before stepping back then shook his head in amazement. "Mell I've never had such a warm welcome from people in all my life, or such unconditional friendship from folks I don't know! I think I'm going to like it here but what I would like to know is how everyone knew I wanted to raise cattle."

Mayor Elton chuckled as he heard Jed's curious question. He pointed at himself then down at Alec. "We can answer that it's very simple you see. The townspeople had been talking before they left to go home. Several days before Giant Bear and Mary returned they took up a special collection as a reward for the both of you, for your service to the town. When Mary and Giant Bear got here to collect Tommy and their things we presented him with the money. But Giant Bear and Mary refuse to take any money of course. So Alec came up with the suggestion of buying two or three horses to give Giant Bear instead of the money. Alec had a mare and a gelding for sale and the Johnson's had a stud they wanted to sell. Giant Bear accepted the horses along with a supply of provisions for his reward. The few townspeople left then asked what we thought you would like and Alec readily answered that you wanted to start a cattle herd. There was ample money to buy the bull and two heifers with a little left over. The remaining money was put into a kitty in the house and will be deposited in the bank for your children."

Mell walked around Jed closer to the mayor with tears in her eyes and hugged him in gratitude as she whispered brokenly. "Thank you for all that you've done for us."

Mayor Elton hugged Mell back for a moment then stepped back and grinned devilishly. "It's the least we could do after all you've done for this town. You know we do have an ulterior motive in giving these cattle to your husband though."

Mell stepped back instantly when the mayor let her go and her voice became soft and protective as her eyebrows rose in surprise. "Oh, and what motive was that?"

John chuckled at the protective note in Mell's voice then he motioned placatingly. "Nothing drastic my dear we just wanted to make sure you were both so happy here, that you would never think of leaving us."

Mell smiled knowingly and she waved with a giggle in the direction Jed had disappeared too as soon as Mell had gotten distracted by the mayor. "I'm sure you've reached your goal already look over there!"

Over by the corral Alec and Jed were talking excitedly already discussing where they would be keeping the cattle and how many new hands they would need. The two men had slipped away while they had been talking and the mayor hadn't even noticed. John laughed as he nodded in satisfaction as he looked towards the excited Jed. He turned back to Mell and pointed towards the farmhouse. "Come on we'd better get those two to the house or all the food will be gone."

Mell smirked in humour as the mayor rubbed his rotund belly in sympathy as it growled at him. They went over and gathered the two reluctant men then headed for the house. Alec looked up at his daughter curiously as Jed pushed him. "Have you and Jed decided where you're going for your honeymoon?"

Mell shook her head negatively as she looked down at her father questioningly. "No we haven't had time to discuss it yet. Why do you ask?"

Alec smiled up devilishly at his daughter as he teased. "Well, Jessica and I want to get married in Boston. We thought you two might like to be there. Jed had mentioned at one time that he had family there so we figured that's where the two of you would be heading."

Mell opened her mouth to say that she didn't know that Jed wanted to go to Boston. When the first part of her fathers statement finally registered. She squealed in delight then bent down impulsively and hugged and kissed her father. Jed quickly stopped the wheelchair before Mell got run over by the wheels as she continued in excitement. "I'm so happy for you! It's about time you decided to marry again. When did you ask her?"

Alec beamed relieved at Mell's approval then squeezed her hand as she stood back up but kept it in his. "Actually, I asked her before you got married but we didn't want to get married with a lot of people since this is our second marriage. So we decided to wait until later."

Jed walked around the wheelchair and shook Alec's hand. "Congratulations! We haven't really talked about this but I had planned on taking Mell across country so she can show me her routine since I need to know how she makes her rounds anyway. After that I figured I would take her to Boston to meet my family."

Mell smiled from one to the other in agreement as she nodded. "It sounds like a good plan to me. Usually, it takes me about a week to make my rounds. Since this is our honeymoon it could take up to three weeks or so I'm hoping. Dad let's say we meet in Boston in four weeks time for your wedding."

Alec looked up at Mayor Elton inquisitively. "Do you think you can get by that long without Mell?"

John's eyes twinkled in delighted mischief as he winked at Alec in conspiracy before looking back at Mell and Jed then nodding that they would be fine. "Yes Kenneth said he would like to remain on as Deputy and Dusty offered to fill in as well until Jed and Mell get back. I told the boys not to expect them for at least a month if not two. Mell's never taken a holiday and with all that's happened around here lately I figured she would need to have time to gather herself together."

Mell hugged the mayor in gratitude. "I'll take both men to the office tomorrow and show them what to do. I'll also make sure to send you a report every so often so you know where you can reach us if an emergency arises."

Mayor Elton inclined his head agreeably as he went behind Alec's chair and took over pushing him to the house. Alec smiled up at Mell inquisitively. "Now that your honeymoon is settled when are you leaving?"

Mell sighed in disappointment at the thought of having to wait even one more day, but they didn't have much choice there was too much to do yet. She looked down at her father and shrugged. "Much as I would like to leave tomorrow I need a couple of days to get everything organized."

Jed pushed the front door open and held it so everyone could go in. Once inside he continued the conversation as he motioned down at Alec curiously. "I think three or four days would be time enough for us. What about you Alec? Are you and Jessica leaving right away?"

Alec shook his head negatively as he looked up at Jed. "No, we probably won't leave for a couple of weeks at least. We want to do some traveling so I need to get everything settled in the office that way you can take over without any trouble."

Jed stopped short in surprise as he gestured down in panic. "Alec, I don't want to take over the running of the ranch. I was hoping that you and your new wife would stay on here."

Alec grinned in delight at the note of dread in Jed's voice then he waved calmly in reassurance. "I didn't mean for you to look after it permanently but we want to travel for a year or so then we will be returning here to live afterwards. Wade will be the one who'll do most of the work. All you have to do is go over things with him once or twice a day."

Mell laughed in amusement at the look of pure relief on Jed's face as he motioned in compliance. "Well I guess I can handle things for a year!"

Mell grabbed Jed's arm in demand as she pulled him along not wanting to wait any longer she was starved. "Come on you guys I'm going to expire from hunger soon you can discuss business later!"

They continued on their way in silence to join their guests for lunch. As they entered the dining room a huge cheer came from all the guests waiting patiently. Alec was pushed to the head of the table and Mell and Jed took the two vacant chairs on his right. The mayor took the seat to Alec's left with his wife beside him.

Mell looked around in surprise Jessica had instructed the men to move the dining room table over and bring in the table from the kitchen. Every available space was being used to seat people so they could eat. Along the wall was a buffet style table, taken from the bunkhouse, heaped with enough food to feed an army.

There were a few faces missing of course since not all of the townspeople could come back but almost everyone that could come had. Mell looked around in wonder there were about seventy guests still here and all of them were packed in this small room, since none of them wanted to miss a thing. Mell continued to look around gleefully at all her friends then her gaze fell on a face she hadn't expected to see here. She leaned over to her father curiously as she pointed towards the far wall at Daniel inquisitively. "What's Mr. Grey doing here? I thought he wasn't coming to the wedding?"

Alec smiled reassuringly over at Mell as he explained what had happened when he had gone over to Daniel's. She nodded thoughtfully when her father was finished his story. "I definitely agree that Brian was going to set him up if things went wrong but he never said what his intentions were for involving Daniel before he died."

The mayor leaned towards Mell inquisitively as she sat back in her chair. "Did you notice that Gloria and Wade's cabin is finished?"

Mell shook her head negatively as she turned then looked at John in surprise. "No, I hadn't noticed how did it get finished so fast?"

The mayor smiled in delight as he chuckled at Mell's shocked look then he waved towards Brad sitting at the far end of the table. "Well it was actually Brad's doing he asked the guests that stayed the whole time to help. He figured it would keep them out of trouble while we waited for you two to show up. He was right too and with all these men working together it only took a week to finish it."

Mell grinned in delight then nodded towards Brad. "Well, I'll have to make sure I thank him later."

Mell turned as the door to the kitchen opened and the rest of the food was brought out. She watched eagerly as the ladies set everything out on the table and she sighed in anticipation. She was so hungry she was sure she could eat a horse all by herself.

Alec caught Mell's attention with a tap on her arm then gestured confidently as she turned to him inquiringly. "I gave Princess to Tommy as a parting gift. I hope you don't mind I know you were eager to see what colour the foal would be."

Mell shook her head reassuringly she was just glad her father had thought of it she hadn't. "No that was a good idea I'm glad you thought of it."

Jessica walked over with a bottle of champagne Alec had hidden three bottles, when they had first moved in here, in the wine cellar hoping for just such an occasion and started pouring some for everyone. Sara was at the other end of the room doing the same. When all the glasses were filled and the food ready the mayor stood up and waited for total quiet.

John smiled in satisfaction, as he looked around at all the silent guests waiting patiently for him to speak. "Ladies and gentlemen it's nice to have everyone gathered in one place for a change. I hope we can do this more often in the future. The wedding feast is laid out on the table and everyone can help themselves, but before we do Alec is going to give a short prayer of thanks."

Everyone bowed their heads obediently as Alec gave the blessing then the mayor still standing continued as he waved at Mell, Jed, Wade, and Gloria. "The newlyweds are to go up first then everyone else will proceed in an orderly manner. When everyone is seated again anyone who wants to make a toast is welcome too. After we eat everyone is encouraged to go into the drawing room for some entertainment where a big announcement will be made."

The mayor sat back down at the excited chatter of the guests as they wondered what could be so important that they had to wait until after Mell and Jed returned. They had all waited patiently for almost two weeks to hear it. That's why they all came back in the first place since John had enticed them before they left to go home with the promise of an important statement. He had told them it was vital to the town and surrounding areas.

Jed grabbed Mell's hand and led her to the buffet table eagerly just as starved as she was. Mell picked up two plates so that she could fix one for her father as well forgetting for a moment that it wasn't up to her anymore to look after her father that would now be Jessica's job.

Mell turned and smiled in approval at Gloria since she was directly behind her then bent slightly to whisper in conspiringly. "Everything looks great! I think I'll give everyone a bonus this month."

Gloria grinned in thanks at the compliment then gestured in exasperation. "You've given us plenty as it is just sit back and enjoy yourself for a change!"

Mell finished filling the plates then took Gloria's advice and concentrated on enjoying herself in the company of her family and friends.

* * *

Everyone finished eating and the men all went out on the porch for a smoke to give the ladies a chance to clean up. The women kicked Mell and Gloria out as well then they cleaned the dining room.

Jessica enlisted the aid of Dusty and Brad to take the side table out of the dining room and set it up in the drawing room against the far wall. They brought out a huge wedding cake and set it in the center of the table. While the men were doing that a steady stream of ladies went in and out as they brought every kind of dessert your heart could desire and set them artfully around the cake.

Dusty and Brad then brought out two large crystal bowls filled with punch then brandy, whiskey, wine, and bourbon decanters were brought out and put on the table at the far end.

Three men from town came in to play music one with a fiddle, one with a guitar, and one with a mouth organ. They would play all night if the guests wanted and there was even someone to play the piano in the corner. All the children had been fed earlier and the older girls were keeping an eye on them.

The couch and big chairs had been removed earlier to give them more room for dancing and smaller chairs stacked against the walls could be used for sitting if you wished.

Everything was finally ready and Jessica went out to let the men know. It wasn't long before everyone was gathered in the drawing room and helping themselves to the much anticipated deserts and drinks. All the guests stood around laughing and joking with neighbours while the band played softly in the corner. You could feel the excitement in the air as everyone waited in anticipation for the mayor to give his long awaited speech.

Mell smiled down at her father in amazement as she motioned around the room. "Wow! I didn't know this room could hold so many people at once and it's still not full. We could bring in another fifty people with no problem."

Alec grinned up at her and nodded but didn't comment as he turned to the John eagerly. "Are you ready yet?"

Mayor Elton rubbed his hands together in anticipation, as he looked down at Alec then winked in conspiracy, before turning to Mell and Jed. He crooked his finger demandingly for them to follow him. "Will you follow us please?"

Mell and Jed looked at each other in bafflement before turning back to John curiously but he was already gone, as he pushed Alec's chair over to where the band was playing, so they had to scramble quickly as they followed obediently. The mayor turned Alec to face the crowd unexpectedly so Mell and Jed had to come to an abrupt halt instantly then they had to sidestep the wheelchair quickly or get ran over.

The band quit playing immediately aware that the announcement was forthcoming and the guests hushed expectantly as they waited for Alec or the mayor to speak. They had all waited patiently for this moment and none of them wanted to miss what was being said. Alec waved for Mell and Jed to stand in front of him then smiled mischievously up at them but still didn't say anything.

Alec looked over at Jed conspiringly then winked at him in explanation. Jed smiled widely now aware of what was happening as he remembered the discussion they all had before the wedding at the mayor's office.

The mayor cleared his throat loudly to make sure he had everyone's undivided attention, but he didn't need to bother, you could have heard a pin drop at that moment. He gestured solemnly towards Mell in explanation. "As everyone knows Mell has been with us since 1806. When she first became our Deputy she passed herself off as a man and none of us looked twice of course. Never would any of us have guessed that a woman could, or even would want to be a Deputy. All we noticed was her height and slightly shadowed face. But from that day on she has changed all our lives for the better. In 1808 Mell became Sheriff, after our Sheriff got himself killed, and she kept our town quiet and lawful. Then in 1810, we found out that 'he' was actually a 'she'. Some people already knew this secret or had guessed without informing us."

At this point the mayor looked directly at his wife in disapproval. Mrs. Elton then turned with a smug smile to exchange glances with Chelsie and Pam. Mary had known as well but she wasn't here. The townspeople laughed at John's disgruntled expression as he gazed at his wife for a moment in obvious displeasure. Mayor Elton harrumphed chidingly at the smug look the three women exchanged then turned back to the crowd as the chuckles died down.

He continued once he was sure his wife had gotten the silent reproachful message then looked around at the guests once more. "Well, most of us were shocked of course and because of our shock we made the mistake of firing her. But lucky for us she didn't leave us completely, and in the four months that she was gone our town became lawless once again. It wasn't until she saved the lives of my wife and unborn child that I finally came to my senses and rehired her as Sheriff. Instead of taking wages though it was agreed that she would take over this ranch on condition that she would look after all the surrounding towns as well. So in 1810 Mell moved onto this ranch and brought her father out here to live with her. Now I don't know about the rest of you but I think we got the better deal."

There was laughter from the townspeople and lots of heads were nodding in complete accord with the mayor that the town had gotten the better deal by far.

John cleared his throat loudly for silence not finished yet and when quiet descended the mayor continued. "Of course at that time there was only one other town besides ours and not too many people lived in it. It didn't take long though for the rumours to spread across the land that people could live out here in peace, without having to worry about outlaws or desperados. So more people started to settle here and another four towns sprang up almost overnight. Now everyone here has heard rumours of the railroad coming. Well it's true and it should pass through our town in another two years hopefully! So our town and the surrounding towns will grow even more and with this new growth unfortunately more outlaws will come. So Alec, Jed, and I came up with a solution to keep our towns from being overrun lawless once again.

There is just no way, that Mell will be able to keep up even with her husband helping her."

Mell turned angrily and tried to interrupt with a fierce scowl on her face but the mayor held up his hand calmly to silence her. She turned and threw Jed a murderous look in the process. Jed just smiled back innocently at Mell then turned back to the mayor expectantly hoping that what was to come would put a smile back on his new brides face. Or he just might end up sleeping in the den by himself tonight.

Mayor Elton took a deep fortifying breath still not sure how Mell was going to take this and continued on hurriedly before he could change his mind. "Now, while Mell is away on her honeymoon every town will elect a Sheriff, and every Sheriff will have one Deputy."

The crowd came alive at that shouting angrily in protest as they threw demanding questions at the mayor all at once wanting to know what was going to happen to Mell. The mayor's speech was completely drowned out something neither of the two men had anticipated when they decided to make this speech tonight. Alec and the mayor looked at each other in concern but all they could do was wait it out.

CHAPTER TWENTY-FIVE

Mayor Elton turned away from Alec and scowled angrily as he looked around at all the shouting people then he raised his fingers to his lips and blew hard so that his whistle would drown out the uproar. Quiet descended immediately. He raised his hands in demand for restraint then bellowed loudly. "Please will you let me finish already?"

Not a sound could be heard as the mayor sighed relieved. He had expected yelling from Mell but not from the townspeople. John quickly continued before they could interrupt him again. "Now before Mell leaves on her honeymoon she and her husband will come to my office then be sworn in as the new Marshal and Deputy Marshal of North Dakota."

There was a shocked hush for a few seconds as the townspeople absorbed that information then suddenly complete pandemonium broke out again. Everyone clapped and cheered their approval.

Mell stood in dumbfounded astonishment totally speechless with such a stunned look on her face that Jed had to laugh as he leaned closer to her and bent down to whisper. "Congratulations!"

Mell turned and looked down at her father as he took her hand to get her attention. Alec grinned up at her amazed look then squeezed her hand encouragingly. "Congratulations!"

The mayor raised his hand for silence once more then sighed in frustration when it took several minutes for quiet to prevail, before he could finally continue. "Mell will now be reporting directly to the Governor of North Dakota. She will then be traveling from town to town throughout the North keeping the peace. Since she has paid for her ranch many times over in the seven years she's been with us. Mell will now get paid wages by the Governor for her services. We will not be seeing so much of her from now on and I think I speak for everyone when I say we will miss seeing her smiling face every day. But I figured it was time to reward her for the many years of service she has given to our towns."

Mayor Elton walked around Alec's chair dramatically and went over to the speechless Mell then took both of her hands in his and kissed each cheek. He smiled at her before speaking loud enough for everyone to hear. "Congratulations Mell. I hope you give North Dakota just as many years and as much wisdom as you have given us. We will miss you when you're away and look forward to the times when it's our turn for your visit."

Mell smiled hesitantly back at him still a little stunned by it all. Not sure if she liked being handed over to the governor without her consent. "Well you sure managed to surprise me this time. I had no idea you were planning any of this. I'm not exactly sure what to say yet since I've been fighting you for the last two years whenever you talked about bringing in a Marshal. I had no idea that you had me in mind for the job!"

The mayor grinned as he let go of Mell's hands then he pointed towards Jed in explanation. "Well you'll have to thank your new husband for that it was his idea to make you the Marshal."

Mell frowned in surprise then shrugged as she motioned with a laugh of irritation. "I'm not sure if I should thank him or be angry at him for doing this to me without talking to me first!"

The crowd chuckled in delight at that and a few yelled out suggestions to Jed on how to appease his new wife trying to be helpful. Jed smiled confidently as he looked around the room at everyone but didn't say anything. He grinned with assurance not really worried.

Mell wiped tears from her eyes as she thought of all the friends she would miss then waved in aggravation. "I don't know if this is good or bad news. I love this town and all my other towns as well. I just always figured on remaining Sheriff here for as long as I could. I'm also not sure if you have managed to give me more or less work. But I do know that I'll be spending most of my time in the saddle now. I also know that I must thank you for the trust you have placed in me and in my abilities to help North Dakota become lawful. I also have to admit that I'll miss all of you when I'm away."

The mayor beamed at Mell one more time then he stepped back to let everyone else offer her best wishes. While she was busy with the others he bent down to Alec troubled as he gestured in confusion. "I'm not sure if she's pleased or not. She doesn't look happy about it."

Alec grinned up at him reassuringly as he gestured calmly. "Just give her a few days to think about it. She'll see that being a Marshal is no different than what she is doing now as Sheriff."

Mayor Elton nodded relieved then stood up straight before turning away from Alec. As he stepped forward he called out loudly so that everyone could hear him. "Could I have everyone's attention again please?"

When he had their undivided focus, John continued. "Anyone who would like to be a Sheriff of our town must go to Mell directly and give their names. She will make the decision as to who goes on the list. We already have a Deputy, as do the other towns, so we don't need to worry about that. Mell will also have to approve of the names for Sheriff in her other towns. After she makes a list of suitable candidates the towns will choose who they want by vote."

The mayor allowed the crowd to discuss the matter of who would make a good sheriff for a few minutes then once more cleared his throat for silence. "I have one more announcement to make. I would like to congratulate Alec and Jessica Donaldson on their upcoming wedding in Boston."

There was more cheering and clapping from the crowd. Alec looked up at the mayor chidingly then couldn't help grinning up at his friend good-naturedly. "You just had to do that didn't you?"

Mayor Elton nodded devilishly as he waved playfully. "Of course, I couldn't miss out on such a good opportunity."

The band started playing softly when the mayor nodded at them. He had arranged it earlier so that once the speeches were finished they would continue so that everyone would start mingling again. Several people came over personally to give their best wishes to Mell, Jed, Jessica, and Alec.

Toasts were given to the newlyweds and the guests helped themselves to more dessert and drinks as they mingled quietly. But none of the toasts given were as exciting as the earlier announcements.

Daniel Grey walked up to Mell hesitantly when he finally caught her alone. He smiled cautiously and gestured in apology as he hung his head slightly in shame. "Mell I have to apologize for my behaviour the other day. All I can say in my own defence is that Brian was so damn convincing!"

Mell smiled in sympathy, not blaming the imbarrassed Daniel at all. She reached out and patted his arm reassuringly. "It's okay Mr. Grey we were all taken in by Brian. I really can't blame you for that."

Daniel sighed in relief, as he looked up then nodded thankfully. "I'm glad to hear that Mell. I've been kind of worried that you wouldn't forgive me."

Mell grinned teasingly as she dropped her hand from Daniel's arm. "I couldn't stay angry with you for long anyway, you've been my father's friend for many years and mine as well."

Daniel nodded thankfully then turned away and went to find Alec to gave him the good news.

A slow waltz started up and Jed walked over to Mell then bent down and whispered suggestively. "Dance with me love."

Mell beamed as he took her hand then led her over to the empty space that had been cleared for dancing. Gloria and Wade joined them right away and after watching for a few minutes several more couples joined them as well. At the completion of the waltz Alec approached Mell in his wheelchair as he grinned up at her teasingly. "My turn for a dance."

Mell smiled down at him thoughtfully trying to figure out how to dance with the wheelchair in the way. She finally bent down so that her head was on his shoulder. Alec grabbed her around the waist unexpectedly and pulled her onto his lap as he laughed at her hesitation. Mell chuckled in delight as she settled herself then put her arms around his neck and her head on his shoulder once more as Alec manoeuvred the chair around the dance floor. When the music stopped everyone clapped in approval they had all stopped dancing to watch Alec and his daughter.

Mayor Elton walked over and claimed the next dance from Mell.

Alec wheeled himself over to talk to Jed since they were both free for the moment wanting to talk business. "Are you still interested in building Chelsie a Goldsmith shop?"

Jed inclined his head as he looked down at Alec. "Of course, do you want to talk to her now?"

Alec nodded that he did and they threaded their way through the guests until they found Chelsie sipping wine and laughing with one of her girls. Chelsie turned in surprise at a tap on her shoulder and grinned at the two men as she lifted her glass in a toast. "Well I must say you sure know how to throw a party!"

Alec smiled up at her in thanks then motioned in apology. "Well thank you Miss Chelsie I'm glad you're enjoying yourself. I hope you don't mind but we'd like to talk a little business with you?"

Chelsie looked at the two men curiously then turned and shooed her companion on her way before turning back to the two men. "Sure I don't mind what can I do for you?"

Alec pointed at Jed then himself in explanation. "Well we both admire your expertise on designing jewellery. I have also seen your beautiful mantel clock at the Saloon you made. We were wondering if you'd be interested in going into partnership with us in a Goldsmith Shop. We would build it and buy all your material. All you would have to do is design the jewellery and merchandise plus manage the shop and we'd all be equal partners."

Chelsie thought about it for a few moments in surprise then shrugged undecided not sure what to say. It had been her dream when she first came to America from Ireland but now she wasn't so sure. "Well I don't know it doesn't seem fair that you two would put in all the capital and still make me an equal partner."

Alec waved dismissively as he shrugged. "We think it's a fair deal because without you we wouldn't have a Goldsmith Shop. Besides I have all the lumber already that we need to build it. It won't cost much except for labour."

Chelsie sighed thoughtfully still not sure she suggested hopefully. "Well it's definitely a good deal for me. Why don't we get together before you two go away and we can discuss it further, that way I have more time to think about it?"

Alec and Jed exchanged glances of perfect understanding and Alec turned back to Chelsie. "We'll come to the Saloon in a couple of days. I need to buy an engagement ring for Jessica anyway."

Chelsie nodded enthusiastically. "Sounds good to me!"

The three conversed for a few moments more about the party then Jed excused himself and went to find Mell. She was standing by the table with a glass of punch in her hand. Jed smiled teasingly at his wife as he bent down to whisper throatily in desire. "Well you definitely look radiant this evening!"

Mell beamed up at him as he bent down for a quick kiss then they turned to survey their guests and both smiled contentedly at how well everything had turned out.

The mayor walked over with a grinning Alec a few minutes later and Alec held up the knife he was holding dramatically. All the guests hushed expectantly as he held the knife by the blade so it was hilt backwards towards Mell to do the honours. "Come on Mell cut the cake I think we've waited long enough."

Mell nodded then looked around for Wade and Gloria and waved them over since it was their wedding cake too. The two couples obediently cut the cake then Mell gave the knife to Gloria to finish up as she took the first two pieces to Alec and the mayor. Jed and Wade helped out and started handing out pieces to all the guests.

Once everyone had a piece Jed took his over to Mell and teasingly held out his piece for her to take a bit. Just before she could bite into it he snatched it back quickly then popped it into his own mouth.

Mell and the guests all laughed at Jed's joke then Mell getting a mischievous look held her own piece of cake out to Jed to bite into invitingly. Jed chuckled knowingly and pretended to take a bite out of Mell's cake expecting her to do the same thing he had done. Mell waited for him to get close to the piece of cake then she all of a sudden thrust it into Jed's already closing mouth and the cake splattered all over his face. Mell laughed uproarsly at Jed's shocked look.

Jed instantly reached out and grabbed Mell around the waist then started kissing her. He ground his mouth against hers making sure her face got just as full of cake as his was.

Alec and the mayor clapped then whistled their approval and the guests all joined in as the couple breathlessly pulled apart. Jed winked at Mell suggestively. She grinned knowingly then all of a sudden grabbed Jed's hand and made a dash for the door leading to the hallway so that they could escape to their room. But instantly the crowed converged on the laughing pair and their escape was foiled.

Mell elbowed Jed and pointed at the door they had been heading for and he smirked good-naturedly as he saw Wade and Gloria make good their escape unhindered. He turned to Mell plaintively as he laughed. "Well at least someone got away!"

Mell chuckled then nodded down at her father in thanks as he handed them towels to wipe their faces on. The two cleaned themselves off then Mell glanced sideways at Jed and winked in conspiracy then both dropped their towels and made another dash for the door. The crowed cheered and clapped their appreciation as the two made good their escape then disappeared.

Mell turned once inside their room and smiled invitingly over at Jed as he closed the door firmly. He leaned back against the door with a sigh of relief at finally getting away from their guests. The two looked at each other for a moment not sure who should make the first move then Jed reached out his hand in hopeful invitation.

Mell smiled teasingly and took a step forward then lightly touched her fingertips to his caressingly but only for a second then suddenly she withdrew her hand quickly and backed away with a sly look on her face. When she was far enough away she stopped and held her hand out to him then waited expectantly.

Jed laughed in delight at the implication of the caress then the quick withdrawal of Mell's hand. He pushed himself away from the door and slowly advanced towards her. When he got close enough he stopped and put out his hand as if to touch her fingertips as she had done. He watched speculatively as her hand got closer but at the last moment he lunged forward and grabbed her around the waist then threw her on the bed. Jed jumped towards the bed hoping to land on top of her. Mell tried to twist away but she was laughing so hard she couldn't move away fast enough.

Jed pinned her down with a growl of impatience, as he claimed her lips, and cut off her laughter with a searing kiss. Mell felt the kiss right down to her toes and they even curled slightly in pleasure at the sensation. She wriggled around imploringly trying to get her hands loose so she could touch him. Jed would have none of that as he firmly held her down refusing to let her hands go and deepened the kiss insistently.

Mell groaned in frustration when she couldn't get loose and waited for Jed to lift up a little then she bit his lip in retaliation for holding her down. Jed lifted his head in astonishment staring at Mell in feigned hurt as his bottom lip came out in a definite pout.

Mell looked up at Jed and tried to look innocent but wrecked it by laughing at his injured look. Jed jumped off the bed suddenly without a word and stood with his hands on his hips still with an appearance of suffering on his face. Mell sat up with a teasing smirk and wiggled her index finger back and forth invitingly so he would come closer. "Oh poor baby come over here and I'll kiss it better."

Jed shook his head in denial still silent and stuck his lip out further as if in a sulk. He backed away instead after a few steps he stopped and watching her closely to see what she would do now. Mell laughed in delight and decided to play his game as she too stood up then advanced a couple of steps. She stopped suddenly in indecision when he backed away and refused to let her get closer.

Mell bit her lip and looked around in confusion trying to decide what to do next. She shrugged resignedly at his refusal to cooperate then pouted for a few moments before getting an idea. Mell motioned in imaginary hurt before turning her back to him. "Okay you stay over there! I'm going to bed."

While Mell's back was turned to him a sly looked came over her face then she hide the look as she checked over her shoulder to make sure he was watching her. When she was sure he was watching and not sneaking up behind her. Mell stood straighter and shook her head of beautiful blonde curls behind her so that all her hair was covering her back. She then arched her back slightly and ran her fingers through her hair as she spread it out enticingly behind her in a waterfall of curls. She turned slightly sideways so that he could see some of what she was doing but not enough for him to see everything wanting to tease him a bit.

Mell brought her hands up slowly making sure her fingertips lightly brushed against her shirt enticingly then began undoing the buttons slowly. When it was open she shrugged her shoulders slightly and let her shirt slide slowly down inch by slow inch until it was at waist height. She held it there for a few moments rolling her bare shoulders impishly before letting it drop to the floor in a pool at her feet.

Mell then arched her back into a steep curve for a second then lifted her hair up again and slowly let it fall back around her playfully. As it fell around her shoulders she made sure to slump forward slightly so that her hair was now shielding her and Jed couldn't see what she was doing. The only thing covering her now was her pant's the binding wrapped around her breasts and her hair of course.

Mell had been watching Jed covertly and smiled knowingly as he caught his breath in anticipation. Jed fidgeting slightly in expectation wanting to see what she would do next but didn't dare move afraid she would stop.

Mell's hands went to the binding on her breasts next and began unwinding it in slow motion. Just before the binding fell away completely she tossed her head so that most of her hair would fall forward over her right shoulder and cover what the binding released. When the binding fell to the floor and Mell's breasts were still beyond his view Jed groaned in frustration. He had to put his hands behind his back so he wouldn't be tempted to reach for her.

Mell lifted her arms up teasingly and reached behind her to gather the rest of her hair forward and at the same time she arched her back slightly so that Jed would get a glimpse of her taut nipples through her hair. When she straightened up again her hair once more covered her breasts completely.

Jed closed his eyes for a moment trying to gain some control of himself he wasn't sure how much more of this he could stand. Mell had watched Jed covertly the whole time so knew when he closed his eyes and she waited for him to open them again. Before she unhooked her pants and let them fall to her hips. She paused for effect tormenting Jed as long as possible before she let them pool around her ankles. Then she stepped out of them and paused again before her hands grasped the garter on her right thigh that held her little pistol. She had to bend slightly to unhook it and her bare bottom showed slightly through her waterfall of curls as she let the garter fall on the floor beside her other clothing.

Jed couldn't wait any longer as he pulled his shirt out of his trousers quickly then pulled it over his head and threw it in a corner. Mell giggled then gasped in open admiration as he dropped the shirt to the floor then undid his pants. Jed hesitated suddenly as he looked towards the candle then he took a step towards it to blow it out. He stopped and turned to Mell in surprise as she shook her head emphatically. "No Jed! Please leave it on tonight I want to see all of you!"

Jed nodded then he slipped his buckskin pants off and walked towards her. Mell groaned in pleasure at the sight of Jed's completely naked body he was just so beautiful to look at! The muscles in his arms bulged as he clenched his fists trying to gain control over his emotions. Mell turned to face Jed fully and took the last step that separated them bringing them so close they were touching slightly then she ran a hand over his chest muscles and giggled when he flexed and the muscles jumped in her hands.

Jed's control fled suddenly as he pulled Mell into his arms completely then backed her up until they were close to the bed. They kissed passionately not able to get enough of each other as they both collapsed on the bed. Jed lifted his head a moment as he panted in passionate apology and looked down at Mell. "I've waited patiently for you to become used to me but now I find I can't hold back any longer. I don't want to hurt you but I must this first time."

Mell put her hands up and framed his face in reassurance as she stared up at him intently. "Jed I must admit I was terrified of you at first, but not any longer. I know it will be painful at first but I'm not some church maid that snivels over a small cut! I've been shot, stabbed, and beaten within an inch of my life. The little pain I'll experience tonight won't bother me. I love you and I trust you. I also need you as desperately as you need me!"

Mell opened her legs to accommodate him and wiggled enticingly until she could feel Jed's manhood at the core of her womanhood. Then she grabbed a fistful of his hair and drew him down until their lips almost met as she whispered urgently against them. "Now Jed!"

She lifted herself up hard just as his manhood plunged inside her. Mell cried out slightly at the slight twinge of pain but it was over in moments then she wrapped her legs around him and squeezed them tightly in demand. Jed paused to give her a moment to adjust then when she squeezed her legs in command he took the hint and drove in to her again and again. There was no way he could hold back now and he threw his head back desperately trying to control his climax. He wanted and needed Mell to join him before he could let go of his own control completely.

Mell arched up insistently then tightened her legs even more as she felt her climax building up. It hurt for a moment almost more than having her maidenhood breached then Mell felt her body give in suddenly and she screamed Jed's name in surprise as she felt him let his own control go at the same time. Jed's seed poured into her and she climaxed again suddenly then layed quietly seeing stars for the next few moments. She came back down to earth slowly and opened her eyes drowsily as she focused on Jed's concerned expression.

Jed grinned in relief when Mell put her arms around him and purred deep in her throat like a contented cat. She pulled his head down for a kiss of satisfaction then released him and grinned saucily up. "Can we do it again?"

Jed threw his head back and roared with laughter. When he got himself under control he looked back down to find her scowling in annoyance at him. "I'm sorry Mell you'll have to give me at least half an hour to recuperate before I can give you more!"

Mell sighed in disappointment as Jed rolled away and propped himself up on the headboard. Mell curled up beside him with a contented sigh as she ran her fingers through his chest hairs teasingly. "Jed, will it always be like this?"

Jed chuckled and shook his head negatively. "No, there will be times when we'll fight and shout at each other at those times we'll turn away. But one thing I'll promise you is that I'll tell you every night that I love you no matter how mad I am at you. I hope you'll do the same thing!"

Mell nodded without comment as she yawned sleepily more tired then she wanted to admit. Jed smiled down at her in gratification he had worn her out. He propped himself up on his side so he could see her face as his tone became serious with just a hint of worry. "Are you mad at me for talking the Mayor into making you a Marshal?"

Mell smiled up at him reassuringly as she shook her head negatively. "No not really. After I thought about it some I realized that I've actually been doing a Marshal's job all along, except a Marshal doesn't concentrate on one or two towns but every town in the state. So the only thing that'll really change is that we'll be in the saddle more and I'll be dealing with Sheriffs rather than Deputies. Plus I'll have to report to the Governor instead of the Mayor. I met him only once and I'm not sure if I'll like taking orders from him he was a pompous ass."

Jed chuckled in delight at Mell's grimace of distaste. He motioned consolingly as he shrugged. "I don't think I've ever met him but I suppose I will now. Well at least you won't have to worry about hired guns going out of their way to try to kill you now that you're not the only one they have to deal with. Although, if they could get past the Sheriff then they might come looking for you."

Jed paused for a moment it wasn't something they needed to worry about now and changed the subject as he leaned down then kissed the tip of her nose tenderly. "I saw you talking with Daniel Grey earlier. Did you two make up?"

Mell nodded thoughtfully as she remembered her obligations with a shudder not really wanting to think about Brian or the others. But as much as she hated thinking of him she still couldn't leave him up there for the scavengers. "Yes he apologized for being taken in by Brian, which reminds me. I should send Brad up to Devil's Rock to bury the dead men up there. Brian must have buried his brothers and cousin since we left them up there because there was no sign of them anywhere."

Jed shrugged dismissively with a scowl of anger. "They can rot up there for all I cared! I don't ever want to go up there again anyway."

Mell sighed irritably it was still part of their jobs, but nodded in understanding at Jed's feelings, then changed the sensitive subject as she asked inquisitively. "I noticed you and dad talking to Chelsie earlier anything I should know about?"

Jed grinned mysteriously then shrugged when Mell slapped him playfully. "It's no secret your father and I want to build Chelsie a Goldsmith Shop. We offered to build it and pay for all the materials. All she has to do is make the jewellery, merchandise, and manage the store. The deal is for a three way equal partnership."

Mell grinned teasingly as she tugged playfully on his chest hairs. "Making your mark on the town already are you?"

Jed smirked smugly then nodded emphatically. "Well of course it's my town now too. So I might as well invest in it."

Mell smiled in relief then gestured plaintively as she changed the subject again. "Good, I'm glad you feel that way already, and how come you never mentioned before that you wanted to go to Boston for our honeymoon?"

Jed shrugged then tweaked her nose mischievously. "Well for one thing I wanted it to be a surprise. I figured we could go across country for a bit so you could show me you're routine. Until we reach a train anyway. I'm not sure how far the railway has come yet, but I figured if we have to, we could always ride our horses to Boston. Even though your routes will change now you still have to visit all your towns and make a list of tentative Sheriffs so we can still go. Plus we have to make a stop at the Governors now so you can be sworn in properly. We can do that after we visit all your towns and this way we can have a working honeymoon. So what do you think is it a good plan or would you prefer to do something different?"

Mell nodded pleased that Jed was willing to have a working honeymoon. "No your plan is fine with me."

Mell paused to yawn sleepily. Jed took the hint and rolled onto his back then pulled Mell closer in contentment. "Go to sleep sweet heart, I love you!"

Mell cuddled closer and curled her fingers in Jed's thick curly chest hairs in pleasure then murmured sleepily in return. "Good night love."

They drifted off to sleep and their dreams were similar. They dreamt of having two or three children together and living to a ripe old age if not tranquilly, at least very much in love.

EPILOGUE

North Dakota 1847

Mell leaned back with a sigh of contentment as she sipped her tea. She eyed her daughter-in-law sitting across from her pensively as she thought back over the years. Pamela, or Pam for short, had married her oldest son Daniel. He was named after Jed's first dead son. It had shocked all of them especially her when Daniel had hung up his guns and decided to become a Baptist Pastor. But Mell was very proud of him anyway, after the initial shock had worn off of course.

Pamela was Giant Bear and Mary's only daughter and had come to live with Mell so she could go to a white school. Pam had her mothers light blonde hair and her father's deep black eyes with a slight dusky look to her skin and high cheekbones, which definitely pointed to her Indian heritage. She was willowy slim with small upright breasts and didn't need to wear a corset to get a perfect hourglass figure, she already had one.

When Pam and Daniel had fallen in love and married. The two newlyweds moved over to Mary's ranch and Pam made it liveable again. Both Mell and Mary had been ecstatic to have their families entwined and the ghost of Brian layed to rest once and for all, as the kids brought love into Mary's old ranch house.

Daniel's twin sister Patricia, or Pat for short named after Mell's mother, had followed in Mell's footsteps and became the second lady sheriff in her home town.

Mell's third and last child another boy that they named John. After Mayor Elton who had died last year and Jed's father who also happened to have the name John, was becoming a rancher like his grandfather Alec much to Jed's father's disappointment and Alec's joy.

The thought of Jed's father made Mell grin in amusement Jed had been right about his father's reaction to Mell. After the initial shock of her being a sheriff and soon to be marshal had worn off of course. As John looked her up and down he smirked in satisfaction. "I expect strong grandsons and tall ones too, from such a good looking woman!"

Mell and Jed had laughed over that for many years.

Her father Alec after being married to Jessica for two years made Mell's dream come true and gave her a sister. Unfortunately for the grief stricken Alec Jessica had died in childbirth, so Mell had to raise her sister as her own. Mell had always felt that little Jessica was more her daughter than her sister because of that.

Alec had given them all a scare after Jessica died and almost died himself, but little Jessica pulled him out of his deep depression with her large green blue eyes and fiery red hair that came with her fierce temper. He was really starting to show his age now though at seventy-eight years old.

Right now Alec, Jed, and their youngest son John were out checking up on the new cattle John had purchased a month ago. Now they had an even five hundred head, which had always been Jed's dream.

Mell's horse Lightning had died quite a few years ago much to Mell's sorrow but not before producing a few dozen healthy offspring.

Mayor Elton's prediction had proven true although he was a few years too early and the railroad went through their town five years after Mell became the new marshal. The towns population doubled within a year and new towns sprung up everywhere across North Dakota. It had kept Mell and Jed very busy. It had gotten so busy that Mell had to hire two more deputy marshals just so they could keep up.

Alec's gold mine had dried up but he had found another one in town when he had invested in Chelsie's Goldsmith Shop. Alec and Jed had tripled their investment since they had built the store for Chelsie. She had to finally give up the saloon since she was just too busy with her new shop to run both.

Mell shook off her reflective mood and turned her attention back to Pam. "Well you look put out today. What seems to be the problem?"

Pam shrugged dismissively but the worry was plain in her voice. "I don't know I've been having these dreams and I'm not sure what they mean."

Mell sat forward instantly in surprise and shock she had been having strange dreams herself lately. She motioned ominously describing her nightmares distressfully. "Dreams of your father calling for help then death and blood all around him?"

Pam shivered in fear as she waved incredulously in alarm. "You've been having them too?"

Mell inclined her head that she was and her gaze became distant as she remembered the last dream two days ago. "Mine always starts out with a white female buffalo running towards your father. Sometimes she goes to him and tells him something then everything is fine. Other times she doesn't go to him but turns away instead. As she leaves blood and death appear all around him."

Mell touched her white buffalo medicine bag that she was never without and knew instinctively that she was the white buffalo in the dream. Somehow she must go and help Giant Bear immediately.

Pam shuddered in panic and dread as she thought of the last dream she had two days ago then gestured apprehensively. "All I see is blood and death with a feeling of urgency to go to my father. Do you hear what the white buffalo is saying in your dreams?"

Mell scowled in confusion as she shrugged pensively. "Yes but I don't understand it. She just keeps repeating over and over again that they must not be forced to marry! An older white man pops into the picture a few minutes later and the white buffalo tells him something important. But I can't hear what she says to him. It's all very confusing."

Pam looked puzzled as she waved urgently. "But who must not be forced to marry?"

Mell shook her head in frustration totally baffled by it all. "I don't know that's all she says to your father."

Pam sighed uneasily as she opened both her hands in supplication to Mell as if she had the answers. "It doesn't make any sense how can two people being forced to marry cause so much death. If my father is in danger why hasn't he contacted us yet?"

Mell shrugged thoughtfully as she mussed reflectively. "Maybe he doesn't know he's in danger yet."

Pam frowned as she looked at Mell meaningfully already aware of the answer but asked anyway. "You could be right. Are you going and when?"

Mell nodded emphatically as she waved towards town in explanation. "I'll leave right away but I have to go telegraph the Governor too let him know I have a family emergency and I'm not sure how long I'll be away. Then I'll let my Deputies know that they're going to have to look after things for me."

Pam scowled grimly then got up as she motioned instantaneously. "I'll run home and pack. I'm not sure if Daniel will come with us or not. Do you think Jed will come?"

Mell inclined her head decisively as she got up as well then waved shrewdly. "Of course, Giant Bear is his friend I know he'll do anything he can to help save Giant Bear."

Pam nodded relieved. "Okay I'll see you in a few hours."

Pam turned away skirts flying and raced from the room without waiting for Mell to agree or disagree more scared now then she had been earlier.

Mell sighed dejectedly. Well so much for her well deserved vacation! She turned and headed for the kitchen to ask Jane to pack provisions for their trip. Gloria had died the year before Mayor Elton had passed on so Jane had taken over. Mell headed upstairs to her room after leaving the kitchen.

At fifty-seven years of age Mell was still a fine figure of a woman. Most people were shocked when they learned her age. The only difference now from thirty years ago was that her hair had turned white. Her face had a few more wrinkles but her body was still girlishly thin even after giving birth to twins then too one more boy afterwards.

Mell and Jed had talked seriously about retiring as marshals this year, but they had decided to wait three more years. Jed would be sixty-five by then and she would be sixty, time enough to retire and spend the rest of their lives together in contentment.

Mell grabbed clothes from the closet and threw them on the bed. She frowned thoughtfully as she stared in surprise at a pouch hanging in her closet, she had forgotten all about it again. Inside were Mell and Jed's wedding certificates as well as Mary and Giant Bears. A deputy's certificate made out to Jed and Giant Bear was inside as well. Getting certificates was a new thing that only started a few years ago. Mayor Elton had them printed out for them as an anniversary gift one year. Mell had asked him to get one for Mary and Giant Bear so that next time she saw them she could give it to them as a gift.

There had never seemed to be an opportunity to give it to them though until now. So she nodded to herself and grabbed the pouch then threw it on the bed to be packed with their things. It would be a good gift to bring them, they could all laugh about the days when....

Jessica came bounding into the room unexpectedly interrupting her contemplation. She waved imploringly in excitement. "I heard you're going on a trip. Would you mind if I came along this time?"

Mell smiled indulgently at her sister but shook her head no. "I'm not sure if you should. I'm going to Giant Bear's village in Montana and it might turn out to be dangerous."

Jessica grinned knowingly then put her two hands together as if in prayer as she tilted her head beseechingly. "I know I heard you tell Jane but I'd still like to come. Please! You've taught me how to protect myself so I won't be a hindrance and who knows I might even be able to help out."

Mell harrumphed in disbelief at the idea of the rambunctious Jessica helping them. It was more likely she would cause more problems, as beautiful as she was. Mell gave in with a smile of surrender at the replica of her mother Jessica. She had never been able to say no to her and this time was no different. She nodded reluctantly then pointed a finger at her and shook it in forewarning. "Okay you can come too but we're leaving

411

in a few hours. If you're not ready you get left behind. Oh, and it's going to be a hard ride so you better wear pants."

Jessica squealed in delight as she grabbed Mell and gave her a fierce hug in thanks. She picked up her long skirts so she could run and raced out of the room in a rush, before her sister could change her mind. Mell shook her head already regretting her decision and wondered if she had made a mistake.

Mell forgot about Jessica a moment later as she cocked her head curiously at the sound of a door slamming and hurried footsteps racing up the stairs. She turned expectantly and waited in anticipation as Jed burst into their bedroom all out of breath. Her gasp of pleasure caught in her throat as she eyed her husband in appreciation.

Even after all these years he still made her heart race in pleasure just by looking at him. His hair was grey now instead of black with a slight hint of baldness on top but he still kept it fairly long. His face had gotten craggier and deeper lined. None the less it was still a handsome face only older. He hadn't lost any of his muscles if anything he had gained more. Most men Jed's age tended to loose height as they got older but not Jed he still stood at six foot six with no hint of slouching. He did have a bit of a potbelly now but hardly noticeable unless you had known him all these years.

Jed inhaled in relief at the sight of his wife standing in front of him unhurt. "What's going on? Pam raced past me like her skirts were on fire and didn't even slow down to tell us if anything was wrong. Then I hurried back here to see what the problem was and I see two pack horses outside being readied for a long trip by the looks of it."

Mell grinned relieved to see him here at least she wouldn't have to go running around looking for him then told him everything about hers and Pam's dreams lately. When she finished Jed nodded not even surprised a little bit as he motioned knowingly. "I've been waiting for something like this to happen but I didn't think it would be this late in the future."

Mell looked at Jed in shocked surprise as she waved angrily in demand. "You were expecting this to happen! Why ever for?"

Jed smiled reassuringly at her tone of astonishment then explained. "Well do you remember back when you were first named White Buffalo by Giant Bear?"

Mell nodded mutely that she did but didn't say anything. Jed frowned pensively as he thought back to that time. "Well later when you were teaching Tommy knife tricks, Giant Bear and I were watching you. He told me that the Great Spirit told him that you would come to him when he was in desperate need but he didn't know when or why he would need you. So I've been waiting for this moment to happen for quit some time now."

Mell sighed in understanding as she gestured around her at all the clothes lying out on the bed. "Well help me finish packing we're leaving in a few hours."

Jed nodded without argument and got to work helping her. A few hours later they were all gathered together in the yard as Mell had predicted. Mell, Jed, Jessica, Pam and an insistent Daniel who refused to be left behind all mounted. They waved good-bye to the people they were leaving behind and raced to save their friends.

* * *

Here ends the story of Mell and Jed. Or does it?

Stay tuned for the next book 'Raven and the Golden Eagle', where Giant Bear and his granddaughter must save their people with the help of a reluctant Englishman. As well as Mell and Jed's struggle to reach Giant Bear before it's too late to save them all.

A BRIEF NOTE TO MY READERS:

For all you history buffs out there that realize my dates do not coincide with actual events. I had to manipulate time slightly so that my third book to this series would have a female Queen on the thrown in England. I used the Cheyenne Indians for the same reason because they were in Dakota as well as Montana and I needed them in both places. So just to set the record straight I'm including a brief summery of actual dates.

—The Cheyenne Indians at one time lived in North Dakota. According to their history they farmed corn, squash, and other vegetables. But in 1776 the Lakota Sioux defeated the Cheyenne and took their land. Some became nomads in Montana like the rest of the Indian tribes. There was some that moved down into South Dakota and they like the Sioux were involved in the Black Hills War in 1876-1877.

—It became known as Dakota on March 2, 1861. The capital at that time was Yankton until 1883. It wasn't until November 2, 1889 that North and South became separated. They formed their own identities at that time.

—Gold was discovered in the Black Hills of South Dakota in 1873, which caused a migration boom that lead to the Dakota Territories popularity and many settlers flocked to Dakota.

—In 1870, the Northern Pacific Railway pushed westward from Minnesota into North Dakota. By 1872, the company had put down 164 miles of main line across North Dakota. Progress was slow because of Indian raids.

—In 1847 a man in Paris named B. Houllier came out with the hammer so that powder was no longer needed for rifles. It was the first single shot rifle.

—In 1857 Winchester made a repeating rifle that had a tube that could hold 15 bullets. Model # 1866 it was to be the most popular rifle used at that time.

—Smith and Wesson also made a repeater rifle in 1854 but it wasn't as good and had to be perfected in the late 1850's.

—Samuel Colt in Paterson New Jersey made the six-shooter on April 1836. That became the most popular revolver.